QUEENDOM OF THE SEVEN LAKES

KING OF THE SEVEN LAKES

Cover design: Marcus Moltzer
Cover illustrations: Nicole Sizer
Mapp illustration: Ellen Liu

This book is a work of fiction. Names, characters, places, and incidents either are products of the author's imagination or are used fictitiously. Any resemblance to actual persons, living or dead, events, or locales is entirely coincidental.

ISBN-978-0-6487299-2-1

Books by the same author

The Fourth Country
The Ruthless Land

The Third Country
Dark Intent
Dark Purpose
Dark Heart

Coming late 2020

Untitled (First Country)

For my family.
My parents,
My grandparents,
My sister,
My friends.

QUEENDOM OF THE SEVEN LAKES

The mind of a queen is a thing to fear.
A queen is used to giving commands,
not obeying them;
And her rage once roused is hard to appease
-Euripides, Medea

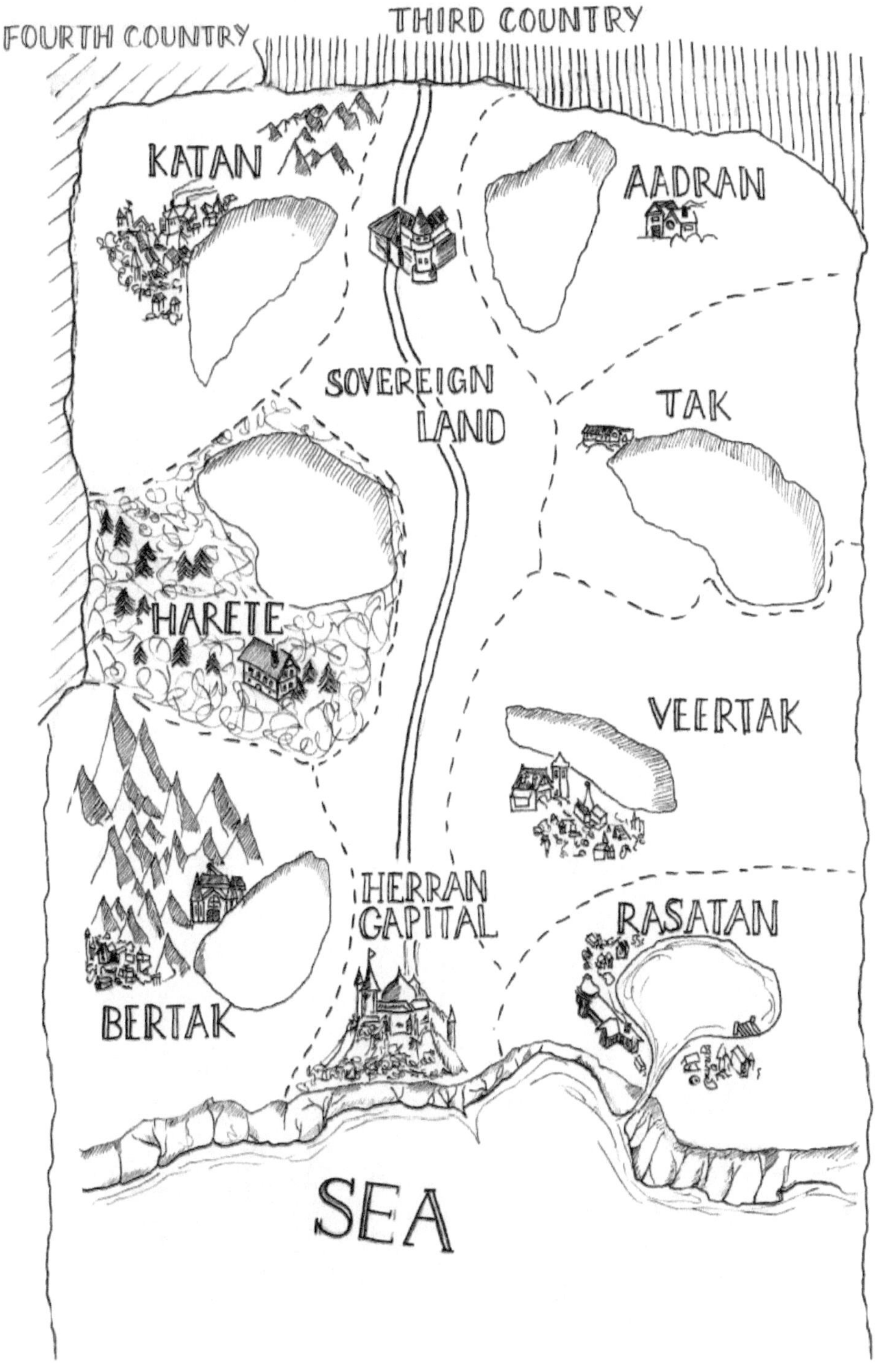

FOURTH COUNTRY
THIRD COUNTRY
KATAN
AADRAN
SOVEREIGN LAND
TAK
HARETE
VEERTAK
HERRAN CAPITAL
RASATAN
BERTAK
SEA

FIRST KILL

The young man's arrogant air was obvious in the way he held himself, the way he regarded everyone around him with the faintest air of contempt. It made it easy to dislike him.

It was why his family's servants were so willing to discuss his habits. For the price of a cheap ale, the assassin had learned everything she needed. People were almost comically friendly when someone else was paying for their drink.

The morning air was crisp despite the promise of heat later in the day. The assassin followed the man through his family's lands. Each step was cloaked in the assurance that his status as a member of the seven families gave him. She slipped from shadow to shadow, barely more than a slip of shadow herself. Her eyes never left her quarry.

Just as she had been told, he stopped at the bank of the stream that fed into the Tak family lake. Here on that very bank he had conceived the child he now refused to claim as his own. The assassin had learned that the previous evening, too. Despite the common knowledge of his indiscreet activity, his word would always persevere over the claim of a lowborn woman. Today however, he was alone. With the precision of routine, he shed his clothes and went into the cool water. The assassin waited a moment longer to ensure they were definitely alone, then she crossed the distance between them. She entered the water with no sound or splash, moving toward him with certain, silent strokes. He was blissfully unaware of his death stalking him, washing himself in the water as though it could wash away the wrong he had done and the contract on his life that his callous cruelty had bought.

She didn't hesitate, taking hold of him and pushing him beneath the surface. He barely struggled, surprise making him inhale the first lungful of water. She held him close in his brief struggle, the heat from his body traversing the cold water across to her own skin. Once she was certain he was dead, she released him and slipped from the river. The corpse drifted in the current. It would soon be found and deemed an accident.

The Family of Assassins guaranteed that death brought by their hand would be indistinguishable from any accident, unless otherwise wished. The girl did not glance back at her first contract. She had been taught well. Her place was not to judge, but simply to be an instrument of death. The Shadow God would be pleased with his newest blooded disciple. She was fourteen.

ONE

"I will take you to the Queen." The servant looked at the assassin then shifted her gaze uneasily to the pile of blades on the table.

Elen-ai had been required to remove her weapons before she was permitted to see the Queen. She had almost snickered aloud when the request was made. Surrendering her blades was a far cry from disarming her, although she felt the weight of their absence. For as long as she could remember, she had always carried some kind of weapon.

No less than two Royal Guards walked on either side of her as she followed the servant along the corridor. Had she not felt so acutely out of place, she would have been fighting laughter. It was an almost sweet naiveté to think that two guards could subdue her.

The Palace corridors alone were indisputably beautiful. The walls were covered with the most exquisite tiles, each tile painted by hand and arranged in a visual feast of geometric design. Delicate light from the midmorning sun coming in through the windows filled the corridors with a haze of colour. Despite the beauty she walked through, Elen-ai was not comfortable in the Palace. The absence of her weapons was disconcerting, but not the cause of the itch at the back of her neck. Her discomfort was caused by the fact that she was walking so openly, so observably. It felt deeply unnatural to Elen-ai who was most at home blending into shadows, slipping surreptitiously along an unnoticed path rather than walking in the open where everybody could see her. Unfortunately – unusually – today she had no choice in the manner of her passage.

Elen-ai counted twenty-three doors as they walked, wondering why she couldn't detect the sound of movement or voices behind them. It was an unfounded suspicion, but she couldn't help but feel she was being deliberately taken through parts of the Palace that were empty. Somewhere from far away, the faint sound of a training drill being called reached her ears. It seemed members of the Palace Guard were practicing.

Elen-ai's escort halted in front of the twenty-fourth door. It didn't look any more or less special than the preceding twenty-three, but the guards and the servant stood a little straighter before the servant smartly knocked on the door and opened it.

From her place just outside the lovely sitting room, Elen-ai looked around at the interior, noting the shadows, hiding spots, entry and exit points, and what could or could not be used as a weapon. The room was a veritable death trap for anyone who was unfortunate enough to be the name on an assassination contract. But then again, most rooms were if a member of the Family had been engaged to kill someone.

"Your Majesty, Elen-ai of the Family." The servant bowed low, all but prostrating herself before her ruler.

The Queen of the Second Country, known also by its inhabitants as the Queendom of the Seven Lakes, rose from her chair, her skirts rustling with the movement. Elen-ai was conscious of the plainness of her own simple tunic and trousers in contrast to the ornate skirts and bodice of the Queen. However, each woman had a role to play, and the job of Her Royal Highness Latana was to look like someone who wielded a vast amount of power. Elen-ai's was to kill people. So while the Queen had her beautiful skirts and long, intricately braided hair, Elen-ai wore simple trousers and shirts and kept her dark brown hair cropped close to her head.

"Thank you." The Queen addressed the guards who had escorted Elen-ai. They hesitated, clearly unhappy with the prospect of leaving their ruler alone in the room with Elen-ai, but the Queen's tone held a clear directive: leave. To disobey would be intolerable insubordination.

"Ah, Lord Silius asked me to remind you about the, uh." The servant who had led the way glanced at Elen-ai uncertainly, clearly uncomfortable with the prospect of completing her sentence in front of Elen-ai.

"Yes, the matter of the justice appointment, I know. Please tell him that I will make my final decision once I have finished with Elen-ai and our visitors from the Third Country." The Queen did not seem to share her servants' discomfort with discussing anything in front of Elen-ai. In fact, in her tone there was almost the suggestion of a rebuke for her servant's conspicuous concern.

Only when the doors had closed did the Queen turn her attention to Elen-ai. "Please, come and join me," she invited the assassin, indicating the seat opposite hers with a wave of her hand. The Queen had not so much invited Elen-ai to be seated as subtly commanded it. Elen-ai obeyed.

The two women sat regarding each other in silence for many moments. The Queen's eyes were the colour of liquid gold, set in a face of delicate beauty. Not all of the Queens who had ruled the Second Country had been beautiful, but Latana was, a fact which inhabitants of the Queendom knew well. However, few were given the chance to see this beauty for themselves, and even fewer this close. Elen-ai had entered a group of highly privileged people without even trying. Her gaze was drawn to the thick gold collar that encircled the Queen's slender neck. While it may have looked like a simple piece of jewellery, Elen-ai knew better. It was worn to prevent her throat being cut by someone sneaking up from behind. A quick glance confirmed that the Queen wore matching cuffs on her wrists. Perhaps they would be effective against a hired sword, but they would never stop a member of the Family.

"Would you care for a drink?" the Queen offered.

Elen-ai had been trained in a great many arts, but the nuances of court etiquette did not number among them. "Yes please, your Majesty," she replied, wondering if instead of accepting she was supposed to refuse to fulfil some elaborate ritual of manners.

"I have juice here, or I could call for something else if you would prefer?" The Queen indicated the pitcher and two glass vessels set on a small table by her side. Elen-ai had never drunk from glass before. Cups and goblets crafted from the material were fiendishly expensive. She wondered if the juice would taste different from glass rather than the vessels from which she normally drank.

"Juice would be fine, thank you," Elen-ai said.

With deft movements, the Queen poured from the jug, handing the drink to Elen-ai. The gold at her wrists flashed as she moved. As she sipped the juice – which was exquisite, Elen-ai reflected that she would much rather return to the quiet simplicity of the Family's home rather than be in this ornate, beautiful room being served juice in glass vessels by the Queen. The distant sound of the training drills had faded, leaving a conspicuous silence broken only by the clink as the Queen poured herself a drink and set down the pitcher.

Queen Latana picked up her own glass and drank. "Now. To business." The quiet firmness of her manner was now entirely focused on Elen-ai. "I presume you are wondering why you are here?"

"Not particularly. The Family offers only one service. Who would you like me to...remove?" Elen-ai chose a euphemism at the last moment in deference to whom she was sitting opposite. Normally she took a small delight in being blunt with people who asked for the services of the Family. She liked to remind them of what they were asking her to do.

"I presume you have heard the rumours of my infertility?" Instead of answering Elen-ai's question, the Queen asked one of her own.

This was not uncommon behaviour. People often felt a need to explain their motivations for seeking the removal of another person. What they didn't realise was that provided they paid, no explanation was necessary. Elen-ai had learned, however, that it was easier to let her clients justify their request. So she simply nodded. The whispers that the Queen was barren had been present at every level of society for many years now. While the Queen had given birth sixteen years ago to a healthy son, no other child had followed, leaving the Queendom without an heir. With every year that passed, the whispers became more agitated and seemed to have more truth behind them than mere speculation. Soon the Queen would definitely be too old to bear children, and that would mean disaster for the country, especially as the Queen's only sister was far too old to be recalled from her marriage to take the throne.

"Regretfully, they are true," the monarch said without any apparent concern for the significance of what her statement implied.

Elen-ai looked at her Queen with polite curiosity. Why this was being confided to her she had not the slightest idea. It wasn't as though she could kill every person who spoke of this. It would leave the Second Country with very few inhabitants indeed.

"Which leaves me with a problem," the Queen continued.

Elen-ai did not speak but was certain that her agreement with that conclusion was evident on her face.

"However, I have a solution. My son will take the throne when I die," the Queen said.

Elen-ai froze. No man had ever taken the throne of the Second Country and for good reason. A Queen could have a child without the father's identity being known. A man could not. The delicate power balance between the

Queendom's seven most powerful families was preserved by virtue of the fact that the monarchical line remained free from any marital allegiance. It ensured that however many power games were played by members of the seven clans, the Queen would always be able to make rulings that were free of any familial obligation. Marriage was a powerful weapon, and the Queen was not somebody's tool to be used for their own power. What Queen Latana was proposing would shatter that precise balance. The Family was not particularly invested in the power politics of the Second Country, but its members were citizens of the Queendom, accustomed to tradition and perhaps more importantly, not immune to the turbulence that such a radical departure from tradition could create. Horror crawled its way across Elen-ai's mind as she considered the Queen's proposal and its implications.

"I know what you are thinking," the Queen spoke calmly, not giving Elen-ai the opportunity to wallow in her shock. It would seem that was something she would have to explore at her own leisure. "My own brothers have voiced their objections enough times. But my mind is made up and I will announce the decision at the Summer Council."

Elen-ai was not surprised to hear that the Queen's advisers – brothers who were trained from birth to serve the Queen in an advisory capacity – objected to this proposal. It was madness and certainly could not have either the best interests of the Queen nor the Second Country at heart.

"Despite the fact that the Queen's word is law, there are always those who would seek to break the law. Especially when they do not like it. My son will make an excellent ruler. Of this, I have no doubt. However, I fear the actions of those who may use this decision to advantage themselves. I fear for his life."

Elen-ai did not offer her own opinion on why someone may attempt to kill the Prince. Nevertheless, she could easily understand why someone may, out of anger at the Queen's decision to spit in the face of hundreds of years of history, be moved to an extreme act. Even she felt a hot flash of rage somewhere deep inside her at the impudence of the Queen to think that she was above her country's history. Somehow she did not think that the Queen would appreciate the contribution. Instead, she asked a question. "Begging your pardon, your Majesty, but I'm unsure what this has to do with me?"

"I seek the services of one who knows best how to slip through shadows and kill undetected. Because of your specific skills, Elen-ai, you are best placed to protect my son's life. The Royal Guard may keep the Palace secure, but I need the skills of someone who can do more than simply patrol. You know from where an assailant would come, how they would come. That is the best way to preserve my son's life, to know from where someone would strike, and pre-empt them before they reach him."

Elen-ai chose her words carefully before speaking. "Your Majesty, I take life. I am not certain that my skills actually extend to preserving it."

The Queen arched an eyebrow, her beautiful face otherwise unmoving. "And with whom do you suggest I trust with the life of my son? The Katan clan? They already have my sister through a marriage. It-" She stopped herself and shook her head. "No," the Queen continued. "The Family's reputation is built upon the fulfilment of its contracts and its discretion. And your unwillingness to kill the Queen or her family members. I would trust one of you with the safety of my son over anybody else, even members of my own Royal Guard." It almost seemed as though she was about to say more, but instead, the Queen stayed silent. Perhaps the words that she almost followed that statement with were "I can't be certain that there won't be someone in the Royal Guard who would seek to kill my son for my decision".

"I haven't accepted the contract yet," Elen-ai cautioned. Members of the Family had the right to refuse any contract put before them. Even one from a Queen. She seriously considered refusing this request.

In wordless response, the Queen pushed a piece of paper across the small table that sat between them. Elen-ai leaned forward to pick it up. Her eyes widened at the amount written on it.

"Perhaps you should tell me more about who you think may harm your son," Elen-ai said cautiously. It would be impossible to turn down such a sum out of hand.

The Queen gave a satisfied half smile, and settled back into her chair, hands curling around the glass full of juice. "I'm not sure what else I can tell you. Once I announce this, I do not doubt that any of the seven families would attempt to take his life if they deem it favourable for their fortunes. Although I do think the Veertak are the least likely to attempt such a thing."

Elen-ai nodded. Everyone in the Queendom knew of the political allegiances and loyalties that existed between the seven powerful families of the Queendom. Even the Veertak, who were the least politically inclined due to their preference for the acquisition of knowledge, had their own quiet ambition to broaden the scope of their power. However, as a rule, the Veertaks were known to avoid violence where possible, instead of using their wits to increase their wealth and standing.

"Aside from that, each family, regardless of their outward loyalty, has members who perceive things differently and would seek to embark upon the course of action that sees my only child dead. I cannot allow that to happen." For a moment a look that was decidedly un-Queen like crossed the monarch's face; the look of a mother terrified for the safety of her child.

"That's not much to go off," Elen-ai noted.

"I know," the Queen admitted. "It's why I've approached the best."

"Flattery won't get you very far, your Majesty," Elen-ai said with a slight smile.

"You don't have children, Elen-ai." The Queen did not ask so much as make a statement. Elen-ai nodded her head in confirmation. No member of the Family had children. If they wished to marry or have children, they had to leave the Family.

"I love my son with everything that I am," the Queen told her. "I didn't think I would. I thought that having a child was a necessary part of my position. Especially…" she trailed off as she searched for the exact words. "Especially given the manner in which royal heirs are produced. However, I loved him from the moment I first felt him kick inside me. And I would do anything to protect him." There was a faint plea in her voice.

"What are the terms of the contract?" Despite the fact that she knew the display of emotion was almost certainly a calculated slip to manipulate Elen-ai, it was uncomfortable seeing her ruler's vulnerability. It seemed that the Queen had known exactly what to do in order to push Elen-ai towards accepting the contract.

"You will become my son's shadow. Wherever he goes, you go. You are not to leave his side. Once it is deemed that there is no longer a significant threat to my son's life, the contract will be completed. He is my only child, Elen-ai. I need to know that he will be safe from any threat." The Queen's voice dropped, a quivering note of fear creeping in.

Elen-ai exhaled slowly, using the time to filter through the facts, discarding the emotion that her Queen was attempting to rouse in order to influence her decision. At the end of her breath, she nodded. "I'll do it."

A genuine smile crept across the face of Queen Latana, touching her golden eyes. "Thank you," she said.

"I assume I start right away?" Elen-ai asked.

The Queen nodded. "I will take you to him. He should be in the middle of his lessons now." She rose, her regal composure absolute.

Elen-ai carefully placed the glass on the table next to the piece of paper on which the Queen had written the Family's fee before she too got to her feet. "One more thing," she said.

The Queen gestured for Elen-ai to continue in place of speaking.

"I'll need my weapons back."

TWO

Elen-ai followed the Queen through the Palace. Neither the Queen nor Elen-ai spoke. Elen-ai was lost in her thoughts, trying to look beyond her instinctive reaction of horror at the prospect of a man on the throne and consider whether the Queen's son would even be a good ruler. She certainly had her doubts. For most of his life, he would have been taught how to advise an unborn younger sister rather than to rule. Not that the Queen's advisers didn't have considerable authority in their own right. But to lead required far more than simply having authority conferred upon you.

As they walked through the Palace, Elen-ai reflected once more that its corridors really were magnificent. She saw several tiny gardens through the windows that they passed and wondered who sat in those lovely, carefully tended outdoor spaces. None of them had any occupants. Elen-ai had been in many different dwellings built from stone or wood, the homes of both poor and rich. No room that she had been in came close to the wealth that she could see merely in the Palace's corridors, let alone the room in which she and the Queen had sat drinking juice.

After several minutes the Queen paused before an open door that led into a larger courtyard. Elen-ai could hear the sound of strikes and heavy breathing coming from outside. She watched the Queen as she looked out into the yard, the corners of her eyes and lips softening at what she saw outside. The Queen took a breath and turned to the assassin, beckoning for Elen-ai to join her at the doorway. Taking a step forward, Elen-ai looked out into the yard in which a young man was sparring with an older, clearly more skilled opponent. Two other men sat on a nearby bench. They appeared to be watching the bout in front of them, but Elen-ai could see the way their lips moved almost imperceptibly. They were talking, and from what Elen-ai could see, they were talking about something that pleased neither of them. She had a strong suspicion that their subject was the Queen's heir.

The Queen lingered in the doorway a moment longer then stepped out into the yard, her appearance arresting the attention of its occupants. The fighting ceased, and the two men on the bench stopped their surreptitious communication and stood.

"Latana," one of the two men on the bench greeted the Queen. Elen-ai presumed that he was one of her three brothers. Surely nobody else would dare address the Queen by her first name, and certainly not in such a brazen fashion.

"Good morning Nikalus," the Queen said, her voice warm with affection. She walked over to him and embraced him, then his companion.

Looking at them together, Elen-ai felt sure all three must be related. The Queen had the same nose as the one she had called Nikalus, while she shared her liquid gold eyes with the other. Beyond that, something about the mannerisms of all three was similar in the way that could only be familial.

"Elen-ai, may I present to you Nikalus and Kaine. My two younger brothers." The Queen turned from her brief conference with her brothers back to Elen-ai. Elen-ai bowed to both of them.

"Nikalus, Kaine, this is Elen-ai of-"

"The Family." The young man who had been sparring cut off the Queen, coming over to embrace her. His opponent had discreetly exited the courtyard at the entrance of Elen-ai and the Queen. The boy was more broad in the shoulders than Elen-ai had initially judged, and already a full head taller than the monarch. He was half a head taller than Elen-ai too, and she was quite tall. Elen-ai judged him to be in the middle of his teenage years, although the way he carried himself made him seem older than he actually was. He fixed a cold look at Elen-ai.

"This is my son, Gidyon," the Queen said, looking fondly at her child. It was a more restrained expression of the one that had crossed her face as she had watched him sparring in the yard.

Elen-ai bowed to the boy - the Prince. "Your Highness."

He continued to regard her with an expression of mild distaste.

"Latana, I must again voice my objection to hiring an assassin to protect our nephew." Kaine spoke directly to the Queen, as though Elen-ai wasn't there.

"Why, Kaine? Do you think that she won't be able to protect my son? That she will not be discreet about her identity?" A look of vexation crossed the Queen's face as she turned to address her brother. His hesitation was all she needed. "You and Nikalus and Sil have all have raised objection to this course of action. You are all telling me what to do, yet none of you is proposing your own solution!" A frustrated note crept into the Queen's voice.

Elen-ai recognised the tone; it was one she heard in her own voice when she was squabbling with her brothers and sisters. There was something profoundly shocking about hearing her ruler speak in a manner that was so terribly ordinary. Then again, Elen-ai had seen her share of supposedly dignified people behave in ways that were profoundly undignified. That came with her job.

"Are you really certain this is something to be discussed in front of our guest?" Kaine leaned around his brother to speak more clearly to their sister, his tone pointed. He was quite handsome, Elen-ai could not help but notice.

The Queen glared at her two brothers, clearly outnumbered but unwilling to back down. "I have made my decision and that is all there is to it. Would you like to stay and complain about something else, or do you have somewhere to be?" she snapped.

Cowing to her authority, the Queen's two younger brothers bid her and their nephew farewell and left the courtyard without so much as a backward glance at Elen-ai.

"Mother, is this really necessary?" Gidyon asked once his uncles had departed. Evidently he did not wish to lend weight to their argument within their earshot. As rude as he was being by speaking about her as though she were not there, Elen-ai had to credit him with his obvious unwillingness to voice his objection in front of anyone other than his mother.

"Gidyon, I believe there is a real possibility of someone trying to hurt you. Just this week our agents heard new reports of things that leave me gravely unsettled. Elen-ai will keep you safe. Of that, I have no doubt." The Queen raised a hand to gently brush her son's cheek. Unlike many boys of his age, he made no move to stop her, instead smiling fondly down at his mother. They had the same smile.

"But there are guards everywhere. They can keep me safe. And I can defend myself."

Elen-ai considered what she had seen of the Prince's sparring practice. He was somewhat competent, but he needed far more practice and tuition before he would be able to fend off someone who was actually skilled with a sword.

"My darling, please do this for me," the Queen asked her son, taking one of his hands in both of hers and bringing it to her lips. There was something fundamentally intimate about the bare display of love for her son. It seemed as though the Queen had forgotten that Elen-ai was there. Not that Elen-ai believed that for a second. It was more likely that this was yet another calculated display to ensure that whatever Elen-ai may
think of the Queen's decision, she would still protect this boy. As much as Elen-ai hated to admit, it was effective.

The Prince relented with a shake of his head and a something that could have been a small smile. "Promise me that it won't be for long, though."

"I promise," she told him. "But for now, Elen-ai must stay by your side wherever you go. Only then can I be sure that you will be safe. I'll leave you two to get acquainted. I must attend to our visitors from the Third Country." She smiled fondly at her son again before casting Elen-ai a quick nod of thanks. Then she exited the courtyard, leaving Elen-ai and the Prince alone together.

Elen-ai let the Prince break the silence. She always let her clients speak first.

"I don't want you around me, assassin," he told her bluntly, all the tenderness that he had displayed toward his mother gone.

"I gathered." She wasn't offended by his distaste for her nor was she surprised that he didn't want her to be constantly by her side, even if it was in the name of safety. Members of the Family were often considered unpalatable company.

"Your kind should not be allowed. My first act when I take the throne will be to outlaw the Family," he informed her rudely.

Instead of giving him the satisfaction of any response she kept her face totally neutral. "I'm sure that when that happens, myself and the other members of the Family will be quite dismayed," she told him in a polite tone.

Uncertain at her lack of response, he glared at her. She couldn't help but notice that unlike his mother's liquid gold eyes, his were vibrant blue, like the colour of water on a sunny day. It was quite arresting. "Just don't get in my way. I can take care of myself," he snapped.

Elen-ai already regretted her decision to accept the contract. She had far more worthy things to do with her time than look after someone who shouldn't even be in line for the throne. If he was going to behave like this for the entirety of the time that she was to protect him it would a very unpleasant experience indeed. The petty thought made its way across her mind that maybe someone would want to kill him because he was so obnoxious. "If you think you can take care of yourself, then why don't you prove it? You and your sword against me unarmed," she suggested.

He considered the offer for a moment then nodded, the arrogance clearly written across his face. It was amusing that he thought he might be able to best her.

She took a step away from him to give him the space to take his stance and bring up the sword he still held in one hand. After that, she gave him to the count of three before she knocked him off his feet and pointed his own sword at his throat.

The Prince looked around, bewildered. His expression suggested he was vainly attempting to understand exactly what she had done. She offered him the hilt of his sword then held out a hand to assist him getting back to his feet. He accepted both, the hostility with which he had initially treated her had gone, replaced with a slight wariness and, oddly, curiosity.

Elen-ai still said nothing. She had proved the point easily. To say anything would simply humiliate him further. He returned her silence, a slight colour creeping into his cheek, which made him look his age. Without uttering a word he turned and stalked out of the courtyard, his back rigid with anger and bruised pride. Elen-ai followed him, her feet making no noise even on the gravel that covered the courtyard. There was something immeasurably satisfying about knocking this boy who would be ruler to the ground. The outrage at the travesty his ascension to the throne would represent was still within her, but the sharp edges to it had been dulled. Perhaps it was petty of her to take such delight in using her unfair advantage to humiliate him, but it had made her feel a bit better.

She followed him through the Palace. They wound their way along a new set of corridors, all as stunning as the first through which she had walked, past more doors and courtyards, and into what she could only assume was one of the Palace's residential wings. Here they passed servants who scuttled to and fro, all of whom averted their eyes as Gidyon and Elen-ai passed them either out of discretion or discomfort, Elen-ai couldn't quite discern which. She wondered whether they were aware of the Queen's plan to make him their heir. Servants did have a way of knowing things that were supposed to be secret. Elen-ai made a note to look more closely at the servants. A careless word from a servant to the wrong person would easily make a threat to Gidyon's life plausible.

The Prince stopped at a door, flinging it open with ill-mannered force. Clearly, he was still smarting over the humiliation Elen-ai had delivered to him.

The only word to describe the Prince's living quarters was luxurious. Elen-ai had to work hard to keep from gasping as she gazed around his private sitting room. The walls were adorned with beautiful tapestries and the space furnished with exquisite items. Elen-ai followed the Prince through the sitting room and into his bedroom which was dominated by a bed that looked as though someone could be lost within its massive confines. Pillows practically overflowed on it. A small bed had been brought in and placed along one of the room's walls. The Prince stood still in the middle of the room, staring at the second bed.

"That shouldn't-" He stopped and turned to Elen-ai, realisation dawning on his face. "Surely you don't have to sleep in the same room as me," he protested.

Elen-ai said nothing, the sarcastic suggestion of course that nobody would ever try to sneak in during the night to kill him remaining wisely unspoken.

Gidyon gave a sigh of anger and frustration and took off his shirt. When Elen-ai made no move to leave the room he glared at her. "Do you need to watch me bathe, too?" he demanded.

She knew that she probably should remain by his side as he bathed, but she couldn't quite bring herself to see him in such a state.

"Let me check the rooms, then I'll wait outside while you bathe," she told him, settling on a reasonable compromise.

He continued to glare at her as she looked around the bedroom, efficiently going through every corner, hiding spot, and shadow to ensure that the room was free from any threat – even a sharp corner on which the Prince may fall and hurt himself. She finally checked the window to ensure nobody had managed to sneak up to the second floor of the building. In the middle of the day, only a member of the Family rendering themselves invisible could do it, but Elen-ai would never allow anyone to accuse her of not being thorough.

"Are you quite done?" the Prince snapped as she moved into the adjacent bathing room - similarly luxurious to the other parts of his suite. The floor and walls were tiled with dark stone that had been polished until it shone. A huge tub sat in the middle of the room. It was filled with water from which peals of steam rose. Another bucket of water, presumably for rinsing, sat next to it. With only one tiny window to allow the steam to escape, Elen-ai could see no serious threat in the room unless someone was hiding in the tub, which they definitely weren't.

She went back into the Prince's bedroom. "I think you should be safe," she told him, enjoying his sigh of exasperation.

While he bathed, she went back into the sitting room. She took the time to herself to examine the room in more detail. A writing desk was on one side. It was clearly used often if the small ink spots on it were any indication. A well-thumbed text on the Queendom's legislation was placed to one side.

She paused her inspection for a moment to make sure that Prince was still alright. The sound of contented splashing reached her ears. Reassured that there was no immediate danger unless he somehow contrived to drown himself, she resumed looking around the room.

Her survey was cut short by the entrance of a Palace servant.

"You're Elen-ai?" he asked. Elen-ai straightened and nodded, unfazed by his clear uncertainty. She wondered if he knew exactly who she was. It seemed likely that the Queen would seek to hide that she had hired a member of the Family from even the Palace staff. But servants did have a way of knowing things they weren't supposed to.

"These are yours," he told her brusquely, jerking his head towards the items that filled his arms.

Elen-ai crossed the room and took the proffered items from him. He all but ran away from her once she had taken it, leading her to suspect that he knew more about her than he should.

Shaking her head, she examined what he had brought her, although the feel of the bundle gave away the fact that her weapons had been returned to her.

THREE

Under the cover of darkness, Elen-ai slipped unseen through the halls of the Palace. Long ago, the lives of gods and humans had touched. In that time, the powers of the gods bled across to their mortal companions. Women and men were able to perform feats that rivalled the gods themselves if legends and myths were to be believed. However, the gods had receded from the mortal realm and the fantastic skills that knowing them brought had been all but forgotten. Yet some still remembered what faith could offer – the Family who had guarded their secrets and followed the way of the Shadow God with dedication, was among the small group of people in the world who still had skills of which most could and would only ever dream. Elen-ai used those forgotten skills now as she concealed herself from anybody who may have seen her, blending her lithe form seamlessly into the shadows of the corridors. Only the most astute of observers would have noticed the slight displacement of air as she passed by them, and even then it was a far more subtle sensation than a person's passage would normally make.

She was completely unnoticed as she passed the patrolling Royal Guards. If she had wanted, she could have killed every one of them before they even had time to realise that their final breath was wheezing out of them. Elen-ai almost felt sorry for them; these men and women were some of the best fighters in the land. But against Elen-ai and the secrets of the Family, the assassin's death would touch them long before they would be able to use the training they had received.

The sprawling complex of the Palace took her through winding twists and turns. In addition to the earlier corridors along which she had been taken that day, Elen-ai passed through several new corridors, adding as she went to the map of the Palace in her head. She quickly moved through the servant's quarters and their far less opulent corridors and stairways. Soon she had the measure of the Palace's design, understanding how the many corridors fitted together in the plan of the architect - or architects - who had envisaged the great building's construction. She passed through the kitchens, empty and scrubbed clean in anticipation for the work that would be recommencing in only a few hours, long before most of the Palace's inhabitants would awake for the next day. She saw the pantry, stocked high with a variety of foods, some so costly that an enterprising thief could make a small fortune from their liberation.

From the kitchens, Elen-ai stole through the dining halls - a grand banquet hall that could seat at least three hundred people and a smaller more intimate dining room which was where she presumed the Queen would normally eat. That evening the Queen had been dining with the dignitaries from the Third Country, so the Prince had chosen to eat in his quarters, saying no word to Elen-ai who had sat on the other side of the room to him eating in her own comfortable silence.

The dining halls led Elen-ai into a series of sitting rooms. She examined those rooms carefully, finding several little spaces in which one could conceal themselves and listen to the room's occupants unnoticed. She presumed the sitting rooms were where the Queen entertained various visitors and charmed them into giving her what she wanted. Indeed, Elen-ai had been in one of those rooms that very afternoon and had capitulated to the Queen's desires like many before her. Each room was different, furnished and designed to create a particular atmosphere and a different message. After moving through all of the sitting rooms, Elen-ai understood that the one in which the Queen had received her was selected to convey neutrality and calmness. The room with the blue walls and dark wooden cabinets was clearly one that held a hint of urgent authority. The room with walls the colour of fresh cream and large soft sofas with pale pink cushions was for seduction. As she moved from the Council room, identifiable by the round table with fifteen chairs, through to the grand throne room where the Queen received petitioners, Elen-ai reflected that the many faces the Queen needed to have must be exhausting. She wondered who the Queen actually was behind the many masks she wore.

After a moment of hesitation – this was her ruler after all - Elen-ai made her way into the Queen's rooms. Her purpose in exploring the Palace so thoroughly was to ensure that there was nothing that could surprise her if an assailant were to make an attempt on the life of the Prince. The first thing drummed into all children of the Family was that knowledge was the most valuable tool an assassin could have at their disposal, more valuable than any weapon. She could still remember one of the Mothers walking through the fish market with her when she had been quite young, only nine or ten years old.

"Look, Elen-ai. That man over there buying the sea eels is a servant of clan Tak. What does it tell you?"

"That someone has disgusting taste in food," Elen-ai responded immediately.

Her dry humour earned her a severe look. "Perhaps. But think about the price of sea eels. They are cheap. It tells you that nobody is in their house in the capital except for servants and that their servants are not well treated. Or perhaps that the Tak family is encountering some financial difficulty. Find out which and suddenly a world of possibility is open to you. Poverty breeds much desperation, an empty house is a perfect place in which to hide, and a disgruntled servant is worth their weight in jewels." The Mother's eyes gleamed as she spoke.

It was a lesson that Elen-ai had never forgotten, especially as her first kill had been a member of the Tak family. One of the Tak's lesser sons had impregnated a girl and refused to acknowledge the girl or his child. The girl was heartbroken, believing that he had truly loved her. Even if he had loved her, she was a laundress and of no worth marrying. Her father, furious at the pain inflicted on his beloved daughter had come to the Family and spent nearly all his savings to exact revenge on the man who had hurt his daughter. Elen-ai had learned of the Tak man's habits by drinking one evening with one of the Tak family's servants. The servant, a man who had little fondness for his employer as a result of their unwillingness to pay their servants well, told Elen-ai of her target's penchant for swimming each morning. The next day Elen-ai had followed him to the stream in which he swum, slipped into the water after him, and held him underneath with the tenderness of a lover. It had been deemed a sad accident. The true skill of the Family lay not in their ability to take life but to make it seem as though that life had not been deliberately taken. Death was useless to most of the Family's clients if it was clearly intended. That was why the Family was so expensive; nobody ever knew if a death was the work of the Family or simply an unfortunate part of life. The Tak son was missed by few, although many other contracts that Elen-ai had fulfilled had been far less just. It seemed the Mothers and Fathers had been gentle for her first time.

The modesty of the Queen's apartments surprised Elen-ai. The seduction, power, or gentle reassurance of the sitting rooms were completely absent, giving nothing away about who the Queen was when nobody was watching. The elegant simplicity of the writing desk, couches and tables was understated despite the significant amount of money they certainly would have cost. Unable to resist the Family's maxim to acquire knowledge whenever the opportunity arose, Elen-ai rifled through the papers on the Queen's writing desk. To her chagrin, there was nothing of particular interest aside from some polite correspondence between the Queen and the heads of the seven families that unsurprisingly, said nothing of any substance.

The sound of voices in the corridor outside reached Elen-ai's ears. She recognised one of the voices as the Queen's. Elen-ai wove the shadows around her more tightly as the Queen and someone else entered the room, clearly in the midst of a disagreement.

"I still don't see why you need to hire a member of the Family to protect him, Latana. If someone finds out, the uproar would be tremendous," the man told her, irritation in his voice.

"You may be older than me, Silius, but that doesn't mean you know better than me," the Queen bit back.

"I've been trained since birth to advise you, to consider everything. You've merely been trained to rule," he told her. He sounded slightly smug.

"That may be so, but you aren't in my position. You've not seen what I've seen, you don't know what it's like to rule. You don't have enough information to have an informed opinion on the matter," the Queen said, sinking down into one of the couches in the room. From her position, Elen-ai had a perfect view of the Queen's face. It was obvious that this Silius was the brother to whom she felt the closest. Elen-ai could see it in the way the Queen's shoulders did not hold the same slight tension as when she had spoken with Nikalus and Kaine, nor did she seem to be in a state of cautious anticipation for what he was about to say. Even her speech was more casual, less considered.

"You're right, I don't know everything on the matter. Because you aren't telling me everything." His voice was soft but firm as he addressed his sister.

"Silius there are some things that you just can't understand unless you experience them yourself." The Queen sounded almost amused, if not slightly tired.

"Were the circumstances in which Gidyon was conceived really that bad?" Silius asked, clearly awkward at asking the question.

His sister threw back her head and laughed in response, clearly delighting in that discomfort. "How long have you wondered if that was my reason for all this?" she asked.

He made an awkward gesture in place of a response.

"Well if you must know, the circumstances of Gidyon's conception were quite fun actually," the Queen told him, a slight smirk on her face. Elen-ai knew that sort of look. It was the look of one sibling delighting in tormenting the other. On the Queen, it was disconcertingly normal.

Silius again did not reply. The Queen's smirk broadened. "There's nothing wrong with enjoying the more physical pleasures in life," she told her brother.

He gave a slight sigh that had her laughing again.

"In the name of the Divine One, you're such a prude sometimes, Silius. Oh honestly, sit down, will you?" she said, sounding slightly exasperated.

He did as she bade, sitting next to her. "Latana, please try to explain it to me," he said gently.

The Queen sighed, her flawless brow furrowing as some private emotion made its way through her. "You know the paternity of the royal line is unknown." She stated a basal fact. Because it was of the utmost importance that the Queen did not become beholden to any one of the seven families through marital ties, she was not allowed to marry. However, the necessity to promulgate the line remained. The solution had been in existence for as long as the Queendom had existed in its current form. Celebrations populated by eligible men from the seven families, following a thorough examination by a doctor, were regularly held, often spanning a few evenings at a time. The Queen would invite the men who caught her fancy back to her bedchamber, but there was a strict understanding that she must take at least two different men to bed with her over the evenings. If a child eventuated, it would be unclear who the father was, offering all the families an incentive to remain loyal to the throne given that it may be one of their own who held it, while also ensuring a reasonable neutrality on the part of the Queen.

Silius nodded curtly to her question, even though a response wasn't strictly necessary.

"I never thought much of it, really. It was something that every queen must do - a duty to produce an heir. And I was given the opportunity to have my pick of eligible and handsome men. I thought that having a child would be necessary. I never thought-" she stopped herself, recollecting her thoughts before she continued. Elen-ai couldn't be certain, but it seemed as though the Queen had caught herself about to say something else.

"I thought that having a child would be easy, that it wouldn't affect me. And then I actually fell pregnant with Gidyon. The first time I held him in my arms my entire world shifted. Suddenly there was this little being that something within me - something so innate, wanted to protect with everything that I was. It made me feel so powerless. I, a Queen, Silius, rendered utterly powerless by a tiny infant. And to think that he was this miraculous product of -" the Queen abruptly stopped speaking, biting her lip and looking down at her lap.

However, if her behaviour was unusual, Silius did not seem to notice. His demeanour had softened completely.

"You know, I felt a similar way when you were born." He reached out a hand to gently place on top of one of hers.

She raised her head with a questioning look on her face. He nodded in response. "It's true. I was brought in to see you right after you were born. You were this tiny wrinkled little thing, so fragile and so delicate. I'd never seen anything more lovely. I think even if I had never been told that it was my duty to look out for you, I would have anyway. I do understand what you mean, Latana. Do not fret."

"He means more than you could ever understand, Sil," the Queen whispered. Elen-ai could see the tears glistening in her golden eyes.

"And you're certain there is a threat to his life?"

"I can't be completely sure. You are the one who hears the whispers, after all, but I do honestly believe someone is going to try and take his life."

"Do you really think that this assassin will be able to keep him safe?" He asked, giving her hand a gentle squeeze.

"I think that if anybody can, she can," the Queen returned.

"And do you think we can keep the fact that we have engaged the Family a secret?" he persisted.

"I think we have no other choice," she replied.

"Alright then, I'll tell the others to stop being so difficult," he relented.

A smile curved the lips of the Queen of the Second Country as she looked at her older brother. "You always were a soft touch, Sil," she teased, although there was no malice in it.

He shrugged, a smile of his own crossing his face in reply to hers. When he smiled Elen-ai could see a strong resemblance between them, and the depth of love he bore for his sister.

"Alright. Bed," Silius said firmly, getting to his feet. There was something humorous about the Queen being instructed to go to sleep like a small child, especially as she nodded obediently and rose to her own feet.

Elen-ai waited until Silius had departed the room and the Queen had gone into her bedchamber before exiting the room, noticing that it appeared the Queen had no servant to help her undress. That fact alone did not surprise her. From what she had seen, the Queen placed a high value on her own privacy. However, something about the exchange she had witnessed made the absence of any servants to wait on the Queen odd.

She slipped out of the Queen's room through an open window, a frown on her face. She had no doubt that the Queen was telling the truth about the depth of her love for her son and the desperation accompanying it to protect her child whatever the cost, but Elen-ai had been watching the Queen's face very closely, and she couldn't shake the suspicion that there was something the Queen had not told her brother. Something that linked to the lack of attending servants. Without any evidence, Elen-ai did not know what it was, although the Queen's certainty that Gidyon's life was in danger seemed too adamant to be simple paranoia. Elen-ai resolved to find out what the Queen had kept from her closest brother. After all, information was the most important thing to any member of the Family.

She found herself in the stables that were almost directly below the Queen's room, the musty smell of straw and feline tickling her nose. Curious, despite the knowledge that she should return to the Prince, she peered into the large area where the kittanae slept, thoughts of the Queen's secret banished for at least the moment by sight of the magnificent creatures. The five giant felines were curled together, an overlapping of paws and heads that looked blissfully comfortable. One was still awake. The sleek animal looked at her with an unblinking ferocity.

Only every ridden – never used to pull a cart, for they would not tolerate such indignity – the kittanae were magnificent animals owned only by the most wealthy of people. The reclusiveness with which they inhabited the depths of forests such as those on the Harete lands or the fringes of the Katan and Bertak lands, combined with their ferocity made them almost impossible to successfully catch. Elen-ai had never ridden one, they were far too obvious for one, but riding the large cats were supposed to be an experience like no other, especially as crossing the country on a kittanae took less than half the time in a carriage pulled by the lumbering hearat.

It was an act of transgression for her to touch the animal, but curiosity overtook her. Elen-ai leapt noiselessly into their pen and stretched her hand out to the one that was still awake. With something approaching trepidation, she placed her hand on the side of the kittanae's neck. Its warmth against her skin was a shock, almost as much as the softness of its fur. Elen-ai ran her hand down the animal's neck, feeling it lean slightly into the pressure of her arm. The beginnings of a purr rumbled in its throat. She stayed petting the animal for a few more minutes, then remembering herself and her task, she left the stable as noiselessly as she had entered it.

On her way back to her mattress in the Prince's bedchamber, Elen-ai detoured through the other residential wings of the Palace, finishing with the one reserved for guests. In the only occupied bedchambers in that wing, Elen-ai found two people. From the clothes strewn on the floor of the room and their possessions, she concluded that they must be the foreign dignitaries from the Third Country the Queen had mentioned in the courtyard and dined with that evening. For a moment, Elen-ai stood in the bedroom watching the two entangled forms as they slept. There was a profundity to the absolute absence of any reserve between the two sleeping people in the way their limbs were entwined that captured her gaze for an extra few seconds. The woman stirred in her sleep, her long dark hair spread around her. In response, the man drew her closer to him. His face nestled against hers, so close it looked almost as though they were two parts of the same whole. Elen-ai looked for a moment longer before she slipped out of the guest wing and back to her contract.

FOUR

While Elen-ai could say many unkind truths about Prince Gidyon, she had to admit he was no slouch. He awoke early and began his day with a light breakfast that was immediately proceeded by a series of lessons. Elen-ai wordlessly followed him wherever he went without once receiving any acknowledgment of her presence from the Prince. She might have thought she had inadvertently rendered herself invisible but for the fact that a servant came and mutely handed her a plate of food at the breakfast table. However, the Prince's animosity toward her did not overly trouble Elen-ai. Her duty was to protect him, not to be liked by him.

The Prince's teachers were a collection of severe individuals, all experts in their respective fields. As far as Elen-ai could tell, none of them posed any threat to the Prince other than possibly boring him to death. She listened as the finer points of mathematics, lawcraft, and economics were imparted to him, trying to keep from tapping her fingers or toes in boredom. Although, while Elen-ai may have been profoundly disinterested in the rates at which various items were taxed, Gidyon was a diligent and interested pupil, listening to his instructors with unwavering attention. As far as Elen-ai could tell, these lessons had been a part of Gidyon's life for as long as he could talk, separating him from any other children who may have lived in or around the Palace. She regarded the Prince during the hours of lessons with a certain curiosity. Seeing someone who had been so abrupt with her display such courtesy and deference to others was quite disconcerting, especially knowing what a solitary upbringing he must have had. That alone occupied her attention during the hours of tedious lessons. Perhaps there was more to this Prince than just youthful arrogance.

Lunch was taken with the Queen in the small dining room that Elen-ai had slipped through the previous evening - apparently, the Prince would often dine there with his mother and uncles for both lunch and dinner. Elen-ai was given a seat at the table rather than being relegated to a corner of the room as she had been at breakfast - the Queen's doing she could only assume.

Gidyon and Elen-ai arrived first, sitting and staring awkwardly at each other across the beautifully set table. The glass wine and water vessels which were placed on the table caught the light, almost blinding in their delicate beauty. The Queen swept in a few moments later. It was a welcome relief. The Prince's surly silence with her was starting to wear thin.

"Good day Elen-ai." The Queen graciously greeted her, a deceptively open smile on her beautiful face. Elen-ai's discovery of the fact that the Queen was guarding a secret seemed at complete odds with that lovely, open face.

"Your Majesty," Elen-ai responded, bowing.

"How are you finding life in the Palace so far?" the Queen asked as she sat.

"So far, very safe," Elen-ai responded politely, sitting once the Queen was seated, and taking up cutlery once she saw the Queen do so. She noted that the delicate plates upon which the lunch was served were from the Katan region's artisans. Even everyday lunch was imbued with wealth here in the Palace.

"Do you hear that, mother?" Gidyon demanded from the other end of the table. "Safe. I am fine. We do not need her."

Elen-ai, however much she found the Prince's attitude toward her distasteful, wholeheartedly agreed with him.

The Queen turned to her son, the charming smile fading from her lips. "Gidyon, how could you speak about Elen-ai in such a tone and in front of her? Elen-ai, I am so sorry for my son's rudeness." She turned back to Elen-ai, extending a hand briefly in an apologetic gesture.

"Honestly your Majesty, there's no need for you to apologise. The Family is not often well regarded," Elen-ai said, throwing a somewhat pointed glance at the Prince who was glowering into his food.

"Others may behave in a manner that a member of the royal family may not," the Queen replied, her comment clearly directed at her son more so than in response to Elen-ai.

Elen-ai recalled the Queen's candour with her brother the previous evening. The responsibility on the shoulders of any leader would be tremendous, even more so one who was attempting to change history. Elen-ai felt for the Queen, trying to balance her roles of ruler and mother to prepare her son to be lead a country that did not want a man to be their monarch. In the Family, all Mothers and Fathers were tasked with only one duty: to prepare the children of the Family to enter the trade of killing. Life was simpler there. Elen-ai thought wistfully of the Family's house with its dark corridors and shadowed halls. She missed the simple quiet and understanding of her brothers and sisters. If she were lunching there, she would probably do so out on the roof. Perhaps she would be joined by her favourite sister, Mari-am. They would often sit in companionable silence on the roof of the Family's house, looking out over the city's rooftops. Elen-ai loved the jumbled collection of houses and chimneys that spread out as far as the eye could see, with the Palace looming on the hill to one side and the glitter of the port on the other. Most days an acute ear could hear fragments of conversation from the street. Sometimes Elen-ai would overhear banter that left her chuckling to herself. It was a far cry from this beautiful room with the Queen on her left and the Prince on her right.

"I want to go to the market tomorrow," the Prince announced, ignoring his mother's reprimand.

"Absolutely not," the Queen replied without even pausing to consider.

"But I go to the market every week," Gidyon objected.

"There is too much risk," his mother told him firmly.

"Isn't that why I have my assassin?"

"What did I just tell you about your manners when speaking to Elen-ai?" The Queen put her hand down on the table with a bang.

He didn't reply but the resentment was obvious in his expression.

"Apologise to Elen-ai," the Queen ordered. "Now," she added when he said nothing.

The Prince breathed in through his nose sharply then looked directly at Elen-ai; the first time he had done so that morning. "I apologise for my rudeness, lady Elen-ai. It was remiss of me to address you in such a manner and I will do my utmost to ensure that it does not occur again."

His overly formal language and the sickly sweet tone were a clear jibe of themselves. It did not escape his mother's attention.

"I do not know what is causing this, but you are utterly insufferable, Gidyon. I did not raise you to be like this," she snapped.

"If I'm so insufferable then I shan't impose my presence on you any longer," he replied, standing and storming out of the room.

Elen-ai wondered whether she should pursue him, but decided against it. She instead sat quietly with the Queen who propped her elbows on the table and buried her face in her hands. After a moment she raised her head from her long, elegant fingers. "I am so embarrassed that you were witnessed that," she said.

"It's alright," Elen-ai told her, shrugging slightly and taking another mouthful of food. Being a guest of the Palace did have some perks. The meal was a delicious medley of fresh vegetables cooked in a rich sauce accompanied by meat so delicious that it could only have been one of the Tak family's lows. She had never eaten anything so fine.

"No, it is not. My son cannot be a good ruler if he is going to be rude to those he finds unpalatable for whatever personal reason," the Queen despaired, rubbing two fingers on each temple in small circles.

Elen-ai didn't reply to that - the Queen was correct. "Does he often go to the market?" she asked instead.

The Queen nodded. "Every week. He likes to talk with the people there. He says that it helps him better understand the lessons that he learns from his tutors." She sounded tired, like a parent at the end of her tether rather than a Queen.

"Let him go tomorrow. I'm sure I can keep him safe from anything that may occur." Elen-ai surprised herself with the offer. She didn't want to do anything to make the Prince happy, but after only one day within the Palace, she was desperate to be among the fuss and noise and mess of the city outside this world of perfect rules and behaviour. In some ways, the Queen's horror at Gidyon's rudeness was more unsettling to Elen-ai than the actual rudeness. She lived in a world in which insults were exchanged on a daily basis. People would frequently treat her rudely if they knew her origin. The Family was often feared but rarely well loved.

"I really do not think that is a wise idea," the Queen objected. "Any hired hand could be waiting for him there."

"I promise no harm will come to him," Elen-ai assured her.

The Queen looked down at her plate of barely touched food and sighed. She made no effort to disguise her discomfort and unhappiness. "Are you certain?"

"On the honour of the Family," Elen-ai promised solemnly.

"Alright," the Queen relented, picking up her cutlery and moving a piece of food across her plate.

"I'll go and find him," Elen-ai told her, taking one final mouthful of the delicious food before regretfully leaving the remains of her meal so she could go and find the Prince.

He was in the practice courtyard, moodily stretching before his fencing lesson. At some time between when he had left the dining room and when he had gone to the courtyard, he had changed his clothes.

"What do you want? For me to apologise to you again?" he demanded when he saw her.

"I convinced your mother to let you go to the market tomorrow," Elen-ai said, not even acknowledging his question.

He stopped and straightened up. "What? Why?"

"Does it matter?" Elen-ai stepped toward him linking her hands behind her back.

"Yes it does. But thank you." It sounded as though he actually meant it.

"There are a few things, though. Your mother seems to think that there is a real likelihood that someone is trying to kill you. I promised her on the honour of the Family that I wouldn't let you die."

"Go on," he said, his expression was guarded but not hostile, which was something.

"You go with guards?" she verified.

"Two."

"There will be five tomorrow. If you speak with someone, you are to stay this distance apart from them at all times." She stepped forward to demonstrate how far she meant.

"They're people from the market. I know them," he protested.

"No, you don't," Elen-ai countered. "And if someone wants to kill you, from any closer than where I am from you now they can do so before anybody - even me - could stop them."

The disbelief showed in his eyes.

"The longest kind of blade that someone can conceal on themselves is this long." Elen-ai drew one of her own concealed weapons to demonstrate. The Prince started at the sudden appearance of the blade in her hand. She continued as if he hadn't reacted. "Look, I hold it out like so," she extended her arm, "and I can't reach you. Any closer and..." She took a half step forward and in another movement that was too fast to see, she had flipped the blade so that the hilt was facing him and brought it to rest in front of his heart.

He took an involuntary step back, clearly perturbed.

"You'll keep that distance, then?" she asked.

He nodded, his eyes on her blade.

The Prince's afternoon was just as tedious for Elen-ai as the morning. She watched as he engaged in a range of combat exercises, silently evaluating the technique of Gidyon's teacher. For someone who wasn't a member of the Family, his teacher was quite good, and she certainly put the Prince through his paces.

After the exercise, Gidyon bathed and met with his mother who had requested his presence in one of the sitting rooms. Wondering how the Prince would behave given the exchange with his mother over lunch, Elen-ai followed him to the sitting room. The Queen had chosen the room that Elen-ai had in her mind dubbed the seduction room. With the afternoon sunlight coming in through the windows, the space was warm and inviting. She imagined that the blue sitting room at this time of day would be far less cosy and much more intimidating as the cool of the deep blue was given an extra intensity by the light. Perhaps she was beginning to get the measure of the court's ways after all.

The Queen had changed her clothes to compliment the room. She wore a dress of soft gold the same colour as her eyes. It was a simple design but the simplicity somehow seemed to heighten her aura of authority, especially given the gold she wore at her throat, wrists and now also in a thin chain encircling her head. Against the midnight black of her hair, the gold gleamed. Whatever she might have been hiding, she was unquestionably magnificent.

"Mother." Gidyon paused at the door and greeted the Queen in a formal tone.

"Thank you for coming, Gidyon," she replied, a smile just touching her face. Elen-ai reflected that the thanks were not really necessary. The Queen had asked her son to do something. His mother or not, she was still the Queen.

"How may I be of service?" Gidyon asked with just a touch of reserve. He too was clearly aware of the fact that he couldn't really have refused the Queen's summons.

"I thought it appropriate that you meet our friends from the Third Country," the Queen informed him, extending her hand in a gesture that clearly indicated she wanted him to come to her side.

The Prince stepped forward, his back stiff even considering the formal doublet he wore. Clearly, he had not forgiven his mother for her rebukes at lunch. Elen-ai slipped into the room unobtrusively and took up a place near the wall. Mother and son stood awkwardly side by side until footfalls in the corridor announced the imminent arrival of others.

The man and woman who Elen-ai had seen entangled in sleep the previous evening entered the room.

"Your Majesty." The woman greeted the Queen first, smiling with what Elen-ai thought to be genuine warmth. It seemed the Queen's charm had worked its magic on these dignitaries.

"Ah, Councilwoman Kuch and Councilman Hart. I'm so delighted you could join us. I'd like you to meet my son, Gidyon. I have yet to announce this to the Second Country, but he is to be my heir. Given the severity of the matters our two countries share, I thought it appropriate he hear at least some of our discussions, given that he may also have to manage these matters." The Queen sharing her appointment of heir before making the knowledge public was a brilliant display of trust that would make anyone willing to call the Fourth country an ally. Noting the uncertain glances directed toward Elen-ai, Latana added "and this is Elen-ai, a trusted advisor." No further explanation was offered or requested.

"Let us continue our talk over some refreshments," the Queen continued. She called out to a waiting servant who immediately brought in a tray of cakes and drinks and placed it on the room's main table. The Queen invited her guests to sit with a gesture, perching herself on the edge of a deeply cushioned chair. "Elen-ai, can we tempt you with a cake?" The Queen turned to address her.

With a small shrug, Elen-ai stepped forward to take one of the delicate deserts laid out on the tray, murmuring a word of thanks to the Queen. She was sure that she should have politely declined, but she had no time for court games, and the cakes looked too delicious for politeness. She bit into the cake as she returned to her position on the room's edge. It was even more delicious than she had thought it would be, a miracle of some clever chef's mastery of sugar, cream, and candied fruit.

"Councillors, I've heard quite a few tales about the beauty of your capital, Oranis – are they true?" The Prince leaned forward, his attention completely focused on the two foreigners and a disarmingly charming smile on his face. Elen-ai tried not to stare at this engaging young man. She wondered where the surly brat that she had followed around all morning had gone.

The man, Councilman Hart, leaned forward in reply. "I daresay it is. Although no story can truly capture the beauty of Oranis."

"Especially at sunrise or sunset." Councilwoman Kuch's eyes lit up as she spoke, her love for the city clear.

"Is it more beautiful than Herran?" The Queen asked, a hint of mischief in her voice.

"Begging your pardon, your Majesty, your own city is very fair, but truly nothing can match Oranis. From the approach when it simply seems to rise from the plain, there's something about it that commands the awe of anyone who sees it, be they a native of the city or a visitor." Councilman Hart spoke with an easy charisma of his own.

"I'd love to see it." A wistful expression crossed the Prince's face.

"Maybe one day you will." Councilwoman Kuch smiled at him.

"Is it true that you were both part of the uprising that occurred three years ago?" Gidyon asked with eager curiosity.

The Councillors exchanged a brief glance. "I didn't realise that so much was known about what happened within the Third Country," Councilwoman Kuch said. "The fact that we are here, as far as I understand, is quite unprecedented. The history of the Godskissed Continent is not one in which the four countries have had much official contact with each another at all."

"You are quite correct, Councilwoman, even many of my teachers do not know of the recent events in the Third Country. I learned it from the merchants and traders, here in Herran's markets. They're terrible gossips."

The eloquence of the Prince's speech surprised Elen-ai as did the breadth of his knowledge. Despite the Family's extensive awareness of events within and beyond the Second Country, the knowledge of the Prince actually exceeded her own in this instance. She had never taken a contract in The Third Country. The country itself was reasonably small, but it while it might not have been somewhere particularly special, the best routes to much of the Fourth Country ran through it. Wealth and significance flowed in off the levies incurred by traders crossing the territory. Yet despite this, the people from the Third Country were curiously insular. All traders from there kept to themselves, even when they were far from home. Elen-ai had heard only vague mentions of rebellion and counter-rebellion taking place. Whispers of legendary figures had accompanied the accounts she'd heard, but such things were more often than not embellishments to make a good story, so she'd paid them little heed.

"How admirable. A young man with a desire to learn of the world around him." The slight emphasis on 'young' by Councilwoman Kuch was not lost on Elen-ai, nor did it seem, the Prince.

"One is never too young to learn, Councilwoman. For instance, I just learned that you are indeed the Councilwoman Kuch who is the subject of several reverential stories," Gidyon replied smoothly.

The expression on the woman's face made it clear that the Prince had unnerved her. It seemed that despite her apparent place within legend, the Councilwoman was not as adept a politician as the Prince or his mother. Hardly surprising, really. The delicate feuds of the Queendom's seven families required leadership that was well versed in the art of discourse and inference. The Third Country did not have such requirements, as far as Elen-ai knew.

"I'm hardly a figure to be revered," Councilwoman Kuch responded once she had regained her composure.

"If you're willing, I would love to hear the events from your perspective," Gidyon told her, abating the discomfort he had caused with a masterful ease.

Her composure recovered, the Councilwoman smiled. "Perhaps if we get the opportunity," she replied.

Picking up on her comment, the Councilman interjected before anybody else could speak. "However, other more urgent matters require our attention."

They were a good pair, despite, or perhaps because of, their unpolished diplomacy, Elen-ai thought.

"Ah yes. The issue of the Fourth Country." The Queen spoke, having watched the exchange between her son and the female dignitary in silence. Elen-ai wondered if she detected a note of pride in the Queen's voice. The Prince certainly had kept a certain mastery of the conversation.

"Your Highness, I'm not sure what your merchant friends might have told you, but in recent years the instability in the Fourth Country has caused concern to both our nations."

The Councilwoman's slight jibe did not seem to affect the Prince. Perhaps because he knew that it said that he had shaken her earlier. "From what I understand, the Lord Protector's interest in keeping the peace amongst her own people is limited. While it has historically been a country of changing powers, its more wealthy members taking control from each other as often as some of us might change clothes, recent instability has meant that some of the Fourth Country's regions are almost autonomous. Most of the time that means that those who maintain control of the areas are not particularly interested in maintaining order for the people who inhabit them, merely in maintaining their own position," he said evenly.

Councilman Hart leaned forward to address the Prince. "That's more or less correct. Recently, parties of raiders have crossed the borders of the Third Country in increasingly violent attacks. Something that used to happen occasionally is now occurring far more frequently. Given that both our countries share a border with the Fourth Country, it is only a matter of time before the one or two raids that your own provinces have seen become increasingly common. The need for a common approach is one that both the lovely Queen and our own Council agree is reasonably urgent."

While Elen-ai was aware of the situation within the Fourth Country, she hadn't realised that things were quite that dire in terms of the lawlessness which plagued the oft-invaded lands. It was a piece of information she filed away to share with one of the Family's Mothers or Fathers when the opportunity arose.

Her attention began to wander as the discussion became one of strategy and mutually agreeable outcomes. Such discussions were not of particular interest to her; the only thing that she was ever sought was finalities and truths, not negotiations that could dissolve as quickly as the blink of an eye. Eventually, the light all but waned and it was time for dinner. The little party moved into the dining room, Elen-ai following them a few paces behind. Her presence had been seemingly forgotten, and that suited her. She had no desire whatsoever to partake in any of the pleasant conversations that seemed to be standard for this sort of exchange.

The Queen's brothers joined them for dinner and the discussion turned to more trivial matters such as music and the best ways to travel a long distance. Elen-ai sat and ate in silence, her own thoughts enough company for her. She watched the Queen, trying to discern what she was hiding from the world, but the monarch gave no indication that she was harbouring any secret. If Elen-ai hadn't witnessed the exchange between Latana and her brother the previous evening, she would never have even been aware that there was something to know.

Finally, the day was over and Elen-ai followed the Prince back to his rooms. He read for some time while Elen-ai meditated on the other side of the room, then he went to bed.

He did not speak a word to her as he climbed into the small mountain that was his bed, nor did she say anything to him. Inwardly she sighed. She did not like the royal life one bit.

FIVE

Rain cloaked Herran, the capital of the Second Country. Elen-ai awoke to hear its soft sound outside the Prince's window. She scowled. Rain was at once a blessing and a curse for any assassin, offering concealment while also giving them away with the droplets that they could not help but leave as a marker of their passage. In the crowded marketplace, anyone could easily sneak close to Gidyon under the guise of a passer-by trying to stay dry.

Despite her hope that the rain would abate, by the time the Prince was to leave the Palace if anything, it had become heavier.

"How far away are you going to stay from everybody?" Elen-ai asked the Prince as they stood in the Palace's main courtyard. He demonstrated the distance, stepping slightly away from her.

She nodded. "Make sure you keep it that way," she instructed him, making no effort to be polite. She already regretted her decision of the previous day to help him get to the market.

The Prince and his assassin set out from the Palace, escorted by five royal guards. The area of Herran closest to the Palace housed the city residences of the Second Country's seven great families. For the most part, the families lived on their estates, but one or two lesser members of the family generally resided in the capital to keep an eye on political developments and report back via either messenger bird or runners. There was no more trustworthy set of eyes than a member of one's own family. The houses were beautiful structures, often several stories high, made from dark timbers – large, beautiful planks from the Harete forest - or stone. Each one was a subtle attempt by the Family who built it to assert their importance and authority. It was obvious in a tower here or an architectural flourish there. However, all of the houses were dwarfed by the Palace both in height and beauty, their darkened forms a mere smudge against the Palace's pale high walls.

In this part of the city the streets were wide, leaving more than enough room for carts to approach or depart the Palace. As they moved closer to the wharves where the market was situated, the streets narrowed as did the buildings. The magnificent, elegant architecture became more cramped, less well maintained. Shops for all manner of things began to appear. The symbols for people offering medical assistance, rare herbs, financial services, or various artefacts appeared in the windows of buildings that they passed. One store even promised genuine Katan plates inside, although Elen-ai doubted how authentic they were. Katan plates were just as rare as fine jewels. The rain kept people inside with the doors firmly closed. On a more pleasant day, a passer-by might be able to sneak a glimpse into the various stores, seeing rows of bottles, wares, or the eyes of a crafty dealer, depending on the store they passed.

They reached the market. Elen-ai was impressed with the pace that the Prince had set. He headed straight for one of the fishmongers and immediately was greeted with an effusive warmth. "Master Gidyon, how d'you fare?" the plump woman behind the stall holding a vicious-looking knife greeted him.

"Mar-ai, it's good to see you." The Prince's warmth was palpable, his smile genuine and open. Suddenly the Prince had become a boy talking with his favourite stall keeper rather than the entitled brat with whom Elen-ai dealt. He didn't even seem to mind the malodorous reek of the fish market.

"How's your lessons going, m'young man?" she demanded, returning to gutting a fish as she chatted with him.

"Always harder, Mar-ai," he told her.

"You must study m'love, it's important. Here - try this," she ordered him, putting down her knife and picking up another piece of fish. "It's best t'eat uncooked." She waggled the piece at him when he hesitated.

Elen-ai sighed as she watched him step forward and take the fish from the fishmonger's outstretched hand, far closer than the distance that she had mandated. Her eyes were on the knife the woman had been using as she waited for it to whip up and be plunged into the Prince's chest. Instead, all that happened was that she pinched his cheek as he chewed and made noises of appreciation.

"You're a good boy t'come out in t'rain young Gidyon." She smiled fondly at him.

"You're too kind, Mar-ai," he told her.

As they kept chatting, Elen-ai only relaxed when he retreated to the distance that she deemed safe. Something about the exchange was niggled at her. Then she realised what it was. The people here did not know that he had been named heir. There was none of the deference – or hostility – that should accompany the knowledge that this boy was going to break hundreds of years of tradition. She wondered how Mar-ai would behave once she knew the truth. Suddenly the knife seemed once again an object of concern.

A slight presence at her side had her tensing, but she relaxed when she recognised the touch on her arm. "My daughter."

It was one of the Fathers of the Family. She wondered how he had found her. She had not sent word to the Family of this outing.

"Father," she greeted him, keeping her eyes on the Prince.

"You took the contract."

"Yes."

The Prince moved on, and Elen-ai followed a slight distance behind. Her Father kept step with her. "And?"

"The Family has been contracted to protect the heir to the throne," she replied.

"I was unaware that there was an heir, Elen-ai."

"You're looking at him," she said, amused to hear his surprised intake of breath.

"Surely not," he murmured. It was unclear whether he was outraged at the decision, as she had been. He sounded more reflective than anything else.

"The Queen is quite determined that her only child will succeed her," Elen-ai informed him.

"And she fears for his life as a result of this decision," the Father deduced. "Not an unreasonable concern. So you are to protect him?"

"More like mind him. Father, I was not trained to mind children." Elen-ai turned to look at her Father, chancing the risk of taking her eyes off the Prince for a moment.

The Father with whom she was speaking was one she had not had much to do with during her childhood; he chose not to partake in the training of the Family's children. Elen-ai had seen him more as she aged, often discussing the finer points of a particular assassination method, comparing preferred poisons or knife designs, but she still did not know him as she did some of the other Mothers and Fathers.

"Daughter, you accepted the contract and you must see it through." His voice was firm.

She returned her gaze to the Prince. He was currently sharing a joke with a fruit seller. "I am an assassin, not a bodyguard," she told her Father, a petulant edge to her voice.

"Elen-ai, you accepted a contract. You must ensure it is completed." There was a note of chastisement in his voice.

"But it is not the work of an assassin to babysit some Prince," she objected.

"You said it yourself, child. We are assassins. The position we hold in this society is safe only because we keep our word. You gave your word to none other than the Queen that you would protect her son. If you break that promise, you bring the Family into disrepute." He spoke calmly but with a firmness that told her she was being chastised.

"And what if I am to stay by the side of this Princeling for years?" she challenged.

"Then you shall stay protecting him for years. You chose to accept the contract, Elen-ai," he repeated before she could say anything else.

"But I never chose to be a member of the Family," she fumed, sweeping her gaze along the marketplace to ensure that no menace lurked waiting for Gidyon. To have him killed here in front of her Father would be quite humiliating.

She felt her Father's eyes on her, flat and dispassionate. "You may choose to leave the Family any time you wish. Nobody will ever stop you," he reminded her.

"You make the choice sound so simple." She gave an angry laugh.

"You are so young, Elen-ai. I wish you could see how loved you are and how all we ever try to do is guide you to be happy." He sighed a little sadly.

"Don't speak down to me, Father." She bristled at his demeanour.

"Do you know who make the best assassins?" he asked. Elen-ai did not reply. Rhetorical questions were a favoured teaching method of the Mothers and Fathers of the Family. "The oldest among us. Not because they are the strongest or the quickest, but because they have the patience to be willing to wait and find the best way to carry out the task. They are willing to take the time to see everything of worth. It is a thought I would counsel you to consider." His words mingled with the cacophony of the market. "If you truly believe that it was a mistake to accept the Queen's contract, then it is a mistake from which you must learn."

Elen-ai began to protest but felt his departure from her side before she could say anything.

It was with irritation that she followed the Prince from the shadows of the market, her eyes everywhere in search of a possible attack. She observed sourly that the Prince appeared willing to be charming and amiable with everybody he encountered provided they were not her. She wondered if these people would view him with the same adulation when the Queen announced that he was not simply destined to be advisor to the next Queen but instead, that he would be their ruler one day. People were very attached to tradition, and she could well imagine that they would be very angry with Gidyon for being the individual who broke a centuries-old custom even if it was not at his instigation.

Gidyon made several purchases, arranging for them to be delivered to the Palace kitchens. It was clear that these transactions were regular occurrences. Yet again, the Prince surprised Elen-ai. She would not have thought him so involved, so invested in the lives of Herran's lowborn.

Finally, the Prince was ready to depart, and they travelled back through the city to the safety of the Palace walls.

Almost as soon as they had returned the summons came for Elen-ai from the Queen. With a shrug, she departed the Prince's side and followed the servant to the Queen. She hoped that Gidyon would not get himself killed during her absence from him. She would doubtless be blamed if he were. Another lecture from a Mother or Father would be tedious.

Today the Queen met her in the blue sitting room wearing black trousers and a simple white blouse. The plainness of the clothes somehow made her seem all the more authoritative. Here was a woman who did not need to establish her command with ornate finery. Elen-ai had taken the lives of many who had. As always, the gold cuffs glinted at the Queen's throat and wrists.

"Did anything happen at the market?" The Queen asked without pre-amble.

The dark wood of the furniture enriched the blue of the walls. With the gloominess of the day, it made Elen-ai feel as though she were underwater.

"Aside from the fact that it rained, nothing of note. Except of course that nobody knew they were speaking with the Prince." Elen-ai looked steadily at the Queen's face, ignoring the slight pool of water her sodden clothes were creating on the floor.

The Queen sighed, her face giving nothing away of her thoughts.

"Why have you not announced your decision?" Elen-ai asked. The Queen may have told her that she would announce appointing Gidyon as her heir at the Summer Council when the heads of the seven families would be present, but Elen-ai couldn't see any reason to delay the declaration.

The Queen regarded Elen-ai for a moment, pursing her lips as she thought. Eventually, she answered.

"Because I am afraid for Gidyon. He does not understand how his life will change once the world knows he is my heir," the Queen admitted. Elen-ai wondered if this was the truth, or simply a reason that the Queen was giving her.

"You must tell your people," Elen-ai implored her.

"You need not tell me that," the Queen responded somewhat frostily. "In fact, I plan to send out the proclamation within a few days, rather than at the Summer Council as I initially told you. I think it will be better if the heads of the families have some time to become accustomed to the idea before I find myself in a room with them discussing the state of the country. That is what I called you here to discuss."

"Oh?" Elen-ai knew her familiarity with the Queen may see her rebuked, but she suspected the Queen was too focused on her son's safety to take issue with Elen-ai's demeanour.

"I do not want Gidyon in the capital when I announce my decision." By the brusqueness of the Queen's tone, it seemed Latana had indeed noticed and taken issue with Elen-ai's informal manner after all.

"He'll be no safer outside it," Elen-ai pointed out.

"This is not to do with an attempt on his life. I fear that there will be much anger from the people in the street. You saw how he was in the market. While I have never accompanied him, I have heard enough to know that he has a special fondness for many of the sellers there. I cannot be sure that their affection for him will outweigh their anger at his new title. I...I would like to shield him from that for as long as possible. Once the people have time to reflect on the change, they may be less vitriolic in the expression of their anger. I wish to protect him from whatever hurt I can, and I think sending him to the country estate is the easiest way to do this."

Elen-ai was silent for a moment. The Queen's desire to protect Gidyon from the near-certain anger of the people was understandable. But there was something else behind the Queen's reasoning that she hadn't been told. "And you still think that someone may try to kill him?" she asked.

The Queen nodded, slipping her hands into the pockets of her trousers. Elen-ai wondered if it was to hide any agitation.

"Can you be any more specific about these threats?"

"No." The Queen replied curtly, making it quite clear she knew something that she was declining to share. While Elen-ai had seen nothing to suggest Gidyon's life was in danger, Elen-ai was certain that the Queen had some other piece of information which suggested the threat was real.

"Your Majesty, if you want me to protect your son, I need to know everything," Elen-ai said, trying not to sound impatient.

The Queen's face remained calm. "I enlisted the services of the Family because you are the best. That means you can protect him from anything that may occur."

"And you can trust me to keep your secrets. You yourself spoke of the Family's discretion," Elen-ai pointed out.

"That is an added convenience," the Queen noted coolly.

Elen-ai looked at the Queen - her Queen. She did not appreciate whatever secret the Queen was keeping from her, but she had absolutely no power to compel her ruler to divulge what it was. "Your Majesty is wise. I'm sure you have your reasons," Elen-ai said eventually. After all, she could hardly expect the Queen to suddenly share something she hid from her closest brother.

"I will send the Councillors from the Third Country with you. It will be a good opportunity to show them our lands." The Queen picked up a piece of paper from the table in front of her and began to scan it, her method of dismissal a clear signal that she was irked with Elen-ai.

Unperturbed by the monarch's anger, Elen-ai left the Queen to find her charge.

For the first time, the Prince initiated a conversation with Elen-ai when they were in his rooms later that evening. "Who was that man you spoke with in the market?"

She paused midway through the task of repairing a seam for one of her pockets which held a blade and turned to look at him. She wasn't even aware that he had been looking at her when she and her Father had spoken. "He is my Father," she told him.

"Your Father?" He sounded surprised.

Realising his mistake, she corrected him. "All the older members of the Family are Mothers and Fathers to us. As those members close in age to me are my brothers and sisters."

"Does that get confusing?" he asked.

"No more than not having anyone to call father," she replied.

She saw the shock and hurt cross his face. He hadn't expected her to be unkind. For a moment she felt bad, but that guilt was overtaken by a chastisement that she let her personal dislike of the Prince lead to an emotional response.

"That was uncalled for," the Prince said softly.

"My apologies." She didn't often apologise. It felt strange doing so to the Prince.

"Are one of the Mothers and Fathers your actual parents?" Gidyon's curiosity clearly was stronger than his impulse to sulk.

"No," she said shortly. When he continued to regard her, she elaborated. "Family members are not permitted to have children. If they want to they must leave."

"So how did you join the Family? I hear you are all trained from a young age." Gidyon stepped forward and came to sit on the chair opposite her.

Elen-ai did not feel entirely comfortable discussing the ways of the Family, but she felt she owed the Prince something following her jibe. "I was sold to the Family when I was very young."

"What!"

"The Family will give people who have an unwanted child money in exchange for that child," Elen-ai said.

"Why would anybody do that?" The Prince seemed genuinely aghast at the prospect.

"Mostly because they don't have the money to care for the child," Elen-ai explained.

"I still don't understand why you would give your child away." Gidyon shook his head to punctuate the comment.

"Members of the seven families are willing to do that all the time," Elen-ai pointed out, trying to be as delicate as possible about the Prince's paternity.

He inclined his head, acknowledging her point. "Do you remember your parents?" he asked.

She shook her head. "The Family only accepts very young children - less than a year old. The only life I've ever known is with the Family."

"Does that bother you?"

She looked at him in incomprehension. "Why would it?"

"Because you never had a choice about being an assassin." He made it sound perfectly obvious.

"Did you have a choice about being the next ruler?" Elen-ai asked, ignoring the fact that she had made a similar comment in irritation to her Father earlier that day.

"No, but that's different," he retorted.

"Why?"

"Because I don't kill people," he told her.

Elen-ai laughed one short bark. "Princeling, your mother will have ordered the deaths of people in her years on the throne. Any ruler does. They just get someone else to do the job for them. When you take the throne, you'll have just as much blood on your hands as me. Probably more."

Gidyon stared at her for a moment before getting up and stalking back into his bedroom. Elen-ai listened for a moment to make sure that no assailant had jumped out from a hiding spot, then went back to her sewing.

SIX

A few days later, Elen-ai, the Prince, and the two Councillors from the Third Country waited in the main courtyard of the Palace, ready to depart for the Royal country estate. The Queen stood before them, her hair in an ornate plait. She wore a dress the colour of new grass and an expression of concern.

"Be careful, Gidyon," she told her son, taking his hands in her own. Her head bowed to him in quiet conference between mother and son.

"I promise I'll be safe," he said. "I have Elen-ai to take care of me."

Elen-ai pursed her lips at the comment. In the days that had passed, he had not spoken a single word to Elen-ai. Given that the Queen had also barely spoken to Elen-ai whenever they had happened to encounter each other, it had made for a certain surrealness to her time in the Palace. Clearly, mother and son shared the ability to hold a grudge.

"I love you my darling," the Queen told him, unabashed at giving her son an effusive hug.

"You be safe too, Mother. You'll be all alone in the Palace." Gidyon's brow crinkled with concern at the prospect.

"I have your uncles to watch over me," she chided him gently.

"Sil is the only one I trust to actually watch out for you," he said, causing her to laugh.

"I won't tell them that." She giggled as she embraced him again quickly.

The exchange was conducted in undertones that only Elen-ai was able to hear thanks to her sharp ears. Despite her irritation with both of the Royals, there was something heart-warming about the tender relationship between them.

The Queen walked with her son to the waiting carriage. The hearat pulling it stood patiently. Now that Elen-ai had seen the kittanae, the poor hearat seemed particularly lumbering, clumsy beasts in comparison to the felines who had a sleek elegance even in sleep.

"I am sorry that I am unable to come with you," she said to the Councillors, "but I trust that Gidyon will be a good host in my stead. Please enjoy yourselves." She smiled with her usual grace and charm at the two foreigners.

"We look forward to seeing more of your country, your Majesty. I'm sure we'll have many stories to recount to you upon our return." Councilman Hart returned her smile with that earnest charm.

With a final nod to Elen-ai from the Queen, the party climbed into the carriage and set off, surrounded by an escort of ten guards. Elen-ai took one final look at the Queen as they pulled away. Whatever secret lay within the monarch's heart, Elen-ai hadn't discovered it yet. She promised herself that somehow, she would.

The carriage itself was a luxurious affair, easily wide enough for four people to sit inside it in comfort. Cushions abounded, as did curtains on the windows that provided both privacy and a shield from the sun. It would take five days of travel on the great road that ran through the heart of the Queendom to reach the royal estate, due to the luxurious pace of the carriage. Elen-ai did not relish the prospect of such a great amount of time in close confines with the Prince, especially given his surly attitude toward her. She told herself that she could always ride outside if things truly became unbearable, but that thought was little comfort.

As the carriage rattled through the streets of Herran, the Councilman fixed her with his gaze. Elen-ai couldn't help but notice how vivid the green of his eyes was. It was almost as captivating as the blue of Gidyon's eyes. "Lady Elen-ai, I still am not certain of what role you play at court." There was something about his voice that made it sound as though he was perpetually amused by some secret joke. If he wasn't so charming it would be quite obnoxious.

Elen-ai shrugged. "I'm not sure that there is that much to say."

"What is it exactly is it that you do? Freya and I can't quite work it out," he pressed.

"Elen-ai kills people, Councilman. It so happens that she is currently engaged to kill people who are trying to kill me." The Prince spoke with his usual charisma, even though his comment was designed to shock. Unfortunately for him, neither Councillor seemed particularly perturbed by the statement. Elen-ai wanted to hit him for his casual revelation about her, especially after the Queen had expressed her desire to keep Elen-ai's trade unknown. She kept that impulse in check – barely.

"Does that mean you're a member of the Family that I've heard so much about?" The Councilwoman leaned forward, her eyes bright with intelligent curiosity.

Elen-ai did not say anything, merely nodding an uncomfortable affirmation and wishing there was some way that she could hurt the Prince for this uncharacteristic lack of discretion. It seemed pettiness had made him reckless.

"Have you travelled much beyond the Second Country?" Councilwoman Kuch asked, not seeming at all concerned by who Elen-ai was or what she did.

"A little. I've been into the Fourth Country a few times, although not recently," she admitted.

"You must know then about the situation there," the Councilman noted.

Memories of the curious land flashed through her mind, the manner in which the men were made to cover themselves, the unusual customs, the excessive choler of the people that was considered ordinary to them. "Somewhat. The Lord Protector seems to arbitrate on the cruelty of her people invading one another as though it were some game, although now that her authority may be threatened, it seems she is willing to be quite cruel in asserting her position. A whole group of landowners do not care about whatever suffering their exchange of lands may inflict on others, simply holding lavish parties for one another while other parts of the country starve. Many people have sought the services of the Family in the hope of changing power favourably." She divulged the information after a moment of consideration, deciding that nothing she said violated the Family's preference for secrecy. Any merchant could have given the same information, and now she may receive information in return for free.

Despite his resentment of Elen-ai, the Prince's curiosity had been aroused and he had listened intently to Elen-ai. "That's so sad," he murmured.

"People struggling for power always ends with innocent people being hurt," the Councilwoman said softly.

"Is that why you participated in the rebellion?" The Prince looked at her, clearly intrigued.

"Yes," the Councilwoman answered, her tone clear that she did not want to say any more on the matter.

Gidyon evidently noticed and did not pursue the issue.

The inside of the carriage lapsed into silence, the Councilwoman resting her head on Councilman Hart's shoulder as she looked out the window. He absentmindedly took her hand in his as he too watched the land pass by. They sat like that in contented silence, comfortably resting against each other, unabashed by the display of intimacy. The Prince read while Elen-ai modified the seam she had been mending a few days earlier. In the many hours of silence when she had been with Gidyon, she had decided that there was a better way in which the pocket could be constructed.

After a few hours, the carriage stopped so that they could have lunch. The Palace kitchens had prepared a picnic for the travellers which they ate by the side of the road. To their left, the mountains that were the domain of the Bertak family were just visible. Within those mountains were the precious metals that enriched clan Bertak. Likely the gold that the Queen always wore at her wrists and throat came from those mountains, although the items themselves would have been made in Herran. The Bertak family did not cultivate artisans to fashion delicate jewellery from the metal they mined in the way that the Katan family employed an array of skilled clay-workers to make the delicate pieces that were so highly prized across the Second Country. It was why the Bertak family were not as wealthy or powerful as they could have been. That was a source of great bitterness for them.

Elen-ai decided to ride outside the pampered comfort of the carriage when they set off again, claiming she could better see the surrounds from there. She was tired of the Prince's clear resentment of her presence and was desperate to be as far away from it as possible. The Councilwoman cheerfully said that she would accompany Elen-ai, to get a better view of the countryside. Elen-ai had no option but to accept the unwanted company.

Contrary to her fears though, the Councilwoman made no attempt to engage her in any meaningless conversation, appearing instead to have a genuine interest in the land as it passed by them. Thus it was Elen-ai who spoke first.

"You and the Councilman - you are married?" she asked.

The Councilwoman looked at her in confusion. "Ashtyn and I are bound if that's what you are asking," she replied.

"Bound?" Elen-ai frowned at the unfamiliar term.

"Our lives are intertwined in union," she explained. "Is that the same thing?"

Elen-ai considered for a moment. "It can be. Not all marriages are for love, though."

The Councilwoman nodded. "That would be a joining."

"Do you differentiate between a marriage of love and politics?" Elen-ai asked.

The Councilwoman shook her head. "No. In the Third Country it is simply that the Kade join and the Pious are bound."

"And the Kade are?" She feigned more ignorance than was strictly true of the goings-on within Third Country, interested to hear how the Councilwoman described her home.

"The Kade follow their gods and the Pious follow the Goddess," the Councilwoman explained.

"So you are Pious," Elen-ai surmised.

The Councilwoman nodded.

"It seems strange to have to different religions existing so peacefully side by side, especially if their customs are so different," Elen-ai commented. Indeed, few in the Queendom knew the Family followed a different god to the Divine One.

The Councilwoman laughed. "Not so different. But there was a time when the Kade ruled and forced the Pious to live as they do."

"What happened?" Elen-ai looked at the Councilwoman. She was looking away from Elen-ai at the gently undulating hills that currently were on either side of the road. Elen-ai wasn't certain that the Councilwoman had the delicate beauty of the Queen, but she was certainly striking in her own way, and deeply compelling. "We rebelled," she said softly.

"And now you can support your own god?" Elen-ai asked.

"Yes." For a moment, the Councilwoman was silent. "What gods do the people of the Second Country follow?" she asked.

"Mostly the people of the Queendom do not pay much attention to gods," Elen-ai replied slowly. "They believe in the Divine One, but do not think overly of its existence. The here and now are the more important concerns."

"Foolish to ignore the Gods. But you don't," the Councilwoman noted.

"No. I pray to the Shadow God." Elen-ai wondered how the Councilwoman had known that she was devout in her faith. Her surprise made her frank.

"Is that the god of the Family?" the other woman asked.

"Yes," Elen-ai said, not elaborating any further. For someone who was not a skilled diplomat, she had certainly found out much that Elen-ai would have told few others. Perhaps sensing she had pushed as far as she could go, the Councilwoman did not ask further questions, lapsing into an easy silence.

Elen-ai had always enjoyed this part of the Queendom. Especially now that it was almost the beginning of summer, the lush green coaxed into the landscape by the spring rains had not yet faded, while the weather was pleasant without being too warm or too cold. The only downside to the time of year was occasional days of rain such as they had experienced when the Prince had gone to the market, but so far the sky was a tender blue that bore no inkling of rain. Elen-ai was grateful for that. It meant that she didn't have to ride in the cabin with the Prince.

That night they set up camp rather than detour off the road into the land of one of the seven families. It was easier to set up a makeshift shelter than travel several days out of their way to impose themselves onto the hospitality of any of the families, as would be required if they were to cross into non-sovereign land.

After checking that no assailants lurked in the nearby area, Elen-ai took herself a little to the side of the camp so that she could pray to the Shadow God. Her talk with the Councilwoman had made her realise that it had been too many days since she had paid her due to the patron deity of the Family. The Family's devotion to the Shadow God had endured while others forgot their gods. One of Elen-ai's earliest memories was the silent prayer of the Mothers and Fathers, seeing them in the home's courtyard one winter morning when the mist still skulked across the ground. The quiet depth of the Family's faith offered in return many gifts, one of them the ability to slip unseen where others would be clearly visible. She prayed kneeling, her focus locked totally on the prayer and the quiet serenity that prayer and her god gave her. Once her worship was complete, she stood, brushing the dirt off her knees.

"What were you doing?" The Prince's voice made her jump. It was an unforgivable oversight that she had not realised he was nearby.

"I was praying," she told him stiffly.

"To what?" As she had learned was the case when he was curious, he had dropped the unpleasant manner with which he normally addressed her. She wasn't certain if she was glad for the reprieve or resentful that he was nice because he wanted something from her.

"The god of shadows," she replied curtly. She figured the easiest way to deal with him was to give him what he wanted.

"Not the Divine One?" he asked.

"No. I didn't think most inhabitants of the Queendom actually gave much thought to truly worshipping the Divine One," Elen-ai added as an afterthought.

"I certainly think there's something else out there aside from this." Gidyon swept his arms wide in a gesture around him. "As apparently do you," he noted.

"Is it a problem that I worship?" Elen-ai snapped.

"No actually. It's just...unexpected," Gidyon replied.

Elen-ai paused for a moment, trying to come up with a response, but inspiration did not strike in a timely fashion. "You should get back to the main camp," she told him. "It's safer there."

Despite her expectation that a snark-infused quip would come her way, nothing eventuated. Gidyon merely accompanied her back to the camp, a thoughtful expression on his face.

The Councillors sat hand in hand by the makeshift fire that the guards had built. Elen-ai looked at them for a moment, fascinated by their perfect unity. They seemed so content with each other, so completed by the other's presence. She had always believed such love a mere myth. However here before her, she saw that she was wrong. Fleetingly, she wondered if she would ever find such completion in another person. The thought that her very personhood would be so tied up in the existence of another was terrifying. She dismissed the notion quickly. To have such a relationship would mean leaving the Family, and she would never leave the Family.

The Prince conversed with the two Councillors over the meal while Elen-ai sat contentedly in her own silence. Eventually, the meal was finished and the conversation petered out. The Councillors and Prince went to sleep while the royal guards kept watch in shifts. Elen-ai dozed lightly, unable to shake the sense that something uncertain loomed on the edge of her awareness. However despite her unease, when she awoke in the morning, no harm had come to any member of the party.

It was as they were breaking camp, when everybody's arms were full of one thing or another, that the attack occurred.

SEVEN

Elen-ai was not by the Prince's side when she saw the first of the mercenaries come seemingly out of nowhere and charge at him, blade drawn. Her yell prompted the Prince to turn and catch sight of his attacker while several paces still separated them. He threw the bundle he was carrying at the approaching assailant, but given he had been tasked with carrying blankets, it was an ineffective defence. Elen-ai dropped what she was carrying and released one of her blades in a motion faster than the eye could see, sending it flying past the Prince's head and deep into the eye of Gidyon's would-be killer.

Before she could get to the Prince's side however, she found herself dodging the scything blow of another attacker. She freed another blade and ducked under his wild swing. She twisted around him, calling upon the skills of the Family to shimmer out of his sight. Confused, he swung wildly rather than stopping as she had hoped he would. His blade nicked her arm, the pain flashing up along her shoulder before she shut it away as a problem to resolve later. Her retribution for the injury was swift. She used the speed built up over many years of training to flank him, drawing another knife and pushing it into his back between his ribs. Even with only a half-second to look, she had picked the correct spot and the knife had found his heart. He fell and she yanked the blade free, throwing it at another man trying to get to Gidyon.

Out of the corner of her eye, she saw three men approaching the Councillors drop in quick succession. She didn't have time to be concerned with the foreigners. Her first priority was the Prince. To let him die, especially at the hands of these untrained ruffians, would be mortifying, especially as she had not noticed their approach.

The sound of their guards fighting off the attackers rang in her ears as she ran over to the Prince's side, the pain in her arm forgotten, his safety her only thought. A third attacker made for him, knocking over the guard who had placed herself in front of Gidyon. Elen-ai cut him down by sliding forward and putting her knife in the softness of his belly. She didn't want to waste any time trying to break through the bone of his chest. Easier to leave him in agonising pain on the ground.

One more person tried to take the life of the heir to the throne, but Elen-ai intercepted her, driving a knife into the woman's arm, twirling around her and then breaking her neck in a sharp, brutal motion.

The sound of fighting stopped, replaced by the ragged intake of breath. There was something quite jarring about the sudden quiet.

Elen-ai turned to the Prince. "Gidyon, are you hurt?" she demanded.

The Prince, arms coiled across his abdomen, did not respond. Elen-ai grabbed him, concern making her rough. She pulled his arms free and gasped when she saw the blood from the slash, similar to the one she had given one of his attackers.

"I need bandages," Elen-ai called out, taking the Prince's weight and helping him to the ground. She couldn't see the cut, but judging by how much blood there was, it was deep enough to be fatal.

"Bandages! Now!" she yelled, pressing her hands to Gidyon's wound. His face was a sickly yellow colour. The smell of gore came to her nose.

Gentle hands pulled Elen-ai back. She struggled against them but whoever had gripped her was far stronger than she had expected and she did not immediately break free. "Let Freya help him, lady Elen-ai. She is a healer of great skill," the Councilman told her.

She stopped struggling and he let her go. Every muscle tense, she watched as the Councilwoman knelt by the Prince who now was going pale, blood oozing sickeningly from his stomach. When Councilwoman Kuch made no attempt to touch him, Elen-ai started forward again, but she was arrested by the Councilman's arm shooting out. "Just watch," he advised.

"But she isn't even touching him," Elen-ai protested, readying a knife to strike him.

"Just watch," he repeated.

Elen-ai kept her eyes on the Prince. Sure enough, he did appear to look a little less like he was on the verge of death. The blood remained on his clothes and pooled on the ground around him, but it did not appear to be increasing in volume as it should be from such a severe wound.

"Oh," Elen-ai realised suddenly, turning to regard the Councilman. "She's-"

"A healer," he replied firmly.

Elen-ai knew that the skills of the Family were not unique, but there were precious few in the Queendom who had any knowledge of the gifts of faith. However, it seemed that the foreigners before her were well acquainted with the gifts of their gods and used them with as much skill as the Family. Perhaps there was more to the legends surrounding these two than she had initially thought. She went to her knees by the Prince's side, her fingers finding the pulse on his throat. It beat strong, if not a little fast. The Councilwoman was sitting back on her heels, a slight smile on her face.

"He should be fine. He just needs rest now," she told Elen-ai. She frowned slightly. "Wait. Ah, it's you. Stay still," she commanded.

Elen-ai looked in puzzlement at the Councilwoman who was staring intently at Elen-ai. "Your arm," she explained after a few moments had passed, the look of intense focus wiped from her face.

Elen-ai glanced at the arm that had been pierced earlier. Her sleeve was bloodied but the injury was healed completely. "I've never met a healer as powerful as you," she told the Councilwoman as she returned to her inspection of the Prince. He was gazing around in a daze but seemed to be otherwise completely fine.

"You aren't afraid of me?" The Councilwoman seemed unconcerned by that possibility, merely curious.

Elen-ai shrugged. "You have been given the gifts of faith. Why is that something to fear?"

The Councilwoman smiled at Elen-ai then turned to her companion. "Are you alright, Ashtyn?"

He came to her side then, helping her up and putting an arm gently around her. "I'm fine, Freya. I didn't even get a chance to be touched. You took care of that before they even came close to us."

Elen-ai looked back to the attackers she had seen drop as she made her way over to the Prince. At the time she hadn't given them any thought, but now that she considered it, she hadn't seen any weapon touch them. It seemed that the Councilwoman's ability to heal could also be used to inflict damage. Tactfully, she said nothing. A few of the royal guards had survived and such a conversation was best conducted away from the ears of those who didn't understand what it meant to be kissed by a god's power. She turned her attention back to her charge.

"Your Highness, can you hear me?" she asked him.

The glazed look in his eye cleared slightly. "We were attacked," he mumbled.

"Quite right."

"I thought I was hurt." He struggled to sit up further, looking down at his stomach.

"You were, but the Councilwoman fixed you," Elen-ai said, her voice imbued with a cheerfulness to deter him from asking too many questions. "Come on, let's get you into the carriage. You need some rest." She heaved the Prince to his feet, giving him some dignity by not draping him across her shoulders, but instead putting her arm around his waist and allowing him to lean on her as she guided him toward the carriage.

"Who were the attackers?" he asked her as they walked. He appeared to be rapidly recovering his wits.

"Not sure. I'll have a look at them once you're inside the carriage," she replied.

"Will it be safe in there?" He sounded concerned, probably afraid at the prospect of facing an actual fight again. No practice sparring could prepare anyone for the unpredictability or fear that accompanied a fight for one's life. Not that the Prince had done much fighting.

"Don't worry, I'll make certain it's safe," Elen-ai assured him.

They reached the carriage and he climbed inside, settling himself among the cushions and looking like a frightened child which, in fairness, was exactly what he was.

Elen-ai clambered to the carriage roof and crouched there, listening for sounds that didn't fit with the aftermath of the fight. She heard moans, the sound of someone weeping softly, and quiet conversation, but nothing that could be even remotely mistaken for someone lying in wait to attack. She climbed back down, giving the Prince a businesslike nod.

"How many do we have left?" she asked the guard standing by the carriage once she had firmly closed the door. The guard seemed to be in a state of shock, standing in the one spot and staring about him. His weapon was held loosely in his hands, but Elen-ai did not think that he was aware of it. She repeated her question, causing him to start.

"Uh, I don't know," he admitted.

"Well go and find out," she suggested, going over to the body of one of the attackers. She heard his footsteps as he plodded away and the murmur as he spoke with one of the other guards and the sharp sob, but those were things she paid no heed. Her attention was focused on the still-warm body.

Some may have felt squeamish about handing a dead person, but Elen-ai was well acquainted with death. There was nothing threatening about a corpse. A corpse couldn't try to kill you. Her search revealed no information of any value. The man's clothes were nondescript and there was nothing on his person that might give some indication of who he was or who had sent him. She conducted the same investigation on the other five assailants just to be sure, but her searches yielded similar results.

Elen-ai straightened up from the final body. She hadn't expected to find anything. These were the kind of brutal, amoral thugs who could be found anywhere and would perform any task without questions provided the right amount of money was placed in front of them. They were completely anonymous, possibly foreigners, the kind of people who had racked up some large debt in an unpleasant place and were willing to do anything to repay it quickly. Elen-ai was nevertheless frustrated. She had hoped someone would have been careless.

The smell of gore and death lingered over the area. It didn't much bother Elen-ai. When she was nine, she had been sent to work in a slaughter yard. Her first task had been poultry, plucking birds from one side, detaching their heads with a swift movement, then tossing the decapitated corpses onto a pile on her other side. From there, she had been given more and more messy tasks. The larger animals were far less pleasant to deal with. After four months in the slaughter yard, she never found the smell of blood or gore overly troubling again.

She walked over to the Councillors who were conferring quietly together, their heads close, arms loosely about each other. They appeared to reach some kind of consensus.

"Did you find anything?" the Councilwoman asked as Elen-ai approached.

She shook her head. "Nothing. The attackers were the sort of brute that's easy to hire and won't care what the task is so long as they're paid – even killing a Queen's son. If I had to guess, though, they would have tried to make it look like a robbery."

"It wasn't?" Despite the question, it was clear that the Councilwoman knew very well that there was more than simple greed behind the attack. Elen-ai saw no point in pretending otherwise.

"I doubt that very much," she replied.

"That's a problem," the Councilwoman said, her expression wry.

Elen-ai quirked an eyebrow, stifling a laugh. Perhaps she was more shocked by the attack than she had first thought. This was not the time for laughter. "I think I should go and consult with the Prince," she said.

"Certainly," the Councilwoman agreed. "We'll do whatever you decide," she added. She seemed completely unperturbed by the events of the day. Whatever she had seen in that rebellion, it must have been quite awful for her to be so unconcerned by the sudden attack, or the near-death of the Prince.

Elen-ai returned to the carriage. The Prince was starting to regain his colour although he still looked very fragile.

"I think we should head back to the capital," she told him. When the Prince didn't respond, Elen-ai continued. "We only have a few guards left, and it seems someone does actually want you dead. There was even a halfway decent attempt to make it look as though they were simply robbers. Not convincing enough, but still, not bad. I recommend we go back to the capital. Hopefully, the guards we have left will be enough to fend off another attack if it occurs."

"No." He said it softly, but with the obstinate tone that she had come to know well.

"No?" she repeated back, incredulous.

"We should go to the Veertak estate. We're only a few hours from Atak." He named the Veertak capital, a town populated almost exclusively by scholars.

"Why?"

"The Veertak are loyal to my mother. It is in their interests to be so. They should agree to loan us some of their guards if we request. That would be safer than just going back." The acrimony toward her seemed to have dissipated in the face of the more pressing issue that someone had tried to kill him.

"Gidyon, all it takes is one member of the Veertak to want you to dead," Elen-ai protested.

"How many guards do we have left?" he asked.

"Five."

"That won't be enough." The Prince's tone may have been firm, but Elen-ai could see the fear on his face. And as much as she wouldn't say to him, he did have a point. All it would take would be for her to be distracted for one second and the Prince could be killed by another assailant. It was good fortune that the Councilwoman and her skills had been there to save him this time, but no healing gift could revive him if he were killed by a lucky blow. She thought for a moment longer, evaluating the benefit of simply returning to Herran straight away or of making their way across to Atak. Her preference was to return to the capital as fast as possible and lock Gidyon safely in the Palace surrounded by the Royal Guards. But she wasn't certain that the Prince would manage. He was clearly terrified despite the veneer of calm he had somehow mustered. That fact alone in the wrong situation could be just as dangerous as a blade. Besides, a former member of the Family lived in Atak. She was sure that she could approach Sam-et for help.

"Atak it is," she sighed.

The carriage with its ornate decorations was far too conspicuous for Elen-ai's liking but there was no alternative. She rode on top of the carriage with the remaining guards riding alongside it. Everyone was tense as they made their way across the countryside, waiting for another attack. She wondered how they felt at the deaths of the other guards, or the fact that the bodies of those who had died had been left by the side of the road out of brutal necessity. Her musing went so far as to be impressed by the fact that those who had survived were so focused on the task at hand. Then again, grief and shock would often dissipate in the face of necessity. Likely, when they got to the Veertak home they would all seek the solace of a big mug of ale.

The Councilwoman sat beside her, having elected again to not ride in the carriage. Had it been anyone else, Elen-ai would have worried that another attack could put them in danger, but after she had seen what the woman could do, she was not concerned in the slightest.

"Thank you. For your help back there," she said after some time had passed. She liked that about the foreign woman, that she did not feel the need to incessantly chatter. People who were not members of the Family often filled silence with empty words. It was tiresome.

Councilwoman Kuch looked slightly bemused. "Why would I not help?"

"To reveal what you can do in a country where that sort of knowledge has been largely lost could be dangerous. More dangerous than being attacked by a band of second-rate hired killers," Elen-ai replied.

"It was once a secret in the Third Country, too," the Councilwoman replied.

"What changed?" Elen-ai asked.

"I was put in a position where I had to reveal my abilities in front of a great many people."

"Why?"

The other woman hesitated. "It's complicated. Anyway, once people had seen what happened, there was no trying to pretend it hadn't. People knew what faith could bestow. There was great concern that it would lead to total chaos. But faith isn't as simple as believing in order to attain abilities. Which you would know, of course."

Elen-ai ducked her head in a non-response. There were members of the Family who did not manage to find that true belief in the god of shadows. They were not cast out, but their role within the Family was limited. Many of them chose to leave.

"May I ask you a question?" the Councilwoman said after a moment of silence had passed.

"Certainly, Councilwoman."

"Please, call me Freya, I have never quite gotten used to the title of Councilwoman." The other woman smiled.

"If you insist...Freya." Elen-ai was never one to stand on ceremony. "Your question?" "I was just wondering why anyone would want to kill Prince Gidyon," she said thoughtfully.

Elen-ai shrugged. "I mean, we've never had a man on the throne before. The mere thought is deeply unsettling. The Queen certainly felt that he would be in danger as a result of her decision to name him her heir. But there are many motivations behind why someone may want him dead. People want another person dead for the oddest of reasons."

"To order someone killed seems very," Freya hesitated for a moment, "personal," she finished.

Elen-ai shrugged again. "Sometimes people come to the Family wanting to eliminate someone in the way of their business interests. Seems pretty impersonal to me." She scanned the area as she spoke. Fortunately, they were travelling on flat land that offered few places for an individual to hide, let alone a large group. The verdant green of the grass that covered the land on either side of the road was almost overwhelming.

"Even then," Freya countered, sounding quite content, despite the brutal events of the day, not to mention the macabre nature of their discussion. She did not say anything else. She didn't need to. There was a certain truth to the fact that wanting someone else dead was quite personal. In some cases, wanting the certainty of someone's death at the hands of another person spoke to a certain coldly intense rage.

"Thank you for your help with Gidyon," Elen-ai said hesitantly. She felt awkward. Members of the Family traditionally only relied on one another. She was enormously in the debt of this woman next to her. It was a new feeling.

"I am a healer first and foremost. It is my duty to heal when I can. But you are welcome," Freya replied, a smile on her face.

Very few words were exchanged between members of the party for the remainder of the journey. There was a certain comfort in the silence that existed between Elen-ai and Freya. Something in what the foreign dignitary had revealed about herself made Elen-ai feel more at ease around her, even while others might have been put off. They had only been travelling for a few hours when they reached the outskirts of the large township Atak. Held by the Veertak and located on the shore of one of the Queendom's seven huge lakes, it was a quaint and peaceful area populated by people whose interest mostly lay more in books than people. Unlike the varying designs and styles of the buildings in the capital, most of the buildings in Atak were low-lying timber structures. The exception was the Veertak's family home and the great library within it. The house was a compound of several stories made of stone to minimise the risk of fire.

The carriage made its way through the streets, drawing barely any glances. Elen-ai was inwardly amused, knowing well the way of scholars and their interest in the outside world. Unless of course, a rival scholar threatened to steal some important discovery. Scholars were some of the Family's best customers, willing to kill for the credit - or suppression - of some discovery. For the most part though, their willingness to kill was limited purely to the world of academia. Nevertheless, that unexpected savagery could have been directed at Gidyon, Elen-ai reminded herself.

Because of the scholars' patronage of the Family, Elen-ai was well acquainted with Atak. She was quite fond of the town, having thought to herself that if she ever had to leave the Family, this would be where she would go. Tranquillity reigned there, for the most part. That tranquillity was uncharacteristically disrupted as the carriage entered the gates of the Veertak home. An elderly man came rushing out to meet the carriage. Elen-ai knew him by sight as the patriarch of the Veertak family, custodian of their knowledge alongside his somewhat fierce, if not adored, wife. Elen-ai raised her eyebrows at his speed, wondering if he would topple over from his forward momentum. For him, a fall would surely lead to an egregious break, although perhaps Freya could be prevailed upon to heal such an injury if it occurred.

Prince Gidyon cautiously opened the door to the carriage and stuck his head out. "My lord Veertak, is everything alright?" He greeted the old man, his voice carrying a note of uncertainty at the unceremonious appearance of the aged man.

"Master Gidyon. I might ask the same of you," the old man gasped, coming to a perilously hasty stop before the carriage. Elen-ai feared that he may crash into the carriage and break several of his fragile old bones.

"How could you possibly know?" Gidyon asked, his face creasing into a frown of puzzlement.

"Why Master Gidyon, your mother. The attack. Have you not heard?" the old man wheezed.

EIGHT

The Prince's face grew quite pale. He tumbled out of the carriage to the old man's side. "Varl what happened?" he asked urgently, formality totally forgotten.

"Word reached us this morning by messenger bird of an attempt on her life that took place last night."

The merit of keeping people in city residences seemed to have proved itself yet again even as the speed with which such information spread across the country seemed almost indecent.

"What happened?" Gidyon all but reached out and grabbed the octogenarian by the shoulders to shake him. Elen-ai worried that such an action may very well snap the Veertak patriarch in half.

"That I do not know," the old man responded gravely. "Don't worry, she's not harmed badly," he added, seeing the stricken look on Gidyon's face.

"Who was behind it?" Gidyon demanded. Elen-ai, watching his face, could see fear for his mother giving way to anger.

"As yet, nobody knows. I'm sorry." Varl Veertak looked with great compassion at the Prince whose composure had utterly deserted him.

Gidyon was silent for several moments, his stare vacant. Then he took a deep breath and with evident effort looked at the old man. "Obviously it's not your fault. May we come inside? An attack was made on my own life this morning. I somehow doubt that they're unrelated." Elen-ai was impressed at the self-discipline it would have taken him to pull himself together like that.

"Divine one! Are you hurt? Of course, come inside at once." Like a clucking mother, Varl ushered the Prince and his retinue inside, greeting the Councillors quickly and with flustered warmth. He looked curiously at Elen-ai whose name was given with no other explanation, but given the tumultuous circumstances of the Prince's arrival, there was no time for him to ask any questions about her place in the party.

"Let us go to the library," he suggested. "We can discuss this at greater length there. We will make up rooms for our foreign friends where they can relax after what I'm sure would have been a most awful ordeal." He truly did bustle, giving distracted orders to servants who were clearly accustomed to vague directives from him.

Elen-ai followed the Prince along the mansion's corridors, every sense on alert. She expected a trap of some sort, the Prince having been lured into the Veertak estate seeking refuge after the events of the morning, in case the first attempt did not succeed. Such complex plans were not unheard of. Certainly, it was what she would have arranged had she been attempting to take the life of the Prince. While she doubted that the Veertak family were interested in killing Gidyon, the surprising ruthlessness of scholars should never be underestimated. Until she had seen more, she could not eliminate them as suspects.

As they reached the library, a servant with a tray of drinks and food met them, placing it on the large reading table in the middle of the room before exiting.

"Oh." Gidyon glanced down at his stained shirt. The blood which had dried on it flaked off as he moved, falling onto the expensive rug on the floor.

"Never mind that," Varl reassured him.

Gidyon took a seat, his eyes hungrily on the plate of smoked meats and fruit. Elen-ai made a motion for him to wait, taking a mug of the slightly warmed fruit juice - a specialty of the Veertak region - and a piece of the meat, and sampling them. When the tell-tale tingle of poison did not reach her tongue she nodded to him and he helped himself. The whole exchange was conducted in a few seconds, but she realised that the head of the Veertak family had been watching with a keen interest.

"Lady Elen-ai, I'm terribly sorry but I didn't quite catch where you were from." He addressed her with the courtesy he would afford someone of the seven families, despite the fact that her name gave away that she was not of such lineage. The suffix -ai or -am for women and -et or -en for men was adopted by all but those who were members of the families of power.

"That's because the information wasn't volunteered," she replied before the Prince could speak.

"Perhaps you can tell me what you know of what happened," Gidyon interjected, either picking up on her reluctance to divulge anything about her identity or simply preoccupied with the news of his mother's attack.

Nodding in deference to the Prince's point, Varl sat down. He opened his mouth to speak but was interrupted by the entrance of an austere-looking woman. Valena Veertak, the matriarch of the family and renowned scholar held herself with the poise of a woman decades her junior. Unlike her husband's wispy white hair that looked as though it had not seen a comb since his sixth decade of life, her hair was tightly plaited to ensure that not one stray strand escaped. She looked every part the authority figure that he did not. The only thing that was similar about their appearance was their eyes. Both had sharp bright eyes that spoke of a keen intellect and spelled trouble for anyone foolish enough to forget it.

"My lady Valena." Gidyon stood and bowed to her, courtesy emerging despite the shocking circumstances of the day.

"Master Gidyon," she replied, her deep voice without any hint of the quaver that often accompanied age.

"Gidyon had not heard of the attack on his mother. He came following an attack on his own life to us to seek shelter." The manner in which her husband efficiently gave her crucial information spoke to decades of practice and partnership.

"Surely the same hand is behind each effort," she replied, outwardly not shocked by the news, logic her primary response. It gave much away about who she was.

"It seems the logical conclusion," Varl agreed.

Understanding flashed between them on an unspoken level, a communication refined over a lifetime together. It reminded Elen-ai of the dynamic that existed between the two Councillors from the Third Country.

"My Lord Gidyon, I do not believe I have met your companion before," the matriarch said abruptly, her gaze turning to Elen-ai.

"My apologies lady Valena," Gidyon had remained standing, his own lifetime of manners at work. "This is lady Elen-ai. She-"

"-is a member of the Family," Valena concluded for him, fixing Elen-ai with an intense stare. Unlike many who looked at her knowing who she was, it was not a look that held judgment, merely evaluation, and perhaps a little consideration of what the presence a member of the Family at the side of the Queen's son might suggest. Beside her, Varl murmured "oh of course," more to himself than anyone else.

The door was flung open once again before anything more could be said. Elen-ai's concern over the Veertaks' knowledge of her identity was pushed aside by the man who walked in. It would be conservative to say he was the most handsome man Elen-ai had ever seen.

"Did I hear-" He stopped and looked at Gidyon, staring with eyes that were a captivating shade of blue. "It seems I heard correctly," he answered himself, not taking his eyes from the Prince. There was something unnerving about the unblinking intensity of his stare.

"Master Gidyon, lady Elen-ai, Erek of the Rasatan family. He is visiting us to conduct research on boat design," Varl said calmly.

"Erek is often in Herran on business. We actually meet quite often when he pays his respects to my mother. Erek, it's good to see you again," Gidyon said, his words soothing the possible awkwardness of Erek's unannounced intrusion into the room.

The man's eyes slid over Elen-ai ever so briefly then returned to scrutinise the Prince. "Master Gidyon, I am so sorry about your mother. I am sure you share our deep relief to learn she survived such a heinous attack." Sincerity imbued his melodious voice as he advanced, still looking at the Prince. He noticed the dried blood on Gidyon's clothes. "What happened!" he exclaimed.

"It would seem my mother was not the only target," Gidyon explained. "The blood is not mine," he added.

"Thank the Divine One. I can only hope that justice was swiftly delivered to whoever would seek to harm you or your wonderful mother," the man said, putting a hand to his chest to emphasise the point.

"That's very kind of you to say, Erek," Gidyon replied, sitting back down and taking a sip of the warmed juice. "But I still don't know what exactly happened to my mother," he added, a pointed edge to his tone.

Valena took a seat next to her husband, picking up a mug of her own. "Please, join us, Erek. We were just about to tell Master Gidyon what we had heard," she said smoothly.

After a moment's hesitation, Erek accepted the invitation, sitting down in one of the room's other luxurious chairs. He leaned forward, adopting the pose of an intent listener.

"What we know is only from a message sent by one of our own within Herran. From what she could gather, a delivery of food brought several individuals into the Palace yesterday late afternoon. They killed their way through the kitchens and managed to actually find the Queen. She was hurt, but the guards intervened before she could be gravely wounded," Valena said.

"Surely the guards would have checked to ensure that the delivery was safe." Erek sounded shocked at the laxity of the royal guards. Elen-ai was not. They may have been well trained, even skilled with weapons, but carelessness was nestled within most people who did the same thing day in, day out. She would know, she had used that to her advantage many times.

"No. Today the delivery will have been what I order from the market on my weekly walk there." Gidyon glanced at Elen-ai. "It seems you were correct about not being able to trust them," he told her, sounding terribly sad. Elen-ai felt sorry for him to be so crushed by the truth of the world.

"We can't fathom why anyone would want to kill your mother, Gidyon. She has been nothing but a fair and just ruler, even if she is currently without an heir." Varl turned to his wife as he spoke. She nodded once to signal her approval of his comment.

"Actually, she isn't," Gidyon said.

Three pairs of eyes snapped to look at the Prince. Elen-ai's own eyes flicked between each face.

"Is there something we don't know?" Valena enquired politely.

"I believe my mother was going to announce it today, but it seems she was," Gidyon hesitated, "distracted by other matters. She has decided that I am to be her heir."

Total silence descended on the room. Elen-ai saw little shock on the faces of the three people opposite her, but she did see the reflexive disapproval against the complete rupture from tradition.

"We heard rumours," Varl admitted. "Although nobody was certain if they were true or not."

An uncomfortable silence followed his words. Eventually, Gidyon spoke. "What my mother wishes is unprecedented, but in studying of our country's laws I have found nothing written which forbids it. I know that it is a change, but you yourself said, Lord Veertak, my mother has been a fair and just Queen. I would ask you to trust her judgment once more."

At some point in Gidyon's life, someone had done a spectacular job of training him to muster himself under stressful circumstances, Elen-ai thought. How he could be so eloquent after such a day, she had no idea.

"You know why there has never been a man on the throne. It could lead to great political turmoil," Varl said gently.

"I've thought about this ever since my mother told me what she wanted to do. Every Queen…consorts with a number of members of the seven families to ensure that any child born is of unclear parentage. This means that no favour can be bestowed upon a particular family as a result of this link. What if I pledged to marry someone of common birth, with no ties to any of the seven families? That way any child I bore would be similarly without any attachment to a particular family. As I am now." Gidyon leaned forward slightly as he waited for the consideration of his proposal to be completed.

"You would marry someone of low birth?" Erek spoke, not bothering to hide his disdain at the prospect.

"Erek, if we only married from within the seven families, we'd be so inbred it would be quite terrible," Valena said to him, her polite delivery lessening the bite of her dismissiveness.

"The idea now, though? You're only what - sixteen years? Something you promise to do now you may not wish to do when the time comes," Varl cautioned him, leaning forward in his chair.

"I'm committing to taking the throne, aren't I?" Gidyon answered, a slight smile on his face.

Varl chuckled in response. He looked at his wife who gave him a slight nod.

"Gidyon, you have the support of the Veertak family," Valena told him.

A slight relaxing of the muscles in Gidyon's throat gave away his fear that the Veertaks would reject his claim. "I'm glad to hear that," he said evenly, his voice not giving away his relief at all.

Erek, who had been watching the exchange spoke then. "Well Gidyon, I can tell you that I personally support your claim to the throne, but I am not sure the rest of my family will. The best that I can do is promise to try and talk them around."

"It is all I could ask of you, and I cannot tell you how much I appreciate it. From all three of you," Gidyon responded, gratitude clearly on his face as he looked at the three adults.

Erek moved first. "If you'll excuse me, I must get back to that research. The faster I finish it, the faster I can get back home and start trying to convince my family that you will be the wonderful ruler I know you can be." Erek stood, gave a little nod of parting and left the room.

Once he had left, Valena snorted. "Don't expect much from Erek's honeyed promises. He has no idea what he just undertook to do. Thinks he can talk his father around? Divine One, he'd have better luck talking a tree out of being timber. His father won't be charmed by Erek's good looks, stubborn, stupid man, and his wife wouldn't say anything even if she did think otherwise, she's so timid," she told Gidyon, making absolutely no effort to disguise her scorn for the head of the Rasatan family. Given that the Veertaks shared a border with the Rasatan lands, it seemed a dangerous move for her to so openly express the derisive opinion. Not that anything she said wasn't commonly held wisdom. Wenden Rasatan was considered a domineering and dogmatic man whose petty tyranny was given free reign by the timidity of his wife, Keela. Some whispers even suggested that there was madness somewhere in the family.

"What will change his family's mind?" Gidyon asked.

"The promise of greater power," Valena answered immediately, putting her juice aside and folding her hands in her lap.

It was true; the Rasatan family was one of the three minor families within the Queendom alongside the Veertak and Bertak families. While the Veertak had never displayed meaningful interest in gaining a greater political position, the desire of the Rasatan and Bertak families for ever-greater riches and importance was renowned. That being said, all of the seven families vied for greater power and importance in some way or another. That ambition was why the tradition of the Queen remaining unmarried and bearing children of unknown paternity had been implemented - to always keep them at arm's length from the throne.

"That's why someone tried to kill my mother and me, isn't it?" Gidyon asked suddenly.

Elen-ai tensed, worried that he had just indirectly accused the heads of the Veertak family of the attack on him and his mother.

"It wouldn't surprise me," Varl shrugged, making no effort to hide his disdain for such behaviour.

"I know this has all happened very quickly, and there is much to consider. Perhaps it may be worth bathing and resting for a little?" Valena suggested kindly.

"I would appreciate that greatly." Gidyon seized upon the suggestion. "I cannot tell you how much your support and hospitality means to me," he told the wizened couple, letting his mask of composure slip just a fraction and exposing the afraid young man beneath.

"I remember when you were very young, and you came to visit us here with your mother. You displayed a desire to learn and a humility regarding the limits of your knowledge even then. Perhaps you don't remember," Valena told him.

"Of course I remember. You brought me into the library - this room, wasn't it? And you helped me understand how I could find books that I wanted." The Prince smiled at the memory.

"You made quite the impression on me then. At the time I thought that you would make a superb advisor to the sister who would follow you. It seems I will have to amend that impression to think you will make a good King," she said gently. Gidyon blushed at the compliment, perhaps the first that he had received in relation to his new position.

"If I could offer you a piece of counsel, though. Perhaps you should not advertise the identity of your companion," Valena added.

"How did you know?" Elen-ai asked. It was the first time she had spoken.

"I have lived a very long time, young lady, and I have seen a great many things. Your kind has a distinctiveness that one learns to recognise," the old woman responded. "But if you are at Gidyon's side perhaps there is more at work here than even I first thought. Do not worry, neither of us will speak of this to anybody else."

The ambiguity of her comment had Elen-ai frowning. Perhaps the old woman knew something in relation to the Queen's secret, but Varl chimed in, moving Elen-ai's thoughts and the conversation, elsewhere before she could ask any questions of Valena. "Our servants should have prepared rooms for you and lady Elen-ai. They should be ready by now. Your Highness," he added, testing out the word.

"Please, call me Gidyon." The Prince smiled at the old man, his whole face lighting up.

Elen-ai remained alert as Gidyon bathed. The grand family home of the Veertaks was made from a grey stone that left the interior of the building somewhat dim. Attempts had been made to counter this through large windows and large fireplaces. This, combined with the crammed bookshelves in nearly every room, gave the grand mansion a deceptively cosy and intimate feel. Elen-ai could hear the tread of people coming and going through the entire house as various scholars came in search of one text or another. The Veertak family guarded the source of its power just as fiercely as the other six families within the Queendom guarded theirs, keeping the knowledge of which they were the guardians inside their very house. While Elen-ai was inclined to believe that Varl and Valena had every intention to support the Prince and his claim to the throne, the constant comings and goings of scholars in search of an obscure text or a consultation with one of their learned colleagues meant that the security of the building was woeful. Anybody could come in and try to finish the job that had been left incomplete that morning.

Gidyon emerged from the bathing room, his hair wet. Something about the washing left him looking his age, his face round with youth. The very adult worries of politics and power games had temporarily departed from his shoulders, sloughed off with the dirt and blood from the road.

He threw himself down into a chair and finally let the fear that he had been containing show on his face.

"Are you alright?" Elen-ai asked.

He took several deep breaths. "I think so," he replied. "It is odd to realise that you are one of the few people I can truly trust," he added. "Normally loyalty can't be bought," he concluded, a sardonic smile twisting his mouth.

Elen-ai didn't know if that was a barb or simply the Prince's struggle to come to terms with the unfaithfulness of the world.

"It seems I am in a predicament," Gidyon continued. "Some member of the seven families wants my mother and me dead."

"Are you sure that it's a member of the seven families?" Elen-ai challenged.

He tilted his head to look at her. "Who else would have the resources and the knowledge to effect such attacks?" he asked.

She couldn't disagree with his point. "You would be much safer in Herran," she said instead, restating her earlier claim.

"But surely they may try again."

Taking her silence as an affirmative, he went on. "But it is not just question of safety. I want whoever is behind this brought to justice. I need to prove to all who doubt me that I can control my people. That I am worthy of the throne. How can I do that if an attack on my mother's and my lives is an unsolved mystery?"

"An admirable objective, but how exactly do you propose to bring whoever ordered this attack to justice?" Elen-ai asked.

"I am going to find out who was behind this," he said, determination making him sit a little straighter in his chair.

"How exactly will you do that?"

She didn't mean it as a challenge, but perhaps it came out that way in her tone. His eyes focusing as he outlined his plan to her. "The only way to do it is to meet with each of the families and request their approval for my claim. It is a reasonable thing to do, especially given my...situation. Support from enough of the families will make the announcement acceptable to the rest of the Second Country. In the course of meeting the families, I'm bound to see something that will give me some indication of who was behind this. That, or someone will try again to end my life – hopefully we can catch them in the act rather than after I am killed."

Elen-ai sighed. How he expected clues to simply manifest themselves, she had no idea. Nevertheless, he had a point in that simply returning to Herran would not necessarily make him safer. And if he was not safe, then her contract was not fulfilled, and she could not go home. "I will follow you wherever you choose to go," she told him. "Aren't you worried about your mother, though?"

"I am," he admitted, hesitating slightly before going on. "If it were simple, I would go back to Herran now and see for myself that she's alright. But this is more important. It's about the stability of the Second Country, not just what I want. That has to come first. I will send her a message explaining what I intend to do. She will understand."

"Just tell me where we go." Elen-ai shrugged.

He nodded. "Thank you for your efforts this morning," he added. "I know that I would have likely died were it not for you."

"Just doing my job," she told the Prince, mentally crediting Freya's help to ensuring that outcome.

Despite it being against her every instinct, she left the Prince for a short while, venturing into the township around which the Veertak mansion was built. The Family believed knowledge was the key to almost everything, and information was sorely lacking in relation to who may have tried to kill the Queen and her son. So she had to see if she could redress this problem. She made her way to the door of a well-constructed little house near the lakeside part of the town and knocked. It was flung open by Sam-et who gave her a beaming welcome and ushered her into the house, showing no surprise at her unannounced appearance. "Elen-ai. What a wonderful surprise," he enthused.

Elen-ai smiled. Sam-et had been one of her brothers, only a few years older than her. They had always gotten along, even on occasion sharing a contract that required more than one person to complete. However, he had fallen in love with a girl that he had encountered on one of his contracts within the Veertak family's region. Because members of the Family were not permitted to be married, he had left to pursue a life with her. Elen-ai watched as he crossed the room, the training of the Family still obvious in the smooth silence of his stride. He picked up an infant from a crib.

"This is Am-ai," he said proudly, presenting the child to Elen-ai for inspection.

Unaware of how she was supposed to hold or respond to the child, Elen-ai leaned forward and gave an approving nod. "She's very...clean," she said lamely.

Sam-et roared with laughter. "Still very much a member of the Family, I see," he said, cradling his daughter close and giving her a loud kiss on the forehead. There was something fundamentally absentminded about his kiss that made it particularly profound. Elen-ai stared, amazed at the transformation of someone who had once taken life without flinching into this doting father.

"I can only assume you're in the region on a contract, Elen-ai?" he asked.

She nodded. "Of sorts. I've been engaged to protect the Prince."

He frowned in confusion. "Prince?"

"The Queen will name her son Gidyon her heir," she explained.

Instead of the outrage that Elen-ai had felt upon learning of the Queen's decision, a thoughtful look crossed Sam-et's face. "To place such a burden on him. Poor lad. So someone's trying to kill him?" Sam-et had always been quick. His departure had been a loss to the Family.

She nodded. "Have you heard anything that might help me know who it is?"

The child started to cry. Sam-et began to sway lightly from side to side to shush her. "Whispers. Nothing certain. I did once hear a rumour that the Queen had a lover, but it could simply be the product of an idle tongue."

"Rumour is rarely based on nothing," Elen-ai mused, watching as her former brother calmed his daughter.

He shrugged as much as he was able to with an armful of infant. "I'll keep an ear out for you, let you know if I hear anything."

"Thank you. I'm in your debt," she told him.

"You're leaving already? Stay, Len-am should be back soon. She'd love to meet you."

Elen-ai privately doubted that his wife would, in fact, be pleased to meet her. "I should get back to the Prince. Make sure he hasn't tripped over his own feet." She rolled her eyes.

She gave him a rough embrace around the child as he accompanied her to the door. "You're different," she added.

"Oh?" He tickled the baby under the chin, eliciting a giggle. Or perhaps a gurgle. Elen-ai had no idea.

"More...content," she said.

"I used to think there was no life outside the Family. There is, you know," he told her. "Be safe, Elen-ai."

She found the Prince in the Veertak library, a stack of books beside him. All the titles related to the gods or supernatural skills. "So you saw," she said.

He nodded. "There was a rip in my shirt, blood everywhere, and no wound. I would have to be pretty thick to not realise. Besides, I've heard the stories about the Councilwoman – her strange magic. I just thought it was made up to exaggerate her feats, but it seems I was wrong."

She wandered over to the books and picked one up. It was old, made by hand as was the case with all books, but with a cover made from some sort of timber. She suspected that it came from one of the other countries, judging by the design on the front. "What have you discovered?"

"Nothing substantial. I would need a lot more time in here to put anything meaningful together, but as far as I can tell, those whose faith is particularly strong have a variety of unusual skills. How that works, I cannot say."

"Is it that important to understand?" Elen-ai asked. She went over to the window. It looked out over the township to the calm, grey waters of lake Veertak beyond.

"To me, yes," he answered, closing the book he had been reading. "But this is not the most pressing matter. I have spoken with the Councillors. They will return to Herran and watch over my mother. You and I leave tomorrow."

"With guards?"

"No. A large party would draw too much attention, and possibly be off-putting to whoever tried to have me and mother killed," he said definitely. "I will say if anyone asks that this is a discreet visit, a personal journey. And if they ask, you are my aide."

She could agree with the wisdom in that approach. In fact, she likely would have proposed something similar herself. A large number of bodies to place in front of an oncoming blade were good and well, but she was too accustomed to stealth, to being able to slip along back roads and shadows. That could not be achieved when being accompanied by a retinue of guards. Besides, the Prince was right, better to lure out his would-be killer with the suggestion that he was vulnerable and naïve.

The Veertak's unexpected guests left early the next morning. The Prince had been treated to a very pleasant dinner the evening before – a Tak low had been slaughtered for the occasion - during which two of Varl and Valena's children were present. While both were older than Gidyon's mother, they deferred to him with a politeness that was not feigned. Try as she might, Elen-ai could not see the Veertak family as a threat to the throne in any way. As she observed the courteous and genuinely respectful treatment of Gidyon, she crossed the Veertak family off her mental list of suspects.

It had been decided that the two Councillors were to return to Herran in the royal carriage. Elen-ai crossed the small courtyard to farewell them, surprised to find that she was sad to part ways with them.

"Thank you again for your help," she said to Freya.

The older woman took Elen-ai's hand in one of her own and pressed her thumb into the palm. "We do it happily." She smiled. "Ashtyn and I haven't had an adventure for a while, so it is enjoyable to do something to help a good cause."

"You are so perfect together," Elen-ai told Freya, shaking her head.

The older woman laughed. "It was not always so," she responded, her eyes crinkling with the emotion of whatever memory the comment elicited. "Good luck," she added, briefly reaching out a hand to touch Elen-ai's shoulder and squeezing it in a gesture of friendship.

"Thank you," Elen-ai replied. "I think we'll need it."

NINE

It seemed the Prince realised he could either speak with Elen-ai, or sit in silence for the entirety of their travel.

"Where did you go yesterday?" he asked after they had been on the road for a little over an hour. The Veertaks had generously loaned Gidyon a small carriage. Two of his original five trunks came with them, taking up nearly all of the space in the tiny vehicle, the rest had been back sent to the Palace with the Councillors. Gidyon sat on the driver's seat with Elen-ai while she drove, holding the reins of the two hearat drawing the carriage. She had been dismayed when he had decided not to squeeze in with the trunks – she had been looking forward to the serenity of solitude.

"I went to see a former member of the Family," she answered, her eyes on the road. Rather than traversing the main road that ran through sovereign land, Elen-ai had elected to take them on a less frequented route running through the Veertak and Tak lands. Gidyon had deferred to her judgment without comment or question.

"Why?"

"Mostly the people who leave the Family tend to see quite a lot of what goes on wherever they end up. It's a habit drilled in to all of us from a young age, noticing things."

"I thought that if you left the Family all ties were cut." The Prince looked confused.

Elen-ai twisted her mouth as she thought of how to explain it. "It's technically true. I think the point is more that leaving the Family requires you to build a life from the very beginning. To whatever extent you still see former brothers and sisters, it is infrequent, and never for very long."

Gidyon looked down, thinking. Then he nodded. "That makes sense. It's similar with my uncles."

"Oh?" Elen-ai casually adjusted the reins to bring the hearat under closer control as they entered a poorly maintained section of the road.

"If they want to marry that's perfectly fine, but they must give up any connection to the royal family, even their name. They have to take a common name."

"I suppose I haven't ever heard of a Queen's advisor with a family," Elen-ai said thoughtfully, manoeuvring the carriage around a particularly large pothole.

The rattle of the carriage as it negotiated the road claimed the silence that fell between them. The road wound along the shore of lake Veertak, the clear day reflected in the water's surface, rippled only by a slight breeze. At one stage, they passed the mill which manufactured the paper that the Veertak family supplied to the rest of the Queendom. Of course, the cloth scraps that were made into the pages came from all over the country in the same way that the animal skins which made the vellum - used for particularly important documents - came from the Tak family's animals. The interconnectedness of the Second Country was woven across the landscape if you cared to look for it.

Despite the fact that she preferred the bustle and activity of the city, Elen-ai had always held a particular fascination for the manner in which the countryside could be deceptively silent. It was filled with uncounted unseen animals going about their business, or the wind through the trees. She appreciated the fact that such noises masked the footsteps of someone coming up behind you just as effectively as the sound of the city, provided you knew what you were doing.

A few people came from the opposite direction, but once they passed the mill, they encountered barely any travellers. It meant that they entered the Tak territory almost completely unnoticed. Elen-ai felt far safer than she had the previous day. This was what she knew, not travelling along in a gilded monstrosity screaming out their presence to anyone even remotely within eyesight.

The landscape flattened out even further as they crossed into the Tak lands. Herds of livestock became visible, watched over by lazy youths and individuals whose age gave them a relaxed competence. Elen-ai pointed as the shimmering blue waters of the Tak lake came into view many hours after they had left lake Veertak behind.

"Can you teach me to defend myself?" Gidyon asked abruptly.

Elen-ai glanced at him in surprise. "What?"

"You had me on the ground instantly when we fought. And when we were attacked yesterday, the only thing I did was get stabbed." He ran a hand over his abdomen despite there being no trace there of the injury he had sustained.

"I started learning how to fight as soon as I could hold a weapon," Elen-ai told him.

"Does that mean I can't learn anything?" he challenged.

She shrugged in thought. He waited for her to respond with no outward sign of impatience.

"I can try. But I can't promise that it will stop you from getting stabbed," she said after she had considered it.

"Isn't that what you're supposed to do?" he asked.

"Well I didn't exactly succeed, did I?" she muttered.

To her surprise, he laughed. "I survived," he reassured her.

So that evening when they stopped, she did her full set of exercises. Lasting almost an hour, Elen-ai rigorously tested and used every muscle in her body, practising kicks, punches, and a series of tumbles and rolls to work her agility, strength, and focus. The Prince spent most of the time watching her, fascinated by the display of physical prowess. It left her somewhat self-conscious, the way in which this young man seemed to observe her with such complete focus.

Elen-ai finished off her practice with a series of held poses, stretching out the muscles she was reasonably certain would ache in the morning. She had let herself become lax during her days with the Prince and she had paid the price when the hired thugs had tried to take his life. It was her good fortune that Freya had been on hand to heal him. But Freya was gone now. Elen-ai could not afford to be in any condition other than her peak.

"Come here," she ordered Gidyon.

He scrambled awkwardly to his feet at her instruction.

"Let me guess. When you were taught to use a sword you were taught that people adhere to certain conventions of swordcraft?"

He nodded.

Elen-ai chuckled. "That's a polite lie told to people who are never going to have to actually fight for their life. When you're in a proper fight, you do anything it takes to win. Don't simply think about the conventions of swordcraft. Think about how you can kick, punch, bite, to win. Can you pull their hair?" To emphasise her point, she circled around him and quickly stepped forward, grabbing a handful of his hair in her fist and giving it a slight tug. "But let's look at other things first," she continued.

As the light faded, Elen-ai made Gidyon practice punching and kicking. He uttered no word of protest, merely doing as she bade with the same obedience that he showed his tutors in the Palace. When she saw that he was growing weary, she called a halt to the lesson and set about making a small fire. Despite the onset of Spring, it was still cool at night. Elen-ai may have been content to simply be a little cold, but she wasn't certain that the Prince's delicate sensibilities would be able to cope.

"You'll hurt in the morning," she cautioned him as they ate the food that had been given to them by the Veertaks.

He shrugged. "I should know how to do this," he said. "Thank you for teaching me," he added.

"Any time." Elen-ai found his genuine gratitude strangely touching.

"Is it safe to sleep?" Gidyon asked as they laid out bedrolls and blankets once dinner was finished. Despite the life of luxury he lived in the Palace, he had raised no objection to the prospect of sleeping in such basic conditions. He probably wouldn't even have said anything about being too cold had she not lit a fire, either.

"I'll keep watch, don't worry," Elen-ai reassured him.

"Don't you need to sleep?"

She shook her head. "Members of the Family are trained to require very little sleep."

"You should still sleep," he insisted.

"I promise I'll be fine."

"I want to take a watch," he said stubbornly.

It was going to be easier to give in than argue. "Fine, I'll wake you to take a few hours' watch just before dawn," she promised.

Satisfied, the Prince obediently went to sleep.

Elen-ai lay down on her bedroll so she was comfortable and closed her eyes, listening to the noises of the night. Insects moved, night animals shuffled. In the peace, she sorted through the cluttered collection of facts about the attempt on the life of both the Queen and her heir in an attempt to start trying to discover who was behind it.

The Prince dozed the next day as the carriage followed the shoreline of lake Tak. The lows from which the Tak family earned their significant fortune remained scattered across the land as far as the eye could see. Elen-ai had allowed Gidyon to take a few hours of watch but clearly, that had been more than the Prince was accustomed to missing of his regular night's sleep. She didn't mind. In fact, she preferred the absence of his questions which had become disconcertingly regular. She had almost preferred when he could barely stand to talk to her.

It took them the better part of the morning to reach the Tak family home. Having driven since it became light, they had been on the road for several hours already. Elen-ai drove up to the gates and nudged Gidyon awake. He blinked sleepily at her then straightened into wakefulness when he saw where they were.

"Gidyon, son of the Queen, here to visit the Tak family," Gidyon said to the guard outside with as much authority as he could muster, given the single-carriage retinue.

The guard dubiously eyed Gidyon, trying to decide whether or not he was serious. When too much time had elapsed the Prince snapped.

"Are you going to leave me waiting all day?"

At this, the guard moved, directing another guard to go and deliver the message to. In the time that they waited for news of their arrival to reach whoever was inside the house, Elen-ai looked around the yard. The carriage waiting in the corner told her that someone else was visiting. The meagre presence of the guards as more a formality than out of genuine concern spoke of the fact that the Tak family was secure in both their fortunes and political position. Neither piece of information was a great surprise. The Tak and the Aadran families – the two most powerful families in the Queendom - were closely aligned. It made sense from a practical point of view: the Aadran family held lands on which grain practically overflowed. Much of their harvest went to feed the Tak animals in winter. In turn, the two families would often combine their produce to leverage better prices for their wares in various markets. That closeness had been formalised through regular inter-family marriages. Their combined wealth rivalled the Queen's. Nobody really wanted to challenge them if it could be helped. It wouldn't end well. That knowledge lent both families a certain security.

The Tak family home as placed on top of a hill overlooking lake Tak. It was a low, sprawling affair constructed of thick timber that could only be from the Harete family's forest. Unlike the Veertak estate, there was no settlement built around the building. Most of the people who lived in the Tak province were scattered, living in homes - or shacks - where they watched herds of lows for the Tak family. The closest to a settlement was the great collection of mustering pens half a day's ride away where the lows designated for sale were driven before they fetched an outrageously high price for those wealthy enough to afford them.

No trees grew near the Tak house, giving it and the immediate area a curiously barren feel. The warm sun beat down on the two waiting visitors in the yard. Elen-ai pondered how the house stayed cool in the deepest summer days.

A man emerged from the main door, his broad shoulders and sun-browned skin speaking of many years' hard work. He seemed almost a different species to the Veertaks whose pale complexions and narrow frames were the legacy of a life devoted to poring over books indoors.

"Master Gidyon," the man boomed.

Gidyon alighted from the carriage, crossing the space to meet the man and clasp his hand in greeting. Next to him, the Prince who had looked so broad-shouldered and tall for his age in the Palace, seemed a thin boy.

"Serek." If Gidyon was aware of the difference in stature between himself and this man, he did not seem it. Instead, the charming diplomat had appeared, infusing the single word with warmth and familiarity.

"Word reached us of the attempt on your mother's life. It's a terrible thing for anyone to even consider." The man continued to speak in a loud tone. It gave the impression of simplicity on his part, but given he was a member of the seven families, that impression was unlikely to be an accurate one. Gidyon's hair shone like spun gold in the sunlight, a stark contrast against the bleached white of Serek's.

"Please come inside," Serek said. "Is this ah," he peered at Elen-ai and their unmarked, modest carriage, "all there is of your entourage?"

"Yes," Gidyon said, as though there were nothing unusual with someone of his position travelling in such a modest manner.

"Ah, well of course. I'll get our people to unpack your trunks. I'll show you and your ah...companion inside." Serek waved to two waiting servants.

They immediately approached the carriage and began to unload the Prince's trunks.

Taking her cue, Elen-ai alighted and came to Gidyon's side.

"Elen-ai, this is Serek, head of the Tak family alongside his lovely wife Karan. Serek, may I present to you lady Elen-ai," Gidyon said.

A light smile touched Serek's mouth. "It's a pleasure to meet you," he told her with a sincerity that she did not quite believe.

As they followed him into the mansion, Elen-ai leaned in close to the Prince. "He thinks I'm your lover," she whispered in his ear, barely managing to keep the amusement from her tone.

Despite the proximity of their host preventing Gidyon from saying anything in reply, his expression of horrified surprise was reward enough.

"You've come in the midst of lunch - Arlena and her son Zekken are here on a business matter. If you're content to forgo a bathe, you would both be welcome to join us at the table," Serek offered.

"Zekken! I know him well." The Prince's voice contained genuine warmth. "I must confess, I would love a proper meal."

Gidyon increased his pace so that he was walking alongside Serek rather than behind him. Elen-ai remained trailing by a few steps. Serek paused and looked back at her in confusion. It was amusing to watch him try to understand the dynamic between the Prince and the woman he presumed to be Gidyon's lover. Elen-ai made no move to offer any form of clarification. It was far too funny to see her charge put in that awkward position.

They passed through the broad, open spaces of the house. Windows lined many of the walls, providing clear views of the land surrounding the house. It was quite pleasant, although Elen-ai wondered how lovely the vista would be in summer when the heat had scorched the grass to a pale yellow. Her personal preference was always for somewhere with shade and shadows.

Serek led them into the dining room, another wide, open affair that offered beautiful views of the surrounding countryside, in this instance, out onto lake Tak. The water glimmered blue in the sunlight, reflecting the brightness of the day into the room. The Tak family home was smaller than the Veertaks' but as equally grand in its own way, if not more suffused with understated yet confident wealth.

The scent of cooked meat met Elen-ai's nose. There was something particularly delicious about the smell. She presumed that it was meat from an animal butchered on that very day. Most of the produce in the markets of Herran was fish caught off the coast on which the capital was located. Keeping the meat of animals fresh for more than one or two days was nearly impossible. Most of the meat Elen-ai had eaten over the course of her life had been outside the city in taverns where it was possible to bring a beast from the surrounding countryside near to the building and kill it there. Since the beginning of her time with the Prince, she had almost eaten more meat than over the course of her entire life.

"Gidyon!" The affectionate cry arose from the man seated at the table who Elen-ai presumed was Zekken. The second eldest child of the Aadran family, roughly of an age with Serek, he had a reputation for his plain face and lovely temperament.

"Zekken." Gidyon returned the warmth, going immediately to embrace the man, who stood to embrace the Prince. Zekken was known to frequently travel into Herran on business for his family. He had dined at the Palace on many of those visits as a guest of the Queen and representative of his family. That, Elen-ai assumed, was how he had come to be on such good terms with the Prince. She presumed his mother would be pleased that a member of her family had the ear of the future ruler. Perhaps Gidyon would find a supporter in the Aadran family.

"Gidyon, you've met Karan before," Serek said.

Gidyon turned to his hostess and offered her one of his charming smiles. "How could I forget? I often think on our discussion about the poetry of Ulate. It made me go back and re-read her earlier work."

Karan Tak was a woman who did not pay particular heed to the preference of being extremely thin, as did some women of wealth. While by no means fat, her curves attested to an appreciation of food as well as other fine things in life, such as poetry and music. This stature made her a somewhat imposing presence. However, under Gidyon's charm, she simply returned the smile, the corners of her eyes crinkling with genuine appreciation for the young man in front of her. "You must sit next to me. I'm very interested to hear what you have to say," she told him firmly.

"I'm so glad you said that," Gidyon responded, keeping a friendly hand Zekken's arm as he leaned forward to speak with Karan.

"And have you met Arlena Aadran?" Karan indicated the woman sitting opposite from her.

"Only once, several years ago when I was very young. But your reputation precedes you, lady Aadran." At this, Gidyon did leave Zekken's side and move around the table to take the proffered hand of the Aadran matriarch.

Her reputation certainly did precede her. The early death of her husband due to an unexpected illness had devastated Arlena, who had adored him. Despite being young enough to re-marry, she never had, managing the family estate with a formidable competence and Zekken as her trusted deputy.

"I've heard much about who you have grown into, young man." She took his hand and held it, scrutinising his face. She nodded once in a definite motion and released his hand. He went over to the seat which had been swiftly set for him with fine Katan plates and glass wine and water cups next to Karan Tak. The Tak family had begun to pay their servants more generously in the last few years. Perhaps someone had made them aware of the perils of a disgruntled employee. The movements of the servants were efficient and unobtrusive.

"Aren't you going to introduce us to your companion?" Karan asked innocently.

Gidyon's eyes widened with minute shock. The manner of their entrance meant that there was no point at which Elen-ai could have been mistaken as a servant, and for him not to introduce her was a terrible breach of etiquette. "Elen-ai, please forgive me. May I present to you lady Karan Tak and lady Arlena Aadran, lord Serek Tak and of course, lord Zekken Aadran. This is Elen-ai, my companion." Only Elen-ai would have caught the slight hesitation before he settled upon describing her as his companion. She suppressed a chuckle. She would enjoy that thought properly at a later time. As it was, she fixed her face into a smile and bowed in what she hoped was the appropriate manner.

"Please, join us Elen-ai," Karan invited her, indicating the space on the other side of her which a judicious servant was already setting with competent speed.

Karan and Serek had an amicable marriage that had produced two children who were a few years older than Gidyon and lived in different parts of the estate, minding their own herds. Karan was the eldest of four other children, one of whom Elen-ai had been responsible for killing – her first kill, in fact. The realisation was not uncomfortable but instead unusual as Elen-ai sat down and looked at the woman's polite smile.

Serek and Zekken resumed their seats and the meal continued. Plates of lightly seared meat were put down in front of Elen-ai and Gidyon, completing the illusion that they had always been present at the lunch.

"I'm sure Serek has already said this, but let me express our relief to learn that your mother was not harmed in that awful attack on her life," Karan said. Perhaps Elen-ai was overly suspicious, but she wondered if Karan's expression of sympathy concealed some darker thought, or darker purpose. Certainly, she was a woman who would be willing to get her hands dirty in pursuit of a goal.

"It's very kind of you to say lady Tak. It was a terrible shock to hear," Gidyon responded, putting down a forkful of his food to address her. He appeared to have no such suspicion.

"Do you have any idea why someone may seek to do such an awful thing?" Zekken asked. There was a note of outrage in his tone. His mother threw him a look that Elen-ai saw but he did not due to the fact that he was focusing intently on Gidyon. She frowned slightly to herself, wondering what was behind such an expression of warning.

"Perhaps this is not the best topic for the table," Serek suggested. Evidently, he had seen Arlena's unimpressed expression.

"Quite right," Arlena added. She was several years older than the Taks which gave her words a certain authority. "How about we move on to more pleasant things. Elen-ai, was it? From where do you come?"

All attention turned to Elen-ai. The Prince opened his mouth, but Elen-ai quickly spoke before he got the chance.

"I come from a merchant family. Cloth, mostly. I met Gidyon in the marketplace one day," she said.

"And how is it you two came to be travelling alone in such a nondescript carriage?" Karan's smirk suggested that she thought she knew exactly how this had come to occur. If she was curious as to why they had decided to stop at the Tak family's residence, she did not ask - yet.

"Well actually we were on the way to the Royal country estate when we were attacked," Gidyon responded.

"Surely not! Are you alright?" Karan exclaimed. Her surprise certainly seemed genuine enough.

"Yes, fortunately. But we thought it best to travel in a less conspicuous manner," he said.

"For a member of the royal family to be attacked on the road. It's outrageous," Arlena added, that outrage clear in her stiffened posture. Her son's contribution and silent agreement was to turn white with shock. Elen-ai, watching the reactions of everybody at the table certainly thought she saw genuine surprise on all faces, but appearances could be deceptive as she – the person who had killed Karan's brother – knew all too well.

"Why would anyone be so audacious as to do such a thing?" Serek's demand was aimed at nobody in particular.

The Prince answered him nevertheless. "It was a deliberate attempt on my life, I'm afraid."

"But this is madness. First the Queen, now you. Why?" Karan interjected.

"Well lady Tak, I can not be completely sure, but I'm reasonably certain that it is because my mother has named me her heir," Gidyon said calmly.

The silence that followed was broken by Serek dropping his glass wine cup.

TEN

The Taks and Aadrans sat at the table for several silent moments, simply staring at Gidyon. He did not seem particularly perturbed by their shock or indeed, that aware of it. He had calmly returned to the meat in front of him as though he hadn't announced something so monumental.

"Are you quite serious?" Karan leaned forward, her mouth a grim slash in a face which had been so pleasant only a few moments before.

"Of course he is. We've all heard the speculation for weeks now." Arlena spoke before Gidyon could respond, her own face far from the visage of someone delirious with joy.

Gidyon sat and ate his meal in silence, letting the quiet argument that took place across the table ebb and flow over him. Elen-ai watched with curiosity, wondering how he was going to respond to the clear dissatisfaction that had met his announcement. Eventually, he put down his cutlery and spoke. "Would you mind if I ask what your objections are?"

"Gidyon, it's not even a question of objecting to *you*, my dear. It's that no man can hold the throne," Karan explained in a somewhat patronising manner.

"So you're concerned about the change this would bring, then?" Gidyon asked, apparently unoffended by Karan's tone.

He waited a beat for everybody to register the uncomfortable tenor to the silence, then spoke again. "Change has always been resisted. My great-great grandmother's reforms on education were met with much resistance. Or her grandmother's decision to allow men to lead families and hold land? She almost faced down a revolt for that. Yet surely the Second Country is better off for those changes."

Gidyon was certainly persuasive. Elen-ai's own lingering resistance to the prospect of him taking the throne was weakened in the face of his argument.

"This is a matter of maintaining –" Karan began to say, but Gidyon cut her off patiently.

"Serek controls the Tak family estate along with you. And he's not even Tak by birth."

"That's different. We're talking about the Royal family," Arlena interjected before Karan could respond. Unlike the younger woman, she did not speak down to the Prince but rather in the cool, direct tone of business.

"What exactly is the concern with a male holding a throne? If it is to maintain stability, I have pledged to marry outside the seven families. Any child of mine will be as apolitical as I am." Gidyon calmly took another bite of his meal after he finished speaking.

"Gidyon, are you certain about that?" Zekken spoke for the first time since Gidyon had made his announcement. He was the only person in the room who looked as though he was actually concerned for Gidyon rather than about the change him being named heir would bring. For someone who was so involved in the maintenance of his family's position, he certainly did not seem to have the heart for the power games of the Queendom.

Gidyon turned to face Zekken. "I have thought long and hard over it, Zek. And it is the best solution. It is my duty to make certain that stability and the prosperity of the Queendom remains. This is the way to do it. And I ask the support of both of your families to my claim." Gidyon turned back to address his later comments to the rest of the room.

"Well I for one have no doubt about your ability to be a good ruler," Zekken said warmly.

"Unfortunately you do not speak for our family, Zekken. I do. Gidyon, might I have some time before I give you an answer?" Arlena's question was not really question. She did not look at her son as she addressed Gidyon, but Elen-ai could sense her displeasure with his rush to offer support that was not his to give. However, unlike Erek Rasatan, who had spoken in open disagreement with the stance of his family, Zekken, despite looking as though he wanted to defy his mother, remained silent.

"Lady Aadran, I would expect nothing less. You would not enter into a business agreement without due consideration. This is not that different. I presume you would also like some time, Karan and Serek?"

"If you please," Serek answered before his wife could.

"Certainly. Perhaps I may take you up on that offer of a bathe, then." Gidyon put down his cutlery and dabbed at his mouth before standing. Elen-ai followed his lead, feeling far less comfortable and confident than the Prince looked.

"Before you go. Lady Elen-ai, may I ask what you think of all this?" Karan's question arrested Elen-ai's escape, much to her dismay.

She faced the table of people whose scrutiny was now turned to her. Being so noticed made her feel profoundly uncomfortable. This room full of people awaiting to hear her opinion on a political matter was a far cry from her preferred place within the shadows. She opened her mouth, then thought for a moment, reflecting that she must look quite stupid with her mouth hanging open.

"I think that Gidyon will make a fine ruler. I've never seen someone with more charm, intelligence, or dedication to his role," she said honestly. "And I've been given a perspective that means that my opinion is an informed one."

"Such admiration," Arlena commented. Elen-ai could not tell whether or not it was meant as an insult, a compliment, or something else entirely.

"I'll have someone show you to quarters," Serek said after a moment, a servant scurrying forward at his words, to usher them out of the room.

Elen-ai and Gidyon followed the servant to rooms which had been prepared for them. To one side was an alcove that housed a large tub. The water in it drained down underneath the house and presumably, down the hill. It was a far less sophisticated system than the complicated pipes that ran through the Palace but a clever one nevertheless.

The high ceilings of the Tak household gave the room a very airy, light quality that most would have found pleasant. However, the tension that had bloomed in Elen-ai at the politics around the table left her unable to appreciate her surroundings. She longed for the silence and shadow of the Family's home in Herran with an acute ache. There was something about the way everybody spoke with double meanings and careful consideration of their own interests that left a bad taste in her mouth, and a lingering uncertainty of what was true or false.

"Do you really think that of me?" Gidyon asked once the servant had left.

Elen-ai finished her inspection of the room and turned to face him. "I do."

Indeed, it was true. The fact that she had no great personal affection for him did not detract from her conclusion that he would make a fine ruler one day. Somewhere between Herran and the Tak estate, she had arrived at a sort of peace with the prospect of a male on the throne, provided that male was Gidyon.

"That's...very kind," the Prince said, an odd look on his face.

Elen-ai didn't bother trying to decipher it. "Either you bathe or I will," was all she said, looking to dispel the emotion of the moment. She still wasn't entirely certain that she actually liked the Prince, but she didn't have to like him to think he would be a good ruler.

Gidyon quickly stripped off his outer clothes, laying them to one side so that a servant could take them and clean them. Elen-ai turned away to afford him some modesty.

"How long will we stay here?" she asked, trying to make the fact that he was naked only a few steps away from her less awkward.

A splash signalled that he had gotten into the bath. "I'm not sure. Perhaps a few days," he called to her.

"Do you think they'll support you?" She idly stretched out her arms. Her muscles, sore from the punishing exercise that she had put herself through the previous evening, complained.

"I would be surprised if they chose to actively not support me," he responded over the slosh of water.

"But that's not the same as actively support," Elen-ai noted.

"Quite right. If I had to guess, I think that they will remain neutral, make no public declaration either way until I have secured a claim by my-self, or lost the ability to make a claim."

"How would you lose the ability to make a claim?" Elen-ai turned, forgetting that he was in the bath. She quickly turned back, hoping that Gidyon hadn't realised – not that she had seen anything of note.

"Someone would likely procure an alternate heir from somewhere." The sound of water being displaced told Elen-ai that Gidyon had gotten out of the bath.

"Do you trust the Taks and Aadrans?" Elen-ai asked, still studying the wall with a concerted interest.

"I do not distrust them," he replied. "You should bathe too," he added.

"I'm fine, thank you," she said automatically, noticing the absence of any significant declaration of trust.

"You are supposed to be my lover, aren't you?" He sounded faintly accusatory. "You can turn around, by the way," he added.

She did as he bade, finding that he had just finished pulling on a pair of trousers and was buttoning them up. "It will be safer if people think you're travelling with a lover rather than a bodyguard," she pointed out. Perhaps she could have posed as a servant, but the discomfort the Prince felt at people thinking she was sharing his bed gave her a sense of juvenile glee.

Again, a look of faint pain crossed the Prince's face. "I do not even disagree. It's just..."

"Not a pleasant thought to think of us as lovers?" Elen-ai suggested when he did not complete his sentence.

"It's an odd thought," he corrected. "Anyway. My lover should be clean," he returned to his original point.

Muttering in discontent, Elen-ai checked to ensure that he wasn't watching, then swiftly removed her clothes and climbed into the tepid water. Grabbing the animal fat bar of soap, she scrubbed quickly then heaved herself from the bath, grabbing for a towel just in case the Prince wasn't quite as respectful of her modesty as she was of his. She wasn't certain why she was so uncomfortable with the prospect of them seeing each other naked – children of the Family often saw each other in various states of undress – but she was. It seemed that her concern was unfounded, though. Gidyon was absorbed in the pages of a book he had pulled from one of the trunks.

Elen-ai went to pull the clothes she had been wearing back on but then reconsidered. Gidyon did have a point about her appearance. If she was to pretend to be his lover, putting back on clothes that were covered in dust from their travels was not going to be acceptable. Holding the towel tightly around herself, she went to the trunk with her clothes in it and rifled around, searching for something to wear.

Gidyon turned to look at her, arching an eyebrow. "Are you alright?"

Elen-ai looked up at him, clutching the towel to her chest. "I'm trying to look the part," she snapped, grabbing the first things that she could find.

"Well you certainly don't look it right now," he commented in a haughty tone.

"Obviously not!" she snarled, slamming the lid of the trunk closed and moving a little distance away from him to pull on the clothes she had found. Fortunately, the black trousers and burgundy tunic that she had grabbed at random seemed to be an acceptable outfit, so there was no need for her to change in front of Gidyon again.

"I wonder what exactly they're discussing," Gidyon said thoughtfully, putting his finger to mark the place on the page as he looked up in thought.

"I could always find out for you," Elen-ai offered as she began to transfer her blades from one set of clothes to the other.

"How?" He looked at her, keeping his finger firmly on the page.

"I could get in unnoticed." Elen-ai shrugged offhandedly, her fingers deftly concealing the blades.

She could tell by the way his eyes took on a faraway look for a moment that Gidyon seriously considered it, but then he shook his head. "I think I'd prefer you by my side."

"Just thought I'd offer."

He threw an amused look at her before returning his attention to his book.

Approximately an hour later a servant came to take them to hear the Taks and Aadrans' decision. In that time, Gidyon had read while Elen-ai had taken the opportunity to pray, sitting in a chair cross-legged and closing her eyes. Despite the unpleasantness of suspense, a curious serenity had descended on the bedroom, perhaps indicative that she and the Prince might finally be getting along.

The Taks and Aadrans had moved from the dining room into a parlour room which contained several stringed instruments on various stands. Elen-ai recalled that Karan was a skilled musician, although she felt there would be no opportunity to verify this today. Perhaps she would be able to learn something else, though, if she watched carefully enough.

The late afternoon sun came through a window, sending a gentle glow onto the walls.

"My apologies for keeping you waiting so long," Arlena said. Given the frequent Tak and Aadran marriages, they were effectively one extended family. As the oldest person in the room, her seniority meant that she was the voice for them all.

"It's no trouble," Gidyon answered easily. He showed no sign of unease or concern, even though the support of these people before him could secure his claim to the throne if they pledged their support to him then and there.

"We have discussed at length the matter at hand. While there is no question about your competence, that is not the only issue at play. Ultimately, we will not speak against you, but Gidyon, we cannot declare our support for you. In this, we remain decidedly neutral." Arlena spoke with a directness that gave no ambiguity or room for argument.

"I appreciate your honesty Arlena. I must say, it is what I would do in your position." Gidyon smiled faintly, ambling over to a spare seat. Elen-ai followed his lead, reclining in an armchair of her own.

"You are very gracious in accepting this news," Arlena noted. "May I offer you a piece of advice?"

"Given the long battle I face with the other families, I welcome your wisdom, Arlena."

It did not escape Elen-ai's notice that Gidyon was calling the matriarch of one of the country's most powerful families by her first name. She was sure Arlena had also noticed it.

"I would be wary of the Katan family. I cannot expect that they would support you."

Gidyon's smile was thin. "I would be a fool to expect they would. Especially given they are the most likely to be able to challenge my claim.

"I researched it this afternoon. My mother had one sister. She married Enges, one of the Katan sons. They have a twelve-year-old daughter, Serenah. My cousin. She would fit a claim if it came to it. Although her father is known, which may weigh against her."

The mystery of what Gidyon had been intently reading while they waited revealed, Elen-ai watched in fascination as he tossed the knowledge of his cousin's possible claim out into the room with a nonchalance she was sure he did not feel.

"Rest assured, Gidyon. If such a claim were to be made public, we would not speak to it, either," Serek noted.

Gidyon's smile was icy. "And in so doing, earn the frustration from both of us."

"Likely," Karan replied with a little laugh. Elen-ai glanced over to Zekken. He stood with his back to the room, staring out the window at the dying light, hands in his pockets. If she was any judge – and she was – his stiff shoulders and clenched jaw suggested he had argued that the Taks and Aadrans should support Gidyon's right to succeed his mother. She wondered why he would have so vehemently supported a male ascending to the throne. Perhaps his anger was a show devised to misdirect attention away from the possibility that the Taks and Aadrans had attempted to kill the Queen and her son in some play for greater power. After all, it seemed everyone was aware of the Queen's supposedly secret decision to name Gidyon her heir. Somehow though, Elen-ai couldn't quite believe Zekken was so superb an actor.

"May I ask your honest opinions?" Gidyon leaned forward, the picture of earnestness.

"Certainly," Arlena responded.

"How likely do you think is it that the Katan family is behind the attempt on my and my mother's lives?"

Voicing such a question left a silence in the room. Zekken actually turned back from his scrutiny of the sunset and looked at his mother, Serek, and Karan. The fact that he said nothing made Elen-ai wonder if he had been directed to not speak at all. She wondered what he had said. She should have argued harder with Gidyon to eavesdrop on the conversation.

It seemed nobody wanted to be the first person to speak. Eventually, Arlena once again spoke for the room. "Nothing is outside the realm of possibility. But I would be very surprised if they were behind those attacks, Gidyon. If it were to be discovered, their credibility, along with any hope of Serenah claiming the throne, would be lost."

Gidyon thought for a moment, then nodded in curt agreement. It seemed then that the matter was settled, and would not be discussed any further.

Dinner was a modest affair; a selection of food brought into the sitting room. Elen-ai made herself unnoticed, sinking into her chair while she watched everybody else. Gidyon appeared to harbour no ill will toward his hosts or Arlena for their decision, conducting an animated conversation with Karan about the works of the poet Ulate. Arlena and Serek spoke in quiet tones about business deals without mentioning anything particularly specific, while Zekken ate in what looked like a moody silence. At one point he came to sit in the vacant armchair next to Elen-ai.

"Take good care of Gidyon, please," he said to her, his face earnest.

It took Elen-ai a moment to realise that he didn't actually know of her place as a member of the Family, but was asking in a more emotional sense. Her fleeting suspicion that he might have been merely pretending to support Gidyon's claim to the throne seemed ever more flimsy.

"I plan to," she replied, her reply somewhat stilted by her initial concern that he may know of her true role at Gidyon's side.

"I can only assume that whatever this is between you two is relatively new," he continued.

"What makes you think this?" she asked.

"I feel he would have told me about something like this. I come to Herran every few weeks on business for mother. I try always to speak with Gidyon when I am there. He is a good young man." Tenderness infused his voice as he spoke of the Prince.

Zekken's unmarried state was the subject of much speculation. Elen-ai's favourite explanation was that he had a particular fondness for the lows of the Tak family. More widely accepted as an explanation though, was that his mother had never authorised a marriage for him because she did not wish to lose her deputy to marriage. It was certainly what Elen-ai had always assumed. Perhaps the fact that he had never gotten the opportunity to be a father himself meant that he had a certain paternal sentiment toward Gidyon. But Elen-ai still found it odd.

"What are you to the Prince, exactly?" she asked Zekken so softly that nobody aside from him could hear it.

Like Serek, Zekken's simple demeanour was a useful tool. The simplicity that Zekken donned remained completely unchanged but for the most negligible tilt of his head as he placed her under a greater scrutiny than had originally been conducted.

"I am his friend, I hope," Zekken answered, his voice just as soft as hers. "I have known him his whole life, and I watched him as he grew up."

"How did Queen Latana let you see him from such a young age?" Elen-ai wondered aloud.

Zekken may have had control over his face, but Elen-ai was not watching his face. She was paying attention to the vein in his throat which jumped at the mention of the Queen's name. "The Queen's reasons are her own," he said in careful reply.

Musing on what she may have just learned, Elen-ai felt it was time to act the devoted lover. "Tell me a story of Gidyon when he was young," she enthused.

Either accepting the diversion or genuinely distracted by the question, Zekken launched into a retelling of Gidyon being only six or seven years old, demanding to play hide and seek and somehow hiding for several hours in plain sight underneath a chair. It was a pointless story that only someone with genuine affection for the child could truly find interesting, but Elen-ai nevertheless played along, laughing where it was appropriate and demanding another such tale when it was finished. As he told her these stories, Elen-ai saw that his face, which she like the rest of the world had initially thought plain, lit up with a certain appeal when he laughed or smiled. There was something peculiarly charming about such reserve in showing such animation and light.

Only many hours later when she lay on the very opposite side of the bed to Gidyon – both of them had refused to allow the other to sleep on the small divan in the room – did she return to the thoughts raised by her conversation with Zekken.

Gidyon was still awake, she could tell by his breathing.

"May I ask something?" she said into the space between them.

His reply was immediate. "Certainly."

"What if a Queen falls in love?"

"The duty of the Queen is not to love one of her subjects more than the others, but to love them equally and well." From the cadence, Elen-ai could tell that he was reciting something he had learned long ago.

"And if she does love one more than the rest?"

"Then she must try to forget it. Why are you asking?"

"I just wondered," she said vaguely.

Gidyon seemed satisfied with her response, lapsing back into silence temporarily.

"Have you ever been in love, Elen-ai?" There was a soft intimacy to his question brought out by the darkness.

She didn't even need to think about it. There was no place in her heart to love anyone other than a member of the Family. "No."

"Alright then, goodnight," Gidyon said comfortably, turning over with a rustle and sigh.

Elen-ai lay in the darkness, thinking about love. The closest she had ever come to something like love was with a tavern keeper in Herran two years previously. He hadn't been her first lover, but he had been the first that had made her want to return to him, which was something. Tavern keepers were treasures to the Family. They saw much and were often unnoticed in their own observance. They often knew the comings and goings of an area's inhabitants more so than many of those individuals' own lovers. Elen-ai had come into Tim-en's bar one evening seeking information about the habits of a particular merchant. He had given her the answers she sought than boldly suggested she remain with him for the evening. While he had known she was a member of the Family, unlike many others might have, he had shown no fear of her. He treated her with an offhand callousness, tender only in the throes of passion.

Elen-ai wasn't even certain if she had liked him that much, yet something about him compelled her to return to his bed again and again. She lost count of the number of times that she had slipped into his room in the latest hours of the night after she had completed some business of her own. No matter how or when she entered the room, he had never looked at her with surprise. He had simply drawn her to him, his body ready for hers, his mouth soft and hungry against her skin. Somewhere between desire and love she had found herself unable to stay away from him until the day he had died in a tavern brawl. She had tracked down his killer and exacted a swift retribution, more out of respect for Tim-en's memory than her own need for some vengeful farewell. Often in the intervening time, she had wondered how much more difficult his death would have been had actually loved him.

That night she dreamed of love and betrayal.

ELEVEN

Gidyon and Elen-ai stayed three more days in the Tak family home. Any animosity that their hosts may have felt toward Gidyon due to the Queen's decision to break with history and make her heir a male was not reflected in their hospitality. He was offered every comfort, shown the greatest courtesy, and even taken on several tours of the Tak estate. Wherever he went, Elen-ai followed, observing their hosts to see if someone slipped, if someone gave away an indication that they may have been involved in the attacks on Gidyon and Latana's lives. She saw nothing conclusive.

One day, they even ventured into the Aadran lands with Zekken, riding kittanae generously loaned to them by the Tak family. The graceful beasts were magnificent to ride on. Elen-ai found the barely-tamed power of the large cat intoxicating, requiring skill and concentration to maintain control of the animal as they sped across the countryside. She could see why they were such a symbol of wealth and power.

It was harvest time, just before the onset of summer. Gidyon seemed mesmerised by the undulating lake of golden-ripe crops. Standing on the crest of a small hill, the trio observed the grain being cut and bundled. There was something profoundly sad about the beautiful ripping sea being thoughtlessly hacked at and taken away piece by piece. Zekken explained that two harvests occurred each year, with every third half-year devoted to keeping the field fallow. Gidyon listened, even nodding at various points, but his eyes were on the dismantling of that magnificent sight.

Over those three days, the temperature suddenly became warmer, as though the land had decided that it was summer time. The twilight lengthened into an extended show of light, and each evening Gidyon would sit and watch it with whoever within the Tak home happened to be idle at that time. Elen-ai seemed to have been accepted as his silent companion, more comfortable to simply observe than speak. Or perhaps her aptitude for slipping into the shadows meant that she was mostly unnoticed.

On midmorning of the second day, Gidyon received a response to the message he had sent his mother from the Veertak estate. The servant brought it into the parlour room where Gidyon and Elen-ai were sitting with Serek and Arlena.

"Pardon me, but a messenger has just arrived from the Palace," the servant said, nervously looking at Gidyon. Word of Gidyon's position as heir to the throne had spread through the house. The servants looked at him with awe, discomfort, or a combination of the two. The Prince either didn't notice or pretended not to notice. Elen-ai was certain it was the latter.

Gidyon took the leather envelope held out to him, offering the servant a smile. "Thank you." He turned to Serek and Arlena. "I may read this in our room, if you would excuse me."

Upon receiving an absentminded nod from Arlena, he turned on his heel and walked out of the room. Elen-ai slid out of her chair and joined him, his constant silent shadow.

Once inside the room that they had become accustomed to sharing, he unbound the leather. Elen-ai took a quick glance at it to determine that it had not been opened before, but the wax sealing the envelope shut was untouched. There were several thick pages. Gidyon read through them quickly, then once more at a slower pace. Elen-ai watched his face closely. She saw flashes of anger, confusion, and perhaps even upset as he read different sections. After several minutes had passed he put down the message.

"My uncle, Silius wants me to come home."

"Is that what your mother said?" Elen-ai asked.

"No. It's what he said. He wrote to me."

"Not your mother?"

"He said she is unable to write following the attack – her hand was injured. So she asked him to write down what she dictated. Which he did. Adding his own comments along the way." Gidyon's mouth was a thin line.

"What does your mother think?"

"According to what Sil wrote, she says that my plan is a good one, but to be careful."

"Does Silius normally contradict the Queen?" Elen-ai wondered.

Gidyon shrugged. "Not in public. If he disagrees with something she wants to do though, he will tell her in private."

Elen-ai thought back to the conversation she had witnessed between the Queen and her brother. For the briefest of moments, she entertained the possibility that Silius may have ordered the attempt on the lives of the Queen and Gidyon. Frustration over the Queen's decision and perhaps even rage over the fact that Latana was appointing a man to succeed her when he himself had been denied that right despite being the first born would certainly be a strong motivation. But she could not dismiss the expression she had seen on his face when talking with his sister. It was a look of profound love, and that meant she could not quite bring herself to find him a truly viable suspect of such a crime.

It was on the third night that she and Zekken spoke alone again. The Prince was engrossed in a game of fa'thong with Karan, Serek, and Arlena. Elen-ai had curled herself into a chair and was reading a book of stories that she had chanced upon. Zekken sat beside her, staring into a glass of liquor. He suddenly looked up at her and spoke, drawing her out of a story about a princess who had lost her memory.

"It seems you prefer to observe than be observed, lady Elen-ai."

Echoing the gesture of Gidyon a few days ago, Elen-ai put her finger to the page to keep her place. "It is difficult to learn when one is at the centre of things, Zekken," she replied, casting a glance over at the adults and Gidyon who were enthralled by the game of strategy and chance.

"What have you learned then?" Zekken asked.

Elen-ai shifted her gaze to him, trying to gauge how intoxicated he may be. Thinking quickly back over what she had seen, she decided that the answer was not very. "That Karan and Serek do not love each other, but are comfortably amicable, which sometimes can be better than love. That your mother has worked hard to ensure that she is not solely dependent upon the Taklows for coin, and that you are the Queen's lover."

Zekken's hand jerked involuntarily at her final comment, although his expression did not change. The liquor jumped out of his glass and landed on his shirt.

"I beg your pardon?" He did not pay any heed to the strong-smelling stain spreading across his shirt.

Elen-ai looked down at the page quickly to note the number and closed the book, smoothing her hands over the cover. "Don't worry, your secret is safe."

"What makes you think this?" Zekken leaned forward, the picture of amused interest, albeit a little bit too interested to be truly convincing.

Elen-ai met his gaze and tilted her head. "Why else would you think that he's your son?"

Zekken leaned forward and dropped his voice further. "Even if I thought that, it's a large leap of logic to claim I'm Queen Latana's lover."

"There's no other reason that she would make certain that you were able to see Gidyon from the time he was born," Elen-ai challenged, her voice just as quiet. It wouldn't have mattered, the other four were totally engrossed in the game on the other side of the room.

"This is preposterous," Zekken told her.

"Then why are you still talking to me?" she asked. The suspicion that had germinated and bloomed in her mind seemed to be completely correct. A tight smugness coiled around her chest at the knowledge that she had discovered what the Queen had kept from everyone, even as some part of her wished she did not know to what foolish depths her Queen had sunk.

"Who are you?" Zekken asked, his eyes narrowing as he looked at her.

"A friend," she said quietly. "My interest is in protecting Gidyon."

Zekken thought for a moment, the grey of his eyes dark in the low light. "Tana did say she would make sure he was taken care of," he admitted finally.

"I think you had better tell me everything," Elen-ai suggested.

Zekken threw a cautious glance at the other side of the room. "Perhaps a stroll outside?" he offered.

The night was not quite as warm as it would be in a few weeks' time, but the chill of even a few days earlier was no longer present. The sound of insects infused the evening air, making it a beautiful night. Elen-ai paid it very little heed, more intent on what Zekken would reveal to her.

"What can I say?" Zekken asked once they had put a reasonable distance between themselves and the walls of the house.

"I think it would be easier if you start at the beginning," Elen-ai suggested.

He took a breath. "If you breathe a word of this to the wrong person, the consequences you invite…"

"I have no interest in gossiping," Elen-ai cut him off, her tone flat.

"Alright then. I suppose I don't have a choice in telling you this, do I?"

"Not really."

"Well, it started at one of the first seasons - when the men of the seven families come to the Queen and -"

"I know what the seasons are," Elen-ai interrupted.

"Of course. Sorry. Well, the seasons are useful for more than just the creation of an heir. It's an opportunity for the families to use their eligible men as informal emissaries. Mother had sent me to speak with Latana about trading directly across the border we hold with the Third Country. At the time, Tana was the heir. She took the throne two years later when her own mother passed. So I went to try and secure the goodwill of a future Queen." He paused and took a breath. "That first night when I saw her she had just turned sixteen. She was a girl. I was just a boy myself. Her hair was down, flowing around her shoulders, and I fell into her eyes. I've never seen eyes quite like hers, you know. I was too afraid to even approach her," he admitted with a little laugh.

Elen-ai suspected Zekken had never told anyone this. Perhaps there was a certain sense of liberation to be felt in telling a secret kept hidden for so long. She said nothing, letting him tell the story at his own pace.

"She took someone else to her bed that first night. But on the second night, I made sure that I spoke with her. Mother had asked me to complete a task and I had to at least try. Quite quickly we stopped talking about trade and started talking about all manner of things. Her beauty was nothing compared to…do you know what an incredible woman she is, Elen-ai?" He paused mid-stride and turned to face Elen-ai, almost entreating her to agree with him.

"She certainly is a formidable woman," Elen-ai said.

"Her mind is the true jewel. And the most remarkable thing happened. She found me worth her time. She took me to her bed that night and has never been with anyone else since."

"Wouldn't that raise suspicion?" Elen-ai asked.

"How could that be proved? Who would want to admit that they had not been chosen by the Queen?"

Elen-ai nodded slowly and resumed pacing down the hill toward the shore of lake Tak. Zekken followed her. "So Gidyon was conceived in that first year?" she verified.

"Yes. And I have been as much of a father to him as I can over the years."

"I assume you were aware of the Queen's plan to put him on the throne," Elen-ai commented instead of asking outright.

She could easily see his face in the dark as he nodded.

"You two have played a dangerous game," Elen-ai said, feeling anger stir within her. "And the outcome might be disastrous for the whole Queendom." The small part of her that had initially regretted that she had discovered the Queen's secret was now screaming. It was far worse than she could possibly have imagined. It seemed almost profane to know of this sort of foolishness in her ruler.

"We cannot help how we feel about each other," Zekken protested.

"But you can help what you do about it," she hissed, anger stoked by his reply. "You and the Queen playing at being a family when, if discovered, it could tear apart the whole country. It makes everything so much harder for Gidyon than it already was."

He looked at her, his face defiant. "People have done worse things for worse reasons."

Elen-ai threw her arms up, the anger sparking into flame. "They say nobody is quite so self-righteous and unwilling to listen to reason as a person in love. I now see what is meant by such a claim." Disgusted, she turned away from him to look out at the expanse of the lake. It stretched away from sight, serene and massive in the calm evening. The white of the moon glistened on the tips of the tiny ripples stirred by the slight breeze.

"Will you still keep him safe?" Zekken pleaded.

Elen-ai sighed heavily, more for show than anything else. "For him. Not for either of you. And if this results in disorder or chaos, it's on both of your selfish heads."

"Will you find out who tried to kill both of them?" Zekken asked, his tone subdued. Probably it was in response to her anger rather than because he truly believed he had done anything wrong.

"That's what I'm trying to do," Elen-ai snarled. She turned and stalked back toward the lights of the house. Halfway there, she paused and returned to Zekken, who was following her at a more leisurely pace. "What does your mother know of this?" she asked, as an uncomfortable thought occurred to her.

"Not exactly everything. She knows of my feelings for Tana, but not that they are returned. Nor does she know the exact nature of my relationship to Gidyon."

Elen-ai breathed out through her nose, willing herself to be calm. Anger was not encouraged by the Family. It did not lead to a well made or well executed plan. "This keeps getting better and better," she muttered to herself.

Without another word, she turned on her heel and stalked back up the hill, taking a running leap as she reached one of the house's walls. She scaled it easily and alighted on the roof, making no sound in her landing or as she moved along the tiles, using the skills of the Family to remove her silhouette from the sight of anyone who may be outside and glancing up. She didn't care if Zekken had seen her climb the wall or what he may have thought. As far as she was concerned, his opinion was irrelevant.

She traversed the extensive length of the house, fragments of conversation floating up to her. She paid them no heed, instead working to make herself as light as possible so that even she could not hear her own footfalls. The roof of the house was peaked, answering her question of where the heat would go on hot summer days. To run along the very apex required quite a degree of concentration. Once she had run back and forth a few times, she had calmed down at least enough to go back inside.

Everybody was still in the parlour room when she finally returned. The game had evidently finished and a discussion on where to find the best tailors had taken its place. Elen-ai was bored with the stifling confines of polite society, yet even her walk with Zekken had been an absence from the Prince's side that she should not have taken, especially given that the revelation of Zekken and Latana's relationship gave yet more motivation for why someone might want to kill the Prince due to the political imbalance he represented. So she returned to her chair and picked up her book once more.

"Did you enjoy your walk?" Serek asked her from across the room.

Inwardly sighing, Elen-ai again put her finger on the page to mark her progress. "The lake is quite lovely in the moonlight," she answered, mustering a smile.

"It's a shame you won't be here in a few weeks, the middle of summer is particularly beautiful. Especially when the flowers on the lake's shore bloom," Karan said.

"I've heard tales of the summer flowers of Lake Tak," Gidyon enthused. "I am sorry that we won't be able to see them."

"Perhaps another time," Serek suggested. The offer certainly did seem genuine.

"I'd like that," Gidyon replied happily.

Elen-ai looked around the room, her eye resting on Arlena. The dowager sat quietly, her head slightly bowed. The restful pose was deceptive. Arlena was clearly deep in thought. The possibility that had entered Elen-ai's mind earlier, that Arlena could be behind the attacks on Gidyon and his mother, returned as she regarded the formidable woman. It was entirely likely that she knew far more about her son's relationship with the Queen than Zekken thought she did. If the truth about Zekken's connection to either Gidyon or Latana were to be revealed, the Aadran family would be disgraced. Regardless of their wealth, power, and the land they held, the other families – even the Taks – would turn on them. It wasn't even outside the realm of possibility that the Aadran family's lands would be forcibly taken from them if her son's affair with the Queen were discovered. The people who lived and worked on them might welcome the forces of another family, one whose members did not seek to break the sacred neutrality that was supposed to be maintained in relation to Royal family. Elen-ai did not doubt that Arlena would take the necessary steps to protect her family. Whether she was ruthless enough to attempt to kill the Queen and the Queen's son – her grandson – was the question. She had seen worse things done by better people. It certainly was a theory that Elen-ai could not dismiss out of hand.

That was a theory to which Elen-ai returned later that evening as she and the Prince lay on their respective sides of the bed.

"Where did you and Zek go tonight?" Gidyon asked.

"Down to the shores of the lake," Elen-ai replied.

"Why did he come back before you?"

Elen-ai paused, trying to decide how much she should tell Gidyon. "I wanted a bit of time to myself," she decided upon.

"Why?"

"He does not agree with his mother's decision on supporting you," she said cautiously.

"Is it because he's my father?" Gidyon asked quietly.

Elen-ai sighed. There was nothing else she could say. "Yes."

Silence came from the other side of the bed. Elen-ai sat up, looking at Gidyon's face. With the Family's skills, she could easily see him in the dark. However, whatever his thoughts were, she could not discern them. "Are you alright?"

He was silent a moment longer. "Yes. It's just odd to know for sure."

"Did you suspect?"

"Not until you asked me about what happens if a Queen falls in love. It made me think about the way Zek is always so nice to me, and then the fact that mother is always just happier somehow whenever he is in Herran. I've never seen anything odd when they have been together, but there is something about her that just seems more vibrant, somehow. I had never thought about it before, but it makes sense, I suppose." He sat up himself. "Is that why someone is trying to kill her and me?"

Elen-ai shrugged, the movement rustling the covers. "I don't know. This evening I wondered..." she cut herself off, unwilling to upset Gidyon with her suspicions about Arlena.

"Tell me." He leaned forward. "Please."

Relenting, Elen-ai went on. "I wondered if Arlena may be behind the attacks in an attempt to safeguard the Aadran family's reputation."

Gidyon considered the proposition, then shook his head slightly. "It's possible, but I don't think likely."

"Why?"

"If Arlena were to organise such an attack, she'd make sure that it would be done properly. She's never seemed to me to be the sort of person who sets up something that may not succeed." He paused for a moment. "Has she ever employed the Family?"

"I can't tell you," Elen-ai responded almost before he had finished asking the question; a knee-jerk protection of the Family's secrets.

"Why not?" Gidyon's eyes flashed in the slight light let in by the gap in the curtain.

"The Family does not speak of its contracts to anyone but its members," Elen-ai told him.

"But if she is behind the attack on me and my mother, knowing whether or not she has had people killed before might help me know it," Gidyon protested.

"I cannot, Gidyon, I'm sorry," Elen-ai was firm. On this, she would not be moved.

He didn't respond but instead lay back down, turning away from her.

Elen-ai stared at his back for a moment longer. Perhaps she should have told him what she knew of the matriarch's business with the Family. But to do so would have unacceptably violated the Family's rules. Regardless, she did not think that his sudden silence was solely due to anger with her. The revelation of his parentage and the possibility of Arlena's involvement in the attempt on his life was confronting simply for her to think about. He probably needed some time to consider everything that Elen-ai had learned in his own way. So she let the issue drop, lying back down herself and remaining in the dark with her thoughts, as she so often was.

TWELVE

They left the Tak estate in the early hours of the next morning. Their hosts farewelled them in the yard as the sun was just rising, its pale yellow rays touching the Tak house's rooftop. Elen-ai could understand why the Taks had chosen to build their house on the top of the hill. It offered the perfect vantage to watch colour seep into or out of the landscape below. It was quite a magnificent sight.

Elen-ai farewelled Karan and Serek, who offered her a polite goodbye. She did actually like them despite the stance of neutrality that they had decided to take on the matter of Gidyon's legitimacy. They were an interesting couple. Not two people who felt a passionate love for each other, but who had been bound by a shared understanding of the importance of family and by the common purpose of keeping that family protected at all costs. It gave them a certain unity. It was also something Elen-ai understood and respected.

Arlena stood with her usual reserve, her son by her side. She nodded formally to Elen-ai, as did Zekken. However, while his mother met Elen-ai's eyes, he did not, staring studiously at her left ear. She wanted to glower at him, her anger and shock at the extent of his transgression against tradition still burning, but to do so would have been noticeably odd, so her face remained politely neutral.

Elen-ai watched as Zekken embraced Gidyon, enfolding the boy in a tight embrace. Gidyon returned the hug, although with less enthusiasm.

He mounted the carriage with no word to Elen-ai and gave one final wave to the assembled people in the yard before they set off.

Only when their little carriage had made its way out of the gates of the Tak home did either of them speak.

"Are you alright?" Elen-ai asked.

He looked down at his lap. "It's strange to think that he has been my father all this time," he said softly, his words competing to be heard against the rattle of the carriage wheels.

"Strange in a bad way?"

He shrugged, a motion that was curiously bird-like. Despite the width of his shoulders, the Prince was still narrow of frame. Some things could only come with age.

"Does it bother you?" she pursued.

Gidyon bit his lip as he considered. "I can't be too angry. I do want to succeed mother. So I can't exactly pick and choose what bothers me, given the unusualness of the circumstances in which I find myself." He took a breath. "But it does bother me. They've kept it a secret from everyone, even me. Having a bond with one of the Families is the one things a Queen is never supposed to do," he added.

"What about naming her son heir?" Elen-ai squinted slightly at the road ahead in the glare of the sun.

Gidyon inclined his head. "See what I mean?" His mouth twisted into a slightly sardonic smile.

Elen-ai nodded. He had a point.

"I just don't understand how they can be so reckless," Gidyon continued after a moment longer, raising his hands slightly to emphasise his confusion. "Just because they are in love or whatever does not mean that they should give in to it."

Elen-ai made a non-committal sound. It seemed some things truly did only come with age. Like understanding the insidiousness of the way a person could get under your skin, lingering there, leaving you aching for their touch, driving you to distraction, to the edge of reason.

"You've read Ulate's poetry, haven't you?" she asked.

Gidyon nodded.

"Have you read her collection of love poems?"

Gidyon threw a look at her. "I didn't know you were familiar with poetry," he said.

"Because you think that members of the Family are only taught how to kill?" she asked, more amused than anything else.

"Well, yes," he admitted.

Elen-ai uttered a short bark of laughter. "Even if that were true, words can be deadly in their own way," she told him. "We are encouraged to know about the world around us. That includes reading works of high literature, or knowing about art." She did not add that such familiarity allowed the Family's members to blend into the circles of people for whom such knowledge was assumed and slip unnoticed to the side of a particular target. After all, that did not detract from the fact that such knowledge in itself could be enjoyable to know and learn.

"Oh," was all he said, causing Elen-ai to laugh again.

"Anyway," she continued. "Those love poems. There is only one collection of them, and they speak of great love, or loss. And of the infatuation with one person that is like an itch, burning you from the inside out, right?"

"You are the flame in the dark, the rain in the heat, the food given to me as I starve. Without you, my anchor, I am lost, cannot find my way," Gidyon quoted.

"Mm, that one's one of my favourites, actually," Elen-ai said.

"You have a favourite love poem?" Gidyon was incredulous.

"That's really not the point," Elen-ai said patiently.

"Even so," Gidyon protested.

"Can we please not become distracted?"

"Sorry. You were talking about the contents of these poems." Gidyon collected himself with not a little visible effort.

"Exactly. I think that the love poems are among Ulate's most powerful, but also in some ways the least refined, of her work. And she didn't write them when she was young. Her younger work was about landscape, or family. So such lack of technical skill can't be put down to a lack of refinement in her writing. No, that rawness is her trying to put into words a consuming passion for another person. Consider what emotion caused a poet who is renowned for her measure and refinement to write not one, but a series of poems that deviate so completely from that precision," Elen-ai said.

"I cannot believe I am having this discussion with you," Gidyon muttered.

"Do you mind!" Elen-ai exclaimed. "I'm trying to make a point."

"Sorry, sorry. I agree. But she's a poet. The job of writers is to consider what it is to be human and explore that through their work," he replied.

"Well that's a different discussion in and of itself on the job of writers," Elen-ai said.

"I still can't believe that you and I are discussing this." Gidyon shook his head in disbelief.

"You know what? Fine. I give up." Elen-ai pursed her lips in irritation.

"You have to admit that this is not something one would expect to discuss with an assassin," Gidyon pointed out.

"How would you know what people normally discuss with an assassin?" Elen-ai snapped, feeling decidedly petulant.

"I'm sorry, Elen-ai. I have misjudged you," Gidyon said, still sounding amused.

In a display of immaturity, she turned her head away from him so that he could only see her profile. That was the final straw for him. He burst into laughter.

They stopped for lunch in the middle of the day. Elen-ai slid moodily from the carriage's seat and pulled out their food, handing it wordlessly to him. Her frustration with his unwillingness to take her seriously had yet to abate. For all his unusually adept capacity to charm various individuals, he had yet again failed to use that charm and insight when speaking with her.

"Elen-ai, I'm sorry about before." He approached her with his food in hand, as though it were an offering of some sort.

She deliberated whether or not she should remain annoyed with him but decided that it was ultimately pointless to do so. Relaxing her shoulders slightly, she made a wordless gesture that indicated she had accepted his apology.

"It was an enjoyable moment of levity, given everything that is going on. Now that I know about mother and Zekken, it makes me feel even more pressured to get the support of the other families and to find out who wants me and my mother dead so badly. If I cannot know I have sufficient support, I cannot be safe. It was already a hard task, but it just seems even more...urgent," he finished somewhat lamely, an unusually inelegant phrasing for him.

"How do you plan to deal with the Katan family?" she asked, feeling a squeeze of pity for him. The dangerous relationship between Zekken and the Queen was yet another concern for Gidyon to navigate in the course of trying to charm or bribe the families into supporting him. It lent a certain sense of precariousness to securing their support, too, lest this be found out and used against him.

He rubbed a finger along the bridge of his nose, a slight scowl on his face. "I know we were initially planning to go to them, but perhaps it may be better to bypass them entirely and just go as far as the Harete estate."

To reach the Katan family residence would require at least three weeks' journey. They resided in one of the most remote parts of the Queendom. The town where ceramics artisans all gathered was practically on the border of the Second Country and the Fourth Country. To traverse the vast plains which housed the clay off which the Katan fortune was spun required the navigation of several ill-maintained roads. Such isolation was the Katan family's preferred method of maintaining a haughty distance from the rest of the Queendom. Their belief that they did not need to frequently come to Herran to pay homage to the Queen due to the substantial wealth that they held was always hidden behind the excuse of their remoteness, although everybody knew that it was a remoteness that they themselves chose to maintain. The marriage of the Queen's younger sister to the Katan family had been an effort to engender some sort of loyalty from them while also conveniently keeping the girl as far away as possible from the Capital so that she could never lay claim to the throne.

"Are you sure that's wise?" Elen-ai asked. As much as she would rather not traverse through the territory of someone known to not have Gidyon's best interests at heart for several weeks, if Gidyon did visit the rest of the families, such a snub would at the very least be unwise, offering them the political grudge that would legitimise a move against him.

"I know, I know," he muttered. "I'll think about it on the way." The weight he had placed on himself to find his attackers and bring them to justice as well as to secure support for his claim to the throne was obvious in the frown that creased his forehead.

She shrugged, biting into a slice of bread. "I'll go wherever you decide," she said around the mouthful.

"Can you show me that move again, Elen-ai?" The question was a sudden change in subject.

"You'll have to be a bit more specific, my Prince," she responded, wondering why he had so abruptly changed topics.

"The kick, you know, to the side." To demonstrate, he awkwardly lifted one of his legs. Unfortunately for him, with his hands still full of food and his balance already poor, he toppled straight onto the ground.

Elen-ai stared at him, eyes wide and mouth paused mid-chew, at this display of complete incoordination.

The Prince looked up at her in surprise, then started to laugh. "You should see your face," he said in between giggles. Breathless with laughter, his blue eyes were vibrant in the sunlight. She saw a small chip in one of his teeth that she hadn't noticed before, and the slight dusting of freckles across the top of his cheeks. Amid the grass he didn't look in the slightest bit regal, he looked like a boy who was carefree and happy. She couldn't help herself. She laughed too, coming to sit beside him, looking up at the sky with the sun shining down upon them. As much of a prat as he could be, and as much as sometimes this Princeling was too haughty for his own good, she could not deny that sometime in the past few days, she had come to like him, and he was no longer simply a contract, but someone by whom she wanted to do right.

After two more days of travel, they crossed back into the sovereign land. The territory encompassed the main road of the Queendom that intersected with the border of the Fourth and Third Countries, off which smaller roads and tracks led into the lands of the seven families. Elen-ai guided the carriage toward a roadside inn that she frequented when she travelled this way. Both she and Gidyon had grown tired of the fruits, smoked meat, and increasingly stale loaves of bread that had been given to them by the Tak kitchens. While Elen-ai had survived on a lot less, she still preferred the luxury of a meal with at least more than two ingredients, if it could be helped.

"Are you certain it will be safe there?" Gidyon worried, asking the question for perhaps the tenth time that day.

Elen-ai looked at him, shaking her head slightly. Gidyon may have known many things, but in other ways he was completely ignorant. "Inns are very safe, provided you don't do anything stupid," she reassured him.

"What if I'm recognised?" he asked.

Elen-ai snorted the mouthful of water she had just sipped out of her nose as she laughed. "You're not that well known, Gidyon," she replied once she had finished cleaning herself up.

"That was disgusting," he informed her.

Elen-ai shrugged and attempted another sip, this time succeeding in swallowing it. "Anyway, we've been practising those kicks and throws. You can always put that to good use if it comes to it." She smirked.

"Thank you for the suggestion. The seat's still wet," he complained, shuffling further away from the drops of water in question.

"Have you thought about how to deal with the Katan family yet?" she asked, diverting the subject away from her hygiene practices.

Gidyon nodded. "I thought I'd invite them to court as honoured guests. That way it seems I'm giving them preference that they cannot refuse, rather than snubbing them by not visiting."

She considered his solution. It wasn't bad. "In the Palace we can keep a closer eye on them, too."

"And we can also prove that their would-be heir is far too unaccustomed to the world of the Court to be a good ruler," Gidyon added as the inn came in to view.

It was a good plan, and Elen-ai was not disappointed to hear that they would see the Katans in the Royal Palace. There was a certain irrationality to her impulse to lock the Prince away, after all, the Queen had been attacked inside the Palace, but she felt as though danger lurked along this journey in many forms, not all of them holding a knife. And she was not skilled enough in the politics and intrigue of the court to detect and deflect that kind of threat.

There seemed to be some unwritten law that all inns required to have a certain universality. They were populated generally by a mix of people who were hard workers looking for a little respite, or a little trouble, or perhaps a little of both, and a great many patrons who were fiercely loyal to whichever inn they frequented the most. While the level of cleanliness varied from inn to inn, they were staffed by the same sort of individual; highly competent and very much able to hold their own in a fight.

The sun had started its descent towards the horizon and both Elen-ai and Gidyon were quite hungry. As soon as they entered the tavern area, Elen-ai's gaze was instantly drawn to the door leading into the kitchen. An appetising smell was emanating from it that didn't necessarily promise meat, but certainly promised an actual meal rather than the sparse supplies that they had been eating over the last few days.

The innkeeper was an elderly woman who was clearing a table. Elen-ai knew her by sight from the previous times she had been at the inn. People sat at various tables either quietly talking amongst themselves or looking with an idle fascination at whatever was in front of them. Most of them were the usual assemblage of people who could be found at an inn that was in the middle of the way to somewhere but not quite anywhere in particular: a bookkeeper, a messenger, several travellers, and perhaps one or two individuals who would give a lonely soul human comfort in exchange for financial comfort. Elen-ai was almost certain that the slender young man with the sensuous mouth was for sale, although she was less certain about the woman who sat next to him who was looking at Elen-ai and Gidyon in cool appraisal. Several such individuals lived within inns for as long as they chose to keep their business there. It wasn't how Elen-ai would want to earn a living, but it certainly could be very profitable, especially if the inn was a good one.

"Can I help you?" The woman who was clearing the tables approached the Prince and Elen-ai, looking them up and down with professional boredom.

"We're after some food. And lodgings for the night," Elen-ai said.

Her only response a nod. The woman turned and marched into the kitchen, easily balancing the crockery piled high in each hand. Elen-ai led Gidyon to a table and sat down, sighing with pleasure at being able to actually stretch out her legs.

"We left our trunks in the carriage," Gidyon leaned forward and said to her in an undertone.

"And?" Elen-ai looked at him blankly.

"What if they're stolen, or gone through?" He glanced about himself nervously.

"Then I will be very irritated," Elen-ai replied, leaning back in her chair comfortably. "I thought you liked to be among the lowborn people, Gidyon." She smirked.

"There's a difference between the marketplace and a tavern in the middle of nowhere," Gidyon said, his unease palpable.

"What exactly are you worried is going to happen?" She linked her hands behind her head.

"I don't know," Gidyon muttered.

The woman came out from the kitchen with two wooden bowls filled to the brim with stew and put them down on the table. "And two ales, please," Elen-ai added.

The woman nodded and returned presently with two large tankards. "Thank you. By the by, that messenger over in the corner, is she reliable?" Elen-ai asked.

The woman gave a noncommittal shrug. "Not the worst messenger we've ever had here. Anything else?"

Elen-ai shook her head, making a gesture of thanks with her hand as she picked up the wooden spoon – a far cry from the delicate metal cutlery that graced the tables of the seven families and the Palace – and leaned forward to start eating. Throughout the exchange, Gidyon had been staring at the tankard as though mesmerised.

"You're meant to drink it, not admire it," Elen-ai advised.

He obediently lifted the mug to his lips and took a sip which immediately set him coughing. Elen-ai roared with laughter. Even though she had anticipated that Gidyon had never drunk the rough ale that most of the country enjoyed, it was nevertheless hilarious to see his eyes water as the potency of the drink hit him.

"You should have warned me," he said reproachfully.

"Where's the fun in that?" She grinned and took a sip from her own mug. She stifled a small cough of her own – it was very strong. "Don't stay angry with me," she implored as she ate, chucking at the memory of his reaction.

He pulled a face and took another sip. "Divine One around us! This stuff is vile. How can people drink it?"

"Mostly it's all people know. Your fancy spirits and distilled drinks are things that most people can't even pronounce properly, let alone afford." Elen-ai spoke between mouthfuls. Whatever other flaws this tavern may have had, its food was good and always had been.

"Mother never let me have luxuries like that," Gidyon protested. "I only was allowed them on special occasions."

"Look around you, Princeling. You have always lived in luxury, regardless of what you may think. But remember that the decisions of your mother, and certain others close to her, affect people here."

"I know that," Gidyon protested.

"Maybe up here," Elen-ai pointed to his head. "But it's different to actually knowing it."

Gidyon threw his hands up. "Sometimes you are so annoying!" he told her, although there was no real fire in his voice. Both of them knew she had a point.

Elen-ai inclined her head as she sipped her ale. "Oh, just give it to me," she snapped, grabbing his mug from him.

"No," he insisted, reaching across the table and pulling it back. "I want to finish it."

"You'll die," Elen-ai said, completely serious.

"Then it'll be your fault," he replied, before drinking long and deep from the tankard that looked much taller than Elen-ai first thought.

The ale took a while to hit the Prince, but soon his speech began to slur and his movements became exaggerated. All things considered, he held his ale surprisingly well. Elen-ai feared he would pass out in the middle of the tavern. When he began to slump in his chair, she paid for a room, asked their cases to be brought to it, and helped the staggering Prince up the stairs to the second level on which the tavern's small rooms were situated. She set Gidyon down onto the simple bed of stuffed straw and a mostly clean blanket. Once he was flat on his back, he immediately started to lightly snore.

He remained asleep for the rest of the afternoon, slumbering off the worst of the ale. Elen-ai passed the time by writing messages to be sent to the Family, using the small area of the room to do some stretches, and praying. All in all, the pace of the afternoon, punctuated by Gidyon's snores, was pleasantly peaceful.

The light had faded almost completely when she could no longer deny the call of nature. She glanced at Gidyon. From time to time, he mumbled something in his sleep, but he appeared to be soundly unconscious. It seemed safe to leave him for the briefest of moments. The day when she could be away from another person's side for more than the shortest time possible would be one of great delight, she reflected as she dashed down the corridor to the privy.

She came back to find Gidyon gone. Fighting the impulse to panic, she made her way back downstairs and toward the sound of a scuffle. As she came into the lower level of the tavern, she was greeted by the sight Gidyon against a wall with three knives to his throat.

THIRTEEN

Elen-ai had never been the fastest member of the Family, but she couldn't imagine that anybody had ever moved as quickly as she did. In perhaps two or three breaths, she had disarmed the three individuals who had looked very much as though they wanted to inflict considerable damage on the Prince, and even put one of them on his back. Their knives now in her hands, she pushed the Prince aside and put herself where he had been only an instant previously.

The two would-be assailants who were still standing looked in surprise at the woman who had appeared to come out of nowhere and taken their knives.

"Gidyon, what happened?" Elen-ai asked, her tone sharp and hard as she held the knives up, ready to attack.

"I woke up and you weren't there, so I came down here." The Prince's mumbled speech suggested he was still feeling the effects of the ale.

"And what, these three people decided they didn't like your face so they tried to stab you?"

"I..."

"Explain yourselves," Elen-ai cut Gidyon off and addressed her question to the people whose knives she now held.

"What's all this about?" Before they could answer, the woman who served them came up to them, hands on hips and a furious expression on her face.

"He upset our game," the person to Elen-ai's left said, glaring at Gidyon.

"Wait, what?" Elen-ai lowered the knives slightly, throwing a brief look of confusion at the Prince.

"I wasn't watching what I was doing, and I stumbled into him." Gidyon waved to the man on the ground. "His cards fell out of his hand, and then..." The Prince trailed off, a delicate blush spreading across his cheeks.

"There was a lot of money on the table for that hand," the woman on Elen-ai's right snarled.

"And what do you expect to achieve by stabbing him?" Elen-ai demanded.

The blank looks that met her question suggested that they had not considered what they were going to do subsequent to taking out their ire on Gidyon with the pointed end of their knives.

"I'll have no fighting of any kind in here," the innkeeper interjected, causing everyone to look at her. "A boy bumps 'nto your game, 'ts an accident, you treat t'as such. Who draws a blade 't such a thing? Honestly!" She swatted at the air to prove a point, her gnarled fingers curving as though she wanted to grab someone by the ear and haul them around the room to teach them a lesson. "And you." She turned her gaze to Elen-ai, the thickness of her speech making her surprisingly intimidating. "I've seen you in'ere before. What's about coming in and causing a ruckus? Who raised you t'mean t'you think fighting's where all things start?"

Elen-ai dropped her gaze, chastened by this woman's anger. "I'm sorry." She offered the weapons back to their owners.

" 'Nd you young man. Watch your walking. You never know who you may't upset if yaren't careful. T' world's full o'fools." She threw a pointed look at the three ruffians who looked quite shamefaced under the might of her wrath.

Apologies were mumbled and the two small parties went their own ways. The commotion had attracted the attention of the tavern's various inhabitants, whose number had grown since earlier in the day. Heads gradually began to turn back to their business and Elen-ai felt herself relaxing once more. This at least was the sort of threat to Gidyon's life that she could protect him from, provided he didn't go stumbling into any more tavern gamblers without her.

"Sorry," Gidyon mumbled beside her.

"It's alright. Like the old lady said, though. You should be careful where you step." Elen-ai slid into a chair, signalling for some food. "You may have been practising those kicks but you're no match for someone with a knife. You do know I was just joking earlier when I said you could try them out tonight, right?"

He didn't respond, merely putting a hand to his head as the innkeeper brought over a plate of something that looked suspiciously similar to lunch with one or two alterations. Elen-ai tucked into the food, simply glad that it wasn't more stale bread. After a moment of hesitation, Gidyon followed her lead.

"We should send those messages tonight," Elen-ai said after she had eaten a few mouthfuls.

"Mm," Gidyon answered.

"Will you write to your mother?" she asked.

The expression on his face was reply enough.

"I take it you're not particularly pleased with her?"

Gidyon looked out across the rest of the tavern as he spoke. "I don't want to talk about it."

Elen-ai scrutinised Gidyon's face. His eyes were completely blue. Some people who had blue eyes also had other colours in their iris; flecks of yellow or green. But Gidyon's eyes were pure blue. When he properly looked at someone, it was quite unnerving. The molten gold of his mother's eyes made anyone looking at them feel as though they were falling into them. The Prince's eyes made one feel as though he could see right through them. It was why his unwillingness to meet Elen-ai's gaze unnerved her so much. She hadn't realised how much she took his competence and control for granted. Sometimes she forgot that he was still a boy on the cusp of manhood rather than a man. Then again, her first kill had been when she was more than a year younger than Gidyon was now. A death that had been exacted upon a member of the family whose hospitality she had just enjoyed for several days. But Gidyon's childhood had been different from her own. He had learned to choose his words carefully, and she had learned to choose her blades carefully.

Leaving him to his mood, Elen-ai ate in a contented silence, occasionally raising her eyes to survey the rest of the room and ensure that there was no potential assailant lurking in wait. A man hurled the door open with great abandon, causing her to momentarily tense in readiness, but amicable cries of familiarity greeted him.

"Al-et, haven't seen you for quite a'time." The old woman who had so competently broken up the earlier altercation greeted the newcomer, giving him a quick kiss of greeting on the cheek.

"That damned magistrate ruled 'gainst me a'few weeks back s'I had t'go t'Herran and appeal." The anger with which the man spoke was understandable, although it caused his skipped lowborn to become even more exaggerated. Local magistrates decided on legal disputes, but they weren't always competent or fair. The decision could be appealed, arbitrated normally by a member of the family from the relevant estate. However, in rare instances, a case may need to be appealed directly to a judge in Herran, or even the Queen herself. Mostly that didn't happen, though. To submit an appeal, the individual had to forfeit days, sometimes weeks, of work in order to make the trek to Herran and wait for the appeal to be heard. Likely, the man, Al-et, had lost a significant amount of money in pursuit of his appeal.

"How did't go?" the woman asked.

The man made a disgusted sound. "The judge ruled f'me, but t'trip took far longer than I expected. I t'was waiting in Herran f'five days, t's not cheap t'stay there. I should'a stayed here a'worked."

The woman guided him to a seat and placed a large tankard in front of him. "T'one's on me," she said, earning a gruff word of appreciation before the man lost himself in the depths of his drink.

"Is there a mirror in the washroom?" Gidyon suddenly asked, seemingly oblivious to the exchange that had just occurred.

Elen-ai looked at him in confusion. "What?"

"Somewhere I can see my reflection," he explained patiently.

"Yes, there was. Why?"

"I should shave before we get on our way," he said.

Elen-ai nearly choked on the mouthful of ale she had just sipped. "You shave?" She made no effort to hide her incredulity.

He looked mildly offended. "Of course I do."

"What do you shave?" She asked. When he simply stared at her, his eyes widening slightly, she went on. "No, seriously. What is there to shave?"

He put a hand to his cheek self-consciously. "I shave my face," he protested.

It took a great deal of self-control for Elen-ai to swallow the ale rather than spit it out all over the table in a gale of laughter. In a voice constrained by that withheld laughter she spoke. "I see. How does that go for you?"

Looking decidedly upset now, he leaned away from her. "It goes fine, thank you."

The muscles of her face fighting to allow the laughter free, she managed to get one final question out. "And uh, are you certain you shave or do you just comb your fluff?"

"I'm going back to bed," he snapped, pushing his food away and standing up.

It was too much. There was something about the wounded pride of an adolescent's masculinity that was universally hilarious, regardless of what position they held. Elen-ai broke down into a howl of laughter, putting her forehead down on the top of the table as the laugh took on a life of its own. She glanced up at Gidyon, whose unimpressed look sent her into further spasms.

Without another word, he set off up the stairs. Elen-ai hastily drained the rest of her ale and spooned up another mouthful of the rejuvenated lunch before following him up the stairs.

Gidyon had stalked into their room and was rummaging around in a trunk. "I'm not talking to you," he informed her as she walked in.

Chuckling to herself, Elen-ai took out several of her knives and began to clean them, putting each one down carefully once she had ensured the blades were free from any spots.

After a time, Gidyon sidled over to stand near her, watching her with his customary curiosity. Certainly, the array of knives would be impressive to someone who had never seen them before. Elen-ai put down the blade she had just finished cleaning. It was the thickness of a few strands of hair and one of her favourites.

"Why do you need so many blades? I thought the Family made the deaths of their contracts look..." he trailed off, clearly uncertain of how to delicately phrase it.

"Not suspicious?" she finished the sentence for him.

"Well, yes." He leaned forward so he could examine the line of wickedly sharp weapons more closely.

"We do. But it's not that simple."

He looked at her, clearly waiting for her to elaborate.

"An unsuspicious death is very different to a death that isn't violent. A brawl can just as easily kill someone as a seemingly-unfortunate fall. If the circumstances look reasonable, people tend not to examine a body too closely for a killing blow delivered by a very skilled hand. But I don't just stay armed to kill one target. Sometimes a member of the Family may find themselves in a tricky situation. After all, most people don't want to die. We have been known to encounter hostility, as surprising as that may sound. Being well armed and ready is important."

Gidyon considered the explanation, then nodded, apparently satisfied.

"Are you still upset with me?" Elen-ai enquired, unable to contain her smirk.

"Yes," he told her, raising his chin slightly and turning back to whatever his own purpose had been.

He did end up shaving that evening, although Elen-ai was not certain that she could see any discernible difference when he emerged from the washroom. She decided that it would not be particularly tactful to say as much, though.

They left the inn the next morning, Gidyon having forgiven Elen-ai's wound to his pride and returning to his normal self. The inn was on the edge of the Harete estate, which itself was composed of a large, sprawling forest. Lake Harete was nestled in the very heart of the forest. While Elen-ai had never seen it – and would not on this occasion either, it was reportedly often so still that it provided a perfect reflection of the forest that came right to the water's edge.

The trees closed in over the track, slightly dampening the noise of the day. The light that came down was filtered through that canopy, a softer yellow than the open brightness that had beaten down on their heads as they crossed the flat Tak plains. Something about the forest reminded Elen-ai of the Family's home. The dense growth of the trees made her somehow think that the quiet forest was full of secrets. She felt more at ease here than she had over the past weeks when being in the homes of those whose political schemes and plans in search of the fulfilment of their own lofty ambition left her feeling a little grubby.

"You seem more comfortable here." Gidyon's comment interrupted her reverie, seeming to read her thoughts.

"I suppose that's because I am," she replied.

"I don't think I've really thanked you for coming with me. I could not have done this without you," he said hesitantly after she said no more.

"You'd have been fine. You'd probably have needed a few more guards, but you'd have been fine," she said.

"No, I didn't mean safe. I meant that you've been by my side. I can talk to you, I can trust you. It, it means a great deal." He reached between them and placed a hand on her arm to emphasise the point.

Touched, Elen-ai found herself lost for words.

"How old are you, Elen-ai?"

His question was a departure from the sentimentality of the moment, but Elen-ai appreciated it. She had never been one for excessive displays of emotion. "At my next birthday, I'll be twenty-two," she said.

"What?" The sound of his exclamation was loud in the muted greenery of the forest.

"You heard me."

"But you're only a few years older than me," he protested.

Elen-ai shifted in her seat. "I am aware. What's your point?"

"I suppose I didn't expect you to be so young. You seem to be so..." He caught himself, biting off the rest of his sentence.

"So what, Gidyon?" She turned to look at him, raising her eyebrows into an anticipatory expression.

"So competent," he finished somewhat lamely.

"That was definitely not what you were initially going to say," Elen-ai accused.

"I don't know what you're talking about." His feigned pomposity made her smile.

She had come to love these moments on the road with Gidyon. Away from the politics and schemes, he was someone else entirely, a boy on the precipice of adulthood who she caught herself thinking of more and more not as her contract, but as her friend.

That night they camped in the forest. The dense growth of the trees meant it was impossible to see the sky clearly, but the glimpses of the night sky in the gaps between the trees made it somehow even more beautiful.

"I must discuss something important with you," Gidyon said once they had finished eating their dinner.

"Mm?" Elen-ai leaned forward to see his face a little better. They hadn't lit a fire that night. It was warm enough for them to go without.

"You know that I have pledged to marry a common woman?"

"I do recall," Elen-ai responded. She hoped he wasn't going to ask her to help him choose a bride. Nothing could be more tedious to her mind.

"Elen-ai." He reached out to touch her hand. "I think it's time that we stop denying what's between us."

Her eyes went wide. "What?"

"I know I'm not the only one who feels it. Elen-ai, marry me." He moved so that he could take both of her hands in his.

"Uh..." She could see his face and the earnest set of his jaw clearly. She didn't move, paralysed by the horror she felt.

He waited for a full minute of awkward tension before he broke, bursting into uncontrollable laughter.

"That wasn't funny!" she protested, yanking her hands from his.

"I beg to differ," he gasped, surrendering to a relapse of laughter.

Elen-ai looked at the Prince's shaking form. "It really wasn't funny."

"It was hilarious," he repudiated as he returned to where he had been sitting before. Every few moments, he would erupt into giggles that he would unsuccessfully try to stifle.

"And what if I would have said yes?" she challenged.

"Would you really have?" That prospect made him dissolve into laughter again.

"Of course not. I would never leave the Family."

"See? Oh, Divine One, that was spectacular." He brought his hands together, making a soft clap.

Declining to reply, Elen-ai shook her head, smiling despite herself. He really had gotten her. She resolved to exact revenge the next evening when he practised kicks and punches under her tuition. It was a petty response to be sure, but that didn't mean it wouldn't be satisfying.

They arrived at the Harete home two days later. On their travel through the massive forest, they had only encountered carts full of the cut timbers that the Harete estate produced. It had been a peaceful bliss for Elen-ai.

Nestled in a cleared valley, the high timber house seemed almost to blend into the backdrop of trees. Elen-ai had never travelled to this part of the country. No contract had ever required the visit of her deadly skills upon people who were connected with the Harete estate. Of course, that did not mean that the Family's presence had not been known here. There was no part of the land where the services of the Family were not sought. From their vantage point, the house looked far less auspicious than the Veertak or Tak family homes. It was smaller, more cosy. It did not announce the excessive wealth that the Harete family possessed, although perhaps that in itself was a testament to their vast fortunes.

The ribbon of the path wound down the valley to lead the small carriage neatly to the house's front courtyard. A girl, perhaps Gidyon's age or slightly younger, ran out to greet them, her long hair streaming untied down her back. She was barefoot and wearing a simple skirt and shirt that hugged close to emphasise a femininity that Elen-ai noticed drew Gidyon's gaze.

"Master Gidyon, we saw your carriage descending."

Elen-ai did not like the breathless excitement with which this girl spoke. It seemed unnecessarily airy.

"I'm sorry, I don't believe we've been introduced," Gidyon leaned down to address the girl, a particularly charming smile on his face.

"I am Rania." She contrived to summon a slight flush that enhanced her delicate prettiness.

"Second-born to Timet and Janyce?"

"The very same," she announced, smiling apparently at the fact that he knew who she was.

"It's a pleasure to meet you. This is Elen-ai, my companion." He gestured quickly, almost dismissively, to Elen-ai.

"Lovely to meet you." Rania barely spared a glance at Elen-ai, her attention was so focused on the Prince. "Please, come inside, both of you."

A servant came forward to take the reins of the carriage from Elen-ai. She handed them over and joined Gidyon in following Rania into the home, a sense of unease at this pretty girl and the Prince's interest in her growing with every step.

FOURTEEN

The Harete family was unusual in that the eldest members who would otherwise lead had given their authority to their eldest son and his wife, Rania's parents. This was because the former patriarch, Lindel, had succumbed to a deterioration of the mind, and his wife, Lilea, had no interest in leading unless it was by the side of her husband. The genuine bond of affection that existed between them did not appear to be present in Rania's parents, a fact which Elen-ai observed as she sat in their parlour room on the lowest level of the house, a drink in her hand and Gidyon to her right. Gentle green light came in through the wide open window that looked onto a small, neatly organised garden which was a world of imposed order against the haphazard wilderness of the rest of the forest.

The two old people warbled at each other quietly in the way that older people tend to do. Lilea's hand was resting on top of her husband's, their fingers gently interlinked. They seemed more interested in being next to each other than their visitor. Their love was a stark contrast to Timet and Janyce, the latter who was quite pregnant. They sat on completely opposite sides of the room, the suggestion of a practised avoidance of each other obvious in the effortlessness by which this outcome had been achieved. Somewhat uncharitably, Elen-ai wondered whether the child in Janyce's womb had been fathered by Timet. That itself was an interesting possibility to report back to the Family, although the Family preferred certainty over conjecture. Elen-ai wondered whether it was worth trying to confirm that suspicion.

"This certainly is a lovely surprise to have you here, especially after that awful attack on your mother's life," Timet said to Gidyon once everybody had come in to the room and settled themselves. The eldest child of Janyce and Timet, a young man named after his grandfather was sitting by his father. Rania had contrived to sit on Gidyon's other side and was smiling enchantingly at him.

There was a certain niceness and cheerfulness to the room that made Elen-ai want to reach for her knives. If she had thought that she had to be on edge in the Tak household, this effusive outpouring of warmth and hospitality made her feel even less at ease.

"Indeed. It is lovely not only to see your home, but also you, and your family, in a setting outside of the Court," Gidyon addressed his response to everybody, although Elen-ai was certain that the comment had one particular individual in mind, though.

"May we be blunt about what brings you here, though?" Timet clasped his hands together.

"I feel you may already be aware of the circumstances which bring me to you." Gidyon's voice was light and open. His posture echoed that apparent carefreeness, leaning into his chair, resting his arm along the back.

"Your mother has decided to name you her heir," Timet supplied the answer. His thoughts on the matter were not discernible from his tone.

"Quite correct. And I've come to ask whether you will support that decision." Gidyon took his arm from the chair's back and straightened. "I won't play games. I know you've likely already heard that the Katan family will almost certainly offer their own potential heir, and I know your land borders theirs. It's an awkward position, but -"

"My Prince," Timet cut him off. "We have always been loyal to the Queen and her family. That is not something that will ever change."

Gidyon sat perfectly still. He evidently expected that he would have had to do more to get their support. "I don't know what to say." He gave a half-smile, looking around the room.

Lilea leaned forward, her hand still in her husband's, her brown eyes earnest. "My dear, your mother and her mother are people Lindel and I have had the good fortune to know, and know quite well. They are exceptional women and you are the product of them. How could our family fail to put its weight behind you?" The earnestness of her tone made the open declaration of support from her son almost believable. But Elen-ai was a cynic.

She turned her attention to Janyce. Despite her position within the family's hierarchy, the woman had said nothing, watching the exchange with a neutral expression. Elen-ai could see tight anger underneath that veneer of neutrality, though. If Elen-ai recalled correctly, Janyce had been born into the Katan family. Despite the fact that anyone who married was supposed to forgo loyalty to the family of their birth, it was a difficult thing to do in practice. Elen-ai decided that she would definitely look further into Janyce when the opportunity presented itself. She couldn't dismiss the possibility that Janyce had her own allegiance that did not mesh with that of the people surrounding her.

"You are far too kind, Lilea. I don't know how to express my thanks." Gidyon's response cut into Elen-ai's musings.

"Will you be staying with us for long?" Rania asked, the enthusiasm with which she asked grating on Elen-ai's nerves.

"At least a few days." Gidyon smiled at her. "If that's alright?" He turned to Timet.

"Please, you and your companion are welcome to stay with us for as long as you would like."

Rania volunteered to show Gidyon and Elen-ai to their room. As they walked through the large home, she maintained an excited chatter with the Prince that conspicuously avoided including Elen-ai. It wasn't so much that the slight annoyed Elen-ai, it was the abject lack of any subtlety on Rania's part that offended her sensibilities. Elen-ai may not have been one for the political game played by members of the seven families and the Court, but she nevertheless appreciated nuance and a well-crafted approach, and this girl seemed to lack either. What was particularly offensive on top of this though, was that Gidyon seemed to not realise or mind, ogling the girl's figure as they ascended the staircase to their room on the second floor of the five-story building.

At the doorway of the room, Rania paused. "We've made up the one bed..." she said, flicking her long brown hair as she spoke. The impracticality of all that hair simply hanging there irritated Elen-ai beyond measure. She couldn't take it any longer.

"That will be fine, thank you," she said, breezing past the girl and into the room.

"I'll leave you to clean up then. I'll just be in the music room, if you want me." It was very clear that Rania's offer was not directed at Elen-ai.

"What do you play?" Gidyon asked, his voice warm.

"Oh, I'm not very good!" Rania exclaimed. Elen-ai thought that if she fluttered her eyes any harder she may lose them.

"I'm sure that's not true at all," Gidyon assured her. "Will you play for me?"

"You'd have to promise not to be too critical. I'd be terribly nervous if you watched me." Her breathy demeanour made a reappearance, and she even coiled a lock of hair around one of her fingers as she looked demurely at Gidyon.

Elen-ai threw herself into a chair to observe the spectacle. The deliberate thud did not appear to be noticed by either of the adolescents caught in what she presumed they believed to be a terribly romantic moment.

"On my honour, I'd never be too critical of you," he promised.

"Well I look forward to you finding me, then." With one final sly smile, Rania set off along the corridor.

Gidyon closed the door and turned to Elen-ai. "Well that went very well I think," he commented cheerfully.

"Are you referring to the discussion with the Harete family or your efforts to impregnate their daughter?" Elen-ai asked casually, crossing one leg over the other.

"What?" For someone who was very skilled at concealing his real thoughts, Gidyon did a terrible job of feigning ignorance.

"My Prince, if I may offer you a piece of advice: beware of the charms of an attractive and interested person. More people have been brought to ruin by lust than I can possibly count."

"She's nice. Nothing beyond that," he protested.

"Just because the Harete family has pledged their loyalty to you does not mean they are without ambition. Being related to the wife of a ruler is a great coup," she cautioned.

"Really, Elen-ai, don't be ridiculous." Gidyon shook his head dismissively.

"Have you ever been with a woman?" Elen-ai asked as the thought occurred to her. It would certainly explain why he was so blind to this painfully obvious ploy.

"That's none of your business!" Gidyon stuttered.

She put a hand to her forehead. "That's all I need. Someone who can be led by what's between his legs because he knows no better," she muttered.

"I'm not going to be led by my groin," Gidyon countered, a blush creeping its way up his neck.

In response, Elen-ai offered a poor imitation of Rania's breathy laugh and flick of hair - difficult given that Elen-ai had very little of her own hair to flick.

"Now you're just being mean," she was told sternly.

"Gidyon, if you want that sort of pleasure, find someone who will want nothing other than coin in exchange for it. That girl can cause you more problems than the entirety of the Katan family's so-called heir," she said.

"That's crude." Gidyon shook his head and turned away from her.

"I can stop a knife coming to you. I can't stop the damage if you mis-step with her," Elen-ai told his back.

Gidyon chose not to respond, walking into the adjacent washroom and closing the door.

He walked out several minutes later, his hair wet and clothes changed. Elen-ai rose and went in for a wash of her own to discover that he had used all of the warm water, almost certainly on purpose.

After she had finished washing in the cold water, she moodily accompanied Gidyon to the music room on the uppermost level of the house, where she was forced to listen to Rania plucking away at a harp and trilling several songs in a rather bland voice. It seemed however, that Elen-ai and Gidyon heard completely different performances, as he effusively praised her every note. Elen-ai would have loved desperately to be anywhere other than by the side of the infatuated Prince, but she could not justify the risk of leaving him alone.

Dinner was slightly less painful, although Rania sat herself next to Gidyon. Thankfully, he was not so foolish as to exclusively pay attention to her, but many of his comments and jokes were clearly not made with her in mind, causing eruptions of giggles or sighs from the girl.

The food was wholesome and good and Elen-ai even enjoyed listening to the conversation when it wasn't between Gidyon and Rania. Clearly, Lilea and Lindel had a close relationship with their son and grandchildren, and the good-natured banter that was flung around the table was a testament to that. Timet's sister and her husband were also present, engaging in the repartee with great abandon, while frequent references to their other sibling - from what Elen-ai could gather, this was the youngest boy, who had married into the Rasatan family - were made. The clear affection that they held for each other would have been quite touching were it not for Janyce's silence. While not conspicuous, it nevertheless was noticeable. There was almost a space around the pregnant woman, as though she were invisible to everybody else. But she did not seem unhappy with her solitude. Indeed, she seemed to have constructed this isolation. She maintained it with a sourness that repelled anyone who may seek to speak with her. The pale blonde hair that framed her face further differentiated her; the rest of the family had curly brown hair. Even her own children did not direct any comment to her. Elen-ai wondered if the woman's distance was because she was hiding something from them, such as an involvement in a plot against the Prince. Certainly, it was the one discordant note in the otherwise perfect harmony that the Rasatans appeared to embody. Something about sitting at the table gave Elen-ai the same discomfort that she felt when holding a fruit that was overripe, sweetness and rot unpleasantly coexisting until the decay won out. Elen-ai resolved to find out more about Janyce Harete as soon as possible, to find out what exactly this family was hiding behind their smiles.

For that reason, much later in the evening after Gidyon and Elen-ai had returned to their room following the bidding of effusive goodnights between Gidyon and Rania, Elen-ai slipped out of the bed she shared with the Prince and out into the house.

She knew that she should probably stay with Gidyon, but she had checked the room and kept her ears out for the sound of anybody moving about the house. The large timbers from which the house was constructed – from the forest surrounding the house – meant that she was able to hear the comings and goings of people within it at this time of night. Wooden floors required far less finesse than the apex of a roof, but wood did have a propensity to squeak when least expected. It gave Elen-ai a confidence that the Prince would not be ambushed without her knowing about it well in advance.

Staying close to the shadows, she made her way to the third level of the house where Janyce and Timet's bedroom was. As she neared it, she could hear the sound of a heated discussion taking place. Curiosity burning, she snuck to the door, flattened herself against the wall, and listened.

"...I'm so tired of you." Janyce's voice came through quite clearly.

"Not as tired as I am of you." Timet's response was infused with a malice that Elen-ai wouldn't have thought possible given the cheerful demeanour he had demonstrated that day. It was satisfying to know that she had been correct about there being something unpleasant lurking behind that open and pleasant manner.

"At least you only have one person to be sick of." The comment was accompanied by the sound of a thump, as though something heavy was being put down. "I'm surrounded here by your parents, your sister and her insipid husband, and our children who your whole family has kept from me."

"If it's that much of a burden for to you to be here surrounded by my family, just leave then!" The explosive delivery suggested that this was an argument that had been conducted a number of times in a variety of ways. The conclusion was foregone and the grievances were always the same; a well-worn path eked out over years and years of bitterness.

"I can't just leave. I have to bear you your final brat," Janyce snarled.

"Yes, well I'm not so certain that it even is my child you're carrying."

That comment was followed by the sound of a sharp gasp. "How dare you." Janyce's voice was low. A different sort of anger was behind it now.

"I wouldn't be surprised if none of the children you've birthed are mine."

"They're more yours than mine. Your parents saw to that, taking them away from me, keeping them close. I was a stranger to them the second they left me."

"You never wanted to be part of my family," Timet accused.

"I was never given the chance," Janyce raged back.

"You never tried. And now you sit in the room like some dark cloud, shaming us all. The Prince and his companion must have noticed that you didn't say a word at all today."

"And pretend that I was listened to when the matter of his position was discussed? Or the decision to encourage Rania to bed him?"

"You don't support him because you want to further your family's ambitions rather than the family to which you pledged your loyalty when we wed." Footsteps sounded on the other side of the wall, coming closer to the door.

"You're despicable." Janyce was the one who had moved, her voice closer to the door.

"And you're just like every Katan I've ever met. Nasty and self-interested. Where are you going?"

"None of your business!" Janyce declared, flinging open the door and stepping into the corridor.

Elen-ai gathered the shadows about her to shield herself from sight. She almost certainly wouldn't have been noticed, though. Janyce was too intent on her dramatic exit than looking at her surroundings to spot an inconspicuous assassin.

"I hope the Divine One curses her," Timet growled once his wife was definitely out of earshot, stomping over to the door and closing it.

Elen-ai followed Janyce, creeping down several flights of stairs and out into the garden in pursuit of her quarry. Nobody else was out of their rooms. Elen-ai heard one or two murmured conversations, even one sigh of desire, but she paid them little heed. She had been in many houses at night and every sound that reached her ears was the sound of a house at peace, with one very significant exception.

The night air held no chill, but it held no warmth either. Janyce rubbed her upper arms in an effort to warm herself. She had neglected to bring a shawl or coat to put over the thin bedclothes she wore.

Elen-ai stood clothed in shadow a few paces away, watching as the unrelenting rigidity that she had seen in the woman's posture melt away, leaving a very human, very alone person.

Janyce paced idly around the small patch of grass that was edged by perfectly maintained flower beds. She didn't seem to have any particular plan in mind. Elen-ai wondered if she came out here often, but it seemed unlikely given the lack of foresight to bring something to keep her warm.

Her arms still wrapped around herself, Janyce's orbit brought her face clearly into Elen-ai's view, illuminated by a ray of moonlight coming down through the clearing in the trees. Elen-ai had never seen such profound loneliness as she saw etched on the face of the woman before her. The intense emotion made her look both terribly young and impossibly old, made more so by the whiteness of the moonlight. It made Janyce's pale hair look luminescent, making her seem almost otherworldly.

Elen-ai was not certain that she could understand what she saw, but she was transfixed by it. It was a sentiment so profound, so intense, that all she could understand was that it had locked Janyce away from everybody around her. The lonely woman paced the small garden. One hand went occasionally to her stomach in the reflexive manner of all pregnant women.

Eventually, Elen-ai decided that she would not glean anything more. No words would be uttered, and no great secret would be revealed through this aimless pacing. Whatever allegiance she may have to the family of her birth, Elen-ai's instinct told her that this woman was too preoccupied with her loneliness to be a part of any particular scheme against Gidyon other than as a reluctant observer as her husband encouraged their daughter to seduce the Prince. Taking one last look at Janyce, she moved back into the house, climbing back up the stairs to the room she and Gidyon shared.

As soon as she entered the bedroom, she knew something was wrong. She went over to the bed to verify that she wasn't, but as she had known from the instant she came into the room that it was empty.

FIFTEEN

Panic threatened for one horrifying, unending moment to overwhelm Elen-ai. It took all the discipline and training she had to quash the sensation and stand completely still, listening to the house. She hadn't been away from the room for long, he couldn't be far away. She could hear everything throughout the house from the sound of the grass being crushed under the feet of the sad Janyce to the breathing of several people, most of them asleep. Amid this, she heard from high up, likely somewhere in the music room, the sound of whispers, of a gasp. As quickly as she could, she climbed the stairs of the house, her feet making no sound. Recriminations swirled in her mind. She should not have thought it safe or wise to leave the Prince, yet she had become lax at the fact that little had happened during the few times when she had previously left his side. At the door to the music room she paused, hearing a furtive rustle of cloth, then she opened it to find Gidyon and Rania locked in a passionate embrace.

At her sudden appearance, they sprang apart guiltily. Elen-ai stood in the doorway, her slight frame nearly blending into the shadows of the house but for her face, illuminated by a candle in the room.

"Elen-ai," Gidyon began, but she stepped into the room toward the two.

"Stop." She cut off whatever he may have been about to say. "You and I will speak later."

Perhaps for the first time, he did as she bade and fell silent. She turned to Rania who was looking at Elen-ai apprehensively.

"Gidyon can be with who he chooses," the girl said, a semblance of defiance peeking through her uncertainty. She lifted her chin, the shadow of a look of pride on her features. Of course, she thought that Elen-ai as someone of common birth, was a lover the Prince could thoughtlessly discard in favour of another woman.

"Why don't you tell Gidyon what your parents instructed you to do," Elen-ai suggested. The soft menace in her voice was terrifying.

To Rania's credit, she did not flinch. "I have no idea what you mean."

"Don't play games with me, little girl. Your parents were enjoying quite the argument just now, and what you had been told to do was mentioned for anyone listening to learn about." Elen-ai advanced on her, her face a grim visage.

"What do you mean?" Gidyon's head whipped from Elen-ai to Rania.

"Tell him," Elen-ai commanded the girl.

"Tell me what?" Gidyon echoed when no words were forthcoming.

"They just thought we may get along," Rania whimpered, her eyes wide and pleading.

"What do you mean?" Gidyon took a step toward her. He was now no longer the lust-struck boy, but once more the Prince, and his words carried an authority that even Elen-ai's menace could not match.

"They said that if you liked me, I should try and..." Unwilling to say the words, she hung her head.

"And what did your family expect to come of this?" Gidyon asked, his face as unmoving as stone. The sudden change in his demeanour was frightening.

"Nothing. I swear." Rania looked up her, her face a mask of wide-eyed honesty.

"The word marriage was never used?"

"Well, maybe once," she admitted.

Gidyon took a deep breath. Elen-ai noticed his hands clench very briefly into fists. "You love your family, don't you, Rania?" he asked.

She nodded, her gaze averted.

"Look at me, please," Gidyon said.

Her reluctance obvious, Rania brought her gaze to him. The vivacity that she had earlier espoused had disappeared and in its place was an uncertain young girl.

"Now answer me. Do you love your family?" Gidyon asked again.

"Yes." Her voice was barely above a whisper.

"Of course you do. Family is the most important thing. Isn't that what we are all told here in the Second Country from birth?"

"Yes."

Elen-ai wondered where he was going with these questions, but stayed silent.

"You marrying me would be very good for your family, wouldn't it? It would bring them much prestige, as well as perhaps a favourable place when it came to dealing with their business. Perhaps it would even bring the ear of the Queen - or the person who succeeds her." Gidyon reached out and took Rania's hand in both of his. "Now I want you to listen very carefully to what I am about to say, Rania. Because I will only say it once. Are you listening carefully?"

"Yes, Gidyon." She sounded almost hopeful.

"If your parents ask you how your efforts with me went, you will tell them that they failed. That you tried your hardest because you did not want to let them down, but I did not accept any of your advances."

Rania nodded obediently. Her hand remained in both of Gidyon's.

"And you will never tell them that I did in fact accept your invitation to meet you here tonight, or that anything transpired between us."

"Of course not," she breathed, a slight smile drawing the corners of her mouth upwards.

"Do you know why you will never breathe a word of this?" Gidyon continued without pausing to allow her to answer, his voice almost gentle. "Because you love your family. And you have the best interests of your family at heart. And if I ever hear a rumour about you and myself, I will ensure that your family is ruined. Taxes, tariffs, a conspicuous absence of invitations to the Court, an absence of blessings on any marriage that may occur between a member of the Harete family and one of the other six families. I will ensure that it is cheaper to buy timber from other countries than from this lovely forest. No, Rania, look at me." His voice retained that gentle quality. Rania's eyes had filled with tears and she had looked down. Elen-ai almost felt sorry for the girl. She saw Gidyon's grip on Rania's hand tighten.

"Your family has pledged their loyalty to me, and your parents offered me their hospitality. And I do not want to harm you or them. But my trust has also been abused, and that I cannot forget or forgive. Do not cry, Rania. Nothing bad will happen to you or your family if you stay silent. You have my word on that."

Tears spilled unchecked down her cheeks as she looked at him.

"Do you understand?" Gidyon asked, his gaze on her unwavering.

She nodded.

"Good girl. How about we all head to bed, then," he suggested.

She nodded again. Only then did Gidyon release her hand. She fled the room, not even seeming to notice Elen-ai, and went down the stairs to her own bedroom. Elen-ai heard the door open and close, and the sound of quiet sobbing commence. She turned her attention to Gidyon who had put his hand to his mouth and looked as though he were somewhere between being deeply abashed and lost in thought.

"Thank you," he said. The fearsome person he had become to deal with Rania had vanished.

The fury that she had been holding in check while he spoke with Rania uncoiled itself. "How could you be so stupid?" she hissed.

Gidyon at least had the good grace to blush. "I thought..."

She cut him off. "No Gidyon, that's exactly it. You didn't think. At least, not with your head."

"I wouldn't have come here if you hadn't been gone when I woke up," he protested quietly.

"Don't you dare try and make this my fault," Elen-ai fumed, keeping her voice low so as not to wake anybody else in the house. "I warned you. I *told* you to be careful. And you still went chasing after her because she promised you – what?"

"I was never going to do anything serious," Gidyon said.

"You and she were alone, here, in the middle of the night. How can you say that?" Elen-ai threw up her hands. "Shadow God, you're just like your parents!"

Gidyon's face froze into place and his expression hardened. Perhaps anger at himself for being so easily fooled by Rania was coming to the surface, lured there by her comment. There once more though was the cold, furious Prince who had so suddenly appeared to reduce Rania to tears. "You have no right to say that," he said. His voice and his eyes were dangerous, but Elen-ai was too busy nursing her own fury to care.

"I have every right. *I* found out that Zekken was your father, *I* found out that Rania had been told to seduce you, and *I* stopped you from doing anything stupid with her. And here you are throwing everything away because some stupid girl bats her eyelashes at you. Did you really think that she wanted nothing from you? Did you really think that the pleasant picture of today was all there was to see?" She made no effort to hide the anger or scorn from her voice.

"Why do you care? Your job is to keep me alive, not to keep me as heir to the throne. That's what you are being paid to do. You are like any other servant. Don't forget your place." Gidyon spat the words at her like bile, his own careful control lost in the heat of his anger and humiliation.

Elen-ai glared at him, the candlelight flickering across both of their faces. "I'll await your orders then, your Highness," she said, turning from him to blow out the candle so that he didn't see the hurt his words had caused across her face.

In darkness she found herself able to speak again. "Is it your wish that we retire for the evening, or do you have other commands?"

Gidyon did not reply, instead leaving the room that had been the site of so much drama and making his way quietly back down to their room. Elen-ai followed him after extinguishing the candle, wordless and distant, suddenly returned to being a stranger to him.

That night, neither she nor the Prince slept. She could not begin to know what was in his thoughts. His cruelty had hurt her deeply. She had not realised how much she had come to view the Prince as a friend, nor indeed how incredibly slender the thread that bound them together was. That was the truth about family; a cruel word or an unkindness between kin could be surmounted with time and an apology. Family was bound together by something intangible but impossible to break. It was why Elen-ai had vowed never to leave the Family. There she would be loved and accepted, regardless what mistakes she may make. Certainly, no family was perfect, and sometimes families did terrible things to one another, yet there was nothing so powerful nor so strong as the ties between members of a family. Gidyon himself had exploited that in his threats to Rania.

Elen-ai chastised herself for thinking for a moment that her friendship with Gidyon was something real, something possibly even enduring. As he himself had reminded her, she was just another of his servants.

Morning dawned. Elen-ai shrugged off the fatigue, accustomed only to a few hours of sleep. Gidyon looked less fresh, the smudges of exhaustion visible under his eyes and in the drawn lines of his face. Perhaps that exhaustion was added to by the betrayal of the previous evening. Elen-ai still could not understand how he, an adept reader of people and their motives, had been so tricked by the simple charm of a girl, but a part of her wondered if he had wanted to believe for a moment that he was just a boy who could engage in a simple dalliance. For anybody else, a romantic meeting with Rania would have been perhaps a little unusual but not something to bring them to ruin. For Gidyon, it was his reputation, his name, his legitimacy, that was at stake. The weight of such an expectation, to be always perfect, to have not the slightest mark against him that might call his capacity to rule into question, must be crushing, even though he never spoke of it. But Elen-ai was not feeling charitable towards the Prince, so she pushed that explanation to the back of her mind and instead labelled him a spoiled, graceless brat.

Despite whatever personal feelings he may have felt toward the family who had sought to leverage influence over him through their daughter, Gidyon was perfectly charming at the breakfast table. Timet had appeared briefly, grabbing a hunk of bread and hurriedly apologising for a speedy departure, citing the need to attend to some logging operation. He also offered an apology for Janyce, claiming that she was not feeling well.

Lindel and Lilea were both in attendance, sitting contentedly at the table, their wizened faces focused intently on the successful passage of food from their plates to mouths. Gidyon made very polite, and patient, conversation with them as he picked at his own food. Elen-ai stayed silent as was her custom, occupying herself with her food and observation of the room.

Rania entered when they were about halfway through their meal, her own face looking as though she had not enjoyed much sleep during the night. Elen-ai had heard her sobs subside after a few hours, but it seemed that the girl had not gotten much more sleep than Elen-ai or Gidyon. Gidyon greeted her with the same charm he had on the previous day. To anyone who was unaware of what had transpired during the evening, there was no difference in his demeanour. For a moment, Rania looked surprised, then she cautiously offered her own smile and greeting.

"Did you sleep well? You look a touch pale." Gidyon's concern sounded so genuine that even Elen-ai believed it for a moment.

"I'm afraid I found it very difficult to fall asleep," Rania confessed hesitantly.

"I hope that you have not been disturbed by my and Elen-ai's presence or our impact on your family," Gidyon said. The veiled warning was evidently not lost on her. She turned an even paler shade of white.

"N-no, your highness. Perhaps I overindulged at dinner," she stammered.

"Hopefully the unease will pass," he said, his face completely sincere.

"I'm sure it will." Rania lowered her head as she scurried to her seat – one as far away from Gidyon as possible.

He appeared not to notice her careful avoidance of him, instead simply returning to pick at his food in apparent contentment.

The morning passed with Gidyon taking a walk through the house's gardens and Elen-ai following him from a distance. What she had briefly glimpsed of the Harete gardens the previous day had only been a fraction of their scope. They were quite spectacular. Were she not still so upset by Gidyon's cruelty and stupidity the evening before she would have quite enjoyed discovering the meandering paths, or even simply sitting in some of the different areas. Hedges were pruned to guide the walker into different sections, some alive with the violent blossom of late spring flowers. Even the kitchen's gardens were artfully arranged, neat lines of vegetables and herbs forming beautiful patterns in the soil.

Some people brush past arguments, not letting words flung at them in anger achieve the objective of getting under the skin. Gidyon and Elen-ai were the other type of person; the one for whom such comments, even though said in the heat of the moment, could not be forgotten or forgiven. It seemed to Elen-ai as they each made their careful way through the gardens as far apart from each other as possible, that whatever friendship may have existed between them was almost certainly destroyed.

Still no word had been exchanged between them when they went inside for lunch. Timet had returned from the work that he was overseeing and Janyce had emerged with her impenetrable sullenness in place. Elen-ai spared her a lingering glance, but there was no sign of the deep distress that Elen-ai had witnessed the previous evening. Her cool mask of indifference was as it had been the previous day. Hiding genuine emotion seemed necessary in order to be a member of a family with wealth and power. It seemed an exhausting task to Elen-ai.

As had been the case with breakfast, Gidyon chatted cheerfully with everyone at the table, even Rania. Elen-ai felt a momentary pity for the girl. After all, she had merely been doing what her family had bid her. As disgusted as she may have been with Gidyon for his blindness to the plan, she was more repulsed by family members who would use their own so callously. It was a timely reminder that the world through she accompanied Gidyon was not her own, governed by a certain ruthlessness that she, an assassin, found left a bitter taste in her mouth. She would be glad to leave this life.

Whatever she may have thought of the Harete family though, when she took a bite of the luncheon dessert, she thought that she had never tasted anything so delicious in her entire life. Gidyon's effusive words of appreciation for the dish echoed her sentiments.

"It's because it's made from fruit which we picked today from our orchards," Timet explained with a disarming smile. "Nothing can beat freshness."

"But it's the recipe, too!" Gidyon exclaimed.

"A secret of the household." Lilea leaned forward in a conspiratorial manner, a smile on her face.

"Forget timber, you should just sell this," Gidyon joked between mouthfuls.

"We're so glad you like it," Lilea reached her gnarled hand across the table and patted the Prince's forearm. Elen-ai wondered how sincere the old woman actually was, or if she too had been a part of the scheme to entrap the Prince.

"I shan't forget your hospitality, or the efforts that the members of the Harete family went to." Gidyon smiled, turning ever so slightly to look at Rania. It seemed unnecessary to yet again remind the girl of Gidyon's promise to her. His comment clearly struck home, she caught the quiver of her lips quickly, pressing them together tightly. However, he made no other such comments to Rania during the rest of the luncheon, simply announcing at its conclusion that he and Elen-ai would depart the following morning. Polite lament over the brevity of his visit was offered, with the return of promises to return and stay longer – delivered with equal politeness.

The rest of the afternoon was an exercise in a similar silence to the morning. This time however, Gidyon spent the time inside, seating himself in the house's library and perusing the books there. The Harete catalogue did not come close to rivalling the collection of the Veertaks, but the bookshelves were filled with a respectable number of texts nevertheless. Elen-ai read on the other side of the room to Gidyon, casting the occasional glance at him, but he refused to so much as look in her direction. She refused to be the one to speak first to try and bridge the gulf that both of them had created the previous evening. She remembered the words of her Father so many weeks ago, about learning from her mistakes. She resolved to not make the mistake again of thinking she and the Prince were friends. Remembering that day, the advice of her Father was inextricably linked with the bustle and sound of the market. Even though she preferred silence and shade, she wished she were back in the market, in Herran, close to the Family and everything that she knew.

SIXTEEN

Gidyon maintained his silence throughout the evening and into the entirety of the carriage ride the next day. In reply, Elen-ai retreated into herself, pretending that he wasn't there. They remained in their respective silences for the entirety of the week that it took them to get to the Bertak family's home, speaking only for the most necessary of communications. There were no more evening lessons on the art of fighting, no more light-hearted banter, no more easy companionship.

Elen-ai watched alone as the Harete forest thinned out until it turned into the flat farmlands that were in the footlands of the Bertak mountains. Despite the expansive number of farms, farming was not really where the Bertak fortune came from. The Bertak lands encompassed a small cluster of mountains in whose bowels were precious metals. Indeed, the metal that formed the cuffs which the Queen always wore at her neck and wrists came from the Bertak mountains. However, despite controlling this resource, the Bertak family's wealth and power did not rank among that of the Aadran, Tak, Katan or even Harete families. An uncharitable soul, and Elen-ai did not consider herself particularly generous, might say that it was because the Bertaks had never put much time or effort into cultivating craftspeople loyal to them to work the resource that they controlled, instead simply seeing the short term benefit to selling off the metal they withdrew from their mountains. Regardless, as a result, the fertile soil in the rest of their lands had been turned into farms that generated extra revenue for the family. This was hardly a singular practice. Any land within the Queendom that was suitable for farmland and not purposed for some other use had foodstuff grown on it. However, it was known that the Bertaks found it particularly egregious that they needed to support their wealth with farmland rather than to simply extend their wealth. This petty embarrassment was compounded by the fact that everybody knew it. The conditions for those who worked in farms on the Veertak estate were markedly different to the other lands they had traversed. Elen-ai watched Gidyon's face as he observed the pitiful existence of the people who worked the farms scattered along the Bertak lands. Perhaps had the Bertak family established a community of jewellers or metalworkers, similar to the scholars in Atak or the clayworkers in the Katan lands, the Bertaks would be wealthier and the people who lived on their land would live in better conditions.

People barely paid the battered Veertak carriage any mind as it passed by. Late harvests were being conducted, or the land was being tilled in preparation for the next planting. Nobody realised that the ignominious carriage carried their future ruler, likely they didn't spend any time wondering who passed by them. Their clothes spoke of the pittance paid to them by those who owned the land on which they worked more eloquently than they ever could have.

The days were clear and warm. Summer had suddenly gone from being a hint on a breath of wind to possible. As they trekked through the Bertak farms on the first day, Elen-ai spied a bird climbing almost vertically into the sky. It looked as though it would fall out of the air, its ascent was so high and so steep. Then it suddenly turned and swooped back down with a reckless speed, lost from sight as it plummeted close to the ground, blending against the faint outline of the mountains' blue backdrop. Elen-ai assumed that the bird was catching some prey, but she preferred to think that it was enjoying the ability to perform such a remarkable feat. She almost turned to say something about it to Gidyon, but caught herself, remembering that he was not her friend. Such comments, such conversations, did not take place between a servant and master.

Elen-ai did not know with what thoughts Gidyon occupied himself during that week. He seemed to draw in upon himself, to be constantly musing on some idea or another. Yet with whatever conclusions he may have drawn, he never seemed satisfied. A look of pensive worry crept onto his face as they entered the Bertak land and never departed, even in his sleep. The absence of any answers as to who had tried to kill Gidyon and the Queen bothered Elen-ai, too. With a would-be killer still at large, it meant she had to continue to stay as close to Gidyon as possible, which was particularly unpalatable given his obnoxious silence.

Due to the absence of any taverns or inns within the Bertak lands as a result of the family's well-known disapproval of 'houses of ill repute', Elen-ai and Gidyon had no opportunity to bathe or sleep anywhere other than under the stars. The closest they came was a small settlement that they encountered on the second day where Elen-ai merely bought some more food to last them until they reached the seat of the Bertak power; the family home. Taverns and tiny townships were scattered throughout the other territories of the Queendom, but not here. The family did not encourage such things, going so far as to prohibit the conglomeration of more than ten abodes three generations ago. The only settlement allowed by the Bertaks in their lands was right outside the entrance to the mountain mines.

They followed the shore of lake Bertak during the last two days of travel. That section of the lake had no shore, merely high cliffs with a significant drop down into waters that moodily broke upon the point where stone met the waves. For those two days, Elen-ai spent much time glancing uneasily at the crumbling edge of the road and the drop into those unwelcoming waters. She kept the carriage as far away from the edge as possible, maintaining an inward commentary of colourful descriptors about the family who seemed not to deem it necessary to maintain the roads within their lands.

These uncharitable thoughts were at the forefront of her mind when they arrived at the Bertak home. It was built from the same stone that made up the mountains, and the cliff on which they had driven. However, unlike the stone which in its natural environment had a vaguely pleasant colour, the slabs of the house had been polished so that they shone a dirty off-white. The house itself was architecturally magnificent; half of it nestled in the mountain at whose foot it had been built, the other half extended almost to the edge of the cliff. Despite the visual spectacle that the house offered both to someone observing it, as well as someone looking out from it, Elen-ai found it a tad ugly, pretensions of grandeur too obvious in the lines of the design. She had no idea for what purpose an observatory on the uppermost level had been built – the mountain would block out much of the sky – but there it sat, a testament to the family's supposed status as intellectuals.

Elen-ai drew the carriage to a stop. Nobody came to greet them. It was as though the house was deserted. She and Gidyon stepped down off the carriage and walked around, waiting for someone to notice their arrival. Eventually, Elen-ai went up to the grand doors, elaborately carved timber that looked as though it were Harete wood, and knocked.

The door was answered by the thinnest woman Elen-ai had ever seen. Despite the warmth of the day, she was dressed in a high-necked full-length dress with sleeves that came all the way down to her wrists. "May I help you?" she asked.

"Are the heads of the family in?" Elen-ai enquired.

"Who wants to know?"

"The Royal family," Elen-ai responded, reining in her temper so that she did not simply snap at this emaciated creature.

"One moment, please," the woman replied, shutting the door in Elen-ai's face.

Gidyon, who was standing a few paces, away gave snort. "Amazing," he said softly. Elen-ai couldn't help but agree with the sarcastic sentiment. It was the first time one of them had spoken to the other without having to.

A few minutes later the woman returned, opening the door wide – quite a feat given the size of the door relative to her. "Please come in," she said.

Elen-ai and Gidyon walked through the huge doorway and into the entrance hall. Various weapons were mounted on the wall, glinting dully in the dim light. As they followed the woman, Elen-ai counted at least thirty different types of sword, twelve spears designs, and sixteen daggers.

They were led through several dark corridors and into a room which overlooked the lake. Here, in contrast to the darkness of the halls through which they had passed, the light poured in, almost too bright.

"If you will be seated, Lady Julyana will be with you shortly," the woman informed them, exiting the room.

Elen-ai and Gidyon exchanged a look of raised eyebrows, their first actual interaction in over a week.

Gidyon wandered over to the window and looked out at the lake below. The sun glinted off its surface, the blue of the water lost in the sparkle of the sunlight. Elen-ai had no idea how he could remain squinting into the glare for so long without his eyes becoming sore. To save her own eyes, she turned her attention to the room's interior. Only two weapons graced the walls in here; a matching dagger and sword. Aside from chairs, a few tables, and a cabinet of bottles filled with what Elen-ai presumed were liquor, there was nothing else in the room.

They were waiting for several minutes before the door opened and a plump woman in her middle years entered. Her fingers were bedecked with various rings and around her throat was a cuff similar to the one worn by the Queen. Unfortunately, while around the slender column of the Queen's neck the cuff was quite striking, it merely emphasised her jowls peeking over the top. The only thing about her which was not rotund was her nose which was curiously delicate in stark contrast to the rest of her. Her mouth had been stained a dark crimson, standing out against her powdered face. She looked somewhat absurd given that only in the capital did people really paint their faces, and even then, only on particular occasions.

Gidyon had turned from the window and crossed the room to greet her. "Lady Julyana. It's so wonderful to see you again." Despite the fact that he hadn't bathed in several days and was covered with dust from the road, Gidyon still managed to be disarmingly charming.

"Master Gidyon." The woman's round fingers enveloped Gidyon's outstretched hands. "Or should I call you Prince?" Her question was delivered with a sly emphasis which had Elen-ai double checking that all of her blades were within easy access.

Gidyon did not seem at all perturbed by her comment. "It seems that news has a way of reaching everyone."

"And I presume that this is your companion who I've heard much about. Lady Elen-ai." Her emphasis of 'lady' made clear her scepticism on the subject of Elen-ai's character.

"Lady Julyana, it's a pleasure to meet you. I am most impressed by your weapons collection," Elen-ai murmured, her anger in check – just.

"Ah yes. All the women in my family have a love affair with weapons of any form. The collection was started by my grandmother, a custom that I have continued." Julyana responded with a dismissive airiness.

Elen-ai bit down on her incredulous question as to whether or not Julyana herself was even remotely adept with any blade other than one that was part of a cutlery set.

"Please, let us sit." The outermost limits of politeness met, Julyana addressed Gidyon, lowering her girth into an armchair. She did not offer him or Elen-ai anything to drink or eat.

"I presume if you are aware of my new title, and even my companion's name, you are aware of why I am here." Gidyon sat after a moment's hesitation. Elen-ai sat beside him, trying to restrain herself from glaring at this odious woman.

"I certainly am. I'm sure it would not surprise you to know that I am also aware of the responses that other people have given you to the question of whether or not they will support your claim to the throne. It was so distressing to hear of the attempt on you and your mother's lives all those weeks ago before, by the way." Julyana interlinked her pudgy hands together, the rings clinking softly. She paused, a look of relish coming over her face. "It has been a long time since the crown has truly needed our support on something. We know you have the support of the Harete family and the Veertaks. And the rumour of a Katans' alternative heir has certainly reached our ears, alongside the possibility that the Rasatan family will throw their support behind this claim. I personally found it interesting that the Tak and Aadran families declined to state their support for you." Her brown eyes looked at him keenly.

"Families as large and powerful as the Taks and Aadrans have the luxury of being able to make such a decision. But even they must tread carefully," Gidyon replied.

"And yet you have one of the other largest families in the Queendom poised to oppose your claim," the large woman pointed out.

Gidyon shrugged. "At this point, it is mere speculation. But if they were to do so, I'm sure that they have their own reasons. Even so, to do so would be a risk. I currently have more supporters than I have opponents."

"The way the Bertaks speak may alter that," Julyana said.

Gidyon inclined his head in acknowledgement of that truth.

"Tell me your Highness, if the Bertak clan were to support your mother's decision to put a man on the throne, what would that mean for our corner of the world?" Julyana leaned back, her fingers still clasped. It looked very much as though she was enjoying this conversation.

"That I could not tell you," Gidyon said. "One would have to wait and see what the future holds."

"Hmm." Julyana looked down at her hands. "I hear you have pledged to marry a woman of common birth in order to ensure your neutrality."

"You hear correctly."

"Yet measures taken to protect neutrality do not always work."

A look of confusion swept across Gidyon's face almost too fast to see. "It's the best I can offer, I'm afraid," he confessed, spreading his hands.

Julyana unlinked her fingers, placing her palms flat against each other and bringing her touching hands up to her face. She performed the act of thinking well, gently tapping her fingertips against each other, with a slight frown drawing her eyebrows downward, creasing the powder on her face. Eventually she straightened up, her pretence of deliberation complete. With a regretful sigh, she raised her eyes to meet Gidyon's. "I am terribly sorry your Highness, but I'm afraid that the Bertak family cannot support your claim to the throne. We must follow the lead of the Tak and Aadran families and remain neutral in this matter. I'm sure you can understand," she added with an insincere smile.

Gidyon's pleasant smile did not waver. "Lady Julyana, you and your family must of course protect yourselves in uncertain times," he told her, his tone warm and understanding.

"I should note that I of course personally wish you success in your claim," she said.

"That is very kind of you," he told her.

"Would you and your companion like to stay awhile with us?" she offered after Gidyon said nothing more.

"It's very generous of you to offer, but I'd hate to impose upon you any further than we already have." Gidyon stood, Elen-ai echoing his movement.

"Perhaps on another trip, then?" Julyana levered herself to her feet with no little effort.

"Of course," Gidyon assured her.

She waddled with them to the front door, back through the dark corridors, their gloom punctuated by the gleam of the carefully polished metal of the weapons on the walls. "Can I offer you anything else?" She made one last cursory effort at the front doors.

"No Julyana, I wouldn't want to take anything from you." She was clearly unable to discern whether or not his response was a barb due to the warmth with which spoke. Elen-ai was.

Julyana waved them off from the front steps, disappearing back inside her ugly ode to the Bertak's perception of their place in the world before the carriage was even out of sight.

Once it was certain that they were away from the Bertak house, Gidyon's anger revealed itself in the most magnificent fashion.

"How dare she!" he exploded.

"Was she ever going to support you?" Elen-ai asked, her own anger only a pace behind his.

"Not unless I promised to marry a member of her family," he replied, the stony wall of silence between them temporarily dismantled in the face of his outrage.

"Her as family? What an awful prospect," Elen-ai commented viciously.

"I'd rather see the Katan girl on the throne than call that fat creature family," Gidyon spat. "Do you know what was the worst thing? The lack of any politeness. We were made to knock on the door. She was playing games with us."

"I could go back and kill her, if you liked," Elen-ai offered, only half in jest.

"It's not worth it." Gidyon shook his head.

"It would be easy. It would appear as though one of her weapons had fallen on her," Elen-ai said.

Gidyon looked at her, his face suddenly wary. "Do you always see the world in ways to kill people?" he asked.

Elen-ai shrugged. "I suppose I do." Uncomfortable with whatever he might have said next, she returned the subject of the Bertaks. "Does she know about Zekken?" Elen-ai asked, recalling the comment about impartiality.

"I don't think so." Gidyon shook his head. "I think she heard it as a rumour but she doesn't know whether or not it's true."

Elen-ai thought back to the look of confusion that had crossed Gidyon's face. Of course, it hadn't been confusion, it had been designed to leave Julyana assuming he knew nothing of any such rumour. An alternative path as an actor would pay him lucratively if he was ousted from the Palace.

The detente between them as a result of Julyana Bertak lasted into the evening. They set up their modest camp and lay on the grass looking up at the sky side by side. While they still hadn't had an evening fighting lesson, it was a marked difference to the previous week.

"You can't get a view like this in the city." Elen-ai gestured to the sky. The still, cloudless night of the early summer meant that a band of yellow lingered on the horizon, the sky above it a light blue tapering into darkness above them, punctuated by emerging stars.

"It is beautiful," the Prince agreed.

"Do you think that they may have been behind the attack on you and your mother?" she asked after a pause.

Gidyon was silent for a moment, contemplating the possibility. "I've been wondering a similar thing myself," he confessed. "I certainly think they are the most likely suspects at the moment. She did not do a very good job of hiding her belief that the Bertaks have been overlooked by the crown."

"I don't see how they can gain anything from you and your mother being dead, though," Elen-ai noted.

"I know," Gidyon agreed.

"The only two families we haven't spoken with are the Rasatan family and the Katan family. If you don't think it's someone in any of the families that we've been to so far, it has to be someone from the last two," Elen-ai said logically.

"You could be right," Gidyon said, clearly unconvinced. "I can't help but feel I'm missing something, though," he said. "Something's bothering me, but I don't quite know what it is. How will anyone take me seriously as a ruler if I can't keep my people in check?" he exclaimed. He drummed his hand on the ground in frustration.

"I wouldn't worry yourself about it. It'll come to you," Elen-ai said, rolling her neck to ease a stiff spot. "Where are we going next? The Rasatan lands?"

"We'll go past Herran on the way to their lands. I think I'd like to spend a few days at home before I go on to see them. Besides, I'd like to have a few words with my mother," he said darkly, his anger with his mother obviously unabated despite the intervening weeks since his discovery of her relationship with Zekken.

"Makes sense. Whatever you'd like to do, I'll do," Elen-ai said comfortably.

"Would you really have gone back and killed Julyana if I had asked you to?" Gidyon asked suddenly.

"I would certainly have considered it. She was rude," Elen-ai said.

"Does it ever bother you? Killing people?"

"Once," she admitted.

"Why not more?" He had propped himself up on one elbow to look at her, but she declined to return the movement.

"It just...doesn't." She couldn't explain it to him any more than she could understand it herself. "If I had to guess it's possibly because I've always been taught that death is natural."

"But you bring death early."

"Who are you to say that?" she challenged gently. "People kill people all the time. If the Family didn't exist, some other group would take its place. Because try as we might, we kill each other. It's in our nature."

"That's a pessimistic view," Gidyon said.

"I don't think it's pessimistic or optimistic. It's a fact." Elen-ai turned slightly away from him so that he couldn't even see her profile, only the curve of her cheek.

Taking the hint, Gidyon fell silent.

Elen-ai was occupied by thoughts of the third time she had taken a contract. This time, the Mothers and Fathers had not been kind to her. She had been sent to eliminate the life of a girl who had fallen pregnant to a member of the Katan clan. The man's aspirations of a good post within the trade administration meant that he needed to have a clear history and this girl was a blight on that because it demonstrated a lack of discretion on his part, given that he was married.

Elen-ai had followed the girl for three days. As was the case with most people who lived in the Katan lands, she was a skilled clayworker, pulling beautiful shapes from sticky clods. Elen-ai had only learned of the motivation behind the contract by listening carefully; the man had unusually not offered an explanation for why he wanted her dead when he had approached the Family. It was a curious inversion to her first kill, and from everything that Elen-ai had seen, the girl was perfectly lovely. The child in her stomach was only just beginning to show, and she hadn't told anybody other than her mother and the child's father that she would soon be a mother. However, Elen-ai's role was not to arbitrate on the morality of the contract but to see it completed. She did not ponder the killing of a corrupt merchant or a brutal farmhand, so she should not question this. So she had killed the girl gently as she slept. She would not have felt a thing.

Beside her as she remembered, Gidyon slipped quietly into sleep.

SEVENTEEN

Their friendship had not recovered from the heated exchange at the Harete home despite the fact that they had resumed talking to each other. Both Gidyon and Elen-ai addressed each other with a measure of wariness, of uncertainty as to what barbs each could and would hurl at the other. But, united by their shared dislike for Julyana Bertak, they had returned to speaking terms. That fact certainly made the trip back to the capital go by a little faster than it otherwise would have. The training sessions in the evenings even resumed, and Elen-ai noticed improvement gradually creeping into Gidyon's technique.

Three days after their unpleasant encounter at the Bertak family home they returned to sovereign land and the main road. Elen-ai was glad. Being on the badly maintained roads of the Bertak estate had left her cranky. Her mood was not helped by the fact that each day had been hotter and stickier than the last, promising rain but failing to deliver it. As they approached Herran, the breeze coming from the sea offered a welcome if not fleeting relief from the oppressive heat which clung to them. On the seventh and last day of their travel, desperate to distract herself from the uncomfortable heat, Elen-ai turned to Gidyon. "Are you any closer to knowing who was behind the attack on you and your mother?"

"I have no idea. Nobody that we have spoken to seems to stand to gain anything from the success of such an attack." He made a gesture of irritation. "I need to find out who it was. How can I be the heir to the throne when someone who tried to kill me and my mother remains at large?" His helpless frustration was understandable.

Given they were absolutely no closer to knowing who was behind the attack, Elen-ai could not help but feel that whoever it was might try again. If someone really wanted another person dead, they weren't going to take stop trying because of one failed attempt.

"People don't just kill for their own advancement," Elen-ai comment-ed, squinting to verify that she could in fact see the city in the distance.

"What else do they kill for?" Gidyon slid her a look of curiosity.

"Killing someone either comes from a place of extreme reason or ex-treme emotion. Reason is generally when people decide the best, or easi-est, way to secure what they want is to eliminate someone. Emotion is when you are generally, not always mind you, unbearably angry with someone to the point that their continued existence is a blight you cannot stand."

"You really think that the reason behind the attack could be the sec-ond?" Gidyon rubbed his chin thoughtfully as he contemplated her com-ment.

"The Veertaks seem loyal, and they seek peace. An upset like that would not serve their interests. The Taks and Aadrans – well, Zekken defi-nitely wouldn't want that, but then again, neither family stands to gain anything in the instance of you and your mother's death." Elen-ai did not repeat her earlier suspicion about Arlena. No matter how she looked at it, she could not believe that the Aadran matriarch would use such a crude way to further or secure her family's position. "The Harete family thought they could further themselves by marrying Rania to you. The Bertaks...I again see no way they would benefit from the murder of you or your moth-er. Maybe the Katans or Rasatans? But it doesn't seem quite right to me. Their best gains are made politically, too. It does seem like the desire to end your life is a very personal one," she concluded.

"I agree." Gidyon sighed in frustration. "I mean, the death of my mother and myself would be an opening for them to put one of their own on the throne, but trying to have us killed is such a risk. It's not what someone who is coming from a place of reason would do." He frowned. "I just cannot help but feel I've missed something."

Beside him, Elen-ai thought to herself that there was some vital piece of information they did not yet have, despite her discovery of Latana's se-cret relationship with Zekken. The knowledge that she did not know some-thing crawled under her skin along with the heat of the day, an irritant that she could not alleviate. Knowledge that was unknown was dangerous.

The city streets quickly negated any relief the sea breeze offered on the approach to the Queendom's capital. The buildings trapped the heat in while also barring the entry of the breeze that had been so welcome on the road. Nevertheless, Elen-ai was fervently glad to be back in the city. She had missed the crowded streets, the familiar atmosphere, the sound of humanity so crushingly proximate. The intense isolation of the previous few weeks with Gidyon was instantly alleviated by simply being surrounded by the noises, smells, and sights that were inextricably associated with home.

The carriage wound its way through the streets, paid no heed by the inhabitants of Herran who were too preoccupied with the task of surviving the stifling heat to take note of one of the many nondescript carriages which passed them.

The sun was reaching its zenith as Elen-ai drew the carriage into the Palace courtyard where servants scurried out to greet them. Gidyon and Elen-ai descended from the driver's bench to face the gaggle of people who breathlessly murmured welcomes to them.

"Master Gidyon, we can have baths ready for you both in only a few minutes," Gidyon was informed.

"That's very kind of you Mal-et, but I think it may be an offer I take you up on in a little while. Do you know where I might find my mother?"

It was strange to hear the Palace servants not address Gidyon as their Prince. Elen-ai had almost forgotten that the Queen had not publically announced her appointment of Gidyon as her heir due to the attack.

"I believe she is in conference with her advisers. She should be finished-"

"I'll see her now, thank you Mal-et. It's good to be home." Gidyon spared a moment to place a hand on the servant's shoulder and give it an appreciative squeeze, leaving the servant looking at him with obvious affection and respect. His thoughtful nature had clearly earned him the love of many who worked in the Palace, judging by the expressions on the faces of the people they passed as they walked through the grand entrance of the Palace. Perhaps, Elen-ai thought to herself, Gidyon would not be rejected by as many of the people as she had once thought.

Gidyon navigated the corridors until they reached one of the rooms that Elen-ai had surmised from her night time investigation of the Palace was used for the Queen's conference with her brothers and advisors. Without knocking, Gidyon opened the doors to the council room filled with maps, desks, and his mother and two of her brothers, all three of whom had turned to regard the impudent individual who had entered without having the respect to at least knock first.

Anger gave way to surprised delight when they recognised Gidyon, the Queen coming forward with her arms held wide to embrace her son. Elen-ai noticed a light bandage on her left hand – presumably the lingering reminder of the injury sustained during the attempt on her life. Gidyon suffered the embrace for as short a time as was possible, then turned to his uncles.

"Nikalus, Silius, I need a moment alone with my mother." He did not speak as their nephew asking their indulgence but as his mother's son, as their Prince.

The two men immediately left the room, casting curious glances at mother and son. Elen-ai was impressed by their deference to their nephew. Latana regarded Gidyon. For the first time that Elen-ai had seen her, she looked older than a woman just leaving girlhood.

"Zek told me that you know he is your father," she said, her face as neutral as ever.

Gidyon stared at her, his eyes so very blue and so very cold. "How could you?" His voice was soft.

"My darling, it's not that simple." An expression of distress clouded the Queen's lovely eyes.

"Don't you dare tell me that. You and my uncles taught me about the importance of duty, the importance of our family's place; that we are more than ourselves. And I find out when I'm on the other side of the country, after someone has tried to take my life – has tried to take your life, that you have betrayed everything you taught me to value and believe?" Gidyon's voice rose as he spoke, becoming louder and louder until he was shouting at the Queen.

If Elen-ai thought she had seen Gidyon angry, the ire she had witnessed was nothing compared to the utter fury he was unleashing on his mother. Yet the Queen did not waver, facing the wrath of her child as straight-backed as ever.

"You don't understand. One day maybe you will." She shook her head sadly. "I know I have failed my duty. There is no excuse that I can offer."

"Failed? That doesn't even begin to describe it." With a violent gesture, Gidyon began pacing the room. "You realise that if this is known by even one person then my claim is ruined, our *family* is ruined. The best thing that would happen is the Katan family put their daughter on the throne. But far more likely is some kind of civil war. Although I suppose it wouldn't matter. We'd all be long dead by then." Anger he had been storing away over the weeks since he had learned of his paternity was unleashed now and had taken on a life of its own. Elen-ai was not certain he could have reined it in, even with his considerable self-control.

"I know what the consequences could be, Gidyon," Latana said, turning to watch her son as he walked. "Are you going to punish me forever for a choice that I made?"

"A choice that you made would be to have a brief affair with him and then break it off. Clearly, that's not what's happened. Even now!" Gidyon flung his hands up.

"I love him," she said simply.

"That's not enough," he flung back at her.

"You're a child, you know nothing of love," she cried, a slight, self-righteous anger creeping into her voice.

"And you're an adult. You aren't supposed to be overruled by your emotions," he returned.

"Enough! I am still your Queen, and your mother, and I do not need to be lectured by you on how I should be conducting myself." Apparently fed up with Gidyon's tirade, Latana raised her own voice. "Do you have any idea how lonely it is to be Queen?"

"So you wanted me to be lonely, but you could not bear it?" There was something particularly wrenching about the look of anguish on Gidyon's face.

"You'll at least have a wife by your side," she thundered.

"A wife who will be the person best suited to be by my side, not the person I may want to take as my wife. How can you ask me to do what you would not?"

Latana stared at Gidyon, her mouth slightly agape. She remained totally rigid for several seconds, then her composure began to crumble. It started with her shoulders slumping ever so slightly. From there, she seemed to crumple in on herself, her hand coming to her mouth and her eyes filling with tears. She began to sob quietly. "I'm so sorry," she eventually whispered.

Gidyon watched unmoving as his mother sobbed. He did not relent, his face still contorted with anger at her betrayal. The Queen walked over to one of the chairs and sat, burying her face in her hands and continuing to weep.

Elen-ai shifted slightly. She felt profoundly awkward at witnessing this very personal exchange. "Should I leave?" she suggested quietly.

The Queen raised her head to regard Elen-ai. An expression of resignation settled across her features. "I hadn't even realised you were still here," she admitted. There was something particularly shocking about the lack of regard for her composure.

"Elen-ai has been with me throughout everything. She knows everything," Gidyon told his mother.

In response, the Queen raised her hand in a weary gesture. "I must thank you for keeping Gidyon safe, Elen-ai," she said, an almost unthinkingly polite comment.

"You are welcome, your Majesty." Elen-ai linked her hands behind her back. "Really, perhaps it would be easier if I left, though. This seems like a very uh, personal conversation."

"No. I would like you to stay here." As Gidyon turned to address her, his posture of anger melted away and a look that could have been one of pleading arranged itself on his features.

She acquiesced with a nod, wishing he hadn't asked. Such displays of temper were so intensely personal. She had no business witnessing the innermost feelings of her Queen.

"Have you finished chastising me Gidyon?" the Queen enquired, her composure restored to her aside from the slightest rasp in her voice from her brief but violent sobbing.

"I have nothing more to say to you," Gidyon informed her coolly.

"Divine One, if you want to throw a child's fit, do not lecture me like you were an adult," Latana exclaimed. "Put aside your anger with me and tell me what you discovered. Our people in the households only know so much of what transpires. Or will you refuse to speak to me like an infant throwing a tantrum?"

It was with no small amount of sullenness that he did as she bade. "Elen-ai would you mind interjecting if I miss anything?" he asked, before launching into a recount of their journey.

Occasionally Elen-ai would correct him or remind him of a detail that he had forgotten. By unspoken agreement, neither of them mentioned the evening that Elen-ai had found him with Rania. Latana's face grew sharper as she listened, seeming to recover her footing now that they were onto matters within her domain: political schemes. When Gidyon told her of Julyana Bertak's behaviour she let out a slight hiss but did not interrupt. Gidyon finished by offering a more abridged summation of his and Elen-ai's conversation from earlier that day.

Latana frowned slightly, turning to Elen-ai. "How can killing someone be so simple? Reason or emotion?"

Elen-ai spread her hands in a gesture that approximated a shrug. "I don't claim to know the hearts of the people who approach the Family, but at their most simple, these are the constants."

"The Palace's sources of information around the Second Country have found no trace of anyone hiring a group of people to make an attempt on either my or your life, Gidyon. Yet someone at least knew enough of our movements to direct people so that they came within striking distance of both of us," the Queen said.

"Therefore the plan behind such an attack came from someone who either lives in Herran or is in Herran often," Gidyon mused. "That eliminates the Katan family, I suppose. They are rarely here. I do not even know how long it will take before they answer my invitation. Unless they worked through someone who does come to Herran often. That would give them a certain distance in the even that their ally is discovered."

"Inviting them was a good idea. Especially given it means they will stay here in the Palace where we can watch them, rather than in their own residence. Visiting the families was also a good idea." The Queen smiled at Gidyon. "My wonderful, clever son. You make us so proud."

Gidyon's face closed like a slammed door. "Who do you mean by us?"

"Our family of course," Latana replied.

"Don't lie to me." His voice became sharp, louder.

"I'm not lying to you."

Gidyon shook his head. "You can't fool me with a charming smile like you can everyone else. When you said 'us' you meant you and Zekken, didn't you?"

His mother opened her mouth but was spared responding by a knock on the door.

"Nobody can hear what is going on inside this room," Latana explained to Elen-ai as she stood up and crossed the room to the door from which the knock had originated. Elen-ai suspected that the explanation was offered to avoid looking at or speaking to her son.

"I beg your pardon, your Majesty," the woman on the other side said.

"No trouble, Len-am," the Queen replied calmly, as though her son was not furious with her, or her rule and authority was not being threatened by unknown attackers and political rivals.

"It would appear that you have visitors." There was a certain familiarity in the exchange between the Queen and the matronly servant. Elen-ai assumed this Len-am was as close to a friend to the Queen as anyone could be. The Queen's words about being lonely resonated in her mind.

"Visitors?"

"At the invitation of ah, Master Gidyon." She held out a piece of paper.

The Queen took it and read it. Elen-ai recognised the letter Gidyon had sent to the Katan family from the tavern so many weeks ago. Latana scanned it quickly then handed it back to the servant.

"It would appear that your invitation has been accepted, Gidyon. You have returned just in time." Latana did not turn to look at her son as she spoke.

"It's not just the Katan family," the servant Len-am said. "They appear to be accompanied by two members of the Rasatan family."

"On what grounds?" Latana pursed her lips, the only sign that she might have been taken by surprise.

"I believe as part of the Katan retinue."

"Tenuous grounds on which to impose themselves on us, especially as guests rather than merely visitors."

"You don't need to tell me that, your Majesty," Len-am replied, none of the Queen's diplomacy in her voice.

At the obvious disapproval, Latana laughed. "Prepare rooms for them, offer them refreshments, and send word to the kitchen that they will need to prepare a special feast for tonight – please also apologise to them, I know it is late notice."

"As you wish."

"Oh, and I think if we are to welcome our guests perhaps we could take a lesson from the diplomatic wisdom of lady Julyana." At this, she did turn to look at her son, a smile of grim purpose on her face. Gidyon, at least temporarily united with her by the diplomatic hostility of the visitors, smiled back at her. The resemblance between them was striking.

"Sorry Len-am, one more thing." The Queen turned back to address the servant as the thought occurred to her. "Double the guards, if you would."

175

EIGHTEEN

While Julyana Bertak's attempt to assert her authority had only made it look as though she was attempting to impose an authority she did not possess, Queen Latana's efforts had a vastly different effect. Leaving her guests to eat the refreshments she had instructed be offered to them, she changed out of the simple trousers and shirt she had been wearing when Elen-ai and Gidyon had first found her. When they met her after washing and changing into fresh clothes, they found Latana dressed in a deep crimson gown that was a simple sheaf on her slender figure. Her hair had been braided and piled on top of her head, she wore no jewellery other than the simple gold bands at her throat and wrists. She looked magnificent.

The Queen's first reaction was to look at Elen-ai's trousers. "You know, skirts can be just as effective a weapon as any," she commented.

"Not the sort of weapon I really use," Elen-ai replied with a slight tilt of her head.

"I doubt your type of weapon will be necessary tonight." The Queen smiled, her beauty almost too much to look at. Whoever had arranged her hair had done a magnificent job of accenting the sculpture of her cheekbones, the arch of her brow – even the shape of her lips was more somehow pronounced, more lovely than normal. To accent those spectacular eyes, a line of black had been slicked along their rim, sweeping up to meet the end of her eyebrows, but that was all.

"Come on, Sil and Nik are waiting for us," she said.

"Will the Councillors be joining us?" Elen-ai asked.

"They left a few days ago. Things with the Fourth Country are...not good. They are going there with Kaine to try and broker some kind of treaty." The Queen let out a little sigh but elaborated no further.

Elen-ai was sorry to hear that the foreigners were gone. She had hoped to see the Councillor who had saved Gidyon's life on their return to the Palace. Had they gotten to know one another better, Elen-ai felt they would have been friends. She fervently hoped that Freya and Ashtyn were safe and that she would one day see them again.

The trio made their way through the Palace to the blue sitting room, Elen-ai and Gidyon flanking the Queen. Guards stood on either side of the door, chatting to a waiting Nikalus and Silius. As the Queen approached, the guards stood to attention.

"Good afternoon." She smiled at them before turning her attention to her brothers. They were dressed in similar clothes to Elen-ai and Gidyon, understated garments which nevertheless underscored the fact that they were members of the Royal family.

"Ready?" the Queen asked.

The two men looked at their sister and Queen. "We stand beside you," Silius told her.

"Always," Nikalus added.

She paused for a moment to spare them a look of gratitude before nodding to the guards.

The doors were opened wide to admit the Royal family and Elen-ai.

"My dear friends, please forgive our delay." Latana exuded a warmth to match the day. Her perfect presentation was a counter to the slightly wilted guests, all of whom had risen and bowed at her entry. They may have been trying to usurp her, but she was still their Queen.

"Latana it is so reassuring to see you well after that awful attack. I'm sure our visit took you by surprise, and that you were of course in the middle of something." A woman who shared Latana's liquid gold eyes spoke first.

"Darling Liita. It has been so long since you left the Palace. I am so glad to see you again, and to have you staying here under our roof, too." The Queen crossed the room to embrace the woman. Once they released each other, the woman turned to the rest of the Royal family.

Elen-ai presumed this must be the Queen's sister - Gidyon's aunt and the mother of the would-be Queen. She had lived with the Katan family from the age of eight as was the custom with any woman other than the heir born into the Royal family. It meant that while she may have been their sister by blood, she was more a Katan than a member of the royal family. Elen-ai wondered if resentment festered within the woman who had been sent away by her family because she was not born early enough. Was it enough resentment to try to extinguish the lives of her sister and nephew?

"Of course you, you remember my daughter Serenah. Although it's been so long since you last saw her, I doubt you'll recognise her." The slight barb was swept aside by the fact that a young girl strongly resembling Liita stepped forward and bowed to the Queen.

"Such a beautiful young lady. And of course, I am sure you all remember Gidyon. My son and heir." Latana's smile dared anyone to raise an objection.

On cue, Gidyon bowed to the room, forcing its inhabitants to return to the gesture.

"And Erek and Keela. It's such an unexpected pleasure to see you both." Latana turned her attention from her sister to the representatives of the Rasatan family. She gave just the barest emphasis to 'unexpected', although it was doubtless noticed by everyone.

"When we received word that Halen, Serenah, Liita, and Enges were coming to court, we thought it would be the perfect opportunity. We are in negotiations for a marriage between our families and seek your blessing." Erek spoke rather than Keela, despite the fact that she would have been the head of the Rasatan family at court. He was just as handsome as Elen-ai remembered. Perhaps more so.

"Does this spell an end to your days as an unwed man?" Latana asked playfully, seemingly not immune his good looks.

"For me, no, but my youngest brother, yes," he replied, his eyes focused totally on the Queen.

"Well you would make a woman very lucky, Erek," Latana told him.

"But my heart beats only for you, my Queen," he said with a sincerity that would have been disconcerting were it not for the easy charm of his delivery.

Latana gave Erek a smirk of amusement before she addressed the room. "Please, let us sit."

More drinks were brought in along with another selection of the exquisite treats that Elen-ai remembered from her first time in the Palace. Meaningless conversation flowed back and forth in an exchange of trivialities and pleasantries. Later would come the reason for this visit, but this was a prelude, an opportunity for the two sides to gain the measure of one another before such a battle. Elen-ai tried her best to remain unnoticed, but her efforts were foiled when Erek came to sit beside her.

"You look as though you've gotten some sun since last we met, lady Elen-ai." He looked at her with those impossibly blue eyes. She felt as though he were looking into her very soul.

She smiled demurely. "Gidyon and I have been on quite the journey," she said.

"I was not aware when we last met that you were a companion who warmed his bed," he said, still looking intently at her. "Although I admit I was curious at the time about what exactly your role was in accompanying him."

She shifted slightly, uncomfortable with the directness with which he spoke about the supposed intimate relationship she shared with Gidyon. She couldn't help but feel he got away with a great deal that others may not as a result of his extraordinary good looks. "He is a remarkable young man," she said by way of response.

"Am I wrong in thinking you are a more worldly individual than he?" Erek asked. It was definitely a question that a less handsome, less charming person would not have even dared ask.

"In some ways." Rather than meet his eyes, Elen-ai looked at the sharp plane of his nose, forming a perfect shape in concert with the angle of his cheekbones and jawline.

"Does that mean he has your loyalty?" His voice was soft enough that nobody else could hear what he was saying. Even if their conversation would have been audible, everybody else seemed occupied by their own conversation. Gidyon, Halen – the patriarch of the Katan family – and Keela Rasatan were engaged in a discussion, although Keela was sitting and nodding for the most part. She seemed terribly unassuming, with a certain hunted look about her, as though she expected someone to jump out and yell 'boo' at any moment. Her timidity made it surprising that she was the mother of Erek. The Queen and her brothers were similarly engaged, speaking with much delightful laughter to their sister and niece, maintaining a pretence that they were a loving and united family. Elen-ai wondered what exactly Erek was asking her. For a fleeting moment, she wondered if he was propositioning her.

"I am but a loyal subject," she answered eventually.

"Aren't we all," Erek muttered. The comment and the edge to his tone piqued her curiosity. Despite his casualness, there was an intensity, an undercurrent of emotion, that he could not completely conceal.

"I'm not so sure I understand your meaning."

He shook his head slightly as if to clear it of a thought. "Do guard your heart carefully, Elen-ai. The Royal family has its own agenda and you may not fall into it," he said, his eyes on the Queen as she laughed at some joke or comment.

"She's very beautiful," Elen-ai commented, seeing the direction of his gaze.

"The most beautiful woman I've ever laid eyes on," Erek replied. "Sort of spoils all other women, begging your pardon."

"I can't disagree," Elen-ai told him honestly.

Erek turned back to regard her with that piercing gaze once more. "You're an unusual woman, lady Elen-ai," he said.

"I'll choose to take that as a compliment," she muttered as she bit into a pastry layered with nuts and vegetables.

He laughed, a charming noise, the accompanying smile oddly, not making him more but less handsome.

The gathering finished shortly, the visitors finally allowed the opportunity to bathe and rest in preparation for the dinner to follow in a few hours. The Queen and her brothers went off to conclude the matter they had been discussing when Elen-ai and Gidyon interrupted, leaving the two of them with free hours until the meal. Elen-ai followed Gidyon out to one of the Palace's courtyard gardens. The air felt almost like liquid enveloping them as soon as they stepped outside.

"Are you alright?" Elen-ai asked.

He shrugged. "I have to be."

"I think it may rain soon," Elen-ai commented idly.

"Blessing of the Divine One. I hope so," he replied.

"What do you think they'll say tonight?" Elen-ai asked, wandering over to a stone bench and sitting on it, stretching her legs out and leaning back to look up at the sky. Sure enough, she could see that fat clouds the colour of a two-day-old bruise had begun to reach across it. Soon they would be above the Palace.

"I still think they plan to challenge my claim. I'm not sure if they will come out and say as much, though," Gidyon answered, coming to sit next to her.

"Your mother was impressive this afternoon."

Gidyon chuckled. "She certainly was. I will not say as much to her, though. I'm still too angry."

"Do you think that you'll get over it?"

"I am sure I will, but right now it doesn't feel like it," he admitted.

"She's only human," Elen-ai offered.

"But she's the Queen. She supposed to be more than just human. How else can she claim people should be ruled by her?" Gidyon said.

Elen-ai said nothing. Gidyon had a point.

The clouds were creeping over the sky now. The contrast between the dark sky and the golden light shining on the courtyard's walls was quite striking.

"I can't say I'm looking forward to tonight," Elen-ai admitted.

"Neither am I," the Prince confessed. "At least the food will be good."

They sat together in silence until the first raindrops started to fall, forcing them to retreat inside.

Gidyon was correct. The food the Palace kitchens had produced was spectacular. Tenderly cooked meat, crisp vegetables, exquisite sauces. Elen-ai had no idea what she ate, she just knew that the display of power and wealth in every bite had certainly convinced her. There was some irony in the fact that the Katans were served a meal that emphasised the power and richness of the throne on plates made in their own lands. However, if Elen-ai had thought the Katan plates she had encountered before were of fine craftsmanship, these were in a completely different class. So thin she feared the servants would break them by simply handling them, the beautiful painting on each was a triumph of artistry. Even a single plate would be worth a small fortune.

The drumming of the rain was a constant noise in the background of the meal. The windows of the dining room had been opened to allow the rain-cooled air in. The breeze swirled gently around the room, doing nothing to alleviate the tension that was slowly building inside.

The Queen remained in the same dress she had worn to the afternoon tea, the only change a little jacket over her shoulders in concession to the sudden coolness, and red stones to match her dress in a line up the outermost cartilage of her ears. The simplicity of her outfit was a contrast to the opulent finery and heavy face paint that her guests had donned. It had the effect of making them look foolishly extravagant and desperate to prove their importance – which of course, they were. The only exception was Erek who wore a simple shirt of deep blue that accented the violent colour of his eyes in concert with the simple black lining them.

Gidyon had changed into a red shirt to match his mother's dress, and he too had opted for simplicity over extravagance. When Erek came to greet the Queen and heir, the three of them looked like an impossibly attractive family thanks to the trick of their garb.

The pleasant conversation of the afternoon was duplicated at the dinner table, punctuated by the occasional toast. Only once the final dish had been cleared from the table did the focus turn to more serious matters. Elen-ai had noted that nobody had drunk more than one or two glasses of any form of liquor despite the abundance proffered to the guests. It seemed everybody wanted their wits about them.

Latana initiated the shift in tone, reclining in her chair with a tall flute of some blue liquid twirled idly between her fingers. Despite the bandage still on her hand, the injury had not caused any her obvious trouble as she ate.

"Now Halen, what is this I have heard about your discontent with recent choices I have made?" she called to him from the other end of the table.

Clearly thrown by the direct nature of her question, the head of the Katan family gaped at her for a moment, the white cream coating his face making him look almost comical. "That is a very strong wording, your Majesty," he said eventually.

"How might you put it then?" She smiled, but it was a smile without any warmth.

"I am concerned by recent decisions. Concerned of course for your wellbeing."

"Come now Halen, you do not need to be coy," the Queen encouraged him.

"I am a loyal subject of the realm," he replied.

"Not a loyal subject of mine?"

His hesitation gave away his position, although nobody had ever really doubted where his loyalties truly lay. "I seek what is best for the people of the Second Country," he said finally.

"And do you believe that the Second Country would be better served with your granddaughter on the throne?"

The silence that followed the Queen's question hung heavily in the room. Shock had stolen the breath from the observers of the conversation between the Queen and Halen. That she would actually ask such a direct question in a world governed by polite side-stepping was without precedent. The only sound in the room for several moments came from the rain outside.

Finally, Halen cleared his throat. "It has been suggested to me that Serenah's claim to the throne may be stronger than Gidyon's, begging your pardon." He inclined his head to Gidyon.

Before Latana could speak, her son did. "I am afraid I will have to take issue with your comment, Lord Katan." He sounded quite amiable. "Not only is she a Katan by birth, but I would also add that being suitable to rule is not simply about birth. Serenah," he turned to address his cousin. "Can you tell me with whom the Second Country's largest amount of trade is conducted? Do you know how many people live within the Second Country? What is your opinion on the laws relating to thievery in place of an unpaid debt? What do you think we should do first and why; repave the sovereign road, rebuild Herran's marketplace, or draft orders for a standing army in case of an attack from belligerent external forces? An answer to any of these questions will do."

The girl looked at Gidyon, her eyes wide and terrified. Her face had been powdered with bronze pigment. It made her look almost like a statue. She opened and closed her mouth several times, but nothing came out. Finally, she looked down at her lap. "I don't know," she admitted in a whisper that was almost drowned out by the rain outside.

"How would you have her rule, Halen?" Latana challenged. "Or would you generously guide her with your wisdom? Please do not take this personally," Latana directed her final comment to Serenah whose eyes had quietly filled with tears.

"She's four years younger than Gidyon." Enges, the girl's father spoke up. "In four years she could learn these things, too."

"I started learning the fundamentals of the Second Country's legal system when I was eight," Gidyon said, almost gently.

"Surely she would also be able to call on her uncles for advice on how to guide the Queendom," Halen pointed out.

"Perhaps, although we would note that the best thing for the Queendom is to have Gidyon or Latana ruling it," Silius said, making no effort to hide his hostility. Elen-ai wouldn't have been surprised if he threw a punch at the older man. She hoped he would.

"I am curious to know what our friends from the Rasatan family think on this matter." Latana interrupted whatever Halen was going to say, turning slightly in her seat to regard Erek and his mother.

Erek leaned forward. "My father has instructed me to convey his concerns about the effect a man holding the throne may have on our country," he said.

"And do you share those concerns?" Latana asked, her head cocked slightly as she met his gaze.

"My Queen, as I am sure you already know, I am in Herran rarely for my own purposes. I am a vessel for my family's wishes." His face was a mask of regretful sincerity.

"You do come to the capital often, and always on the business of your family. You are very lucky to have such a devoted son, Keela," Latana said.

"I am." Keela smiled timidly at the Queen. She seemed shocked at being directly addressed. Indeed, the fact that Erek referred specifically to his father's views on the matter of Gidyon's position rather than his parents' spoke to the utter domination of the poor woman.

Latana surveyed the people sitting at the table, her lips slightly pursed. "If I did not know any better, it would seem that you were planning to move against me, Halen, and that the Rasatan family is in support of this. That sounds like treason to me."

"Your Majesty, your sister is married to my eldest son. Your niece is my granddaughter. We are here as guests at your table. Such a phrase is ugly and unnecessary." The boldness with which he contradicted the Queen validated her words even as he proclaimed otherwise.

"I must say, that is a great relief to hear, Halen." She bestowed on him one of her lovely smiles. "I was always certain that you were a loyal subject of the Queendom rather than a pathetic usurper, trying to eke out more power in the guise of acting in the best interests of my people."

Elen-ai was amused to see him turn a shade of light purple underneath the white face paint as he struggled to find a way to respond to the Queen's insult without proving her correct. She heard Gidyon give a little cough that she would have bet everything she owned was in fact a concealed laugh.

"Well, yes," Halen said eventually in a most inelegant manner.

Liita smoothly interjected. "In any case, I am sure that the question of Gidyon succeeding you is not a serious possibility for a great many years. I'm certain that all of us at this table wish on you the blessings of the Divine One for many more years of your reign."

It was impossible to know what the Queen truly thought of her sister's comment, but she smiled and nodded. "You are quite right, Liita. I must confess, I always assumed there would be some consternation in the immediate aftermath of Gidyon being named my heir. I am sure that with time, any concerns that may be felt will be allayed, one way or another."

The finality of her words moved the conversation on, but Elen-ai saw the slight tightening around Halen's jawline and the briefest of glances between Liita and Enges. The matter was most certainly not finished.

The dinner dragged on for a little while longer, but following the diplomatic altercation between Latana and Halen, the mood had changed completely. The rain continued to fall, an unabated patter that sounded outside the windows, intruding into any pause in chatter. Eventually, the Queen stood and bade all of her guests a good evening, which concluded the meal. Elen-ai followed a pensive Gidyon back to his room.

"I assume that they won't give up, then," she said once they were in his sitting area.

"I would stake a significant fortune on that, yes," he affirmed.

"How?" she wondered aloud.

He sighed, falling into a chair and running a hand through his hair. "I imagine several legal claims challenging my right to rule, put up by someone else of course, attempts to generate popular support for Serenah as an alternate ruler to me, and a variety of other petty schemes." He lowered the hand that had been entangled in his hair to run a finger up and down the bridge of his nose. "It just makes me so angry that they think Serenah would be a good ruler. She clearly knows nothing about anything related to statecraft. I don't even know if she really wants to be Queen. It's not right."

He made his hand down in a fist and brought it down to thump on his knee. "And what's this about the Rasatan involvement? I don't understand what they're playing at," he exclaimed, his speech unusually inelegant. "Might they have somehow been behind the attack on me and mother, on behalf of the Katans?"

"I've been wondering that myself," Elen-ai commented. "I can only assume that they've been promised something if they support and aid the Katans."

"I wish I knew what's going on," Gidyon said, clicking his tongue in frustration as he stared at his still-clenched fist.

"There may be a way to find out," Elen-ai offered.

His head snapped up to look at her. "I'm listening."

"I could get into their rooms now and see if I could find anything."

Gidyon pursed his lips, seriously considering the offer. "Are you certain you could get in and out unnoticed?" he asked.

She snorted in response, giving him a look of mild offence. In reply, he held up his hands, palms outwards. Then he grew serious. "Do it," he told her. "You should be able to get to their rooms through here." He got up and fetched a paper scrap, sketching a rough map of the Palace for her.

It took her one minute to change her clothes and slip out of Gidyon's room, the sound of the rain surrounding her as she moved through the Palace.

NINETEEN

The rain had well and truly settled in. It was a gentle beat that would have masked Elen-ai's footsteps, had they made any sound. She made her way to the visitors' wing, easily remembering the Palace's layout from her first night time expedition. Leaving the corridor, Elen-ai slipped outside to one of the small gardens within the wing. Recalling where Gidyon had told her Erek Rasatan's room was, she found the window and swiftly scaled the wall. The window was open. The stone walls of the Palace had soaked in the heat of the previous few days and every room was still stiflingly hot without the respite of the cool night air. It was almost too easy.

The sound of discussion between Erek and his mother surprised Elen-ai, not because she had not expected them to confer at this hour, but because it was very clearly a heated argument that she heard. Elen-ai slipped through the window, conscious of the water clinging to her clothes. Fortunately, a little rain had been blown into the room already so the drops from her clothes joined the ones already there unnoticeably. It didn't really matter though. Erek and his mother were too engrossed in their exchange to notice some extra water in the room.

Elen-ai stared in wonder at Keela as she addressed her son. Gone was the timid woman who had barely uttered two words throughout the afternoon refreshments and dinner. In her place was a bastion of terrifying authority. She wore the same face, but the features were arranged in a totally different way. Her mouth was a snarl, her eyes were suddenly narrow and focused, and flashing with malice. Elen-ai had entered the room midway through Keela administering a spectacular beration to Erek.

"...and you just sat there moping at that stupid creature for most of the night. You said none of what we planned you would."

Erek who normally seemed so supremely confident was sitting look-ing up his mother, an abashed expression on his face. "I'm sorry mother," he said, his voice plaintive and pathetic.

"Sorry? There are bound to be questions about our loyalty to the Katans now. We were supposed to present a show of solidarity with them to secure our allegiance," she snapped.

"I had to respond to what was being said. When we discussed how the evening would go, we didn't expect Latana to discuss the situation so plainly," he whined.

"Don't think for yourself, it never ends well," she told him nastily.

He looked down, the hurt obvious on his face. "Father told me that in such situations..."

"Your father is a bigger fool than you." She cut him off, flapping a dismissive hand at him. "Be quiet for a moment. I need to think." She put one hand on her hip and brought the other to her chin, turning away from him and pacing the length of the room. She came within a hand span of Elen-ai but turned around before she actually touched the assassin. "Why didn't you tell me about Latana and Zekken as soon as you found out?" She sounded exasperated, the raw bite of her anger lost in contemplation.

"I...I don't know." Erek kept his eyes on his mother as she returned to her previous spot in front of him.

His response seemed to rekindle her anger. "Well I do. It's this ridicu-lous infatuation you've had with her ever since the first Season. It's made you blind to her incompetence as a ruler and what should be done to stop her, and to put our family in a position to be strong."

"I'm not in love with her," he protested, but again his mother cut him off. From the look on his face though, Elen-ai had to agree with Keela's as-sessment that Erek was infatuated with the Queen.

"Why else would you spend so much time and coin tracking down half the servants and messengers in the land to put together something that has been so well hidden?" Poison dripped from her tongue as she ad-dressed him.

"I knew she was doing something she shouldn't have been. I knew it," he exclaimed.

"Because she wouldn't take you to her bed again? Really, Erek, I don't know why you think you're so special." Keela's contempt for her son made

Elen-ai's skin crawl. None of her Mothers or Fathers would ever speak to one of the Family's children like that.

"You see the way she treats me. She flirts with me, she acts as though I'm one of her favourites, but aside from that first time, she has never invited me back to her bedchamber. I knew just knew something was wrong. I knew she was hiding something."

Keela snorted. "Well I suppose your obsessive snooping did uncover something we can use. Why you had to be so impudent in that attempt on the life of Latana and that...." The sound of sobbing cut her off. She lowered her gaze to her son.

Erek Rasatan, the most handsome man Elen-ai had ever seen, was crying like a small infant. "He's just as likely to be my son, and they took him from me, mama. Being by her side, being the father to her son, it should have been me. I just wanted to take him away from them and scare her," he gulped in between sobs.

His mother stepped forward and pressed his head to her stomach, rocking him gently back and forth. The abruptness of the shift from vindictive spite to maternal care was disturbing. "I know my darling, I know. It's alright. I've always said you were destined for great things. You're right, it should have been you she took as a lover. There now, there's no need to cry." She murmured the platitudes to him with disconcerting intensity.

Gradually he stopped crying, quietened by Keela's soothing. She took his face in both of her hands, leaned down so that she could look directly in his eyes and spoke with the firmness of someone addressing a small child. "No more of your own plans, hm? If we decide that the way forward is to kill that fool and her child, you wait for me to organise it. From now on you'll do what I tell you?"

He nodded obediently. She kissed his forehead gently. "That's my boy," she crooned.

Elen-ai had seen enough. She climbed silently out of the window and returned to Gidyon's rooms.

"Well?" he demanded the moment she came in.

"I suggest you sit down," she advised him. When he had done as she bade, she continued. "I know who was behind the attack on you and your mother and why." She held up a hand to forestall his questions, searching for the best way to explain what she had learned.

"It would seem that Zekken may not be your father. The uh, the Season in which you were conceived was the only time the Queen was with someone other than Zekken."

"Erek," Gidyon surmised quickly. He did not seem to be particularly upset by the revelation, but Elen-ai expected that may come in time. For now, he was too busy trying to see how this information might change the situation.

She nodded. Now that she knew, she thought she could even see a physical resemblance between the Prince and Erek. Certainly, he didn't look like Zekken in the slightest.

"How did you find this out?"

"Luck, really. He was talking with Keela. She's not at all what she seems, by the way. She's awful."

Gidyon raised an eyebrow at this news but said nothing. Elen-ai continued, still choosing her words with care. "From what I gathered, Erek is quite in love with the Queen and he couldn't understand why she had never invited him back to her bedchamber. It seems he spent quite a lot of money finding a number of servants, or people who might know something, to try and learn what your mother was doing and why she may not want him to uh...well, you get the idea.

"I suspect he spoke with enough people to realise the existence of the relationship between Zekken and Latana. I can't exactly know his thoughts, but from what I heard, discovering that the Queen had taken a lover that was not him prompted him to arrange an attempt on the lives of both you and your mother."

Gidyon was silent for a moment as he considered the information. "He is in the capital often on family business. He would likely have enough knowledge of the goings-on within the Palace to give any assailants the information that they used to get to us. But I don't understand. Why would he try to kill me if he might be my father?"

"The way Keela was treating him, and the way he was behaving...I'm not sure that he's entirely sane." Recalling the sudden change from Keela's nastiness to her cossetting of Erek made Elen-ai feel vaguely nauseous. "He's a terrific actor, able to seem normal in public especially because of his looks, but I think, if what I saw was any indication, he's not quite right. The most unstable of individuals can be the most deceptive," she elaborated.

Gidyon was silent for a moment longer. "We need to go to mother with this. Now. Not only did he try to kill us, but he knows about her and Zekken." He got to his feet.

As she followed him through the Palace, Elen-ai wondered if Gidyon was seeking action to distract himself from thinking too much about these recent revelations. The rain pattered softly outside. Its gentle tap-tap generated a sense of understated urgency that nestled itself somewhere in Elen-ai's stomach.

Gidyon knocked sharply on the door to the Queen's chambers, ignoring the curious looks that he was given by the two guards outside it. Latana answered almost immediately. Evidently she too had not been asleep, although she was wearing bed robes and her hair had been let loose from the elaborate braids it had been piled into that afternoon and evening. Even her collar and cuffs had been removed, giving her a certain look of delicacy.

"Gidyon." Her surprise at her son's sudden presence was undisguised.

"Elen-ai found out something." The seriousness of his tone had her immediately stepping aside to admit them. The room looked exactly as Elen-ai remembered it, barring a few papers strewn about rather than neatly stacked and put aside.

"I was just reading over some petitions for new buildings in the market district," Latana explained distractedly, gesturing to the pages on the couch.

"Why didn't you tell me Erek might be my father?" Gidyon's question cut across her demeanour, freezing her in place.

"I didn't think it was important. We never thought it likely. How do you know he was the other?" Her words were careful, like she was picking her way across a floor strewn with burning coals.

"Elen-ai overheard him speaking with his mother. He knows about you and Zekken."

Latana's face turned quite white. "How could he possibly know? We've been so careful."

Gidyon was obviously unimpressed. "He's obsessed with you."

"If I understood what I heard, he sought out a number of servants and messengers. From there, I would imagine he tracked your respective movements and figured it out," Elen-ai interjected before Gidyon could launch into another tirade against his mother's relationship with Zekken.

If possible, the Queen paled further. "I always just assumed he was being unnecessarily exuberant," she mumbled, putting a hand to her mouth and turning slightly away, as if to give herself space to think.

"We can consider the whys and hows of it later, mother." Gidyon cut off her musing. "There is a problem in front of us as well as an opportunity, but I think we need to act quickly."

Latana turned back to face her son, her eyes devoid of the confusion and shock that had filled them only a moment before and instead sparkling with purpose. "Someone taught you well, to see opportunity within a problem." She smiled at him, never once losing that focus.

"I learned from the best."

She reached across the space between them and placed a hand on his arm, letting it rest there for a moment before crossing the room to summon a servant. "Please bring Erek Rasatan here," she ordered once her summons was answered.

While they waited for him to arrive, Gidyon cleared his throat. "Are you sure this is the best way to deal with him?"

The Queen threw her son an amused look as she went into her bedchamber, returning with a deep purple robe which she tied firmly about her waist. "He will be uncertain about why I called him here due to the late hour. Now is the perfect time to confront him and bend him to our purpose. Besides, he is only a man." She ran her fingers through her hair to remove any knots, shaking it out behind her. "Thank you, Gid," she added, the only moment of hesitation in her certainty.

"I still don't forgive you. We will be having many words once this mess is sorted out. You do realise we wouldn't be in this predicament were it not for you?" He folded his arms across his chest.

"I will not apologise for my choices," Latana told him sternly.

He shook his head. "I pray to the Divine One I will not be so arrogant when I rule."

"The very act of you taking the throne is arrogance incarnate, my son," his mother retorted, turning away from him to address Elen-ai. "You have done the Second Country a great service not once, but many times over. I do not know how to thank you."

Elen-ai suffered the gaze of the Queen, feeling herself falling into pools of liquid gold. It was little wonder that Erek was so desperately infatuated with her. There was something utterly irresistible about Latana. "I am simply fulfilling the Family's contract, your Majesty. But perhaps I should not be here for this," she suggested.

"No, I think you have earned the right to stay," the Queen countered. She offered Elen-ai a smile that set her whole face alight.

"As your Majesty wishes," Elen-ai acquiesced.

Erek arrived quickly. Since Elen-ai had left his room, he had changed his clothes, wearing casual attire that one may don in the hours after dinner and before bed. From what Elen-ai had seen though, he would have chosen those clothes carefully despite the casual air they exuded.

In the man who strode into the room, there was no sign of the cowed, child-like being who had been subject to his mother's abusive tirade. The charm and confidence were as ever. The difference was unnerving.

"Your Majesty." He bowed low as he entered. Seeing Gidyon, he offered him a bow too. "To what do I owe this pleasure?"

From her inconspicuous place in the corner, Elen-ai watched as the Queen put on her most charming smile. "After the events of this evening, I thought it may be worth having a more intimate discussion over the matters at hand."

His smile did not waver in the slightest. "I am sure Gidyon has told you what I said to him in the Veertak home. I personally think he would make a superb ruler, although I do wonder about his decision to marry a lowborn woman. Nevertheless, my father's word is what I ultimately must respect."

"What about your mother's?" Gidyon chimed in, his eyes – so similar to Erek's now that she looked – wide and innocent.

Erek gave a little laugh which he accompanied with a dismissive shrug. "I love my mother dearly, but she doesn't really have the head for such matters."

Latana smiled but the warmth had left her face. "Of course."

"I'm sure there must be something I can do to help you both, though." Erek took a step toward the Queen and took her hands in his, looking earnestly into her face.

"You could start by not making any more attempts on the life of Gidyon or myself." Latana did not move, nor did she alter the polite lightness of her tone.

Erek's reaction was almost imperceptible to the casual observer, merely a slight stiffness stealing across his face before the charming mask slipped back into place. However, he was not in a room of casual observers. He was in a room with three individuals who were accustomed to watching and reading people. "How can you think I would do such an awful thing?" He sounded genuinely bewildered.

Latana yanked her hands from his. "I am aware of everything. Please do not try and lie to me, Erek. How could you?" Her question was soft, almost gentle.

His face crumpled. Such small pressure from the Queen and he was suddenly just as he was with his own mother. "How could *you*? What does he have that I don't? That you would think of him as Gidyon's father even though it could just as easily be me?"

Elen-ai watched Gidyon's face as he regarded the man who may have sired him whine at the feet of his mother. As usual, she was unable to discern what he was thinking.

"Is that was this is about? Why I did not take you as my lover?" A note of disgust crept into Latana's voice.

Erek grasped for her hands again, but she drew them out of his reach. "Please just tell me you care for me too," he begged. It was uncomfortable to witness this display. Elen-ai found that she could not look at the pathetic spectacle directly.

Latana allowed her disgust to show on her face. "I will tell you no such thing. Instead, I will tell you what you are to do now if you do not want me to imprison your entire family."

Elen-ai didn't see Erek draw the knife. The discomfort that his desperate mewling instilled meant she had averted her gaze, choosing instead to try and gauge how Gidyon was reacting to this display. She only saw the glint of the knife out of the corner of her eye as he drove it all the way into the base of the Queen's unprotected neck.

The skills of the Family gave her a speed none could match, but even she couldn't make it across the room in time to stop the knife from plunging into Latana's delicate flesh. Gidyon's cry rang in her ears as she wrenched Erek off the Queen and violently twisted his neck to end his life. His body hadn't even hit the ground before she had wheeled back to the Queen.

Gidyon pushed her aside to get to his mother, paying no heed to the red, red blood that soaked into his clothes as it poured out of the wound in her neck. He screamed for help as Elen-ai came to the other side of the

Queen, placing her hands on the wound in a desperate attempt to stop the blood as it gushed out.

Somewhere, members of the Royal Guard called frantically for someone to come and prevent the Queen's death, but all Elen-ai could focus on was the softness of the Queen's hair as she cradled Latana's head. Beside her, Gidyon was whimpering, or perhaps he was just repeating 'no' over and over again. The look of surprise on Latana's face unsettled Elen-ai the most.

Hands pulled her away as a number of people descended on the Queen to try and save her, but Elen-ai was too familiar with death to cling to false hope. She knew the Queen's end was inevitable.

TWENTY

Gidyon's howl of anguish signalled the terrible truth: Queen Latana was dead. Elen-ai fought her way through the shock that was threatening to engulf her and crouched next to Gidyon. The boy was sobbing as he held his mother's body. Tears had yet to make their way to his eyes despite the cries that wracked him. Somehow it made his grief all the worse to witness.

"Gidyon, look at me," Elen-ai said. When he did not seem to hear her, she repeated herself.

The room was a maelstrom of activity, yet a space around the Queen, her son, and Elen-ai still existed. The horror of the Queen's murder was keeping people away, but that would not last for long. The Prince looked up at Elen-ai, his eyes dulled by the momentousness of the events that had transpired so quickly.

"Gidyon," Elen-ai spoke urgently. "Erek attacked the Queen, you don't know why. It seemed he just became mad out of nowhere. You pulled him off, not in time to save your mother. In the struggle, his head was hit. Do you remember?"

He looked dully at her and she feared that he would not understand what she was telling him. He nodded slowly.

"Tell me what happened," she instructed. Her heart broke for what she was doing to him, but she didn't have the time to be gentle. Her duty was to protect the Prince and this was the only way she could do that now.

"Mother and I met with Erek to try and convince him to support my claim. Suddenly he went crazy. He pulled out a knife and stabbed her before I could do anything. I fought him, he hit his head and he fell down." He even managed to sound as though he believed it.

"Good," she told him. She rose to leave but he reached out a blood-soaked hand and grabbed her sleeve.

"Please don't go."

"I'll be right back, I promise," she told him.

"Where are you going?"

"To take care of something."

He didn't understand, he just stared at her, his hand still clinging to her sleeve. "Gidyon. I'll return quickly," she reassured him. "Trust me," she added when he didn't move.

He nodded and let her go, dropping his head back to look at the Queen's lifeless form.

Elen-ai slipped out of the room as Silius entered it wearing a dressing robe the same colour as the Queen's eyes.

Catching sight of his sister's corpse, he let out an oath. "Divine One, what happened? Tana!"

Amid the new commotion Silius' arrival had caused, Elen-ai sought out the maid Len-am who had brought the message of the Katan's arrival to the Queen earlier in the day. She was taking a risk in trusting the woman, but it was a calculated risk. Dressed in her own bedclothes, the servant had come running quickly to answer the cries for help. She stood, looking in stupor at the Queen's body, still cradled by the Prince.

"I need your help," Elen-ai said.

She looked at the still-wet blood on Elen-ai's hands and clothes. "What happened?"

"I didn't think he was a real threat," Elen-ai said simply, indulging herself for a moment and wallowing in guilt. This was twice she had become complacent. This time though, that complacency had cost a life. "But I need to make sure this is all that happens. For the Queen's sake."

Len-am nodded despite her obvious confusion. "What do you need?"

"Show me where Keela Rasatan's room is."

Len-am threw a glance at Erek's body, at the present paid no heed by anyone. Whatever suspicions she may have had, she kept them to herself as she turned and led Elen-ai through the Palace, winding through the servant's staircases and corridors where they remained unseen. The rain pattered down outside, muffling the servant's footfalls. Elen-ai's were as ever, silent. She could hear the sound of running in the grand corridors of the Palace. As news of the Queen's death spread, it seemed people were taking the fastest rather than the most discreet route.

Nobody was in the corridor outside Keela Rasatan's rooms.

"I need your shirt," Elen-ai said, stripping off her own soiled shirt. Len-am did not even hesitate. She took off the requested garment, holding it out to Elen-ai who used it to meticulously wipe all the blood off her hands. She looked at her trousers for a moment then stripped them off too. The air was still warm enough that even in her underthings, she was not chilled in the slightest. Len-am did not seem to be concerned that she was in her own undergarments. Instead, she simply held out her hands expectantly for the dirtied clothes.

"Wait for me here," Elen-ai told her, opening the door and slipping into the bedchamber. Using the skills of the Family it was easy to see the room in the dark and find the slumbering form on the bed.

Elen-ai crossed the room and regarded Keela for a moment. In her sleep her face held a certain malevolence that was masked when she was awake. Keela's breathing was smooth and even, undisrupted even as the assassin stood over her.

Elen-ai gave a swift and merciful death, smothering Keela Rasatan as she slept. Unlike the Queen who died in confusion and pain, Keela felt nothing. It seemed unjust. Once she was satisfied that the woman's life had departed, Elen-ai cast about the room for a way to conceal the fact that her hand had brought this death.

Fortune was with her. Keela had a room several floors up with a large window that would let in the morning light. Elen-ai quickly heaved the still-warm body up and over the sill. She heard the thud as it hit the ground, muffled slightly by the rain.

Elen-ai left the room, taking her soiled clothes from the waiting Len-am and pulling them back on. The blood was starting to dry, making them stiff. "You went to inform Keela Rasatan of her son's death. She seemed wild with grief but screamed at you to leave so you did," Elen-ai instructed her.

Len-am didn't even hesitate before she nodded in reply.

They returned to the Queen's rooms in the silence, broken only when Elen-ai turned to Len-am. "You don't seem surprised," she commented.

In response, she was offered a knowing albeit weary smile. "I've been the chief servant to her Majesty for the whole time she has been on the throne. There isn't much that occurs that I don't at least know about. I know who you are."

Elen-ai wondered if Len-am knew about Latana and Zekken's relationship, but she did not ask. There were some things that were better left unsaid. The rest of their return to the Queen's rooms was undertaken in silence punctuated only by the patter of Len-am's footsteps.

Silence had settled over the room that held the Queen's body. Silius had joined Nikalus. Both were seated, their shock and disbelief etched into their postures. The Queen's body had been moved from its position slumped on the floor and instead laid on the couch. Erek's body had been removed. Elen-ai felt sorry for whoever had to handle the mundane details of this death; handling the corpses, or scrubbing the Queen's blood from the rug. Despite her familiarity with death, the prospect of cleaning the Queen's blood from the rug seemed somehow terribly sacrilegious. She hoped that the rug would just be burned.

Servants and guards moved quietly around the room. It didn't look as though there was any specific purpose to their movements. They seemed the actions of people desperate to have something to do rather than look at the body of their beloved Queen laid out in a terrible semblance of repose. Gidyon now stood at the window, lost in his own world. Something about the way he held himself kept everyone away from him – even Elen-ai.

The long slow tolling of bells began to sound from somewhere within the Palace compound. The length of each toll filled the air with a profound sorrow. Everybody in the room went totally still, waiting for the rest of Herran's bells to join in. It was only a few minutes later that the sound of all the other bells in the city could be heard. The last time the city's bells had sounded in such a way was sixteen months after Gidyon had been born when his grandmother had succumbed to a virulent winter flu. Elen-ai herself had been a relatively young child at the time, but she remembered the way the peals of lament had transformed the capital so suddenly, changing it from a vibrant and busy place to somewhere with sadness and mourning that swept through every corner, leaving no stone untouched by the weight of grief.

Gidyon stirred. He turned from the window. His eyes were red and tear tracks had etched themselves down his face. "We need to prepare mother for the funeral. Can someone please fetch the doctors?"

There was a rustle as though the room were awakening.

"I also want to speak with the Katan family," Gidyon added.

"Perhaps that can wait until the morning?" Silius raised his head to address Gidyon.

"I think not." Gidyon contradicted him with a firmness that gave no room for further discussion.

Silius did not try to push his nephew. "Where would you like to meet them? I'm not sure here is the best place," he said instead.

"The blue sitting room." Gidyon sounded so certain, so sure of himself. Elen-ai wondered whether he actually felt that certainty.

"Should you perhaps change?" Silius suggested, looking at Gidyon's blood-stained shirt, the red of the Queen's blood darker patches on the fine red cloth.

Gidyon glanced down. "No. Let them see. Elen-ai?" He swept from the room, not glancing at his mother's body laid out on the couch.

Elen-ai followed him silently. She did not ask if he was alright. It was a preposterous question to ask. "Keela will not be a problem," she said instead.

"That's where you went?" was all Gidyon asked.

She nodded. He said nothing further.

They reached the sitting room. Gidyon did not sit. He remained on his feet, a stillness that concerned Elen-ai settling over him. A glassy look which spoke of thoughts far from the present flickered over his eyes.

The door opened and Silius and Nikalus came in. Focus came back into his eyes as the two men entered. When they crossed the room, his two uncles simply each rested a hand on his shoulder before selecting seats for themselves. Gidyon said nothing, but Elen-ai saw him work to swallow, and the sheen of unshed tears cross his eyes.

The knock on the door a few moments later signalled the arrival of the Katan family. They piled in, Liita, Enges, Halen, and of course, Serenah. All of them were in their nightclothes, and from the expression on their faces, it was clear that they knew but clearly did not believe what the toll of the bells was telling them. From Liita's gasp, Elen-ai assumed she had noticed the blood still on Gidyon.

Before any of them could say anything, Gidyon spoke. "Erek Rasatan killed my mother tonight."

Halen's eyes widened in shock. "What! Divine One around us."

Gidyon cut him off. "He came as part of your retinue, Halen. Tell me why I should not find you responsible."

For several moments, the man's mouth hung open in shock, elongating his face in a manner that would have been comical were it not for the circumstances. He shook his head slightly, sending his jowls fluttering.

"Your Highness," he began, but again, Gidyon cut him off.

"Your Majesty, you mean."

Halen looked at the boy before him who was young enough to be his grandson. The silent support of Silius and Nikalus and even Elen-ai in conjunction with the seriousness of the Queen's death left him totally dumbstruck. Elen-ai hoped he would refuse to recognise Gidyon's title so that Gidyon had a reason to arrest him. However, years of political nous meant that he was wily enough to not quite fall into that trap. "Of course. My apologies, your Majesty. If you wish to hold me responsible for Erek's actions, I understand but would ask that you do not punish my family for my lapse in judgment. Where is Erek now?"

"Dead." Gidyon's voice was flat. "I killed him in the struggle."

Again, he rendered Halen speechless. In this silence, Gidyon spoke again. "I can only trust that you would not have wanted harm to befall my mother or me in any way, especially given that you are our guests. Erek's madness is – was – his own and you cannot be blamed for failing to see it. None of us did. You are all more than welcome to remain in the Palace until the," he paused. "Until the funeral."

With Gidyon rescinding his threat, the entire Katan family visibly relaxed.

"We can't possibly impose upon you during this difficult time, we will return to our house in Herran in the morning." Halen's gently mournful tone had Elen-ai clenching her jaw. "I imagine this will be a difficult time for you. Your young years may find you lacking in some ways. I hope you will feel you can come to me for any advice you may need," the man added, his face a picture of sincerity.

Nikalus cleared his throat conspicuously, causing Gidyon to give a reflexive, empty smile. "I'll keep your generous offer in mind Lord Halen."

The silence that followed gave a clear indication that as far as Gidyon was concerned, the audience was over. The Katans departed the room in a silent awkward shuffle. Once they had left, Gidyon turned to look at his uncles and Elen-ai. She could see in his face that he was focusing on the matter at hand to keep himself together. It was heartbreaking. "He's unbelievable," Gidyon said quietly, running a hand through his hair, heedless of the dried blood still on his hands.

"He's unlikely to do anything now," Silius commented.

Gidyon pulled a face.

"Perhaps you should try and get some sleep, Gid," Silius suggested, his voice gentle. "We can discuss this at greater length in the morning."

This time, Gidyon did not disagree with his uncle. "Elen-ai?" He looked to her with vague, unarticulated uncertainty.

"I'm here," she reassured him.

Gidyon's uncles watched him with concern as he left the room, but both seemed at a loss for what advice or guidance they could give. Elen-ai could hardly blame them. She couldn't begin to understand how they were wrestling with their own grief while trying to discern what was best for the Queendom, and their nephew.

As they walked to Gidyon's rooms, Elen-ai thought that it seemed impossible that such little time had passed since they had ventured to back to his rooms after dinner. Latana had been alive only hours previously. Shock and disbelief hovered on the corners of Elen-ai's perception of the world, but she had the privilege of being familiar with death. Gidyon was not so accustomed to such things and it was his mother who had died. She knew that Gidyon was yet to be fully struck by what had transpired. When he finally did truly realise what had happened, it would be awful.

Once in his rooms, he finally washed his mother's lifeblood off him. He emerged in his bedclothes, looking no more refreshed. Elen-ai silently went into the bathroom, filling the tub with water and scrubbing at her own skin. She never ceased to be amazed at the way blood seemed to grind itself under even the shortest of fingernails. When she came out she found Gidyon simply sitting on his bed staring blankly at the wall.

"Do you need anything?" she asked.

Grief is a curious state of being. While two people can feel grief for the same person, more often than not they will experience it differently. For that reason, Elen-ai had always viewed grief as a feeling that was distinctly isolating.

"Do you think I should move rooms?" Gidyon asked rather than actually answer her question. "A ruler should have, I don't know, more grand rooms, don't you think?"

"I think you should have whatever rooms you feel most comfortable in," she replied, coming to sit beside him on the bed. "Will you be able to sleep, do you think?"

He shrugged, scratching his cheek with one finger. "I suppose I should try," he said.

"Whatever you want to do we'll do," she told him.

"This is my fault," Gidyon said, clearly not hearing her, too preoccupied with his own thoughts, his own grief, his own shock.

"No it's not, Gid." She was surprised by how vehemently she wanted him to believe her, to understand that he wasn't responsible for the crime of another man.

"If I hadn't made us go straight to her rooms –"

Elen-ai spoke over him. "He may have done something like that on another day. He was clearly not sane. You didn't see how Keela was with him. I can't imagine what it would have been like to be raised by her."

"Keela. She knows about mother and Zekken, you said." Gidyon looked down at the sheets with a frown on his face.

"I took care of it, remember?"

"Oh yes, so you did." He blinked.

"Look, I'll dim the lights. Try to rest, alright?" She stood and dimmed the flames that illuminated the room rather than extinguishing them completely, leaving a soft glow in the room. She did not want to leave Gidyon in the dark. Not tonight.

Rather than going to the cot in the room, she returned to the opposite side of the bed to him. After a moment, he lay down, and then she followed his action, lying back against the softness of the mattress. It was still a warm enough night that neither of them needed blankets. As they lay in the soft half-light, Gidyon's hand crept across the bed to find hers.

Elen-ai did not sleep that night and she could tell from his breathing that Gidyon did not either. The tolling of the bells was a constant note that endured through the night and long into the next day after they arose.

TWENTY ONE

The Queen's funeral took place on a spectacular summer day one week after her death. Elen-ai had barely left Gidyon's side through that week, from the morning he rose bleary-eyed from grief and the sleepless night, sitting through a series of discussions on the necessary actions to follow the tragedy, up to the funeral itself. It had been an awful week. The days had blurred into one another, filled with endless offers of condolences, decisions, and directives. This was all conducted to the background of numb shock, a sense that the world was somehow out of balance in some indefinably significant manner, and would never be right again.

The funeral procession wound its way through Herran's streets in the requisite showing of the body. The capital was still in shock, people thronging in a silent crowd to see for themselves that their adored Queen was actually dead. So profound was the people's grief that Gidyon had been required to order the bells to cease ringing two days after they had first sounded, otherwise it was likely they would still have been ringing as Latana's body was carried through the streets. Gidyon was dressed in mourning silver. The only splash of colour on him was the purple sash that cut his torso in two, denoting him as the ruler of the Second Country now. Silver was not his best colour, especially after several nights of little or no sleep. It served to emphasise the shadows under his eyes and the slightly jaundiced pallor to his skin. All things considered, though, he was doing a remarkable job of holding himself. He had only succumbed to true anguish once, on the third night after Latana's murder. The rawness of his grief, evident in every aching sob had been terrible to hear. Elen-ai had been the only person who had seen the true face of his grief. She had run a hand across his back as he cried, the only gesture possible to offer someone so profoundly grief-stricken; the reminder of 'I am here'.

In her own mourning clothes of silver, Elen-ai felt like some kind of fish, moving through the stream of the capital. She could pick out members of the Family at various points in the crowd, their inconspicuousness marking them out to her as though they wore some kind of sign. She knew they too saw her among the funeral procession, even though very few other citizens would have noticed her walking inconspicuously between Varl and Valena Veertak, and Arlena Aadran.

The morning following Latana's murder, the Palace's messenger birds fastest messengers had departed for every part of the land. Members of the seven families had begun to arrive in the capital over the following days, coming to offer their condolences to Gidyon and prepare themselves for the funeral. The remainder of the Katan family had arrived mere hours before the funeral, coming by the fastest possible means, most of them having travelled through the nights in order to arrive in time for Queen Latana's funeral.

Elen-ai glanced at Varl as the procession passed the harbour's most scenic point. He was clothed in silver that somehow managed to clash magnificently with his white hair. Tears trickled unchecked down his wrinkled cheeks. Beside him, Valena reached over and took her husband's hand.

There was something obscene about the beauty of the day. The harbour water was a brilliant blue, sparkling in the sunlight. Not a single cloud marred the sky, and the sun shining on Herran's buildings lent the city a particular radiance. Yet nobody was able to appreciate the magnificence of the day, for borne through the streets of the capital was Queen Latana the Fourth, the most beautiful Queen ever to grace the Second Country.

At the city's merchant bank, Elen-ai glanced at the tall, stern building on her right. Arlena Aadran came into her view, walking as straight-backed as ever, the silver of her dress almost the same shade as the grey which coloured most of her hair. Elen-ai thought she saw a shadow of Gidyon in the arch of her brow, but then again, she could swear that Wenden Rasatan, Erek's father and Keela's husband, had the exact same nose as Gidyon. The man in question walked alone, whatever shame or personal grief he may feel at his son's crime and the apparent suicide of his wife, hidden. Gidyon had deliberated on banning him from the funeral but ultimately decided against it. The Rasatan reputation was already in tatters as a result of Erek's actions, and it seemed cruel to humiliate the man who had lost not only his wife and son but also his family's credibility.

A wheeze caught Elen-ai's attention and she saw Julyana Bertak struggling to remain silent in her efforts to keep up with the procession's pace. She wore a silver dress that looked as though it had been made for a far less substantial woman. Elen-ai somewhat nastily thought that the choice of a sleeveless bodice was an unfortunate one. Pink from the heat, her arms looked like two slabs of cured meat. Elen-ai gleaned a sliver of amusement from the fact that the woman's husband was a man of such slight stature that it looked as though she could squash him if she mistakenly sat on him. It was a welcome levity given the sorrow and concern that had weighed so heavily on her over the last week.

After the necessary rituals and prayers were performed in front of the city's temple to the Divine One, the procession made its way back to the Palace along a different route. Elen-ai heard weeping from among the crowd. The genuineness of the grief of the lowborn deepened Elen-ai's own grief. Despite her anger at the Queen for her reckless relationship with Zekken, like any member of the Second Country, she had held a love for her Queen that was intertwined with her love for her country. The Queen's untimely death was a profanity and the fact that she had been murdered simply extended the underlying shock and outrage at the fact that even Queens die before the time.

As they neared the Palace, the people lining the streets ceased to be the lowborn residents of the city and became the members of the seven families and their households gathered outside their city residences. Elen-ai glimpsed Rania among the Harete family, her pretty face stricken. Her parents walked in the procession, the pregnant Janyce supported on Timet's arm. Their acrimony was obvious to anyone who looked, her body bowed away from him despite the arm on which she leaned.

The procession passed the Aadran residence and Elen-ai could see Zekken standing with his other family members. He looked utterly devastated, his appearance barely presentable. His eyes were red and his face was puffy in the way that signalled he had shed a great many tears and was likely holding them back now. As the procession passed the Aadran family, his gaze flickered between Gidyon, the boy he believed to be his son, and the body of Latana, his adored lover, before he succumbed to sobs that he muffled poorly with his arm.

The procession re-entered the Palace compound, led by Gidyon and his two uncles – Kaine was unlikely even to have yet received word of his sister's death due to his diplomatic journey to the Fourth Country. The three men accompanied Latana's body into the incineration house. From a window in the Palace Elen-ai had watched the armfuls of wood being prepared for the fire that would consume the Queen's form in the early hours of the morning. When the sun set, the fire would be lit and the Queen's ashes would rise into the night sky and drift over her country. The funeral procession, the heads of the seven families and Elen-ai, milled in the yard that surrounded the little stone room.

It was mid-afternoon and the sun would not set for several more hours. However, tradition dictated that nobody was permitted to leave until the Queen's funeral pyre was lit at sundown. The Palace servants brought out water and Elen-ai gratefully drank. The walk had taken several hours, and the heat of the day had made it seem even longer. Chairs were also brought out, and several people gratefully sank into them.

The courtyard descended into the stillness of the vigil required by funeral custom. The sun lapped at the procession. Elen-ai could smell the salty tang of sweat as the gathered individuals perspired in the heat. She wondered whether it was hot in the incineration house and whether Gidyon had been offered a drink.

The hours passed slowly, punctuated with the occasional clearing of the throat or rustle as someone shifted in their seat. In different circumstances, Elen-ai might have enjoyed the extended period of silence, but today, surrounded by people whose boredom and grief were all a part of a game that left a sour taste in her mouth, Elen-ai wished she were in some other part of Herran, mourning the Queen in the noisy lowborn way. Finally, the sun dipped below the horizon and the Palace bells gave one single toll in recognition of the day's end. The door to the room opened and the men of the Royal family emerged. A flaming brazier was brought to Gidyon with a solemnity that befitted the moment. He took it, his hand steady, and turned back to the entrance of the room. Elen-ai glimpsed a small mountain of carefully piled wood before Gidyon touched the brazier to the nearest branch. The flame ran along the wood and out of Elen-ai's sight, but she saw the glow reflected on the room's walls which meant the fire had caught.

The heavy metal door to the incineration room was swung shut and firmly latched. Elen-ai looked up. Against the darkening sky she could see a trickle of grey smoke curling from the chimney. She wasn't certain, but she thought she could faintly smell the meaty, slightly sweet scent of burning flesh. It seemed almost impossible that in the stone structure before Elen-ai were the final remains of her Queen.

The funeral now complete, the members of the procession eased their stiff limbs and wordlessly entered the Palace. The funeral feast would be served following a short break to allow those who had been outside in the baking afternoon the opportunity to refresh themselves.

Elen-ai followed Gidyon to his rooms. He did not seem to have been particularly affected by the heat of the afternoon, but his air of malaise told her that his mother's funeral had, unsurprisingly, been deeply distressing. Once in his rooms, he exchanged his shirt for a fresh one and sat down on the couch, resting his head in his hands. Elen-ai changed her own tunic, carefully transferring all of her blades across into the new garment. She did not bother Gidyon with pointless conversation. If he wanted to speak, he would.

"I wish I didn't have to go to this dinner," he said softly, the defeat in his voice more upsetting than the sadness he exuded.

"One more night, then it will be done." Elen-ai did not seek to soothe or cajole, she simply sought to pull him through for one more evening. There may have been a time when she would have suggested he not go, but she knew him well enough by now to know he would never even entertain the notion. It was his duty to preside over the funeral dinner for his mother, so he would go.

He sighed. "I suppose you're right. Alright, let's go." He stood, his face slack with exhaustion and grief, and led the way into the banquet hall.

The immediate members of the seven families were in attendance at the funeral banquet. Elen-ai could hear the soft hum of their conversation as she and Gidyon approached the room. Outside the door, Gidyon paused. She saw his shoulders slump for a fraction of a moment then heard him take a deep breath and pull himself up straighter. He nodded to the guards and they opened the doors. With everybody wearing mourning silver, the room looked like a shimmering pool. Gidyon strode in, commanding the total attention of the room, the purple sash a contrast to the sombre tones. Elen-ai slipped in after him, as always, an unobtrusive footnote.

Everybody sank into a deep bow. Regardless of their allegiance to him as their ruler, he was nevertheless the reigning monarch, and a week ago he had lost his mother. Nobody would have dared fail to prostrate themselves before him. Even Elen-ai sank into a bow, although she kept a sharp alertness about her. She had failed the Queen one week ago, and she would not fail again.

The dinner commenced to a backdrop of music. The musicians played soft and gentle pieces which entrenched a sombre mood. Normally for a feast of this scale, the tenor of the music would be lively and cheerful, creating an ambience which urged diners to greater heights of cheer and merriment in a reminder of the fact that the Palace was able to hold the finest parties, amongst its other many points of authority. Tonight however, such cheer was out of place. As such, conversation never rose above a discreet murmur and no laughter sounded.

Elen-ai wandered over to the Veertaks, smiling at Varl despite the circumstances.

"My dear, I'm sorry we haven't had the chance to speak since we arrived." Varl returned her smile, his wrinkled face crinkling around the sadness that had settled on it.

"Gidyon's been very busy," she replied.

"Is he alright?" Valena came to her husband's side, putting a hand on his shoulder. Without even seeming to realise it, he reached his hand up and across to cover hers.

Elen-ai gave a small shrug. "His mother just died. He is as well as can be expected."

"I do not envy him the task ahead, especially given the obstacles some may place in his way," Varl said, casting a pointed glance in the direction of Halen Katan and his wife, Lilea, who were quietly conferring with Julyana and Aydrien Bertak.

"Have they no shame?" The little man practically vibrated with anger.

"My darling," Valena's voice contained a note of warning.

"How dare they?" he uttered.

"You are not to go over there and berate them," Valena told him sternly.

"I would never do such a thing," he protested, his eyes still on the little conference taking place on the other side of the room.

"You are a terrible liar and a good man. And I love you," she told him quietly. "But if you go over there and tell them off, I will have to stab you with a serving fork to prevent you from doing so," she added.

Elen-ai let out an amused breath. She actually believed that the dignified woman would make good on her promise in order to prevent her husband causing a worse scene.

Wenden Rasatan wandered over. His features were an echo of his son's, albeit without the striking good looks. Elen-ai wasn't certain if it was the haunted look he had adopted that made him so distinctively less handsome than his son, or if it was a slightly different arrangement of the component parts that meant that while he was good looking, Erek had been startlingly attractive. "Hullo Varl, Valena," he said.

Elen-ai had noted the elliptical orbit of his path through the room, his momentum spurred on by the polite dismissals from anyone with whom he had tried to converse. Even the Veertaks looked mildly uncomfortable by his presence.

"Hello Wenden, how are you?" Valena said, her question reflexively polite.

In reply, he spread his arms a little bit. "I could be worse I suppose." He gave a sad little smile that was surprisingly endearing.

"Are your other boys here?" Varl asked.

Wenden shook his head. "I thought it perhaps best if they didn't come. I'll head straight back tomorrow with..." He trailed off, although everybody present knew how that sentence would have finished. The bodies of Keela and Erek had been preserved for transport so that they could be appropriately sent off. While Keela would be given the traditional funeral by fire, Erek would, like all criminals, be buried. It was a twofold shame, to have a son who had committed regicide, but also whose resting place would be in the dirt with his final fate to be consumed by worms and rot. The prospect made Elen-ai shudder with revulsion.

The evening dragged on, a necessary unpleasantness to finish the formalities of the Queen's death. Gidyon departed at the appropriate time, not a minute earlier or later. She had watched him carefully avoid Zekken who tried to approach Gidyon several times throughout the night. On each occasion Gidyon had somehow managed to find someone else to speak with or somewhere else to be. She almost felt sorry for Zekken. He looked like a spectre of the man Elen-ai had met on the Tak estate. He and Wenden even seemed to resemble each other somehow, both men seeming lost as a consequence of their grief and shock.

In his rooms, Gidyon read over several documents that required his attention. Elen-ai sat silently watching him, preoccupied with thoughts of the horror of being buried and the look on Wenden Rasatan's face. The Veertaks had ultimately been kind to him, speaking with him far longer than anybody else, but even they had to consider their reputation. Being too friendly with the father of the man who had killed the Queen was not going to hold their family in good stead, so they too had extricated themselves from the conversation with haste. After seeing him, Elen-ai wondered how he had ever gained a reputation for being so ruthless and authoritarian. He had simply looked like an ordinary man to her.

Two days later, Gidyon paused in between his many meetings and turned to Elen-ai. She had never thought that the position of monarch would require so much work, but since Latana's death, she had been by Gidyon's side for meetings with various individuals who held positions that she did not even know existed, while he had read reports, and of course while he had listened to petitioners. He handled each of his duties with a dignity and calm that belied the fact that he was only about to turn seventeen and had just witnessed the murder of his mother by the man who might be his father.

"Elen-ai." From the way he said her name, Elen-ai knew that he was about to say something she wasn't going to like.

"I have given the matter of your contract considerable thought," he continued.

She frowned, uncertain of where he was going with this.

"My mother signed a contract with the Family to ensure it was safe for me to be able to ascend the throne. I have ascended the throne."

"Yes, but –"

He held up a hand to silence her, his face grave.

"You have fulfilled your contract, and I cannot expect or ask you to stay beyond the fulfilment of your contract."

Something that felt like panic bloomed in her chest. "You could take out a new contract with the Family," she suggested, hoping that she did not sound desperate.

He smiled, sadness in his eyes. "A contract to what? Protect me as ruler? You'd have to be with me for my entire life."

She opened and closed her mouth, uncertain of how she could respond. From the sad smile on Gidyon's face, he had apparently anticipated this. "I have arranged for the payment my mother promised to be made available for the Family to collect as they wish," he continued.

"I could stay just a little longer, just until things settle." She was starting to sound almost hysterical. Something about the prospect of leaving Gidyon alone, without her protection or companionship made distress secure itself in the pit of her stomach.

"Elen-ai, your contract is fulfilled." It seemed wrong that he was the one comforting her, but the gentleness of his voice made it clear that was exactly what he was doing.

"Gid." She was begging him, although she didn't know exactly what for.

"I've made my decision, Elen-ai," he told her. "Thank you. For everything. I am supremely lucky to have a friend like you." He embraced her. It was the first time that they had ever hugged.

She wanted to tell him that she was sorry she hadn't saved the Queen, that she was sorry for the fact that he was so terribly alone and facing the possibility that once the grief and shock of the Queen's death wore off the people may refuse to be ruled by a man. Instead, she held him close, feeling the slenderness of his form that gave away his age.

"It has been an honour to stand by your side," she told him, fighting to keep her voice from breaking as she felt tears threaten to fill her eyes.

TWENTY TWO

The Family's home was cool and dark, and a welcome sanctuary from the heat of the day. As Elen-ai stepped inside the familiar walls, she inhaled the slightly spicy scent that she simply knew as 'home'. It felt indescribably good to be back in the place where she had grown up, where everything was deliciously familiar. She could hear muffled noises coming from one of the rooms; probably a Mother or Father giving lessons to a group of the Family's children. She smiled at the familiarity, relaxing fully for perhaps the first time in a great many weeks.

The beautiful house was a mixture of timber – fine Harete wood – painted a dark colour and cool stone with high ceilings and floors that were heated ever so slightly in winter and somehow managed to remain cool even in the depths of summer. Despite having a great many windows, they were almost always covered by dark purple curtains, which meant that only a little light was let in by any one window. This created a row of thin rays of light punctuating the shadowy corridors. Elen-ai had always found it quite beautiful to walk along such corridors in the middle of the day, watching as motes of dust danced as they were caught in the beams.

She intuited rather than felt the appearance of one of her Fathers beside her.

"My daughter." Did she detect a hint of warmth in his voice, or was she succumbing to sentimentality?

"Father."

"It is good that you are back home with us." His face was totally impassive, as though he were making an idle comment about the heat of the day rather than bestowing on her an unusually high compliment.

"It is good to be home," Elen-ai responded, her own voice neutral. The calmness of being home, of being within those walls settled on her, smoothing away the excesses of emotion, of worry, anger, or sadness.

"I trust that you have not become lax during your lengthy time away from us."

"Of course not." Privately, Elen-ai worried that perhaps she had not done as much as she should have to ensure she remained in peak physical condition. She had made sure to do exercise every day, but it had often been done in whatever space was available to her and only within the time permitted.

The Father said nothing, he merely began to walk along the corridor. He did not have to tell Elen-ai to follow him. Any member of the Family who was away for an extended period of time was required to prove their capability upon their return. If they failed to demonstrate their competence they would not be permitted to take a contract until they returned to the peak of their abilities.

The courtyard felt particularly warm after the refreshing coolness of the inside of the house. The Father remained motionless by the door. "The roof," was all he said.

Elen-ai glanced up at the series of railings and ledges that were on the side of the house. There was an abundance of hand and footholds to get onto the roof from the ground, but the difficulty was not in finding ways to get up but in the speed that she was required to demonstrate she still possessed. She took a breath and launched herself at the wall, propelling herself up faster than a normal eye could follow. Within two breaths she had ascended the three-story building and stood on its roof, looking down at the suddenly small figure of her father. She saw his nod of approval and slipped quickly down the wall to stand back in front of him.

He directed her through several more exercises, forcing her to prove her speed, agility, silence, and then finally he stood in front of her, naked blade in his hand. She swallowed. Many who were required to prove themselves failed at this final stage. She did not want to be one of them.

She did not draw any of her blades. To do so would have been the mistake of an amateur. She did not know how the fight would progress and as such, she did not know which of her blades she would require. He came at her quickly. To anyone watching, it would look as though she simply swayed from one side to the other as she evaded his attacks, but she moved much faster than that. She kept her feet in place, refusing to give any ground. Another mistake made by many. She tried to sweep his arm aside with her forearm but he anticipated the move and came at her with his other arm, another blade appearing in his hand. Now she moved, having expected this tactic herself. He had taught her how to fight with knives, after all.

She spun on her foot, using the momentum she had generated with her forearm to pivot around him, now drawing a blade and thrusting it toward him. Anyone watching might have mistaken the movements of the two for dance, so graceful were they. In reply, he curved his body just out of her reach and he too spun. Elen-ai now drew a second knife, twisting herself in a counterpoint to his movement so that her knife came to rest at his neck when they both stopped. Their dance ended abruptly. Elen-ai held the blade there a moment longer to forestall any trick, lowering it only after he inclined his head in the tiniest of nods. She stepped back and he turned to face her. Something akin to approval flickered across his face. "You are a credit to your teacher," he told her, a shadow's smile on his face at the compliment he had given himself.

Dismissed, she went back inside the house, once more feeling the world outside the house recede as she entered its shadow. She navigated the stairs to the small bedroom that was hers. Members of the Family did not really own many possessions aside from their blades and perhaps a few clothes. There was no real need for anything else. As such, they could claim one of the narrow rooms furnished with a plain cot and blanket as their own, or move between them as they chose. Elen-ai was in the minority of the Family that chose a permanent residence for herself. She couldn't quite say why, but she liked the idea of knowing where she was going to sleep each night.

She slipped back into the routine of the Family as easily as though she was awakening from a strange dream, rising early to exercise, and eating her lunch on the roof with Mari-am on the days when she and her sister were both in the house. There was a comfort to returning to what she knew, a certainty of who she was and of what she was supposed to do. Contracts arose and she took them, escorting her targets to death. The summer wore on, the heat settling over the Second Country like a blanket. The wrongness to the world that had descended after Latana's death slowly receded – or rather, it became familiar enough that it ceased to be noticeable. A date for Gidyon's coronation was set, and the country began to consider the prospect of a man on the throne. Elen-ai heard all side of the argument as she passed through various residences, but it was as though she were hearing it from afar, unable to accept that these references to the boy King – or the imposter King – were in reference to the Gidyon that she knew.

Whispers reached the ears of the Family about the machinations of the seven families – the attempts of the Katan family to subvert support for Gidyon, and the fact that most of the families were hiring and training an unusually high number of people for their household guard. Regardless of whether or not individuals supported Gidyon, the people's unease about being ruled by a man was palpable, picked up in the myriad of conversations that were exchanged in places where nobody from the Palace would even have heard of. Rumours and reports even trickled into the Family of the increasing instability within the Fourth Country and the posturing of its leaders towards the Second and Third Country in an attempt to distract their population from this ongoing problem. However, the actions of people in power and the games played between them were no longer Elen-ai's concern. She put the reports that she heard to the back of her mind and focused on the simple and easy known parts of her life.

Around the peak of the summer's heat, she began to take part in training the Family's young children. It wasn't a task that she had done much before, preferring instead to take contracts, but now she found a curious satisfaction in walking through a group of children and correcting their grip on a knife, or coaching them through a particular flip, even weaving shadows around herself to show them what they may do in a few years' time provided they were able to find faith in the God of Shadows. It was disconcerting when they called her Mother, but something about it was natural, too. Many of her own brothers and sisters had already adopted the title of Mother or Father when dealing with the Family's youngest children. Perhaps it was time she joined them.

Even though on reflection it shouldn't have, she was initially surprised that what she had seen during her time with Gidyon was considered too valuable to the Family to remain only in her head. She was often asked to join the discussions in which the Family shared the information that their members had collected. Privately, she felt that she knew far less than was assumed, but she obliged the requests for her presence, contributing a comment here or there when she had something she could add. It was in one such meeting that the subject of Gidyon's marriage arose.

"The Haretes are apparently still hopeful that the Kingling will marry their daughter," one of the Mothers said.

Elen-ai could not contain her snort. It elicited the attention of the room's members, who all turned to regard her with expectant expressions. Elen-ai composed herself before she elaborated. "They can hope but Gidyon will not. He has pledged to marry a lowborn woman."

"Surely the support of one of the four largest families through a marriage would bring him enough strength to secure his claim to the throne," pointed out Wyn-et, one of Elen-ai's brothers.

The shake of her head was one curt motion. "Perhaps, but it breaks the neutrality that the royal family is supposed to maintain. He would never do something that would endanger the peace of the Second Country for his own immediate power."

Given the obviousness of what she had just pointed out, Elen-ai was surprised to see the expressions of surprise and confusion on the faces of the others in the room.

She received an explanation for the expressions only a few hours later. A Mother found her in the practice yards while she was going through a series of flips and twists as part of her daily practice.

"My child, may I have a word with you?"

With a shrug, Elen-ai jumped off the bar that she was on and landed noiselessly in front of her Mother. A vague sense of worry prickled in the back of her mind, but she told herself to cease being silly. She had done nothing wrong.

Her Mother led the way through the large house to one of the small rooms normally used for private meditation and prayer. With a gesture, she indicated that Elen-ai sit. Elen-ai did as she was bidden, descending to sit cross-legged on the floor in one fluid movement. Even though she had bested her Father at the trial upon her return, she was only now returning to the full extent of her capabilities and movements. Perhaps he had been gentle with her.

Her Mother sat too, facing Elen-ai. For a moment, the only sound was their barely perceptible breath. With the door closed, hardly any light came into the room, although that wasn't a problem for either of them. Finally, her Mother spoke. "The Family is neutral when it comes to the Royal Family aside from our interest in knowing what is about to transpire."

Elen-ai nodded. It was, of course, the most basic rule of the Family.

"But perhaps you are not quite so neutral in how you view the King-ling."

Despite the gentle tone, Elen-ai was stung. "Whatever my personal views on Gidyon, it does not mean that I do not share the Family's neutrality," she protested, a very real fear welling up inside her. She thought of those members of the Family who had left because they were no longer aligned with what the Family asked of its children. She did not want to be one of them.

Her Mother smiled at her. "I am not accusing you of anything, Elen-ai. This is merely an observation that has been made. It is not a shame to have your own opinion."

"But I don't want to leave," Elen-ai blurted out, horrified by her lack of self-discipline.

"Why would you leave?" A look of slight confusion crossed her Mother's face.

"If I don't share the Family's neutrality," Elen-ai replied. "It would be as if I wanted to have a child," she continued.

"My child, those who leave us do so because they wish to leave us. We have never made any of our children leave us, nor will we."

"Oh," was all Elen-ai could say. She had never really thought about it that way. She had always assumed that love with someone outside the Family was prohibited rather than perhaps being incompatible with want-ing to remain a member of the Family.

"I will be frank with you, Elen-ai. The Elders have agreed that given the uncertainties surrounding the Kingling and his rule, we need more information on the goings-on of the Seven Families and the Palace."

Elen-ai nodded, privately agreeing with the assessment. People would always want to kill one another, ensuing coin aplenty for the Family. But it was a different matter entirely for the Family's position within the Second Country to be secure. If Herran looked like it may become a place of war, Elen-ai knew that the Family had contingencies to move to a safer area. The Family protected its own no matter what, and if their home was in the middle of a battlefield, safety could not be assured. But if they did not know where fighting was likely to occur, such measures could not be taken. If there was anything that Elen-ai had noticed at the meetings that she had been requested to attend, it was definitely that the Family did not know enough.

"Perhaps you could be persuaded to return to the Palace and find out what we need to know," her Mother said.

"But –"

She was cut off. "You want to help this Kingling. There is no shame in that. We need information so that we can keep our children safe. It makes sense."

Elen-ai shook her head. "I don't want to leave."

"Elen-ai," her Mother's voice was so gentle. "You do not have to accept."

"Surely if I did I would be taking a side, though," Elen-ai worried.

"You would not be there as a member of the Family."

Elen-ai raised a hand and pressed it against her cheek, trying to comprehend what was occurring. "Are you saying I should go back?"

"Do you believe that Gidyon should be King and that you can help him do that?" her Mother asked.

Elen-ai was silent for a long time. She had made a very deliberate decision to not ask herself such questions since her return. She was a member of the Family and her time with Gidyon had been in fulfilment of a contract. That contract had been completed, and she was obliged as a member of the Family to return home. Yet now that she allowed herself to consider the matter, she thought about Gidyon's desire to do right by his people, of the skill with which he dealt with the members of the seven Families. She thought about the grief that he had not allowed himself to feel for his mother because he had instead been obliged to attend to matters of state. Finally, she thought that at nearly seventeen, he was already a spectacular young man, and if he was given the chance, he might in fact be a great man and a great King. She looked up at her Mother. There was no judgment, no anger in her face, merely a serene acceptance of whatever Elen-ai chose to do.

"Yes," Elen-ai said. "I do."

THE FIRST SEASON

Golden eyes stared back at her from the mirror. She searched her face for any trace of the trepidation she felt whirring in the pit of her stomach, but years of conditioning and training kept her features smooth. Her dark, lustrous hair was styled to flow down around her shoulders so she would need help un-picking the style. Her gown was magnificent, a deep green with sumptuous embroidery across the fabric. But it too, was simple in design. It could be removed by her own hands, or by one unaccustomed to the workings of in-tricate women's clothes.

Her composure cracked and she raised a hand to her bare throat where the delicate flesh glowed white. Her mother had told her that she would find it thrilling to walk among the gathered young men and select who she would take to her bed, wanting nothing more from them other than a night of pleas-ure and the possibility of a child. Yet she did not find the prospect thrilling. She found it daunting. But that kind of weakness was not allowed in a Queen-to-be.

A knock at the door preceded the entrance of her favourite brother. His hair already thinning, even though he was still a young man, he regarded her with a gentleness he reserved exclusively for her. "How are you feeling?"

She swallowed. "How do you think?"

She could see the struggle within him. Upholding duty and tradition was an obligation that defined all her brothers, but him the most. Yet he had always been protective of her and sought to shield her from harm wherever possible. Given their birthright, that was often not achievable. "It's only a few nights." He sounded unconvinced.

Her sigh sounded, to her own ears, far older than that of a girl of six-teen. But then again, she was more than a mere girl of sixteen. "I'm sure it will be fine after tonight. I simply don't know what to expect, is all."

"Are you ready?" he asked.

She considered saying no, but she knew that would change nothing of what needed to come next. She pressed her lips together and nodded once. She felt her posture slide into the position it assumed whenever she was out-side the privacy of her personal rooms. With her shoulders thrown back and her head held high, she felt false confidence slip through her so smoothly that she could believe it was real. Regardless of how she may feel, the gathered men were there for her to speak with, dance with, and take to her bed as she pleased.

She walked through the corridors of the Palace and knew she appeared to all as Latana the princess rather than Latana the girl, radiating cool, composed authority with each step she took.

The doors open and the crowd of young men in the room bowed low before her. Her eyes swept over their assembled heads and she smiled to herself. She'd find the most handsome man here and take him back to her bed. She didn't need to fall in love, after all.

NO SPACE FOR REGRET

The girl was two years older than the assassin who had been sent to kill her. It was easy to like her. She had a face that frequently gifted those around her with a smile, a gentle voice, and eyes in which many had found hearts they thought hard, inexplicably softened.

Since her first kill many months previously, the assassin had taken a myriad of lives and felt nothing at the death her hands brought. But this girl had given her pause. It seemed profane that the girl was to be killed for the indiscretion of an ambitious married man. If only the farmer who was so obviously smitten with the girl had been more bold in voicing his affections, if only the girl had not been quite as fertile as she evidently was, if only the contract had been given to some other member of the Family. But the assassin had been taught that such conjecture was pointless. The farmer, for all his adoration now, may develop a destructive fondness for drink or violence as the disappointments of life weathered him, the girl was doomed to fall pregnant to someone at one point or another and childbirth was just as dangerous as loving the wrong person, and any other member of the Family would have completed the contract.

She dismissed the regret prowling in her mind. It was not her place to question the death she brought. She kept the shadows wreathed around her, shielding her from sight. The girl slept, her face peaceful in repose. The assassin crossed the room and stood over the older girl. Had she not been sold to the Family when she was but a babe, this might have been her. That thought too, made her hesitate.

It was the years of discipline that made her smother the girl. She was so gentle that the girl would not have felt a thing. The slight upward curve of her lips was still there, even in death. The assassin looked once more on the girl's face, the bloom of life fading slowly from her cheeks, then she left the room, pushing away the vague sense of guilt.

AN ENCOUNTER

The assassin's nimble fingers sorted through the cupboard's contents. Most household's stores could be deadly – in the right hands. His were the right hands.

Within moments, he'd learned all he required. He exited the house as unnoticed as he'd entered it. There were a few more scraps of information he wanted, but the outcome of his presence was as certain as the passage of the stars overhead. He headed for a tavern near enough as to be useful, but not so close as to be suspicious.

Training enforced so thoroughly that it had become second nature meant he took in every aspect of the room; the number of people and where they were gathered, the presence of potential threats, what he could use as a weapon if he so needed. A glance would easily give up to any observer that the tavern was well kept, but he discerned that in a myriad of minute ways – the recent re-application of finish to the wooden tables, the absence of soot-stains on the ceiling, even its very layout. Someone loved this tavern very much. He made his way to the counter where a young woman stood, casting a perceptive eye across the room.

She noticed his approach – many would not have – and gave a wry grin that offered much and promised nothing. "Good evenin' stranger."

It was not simply training to blend in that had him smiling in return. "To you, too. Ale, if you will."

As she filled a tankard for him, she kept her gaze on the merrymaking group dancing to the lively tune from a bard's instrument.

"Expecting trouble?" He could not help but ask.

Her eyes never left the group as she exchanged tankard for coin. Her hands bore the unmissable signs of someone familiar with all manner of tools. It was clear who kept the tavern in such good order. "Naw, not really. But the more I keep me eyes sharp, the less trouble I see."

He liked the sound of her voice, the alternate smooth lines and rough burs. Contrary to his plans, he remained at the bar as the hours wore on. She was a willing and excellent conversationalist, and brooked no nonsense, it turned out. She broke up a brawl with a fighting style he admired from his place at the counter.

The night drew to a close and only the assassin and the barkeep were left. "Closing time," she noted with that irresistible voice.

"Indeed it is. I don't suppose you'd like company for the rest of the night?"

She looked him up and down, making no effort to hide her appreciation for what she saw. "I think you're more trouble than you're worth."

"Sure about that?"

Her smile was flirtatious but her words were firm. "I'm not the sort that takes a different man to my bed each night."

He stepped back, more disappointed than he thought he'd be. "Can't blame me for trying."

As he walked to the door, her voice arrested him. "Perhaps if you're back tomorrow, or the day after, I may change me mind."

He threw one last look at her, and that was his mistake. The way she leaned against the counter brought out the curve of her waist, the muscles in her arms. Something about the light from the dying fire picked up the colours of her eyes. The sight of her was etched into his mind.

Suddenly, the idea of finishing his contract and going back to the Family, never returning, never seeing her once again, seemed intolerable.

"Maybe I'll just have to come back, then," he said.

KING OF THE
SEVEN LAKES

*A
woman of hot temper – and a man the same –
Is
a less dangerous enemy than one quiet and clever.*

-Euripides, Medea

THE FAMILIES OF THE SECOND COUNTRY

The Royal Family

For centuries, the Royal Family have overseen the stability of the Second Country underneath the firm hands of their queens. Following the sacrilegious murder of Queen Latana, in a complete breach of custom, her son Gidyon ascended the throne. Despite his gender, those who have observed him have commented on his intellect, sense of duty, and political nous. Guided by his uncles, Kaine, Silius, and Nikalus, in the first year of his reign, Gidyon ruled over a country divided. While some supported him, others were less enthusiastic in their willingness to be ruled by a man, and others still saw an opportunity to further their own power.

The Aadran Family

Presided over by their formidable matriarch, Arlena, the Aadran family possesses enormous wealth. They have had longstanding familial and business connections with the Tak family, which has entrenched their position of power. However, were it to become known, the illicit romantic relationship between one of the Aadran sons, Zekken, and the late Queen Latana, would see them shunned by even the steadfast Taks. Their social, and ensuing economic, ruin would be complete were it also known that Zekken believed himself to be Gidyon's father. The only thing worse than a queen conducting an enduring love affair with a member of the Seven Families would be if she knew who had fathered her child, decimating the neutrality her position was supposed to enshrine.

The Rasatan Family

One of the lesser of the Seven Families. Their fortunes were ruined when Erek Rasatan killed Queen Latana. Few know that underneath his unusually handsome visage lurked a deeply unstable mind. Erek's instability was preyed upon by his cruel mother, Keela, who despite her outward timidity, was best described as a masochist. Upon Erek's death in a struggle following his murder of Latana, Keela apparently killed herself. While Zekken and Latana may have considered themselves Gidyon's parents, at the first Season – the events at which royal children are conceived – Erek also made himself a contender for Gidyon's paternity. Following the scandal of Erek's regicide, the Rasatan family have become shunned by polite society and much of the power they held has been lost.

The Katan Family

Despite their powerful wealth generated by the spectacular ceramics spun from the clay within their lands, the Katan family have always been greedy for more power. The remoteness of their lands made marrying Latana's sister into the family seem like a good way to remove her as a direct challenger to the throne, as well as being a Royal gesture of goodwill to the Katan family. But the move also produced a girl now being touted as an alternative heir to the throne. Serenah's claim is especially strong now that a man sits on the throne in contravention of tradition. The patriarch, Halen, aggressively advocates his granddaughter as the rightful queen of the Second Country and will use any opportunity to put her on the throne. In the instance of her being placed on the throne, he would be adviser to her, and strongly encourage her to implement whatever policies he desired. Certainly, this likelihood makes a compelling case for the current system and the impartiality it ensures.

The Bertak Family

A lesser family, and famously resentful of that fact. While they mine precious gems from the mountains of their estate, they lacked the foresight – and now the capital – to establish master artisan workshops to cut or set these gemstones, and thus the wealth that enables true power eludes them. The Bertaks' manners are almost as minimal as their willingness to do anything that even vaguely promises them power is strong.

The Harete Family

Making their money from the timber of the forest that lies across their land, the Harete family is perhaps the most enigmatic of the Seven Families. The bitter enmity between husband Timet and his wife Janyce (by birth, a Katan) is a poorly concealed secret. Like all of the Seven Families, they seek to further their power and have demonstrated a certain breed of unscrupulousness in the pursuit of it. Their most recent attempt was to instruct their daughter, Rania, to try to seduce Prince Gidyon when he visited them prior to his mother's death. Were it not for intervention, Rania's charms might have succeeded, too. Certainly, it did not endear them to the Prince.

The Tak Family

Historically allying themselves with the Aadran family, the Tak make their fortunes from livestock. Their wealth offers them the luxury of being able to claim neutrality in a great many circumstances so that they can always side with whoever ends as the victor. Led by Serek and Karan, the Tak family would be a powerful political ally.

The Veertak Family

A family of scholars, the Veertaks have always been more interested in books than politics – just. Their leaders, the aged but sharp-witted Valena and Varl, have steadfastly put their support behind the Royal Family. They alone know the true identity of Gidyon's mysterious companion, Elen-ai, but have vowed to maintain this secret.

The Family of Assassins

Some may dispute their place on this list. However, the Family of Assassins was formed in the infancy of the Second Country following the great wars of the Godskissed Continent. The Family takes in children only a few months old and its Mothers and Fathers train them to become masters of every weapon, as well as disciples of the arts gifted by the Shadow God. If someone's name is on a contract taken out by the Family, their death is all but assured. No fighter alive can match the skills of the Family. Their one rule: they will not take the life of any member of the Royal Family. The Family's loyal daughter, Elen-ai, was contracted by Queen Latana not to kill but to protect Gidyon following her decision to name him her heir. Initially reluctant to accept the contract, Elen-ai's reservations seemed to be confirmed by the Prince's distaste for her origins. Yet, somehow, she and the Prince became friends, and she returned to the Palace following his coronation in an unofficial capacity to assist him. While she might have the blessing of some of the Family, acting as a sort of informant for them, this arrangement is not unanimously supported within the Family.

ONE

Pulling her scarf more tightly around her in a valiant fight against the cold, the assassin hurried toward the Palace. She moved with lithe grace, habit pushing her to stay close to the shadows. The inclination to remain in the darkest, most unobtrusive part of wherever she went arose from the training instilled in her from the youngest of ages.

Elen-ai passed barely anybody as she ascended the hill to the Palace, where it occupied the highest point in the capital. Even now, despite months of living there, it felt strange to be climbing the broad street to the sprawling complex rather than winding her way through Herran's lanes to the Family's home. Opulence was all very good and well, but nothing could ever compare to the familiarity of home. But the information swirling in her head took precedence over any sense of being out of place. Despite the prowling sense of urgency in her stomach, she paused at a shrine to the Divine One decorated with coloured ribbons and flowers. It was the fifth shrine she had passed since leaving the Family's home. A year ago, there had been no such shrines in the Second Country, only the temple to the Divine One in the heart of the capital. Now, it was almost impossible to walk for five minutes without seeing one. Tensions between the Seven Families and the Royal Family had not yet led to any true instability within the Second Country. The roads through the Second Country were still reasonably safe to traverse, and there were no shortages of any food or material, but people were worried.

Some of the Seven Families, like the Veertaks, remained steadfast in their loyalty to the crown, but others had taken advantage of the recent political instability to try to subvert the authority of the Palace and increase their own wealth and power. Of course, while those seeking to gain – or at the very least not lose – power always had enough to eat and trained fighters to keep them safe, the lives of most others were less secure. Problems wrought by the squabbles of the powerful always affected those who lived at the pleasure of the wealthy. The lowborn were keeping a sharp eye on what transpired between the powerful families of the Second Country, and it was obvious that they were worried by what they saw. The concern the shrines represented in turn worried Elen-ai. People often turned to faith in their gods when faith in their leaders faltered, and when people no longer had faith in their leaders, they were often not particularly averse to seeing those leaders leave. Often bloodily.

It was one of the reasons the Family of Assassins would accept a contract on anybody of high or low birth, provided the client was able to pay: the Family did not discriminate. The only strict exception to that neutrality was an unwillingness to touch a member of the Royal Family. Their deaths would cause too much instability, and the Family liked being situated in a prosperous, war-free country. It was good business. The Family's home was in an area that straddled the less dangerous parts of the poor district and the residences of individuals whose wealth offered them some measure of comfort, where the buildings ceased to be made entirely from timber and the more sturdy construction of stonework crept into the designs. In some ways, the Family's home was situated in a space of perfect neutrality between the high and low born, echoing the Family's apolitical nature.

As Elen-ai progressed through the wealthy district, each shrine was grander than the last. Those erected by the poor were all hastily made from whatever materials could be spared – a sun clumsily carved from a piece of scrap timber, a wooden sphere painted yellow or orange, even a simple cloth banner with a sun symbol embroidered or crudely drawn on it. Not so the one outside the fencing arena of the Artisans Quarter. Some fortunate woodcarver would have received a handsome commission for the work. Even the arena, which was easily distinguishable by the height that enabled many people to crowd in to watch the match, was of better construction than those arenas in poorer parts of the city. This one was built mostly from stone and had a fresh coat of paint on the door. Elen-ai could easily imagine the wealthier members of Herran's society cheerfully coming here for an evening's entertainment. One of the favourite pastimes of the Second Country's residents was to watch several fencing bouts across an evening. A night's entertainment would start with matches in which contestants fought with dulled blades and were limited to touches, then progress to first blood as the determinant of victory, and then finally to unrestricted fighting when victory was only determined when one fighter yielded – or died. Those final matches were the most eagerly anticipated. Many a lowborn citizen had made a comfortable fortune from their prowess with a blade, especially those lucky few to be sponsored by one of the Seven Families looking to add a champion fencer to the things about which they could boast. Elen-ai wondered if the shrine was visited by the competitors before they came to fight. Not that a simple shrine to the Sun God would protect any of the contestants from a well-aimed strike, but people liked to believe that something larger than themselves watched over them. Elen-ai personally preferred to place her faith in quick wits and rigorous training.

Predictably, the Katan family's shrine to the Divine One outside their city residence was taller, wider, and more splendid than all of the others combined. Despite her desire to be out of the bitter cold, Elen-ai crossed to the other side of the street so she could better regard it. She snorted in amazement at the gold that covered the orb at the centre of the sun symbol and the gems embedded in the point of each ray emanating from the sphere. Such an extravagant display of wealth did not surprise her in the slightest. Halen, the leader of the Katan family, had aspirations for his granddaughter to be put on the throne. It didn't matter to Halen that Serenah was woefully inadequate as a potential ruler. He did not care that a ruler who had not been trained to possess the neutrality and even-handedness that was crucial when managing the delicate politics of the seven ambitious families, could be disastrous. The presence of a man on the throne following the brutal murder of Queen Latana was reason enough for Halen to justify the even greater instability he risked unleashing by trying to make his granddaughter queen. Though Elen-ai had only met the man once, it was a genuine pleasure to despise him. That vehement dislike was only compounded by what she had just learned about his actions. The rage that left a sick feeling in her throat fought with tense concern at what Halen's ambitions might mean. Taking one final look at the vulgar statement to Katan self-importance, Elen-ai continued on her way.

The ascent up the hill to the Palace offered progressively lovely views of Herran and the harbour around which it had been built. As she climbed higher, the city's rooftops fell together in a curiously harmonious patchwork of reds, greys and blacks, regularly interspersed with curls of smoke hanging softly in the cold air. With distance, even the ramshackle timber houses of the city's lowborn areas were beautiful. Elen-ai paused to turn and look back to the city. She swept her gaze along the crowded streets to the stone blue of the water in the harbour. In sunlight it would sparkle with unparalleled radiance. Today, however, the colour of the overcast sky was mirrored in the grey waves. She couldn't help but think that it suited her current mood.

Finally, she reached the Palace gates. Nearly the height of three people, the Palace's walls were an imposing sight, only rendered plain by the magnificent structure that rose behind them. Made from pale stone that glowed even in the lowest light, the immense complex was home to the Royal Family. Since the formation of the Second Country, its queens had resided within the Palace walls where they had managed the delicate power balance of the country's seven wealthiest families. Glimpses of the Palace could be seen from almost anywhere in Herran, but up close, there was something awe-inspiring about the elegant buildings.

Elen-ai wasn't sure she would ever become accustomed to so brazenly passing through the main gate. Her preferred method of entrance and egress was always the least noticeable one. Assassins who were spotted were not particularly successful in their trade, nor were they particularly long-lived. It was odd to realise that she even recognised the guards who stood on either side of the gates, nodding a quick greeting to them as she passed and receiving one in return.

For a moment, Elen-ai contemplated entering through the servants' door. The entrance was far less conspicuous than the grand doors of the Palace through which people of high birth, or high importance, entered. However, to enter through the servant's door would be more cause for attention given her place by Gidyon's side was well known. So, in defiance of every instinct she had ever cultivated, she gritted her teeth and ascended the stairs to the grand entrance. The door was opened for her and she walked out of the cold into the grand foyer. The foyer was its own testament to the wealth and power of the Royal Family. Several stairs and doors led away from it, hinting at the expanse of the Palace beyond. The foyer itself was huge. Every part of its walls was covered in murals painted by the most skilled artists of the time. Even the ceiling was painted: a blue sky, complete with clouds.

Elen-ai had always found it odd to simulate the open sky while inside, but most people seemed to think it a stroke of the painter's genius. The first time Elen-ai had been in the space, she had been too curious as to why a member of the Family had been summoned by the Queen to actually notice the magnificence of where she was. Now, she had seen the foyer so many times that its splendour was almost lost on her.

Elen-ai made her way through the maze of breathtakingly beautiful corridors with a comfortable familiarity born from months of living there. Sadly, the stone out of which the walls had been built, despite the beauty it offered, held in the cold, encouraging swift passage through the building. Once more, Elen-ai thought wistfully of the Family's home. A clever system spread the heat from a fire throughout the home's walls. It meant that the whole building was a sanctuary from the chill of winter, unlike the Palace where one had to all but run from wing to wing in order to stay warm.

She was struck anew – as she always was – by the strangeness of being greeted by servants as she passed them. Never before had she been so recognised. Indeed, when she reached the council chamber, the guards at the door simply moved aside for her as they saw her approach. While there had initially been some element of novelty that made the experience somewhat enjoyable, she had never managed to shake the discomfort that such special treatment evoked. Anybody who was given immediate, unrestricted access to the most senior members of the Royal Family was uniquely privileged as well as uniquely conspicuous. It went against everything she knew to be at the centre of such attention.

At the opening of the doors, the room's occupants halted their conversation. Maps and charts pinned to the walls, with no regard for the plasterwork, all spoke of warfare strategies. However, the well-groomed and well-dressed men who were conferring inside seemed totally incongruous with war and fighting.

"Well?" The youngest of the group, handsome and authoritative despite his lesser years, seemed to recover himself first. He strode across the room to greet Elen-ai, who was privately delighting in the room's warmth.

Most people in Elen-ai's position would have bowed, faced as they were with their monarch. She did not. Gidyon and Elen-ai had been through too much for such formalities.

Every time she saw Gidyon, it seemed there was a further ageing in his face. At seventeen years old, it seemed hardly fair that the burden of ruling had been thrust upon him, let alone the burden of being the first male to sit on the throne of the Second Country.

His advisers, also his uncles, looked at her expectantly, waiting for the news that she had promised to bring. She remembered the hostility with which they had opposed her presence when Gidyon's late mother, their sister and queen, had engaged Elen-ai to protect Gidyon prior to the public announcement of her decision to make him her heir. Fearing violent reprisal for her boldness to go against centuries of tradition, she had engaged the Family, reasoning that an assassin would know best how another may try to take Gidyon's life. Elen-ai could still recall the suspicion and unease with which the Queen's brothers and advisers viewed the decision to have an assassin protecting the Prince. But their hostility toward Elen-ai had melted away in the face of Elen-ai's obvious loyalty to Gidyon. Perhaps a slight reserve remained, but she could hardly blame them for that. A member of the Family within the Palace was unprecedented. Then again, they were living in unprecedented times.

"The news is not good, I'm afraid," Elen-ai said. She made no effort to hide the grim tightness in her voice, or on her face.

A look of weary resignation flashed across Gidyon's face. He must have been very tired. Normally trying to discern what he was thinking or feeling was impossible. The duties and obligations of the throne not only robbed him of hours of sleep but weighed heavily upon him, too. Even Elen-ai, who was accustomed to very little sleep, would often take herself to bed long before him. It wouldn't be untrue to say that she worried about him.

"Let's have it then," Gidyon said. His face was totally impassive once more.

Elen-ai reported what she had learned at the Family's home: "From all accounts the Katan family is training a small army." She linked her hands behind her back while she observed the reactions of the men.

Silius, the oldest of Gidyon's uncles, displayed his anger in the tightening of his face and the flare of his nostrils. His two brothers, however, were less restrained, expressing their anger and dismay with muttered oaths and profanities. For his part, Gidyon absorbed the news with no visible reaction. After a moment, he let out a slight sigh.

"So it's for what we've been preparing," he said, his voice utterly even. He walked back to the table, Elen-ai falling into step beside him.

For a while, the five of them stood there in silence as the implications of her information were fully considered. During her walk to the Palace, Elen-ai had arrived at the conclusion that Gidyon and his uncles were no doubt drawing now: if Halen Katan would not be given the throne, it seemed he was willing to take it by force.

TWO

Almost all coronations are undertaken with a certain undertone of unacknowledged sadness. In most instances, this makes sense, as the coronation is taking place due to the previous monarch's death. Gidyon's coronation, however, had been characterised by overwhelming grief and confusion, if not also the muted undertone of outrage. The murder of Queen Latana by the deranged Erek Rasatan had plunged the Queendom of the Seven Lakes into a profoundly shocked mourning. Gidyon's mother had been beloved by her subjects, even though she hadn't yet produced a girl to one day take the throne from her. The fact that she had named Gidyon her heir and had been planning to do so for some time left her people in a tricky position: accept the decision of their unjustly murdered queen, or look upon this as a move that destabilised the political balance of the Second Country while ignoring generations of history and tradition. At first, the grief and shock had meant that not much thought had been given to who succeeded Latana. But as time wore on, it seemed most people had arrived at an uneasy middle ground: not violently opposed to the prospect of a man on the throne while remaining deeply uncomfortable with it and what it may mean.

What people didn't know was that Erek might have been Gidyon's father and he had killed the Queen in a jealous rage following his discovery that Latana had, unbeknown to anyone, been conducting an affair with Zekken Aadran for several years. The only thing that made this worse was that Zekken considered himself Gidyon's father, as Gidyon had been conceived during the Queen's first Season – the only time that Latana had actually adhered to protocol and taken more than one man to her bed. Had this been public knowledge, support for Gidyon would have fallen away entirely. It was of the utmost importance that the Royal Family remain neutral. That was why the Season theoretically ensured that the father of any child produced from the liaisons between the queen and eligible male members of the Seven Families during the few days of feasting and socialising was never known. It meant that the queen's children were not obligated to any one of the families. Fears over whether as a man Gidyon could keep the Royal Family's neutrality intact would boil over into infuriated rejection of him were the Queen's lapse in judgment ever known.

However, shock had still been the dominant emotion on the day of Gidyon's coronation. He had walked through the streets, taking practically the same route of his mother's funeral procession, all the way through Herran until he arrived at the Temple of the Divine One where he was officially blessed by a Priest and Priestess before making his way back up the hill to the Palace. However, unlike Latana's funeral parade when he had been surrounded by his uncles, Elen-ai, and the heads of the Seven Families, this path he had walked alone, still wearing the silver mourning colours underneath the purple and gold cloak that fell from his shoulders. The streets were no less crowded than at Latana's funeral, as the people lined up to lay their eyes on the man who dared take the throne.

In truth, Elen-ai could think of nobody better to rule. She had accompanied Gidyon through the Second Country following an attempt on his life, orchestrated as it turned out, by Erek Rasatan. He had undertaken the journey to both gain the support of the Seven Families for his claim to the throne and try to determine who was behind the attack. Following her initial impression that he was a brat, Elen-ai had arrived at the realisation that in fact he had the makings of a great ruler. It was why she had helped him to discover that Erek Rasatan was behind the attempt on his life. It was why she had returned to his side, even after he had tried to send her back to the Family.

That hot, late summer evening on which she had scaled the wall of the Palace and crept through the grounds was inscribed on her memory. She could still taste the scent of the night-blooming flowers in the garden that she had used to gain entrance to the Palace building. Guards patrolled at very commendable intervals, but Elen-ai moved past them, invisible to anyone, even if they were looking directly at her. The Family's devotion to the Shadow God gave them skills that less enlightened individuals might term magic. The Family had always termed them forgotten skills, capabilities that might once have been possessed by all in the time when the divide between gods and humans had been less clear, but had been forgotten when the veil between divine and mortal had grown almost impermeable, and most people in the world simply viewed their god as an oath to be used in emotional moments.

She effortlessly remembered the way to Gidyon's room, even though the number of days she had spent in the enormous, complex Palace had totalled only a few. She entered through a window that had been carelessly flung open to allow the scant night breeze in to cool the room. Given that Gidyon's chambers overlooked a sheer wall that no ordinary person could climb, Elen-ai hadn't been particularly outraged that the window had been left open, although she was certain whoever had opened the window had not ever considered that it may invite danger to Gidyon's side. She found the room empty and settled herself in a chair to wait. True to form, when he had finally come in, he didn't seem surprised in the slightest to find her there.

"What are you doing here?" he had asked calmly, blue eyes fixed on her as he shrugged off the ceremonial jacket, sighing slightly in relief to be free of the restrictive garment.

"I want to help you." Elen-ai remained seated. The formality of standing at her ruler's entrance, let alone bowing to him, was already long behind them.

Gidyon arched an eyebrow. "I told you that your contract was fulfilled." He crossed the room and poured himself a measure of something from a tall bottle. He didn't drink it, though. He merely swirled the liquid around in the glass vessel as he gazed into its depths.

"I..." Elen-ai faltered, uncertain of what to say, of how to convince him that she should be by his side. So she said nothing, allowing her silence to speak for itself.

Gidyon did not immediately say anything. "Are you certain?"

There was a certain tightness in the way he asked that gave the question a weight and meaning it otherwise would not have had. Gidyon had his uncles, but being the ruler of a country, especially the first male ruler, left him apart from everybody else, and perhaps the only person who knew that, along with his other secrets, was Elen-ai.

She hadn't even heard the end of his question before she was nodding. "Gidyon, I am yours to command." She was surprised by how seriously she meant it.

He took a sip of his drink. Elen-ai knew the action wasn't because he had any great fondness for liquor. She had once nearly killed him by making him drink ale. She would have bet that the action was to mask some emotion that he didn't want her to see, to give him time to compose himself. "You are free to go at any time—"

"I am here, Gidyon," she interrupted him, her voice firm.

"I will have rooms made up for you. Sleeping in my room is perhaps not appropriate." His voice was rough with emotion and his eyes perhaps a bit brighter than normal, but Elen-ai pretended not to notice either of those things.

"It's a good idea. Although people will still probably assume we're lovers," she said, the slightest hint of mischief in her voice.

"And you will need a new wardrobe," he continued, as though she hadn't referred to the assumption that had been made about them in the spring when they were travelling through the Second Country. He had been mortified by that assumption, even after Elen-ai had pointed out it hid both their purpose and her position as a member of the Family. It seemed he was still mortified by it now.

"What?" Elen-ai made no attempt to mask her horror at the prospect of a new wardrobe. She was perfectly comfortable in her own clothes

"Well, we need an explanation for you to be here. Given you are low-born it would be plausible to say that I have taken you on as a special advis-er."

Elen-ai nodded. What he said made sense. Only those born into the Royal Family or the Seven Families had an unbroken first name. It meant that the moment they introduced themselves, it was clear they were someone to be treated with appropriate respect – or disrespect, depending on your atti-tude. Indeed, all lowborn women had the suffix -ai or -am at the end of their names, while men were given the suffixes -et or -en. From the second that she was introduced, everyone would be aware of the station of her birth. Yet that was advantageous, as it meant that she could easily claim credibility within the Palace as Gidyon's liaison to the people, something he most defi-nitely was in need of given the complicated mix of feelings with which he was viewed by most of his subjects.

Gidyon continued, sounding completely serious. "Well, if you are to take such a title, you must look the part. That means a new wardrobe full of beautiful clothes."

"I regret coming back," Elen-ai said. The idea of being fitted for a variety of clothes, or even of being forced to be the subject of a discussion about the fabrics and colours that best brought out "the depths of her dark eyes" and "complemented the colour of her skin" (phrases she had heard used in several tailors and been thoroughly grateful that she was merely passing through), seemed the most awful torture that she could ever envisage for anybody, let alone herself.

Gidyon nodded as he came to sit next to her. "Oh yes, a beautiful collection. An abundance of clothes for you, in fact. And many, many dresses." He sounded so sincere that for one horrifying moment, Elen-ai believed that he would force her into a dress.

"Well played," she muttered as she took the glass flute from his hand and drained the expensive vessel of its very fine contents. The feel of the cool glass against her fingers was a shock. She had only ever held glass drinking vessels on a select number of occasions – most of them during her time with Gidyon. "I am yours to command, my King," she repeated her earlier statement, although the false sweetness to her tone undercut the gravitas of the comment. "And I can't imagine a better way to use my many skills than putting me in a dress," she added, dropping the sickly sweet tone and adopting one of most fervent sarcasm.

Gidyon chuckled. "I've missed you these last weeks," he admitted, leaning back into the cushions of the couch. He seemed too tired to pretend he didn't want her there any longer. His expression sobered as he put his hand on hers for the briefest of instances. "Thank you, Elen-ai." The emphatic gratitude had brought unexpected tears to her eyes.

Now, standing in the council room, considering the implications of Halen Katan's actions in his attempt to take the throne, that summer evening seemed an age away. If Gidyon had seemed tired then, it was nothing compared with the fatigue that constantly seemed to weigh on him now. The escalating belligerence of the Fourth Country, who seemed disinclined to curtail the border raids resulting from their own political instability, the hostility within the Second Country to a man on the throne, the actions of Halen and his allies to destabilise Gidyon, and of course, the normal requirements of being a ruler, had aged Gidyon far beyond his seventeen years.

Gidyon leaned on the table at the room's centre. He looked down at his hands as he spoke. "All right then, let's have it."

Elen-ai spared a moment to share a glance with Gidyon's uncles. They all looked as though they were bracing themselves to be severely beaten.

"As we know, the Katan estate is one of the most remote in the Second Country. It seems Halen has been using that to his advantage, training a small army without anybody noticing."

"How is he arming those people? We control where weapons are made," Silius asked. His features, which naturally fell into a disapproving expression, had arranged themselves in a look which was even more unimpressed than usual.

Gidyon answered before Elen-ai could. "The Fourth Country is trading directly with him. His land shares a border with them, after all."

"Of course they're trading with Halen." If Silius' lips were pressed any more tightly together, they would disappear.

"What do we know about this?" asked Kaine, Gidyon's youngest uncle.

Gidyon shrugged as he turned to look at the war charts on the wall. Elen-ai wondered if he was thinking about how he would fight Halen on a battlefield. The thought perturbed her. War had not touched the Second Country for centuries thanks to the manner in which power had been divided and the impartiality of the queens. It need not touch the land now but for the small-mindedness of certain people.

"I only know that there are discrepancies in the trade reports they have been providing us," Gidyon said. "I thought they were incompetent or being deliberately vague..."

"I know a trader from the Fourth Country who is often in Herran," Elen-ai volunteered.

Gidyon remained looking thoughtfully at the charts. "Would she know anything?"

"Would it hurt to ask?" Nikalus, Gidyon's other uncle, asked.

Taking Gidyon's lack of further comment as an approval, Elen-ai said, "Next time she's here, I'll speak with her."

"Where would we be without you, Elen-ai?" Of Gidyon's three uncles, Kaine had taken to her the most. Given to mischief when the situation permitted, he winked at her across the table, gesturing with a small inclination of his head toward Silius who was clearing his throat in preparation to voice an objection.

"We do have our own informants who can find out the goings on within the Seven Families, and beyond," Silius pointed out to his brother coolly, apparently playing right into Kaine's verbal provocation.

Elen-ai swallowed a smile as she again caught Kaine's eye and saw the satisfied twinkle there.

Gidyon, who had seemed to be lost in his own thoughts and had missed the baiting of Silius, turned back to face his uncles. "Yes, but we have something they do not. An Elen-ai." He glanced at her, a tiny smile on his face. It brightened him, made him almost look his age. All too quickly, the smile was replaced by the solemnity that had become customary for him.

"And Halen?" Kaine prompted.

"The Council of Families will take place in a few days. I will wait to decide how we act until after I see what he does there," Gidyon said.

Silius gave a satisfied nod.

"We were just about finished here before Elen-ai came in. Is there anything else pressing?" Gidyon looked at his three uncles, his family. They shook their heads.

"Good. I believe I have a mathematics class that I should attend. My poor tutor, Gled-am, has come here for the last three days and each day has been sent away not having seen me because I have had to attend to something else. I am determined to see her today. Elen-ai, will you walk with me?"

Every so often, it was almost possible to forget that Gidyon was in charge, that he could end or start meetings as he pleased. Then he would decisively conclude matters, and the absolute certainty with which he conducted himself made it impossible to ever doubt his authority.

As Elen-ai walked out of the room with Gidyon, she was curious, not for the first time, how his uncles felt that he confided in her above anyone else. But the thought was driven from her head by her friend's slight frown.

"How worried should I be?" Gidyon asked as they walked.

"How worried are you?"

He chuckled without mirth. "Oh, very good. We'll make a statesperson out of you yet." He slipped his hands into his pockets. "Do you think we can get away without war? I really would prefer not to be known as the king whose reign saw the first war in the Second Country since the modern state's inception." It did not escape her attention that Gidyon had waited until there were no guards or servants nearby who might hear the question before he asked it.

She looked at the beautiful tiles they walked past. The gentle geometric arrangement was curiously meditative. "I honestly don't know. Perhaps we may be able to corner Halen so that he feels he cannot march against you."

Gidyon made a sound that suggested he was not optimistic. "Where is he finding these people who are willing to march against me, anyway?" He sounded curious more than anything else, but Elen-ai knew that frustration lurked underneath his voice.

"I'm not so certain that they're willing to march against you as much as unwilling to resist the lure of his coin," Elen-ai said.

"Are people that untethered to the throne?" Gidyon sounded genuinely shocked.

"The throne on which your mother sat, no. The throne on which you sit..." She let the unfinished sentence complete itself. It was not necessary for her to say that the people did not love him as they had his mother. Few monarchs could be loved in the way that Latana had been adored. But Gidyon's sex made it even more difficult for the people to come close to loving him with the adoring fidelity with which they had regarded Latana.

To Elen-ai's amusement, Gidyon cursed under his breath. It was not something he did often.

"Are you sleeping enough, Gid?" She asked the question even though she knew what the answer would be.

Gidyon threw her an amused look. "Of course I'm not," he replied. "Divine One, it's cold," he added, pulling his jacket around himself more securely.

Without thought, Elen-ai unwrapped her scarf and offered it to him. He waved her offer aside. "I'm all right, but thank you."

With a shrug she draped the garment back around her neck. They were nearly at the room where Gidyon's mathematics tutor was waiting. He had ordered that every effort be expended to make the poor woman comfortable while she waited for him to find a spare moment in which he could see her.

"Do you really think we're going to end up at war?" Elen-ai asked, unable to resist asking the question that had preyed upon her mind since she had learned about Halen's actions.

Gidyon stopped and looked properly at her. As was his custom, he did not answer her question immediately. She could almost see him choosing each word.

"Honestly, I don't know. But I'll do everything I can to try to stop it."

She could see the weariness in the shadows smudged under those violently blue eyes and the tiny lines that had worked their way into the smooth skin of his face. She worried that among the spun gold of his hair she would soon be able to see streaks of grey. However, none of that marred his beauty. If Erek was his father and not Zekken, Gidyon had definitely inherited the man's good looks. Erek Rasatan had been the most attractive man Elen-ai had ever seen. In some ways it was sad that he had been so tormented by his unassuming yet cruel mother to the point that his own sanity was so tenuous.

Elen-ai wanted to take her king in her arms and hold him close, lift the burden of everything – the question of who his father was, grief for his mother, worry about his position, and everything in between – for just the slightest of moments. But despite their closeness, he was still her king, and that was one line she could not cross. She kept her arms at her sides as he walked away.

THREE

Twice a year the Council of Families was held. It was the occasion on which the heads of the Seven Families would come to Herran and meet with the queen – or king as the case now was. It was first conceived as a mostly ceremonial occasion when the families would formally present their taxes to the queen in a demonstration of their fidelity to the crown. However, over the years it had also become a time when the Seven Families would convene with the queen to negotiate over administrative and political matters such as rates of tariffs or the maintenance of roads through various parts of the Queendom. It was also considered a forum in which the power politics of the Seven Families were exercised, for allegiances to be subtly displayed, or challenges to be made to one another. This was Gidyon's second Council as king, but the first had been so soon after the death of his mother that all of the families had maintained a certain respectful restraint. In the intervening months, that decorum had apparently fled and the power games had returned with vengeful intensity, amplified by the underlying knowledge of the Katan desire to usurp Gidyon's authority.

The leaders of the Seven Families and Gidyon sat in a room of understated magnificence at a large circular table. The varnish on the table's wooden surface reflected the flickering light of the fire that fought the chill trying to make its way into the room. Elen-ai stood against one wall, nearly invisible among the shadows. Nobody had made any comment, although she was certain her presence was not entirely unnoticed. She had met all of the family leaders the previous year, when she had been introduced as Gidyon's companion and assumed lover. It was the monarch's prerogative to allow an adviser into the room, although this convention was more observed in not being exercised. Her lowborn status made it less affronting than had it been one of Gidyon's uncles, especially as she had never once opened her mouth to yawn, let alone utter some comment that might upset the delicate political construction of the discussion.

This was the third, and thankfully final, day of the Council and the second day Elen-ai had quietly observed the proceedings. She had blessedly managed to avoid attending the first day of the Council by going down into Herran to determine when her merchant friend from the Fourth Country would be docking. She had taken her time, ensuring that she missed almost the entirety of the day. The other two days, she had not been so fortunate, and could find no excuse in the face of Gidyon's request that she observe, as perhaps she might notice something he missed. She could hardly wait for the Council to be concluded.

"Your Majesty, I'm just not certain that we should be made to subsidise the instruction of teachers. After all, the mandatory education of our people in letters and numbers is an edict that does come from the crown," Karan Tak said. She was a broad woman whose firm demeanour left no doubt of her competence, and while Elen-ai normally quite liked Karan, she found herself disagreeing with the Tak stance on this particular matter.

"So how do you propose teachers are paid, then?" Gidyon asked calmly, his fingers interlinked on the table in front of him. He did not appear to be particularly put out by the understated aggression with which Karan had challenged him.

"Well, the Veertak family could always—"

Valena, the matriarch of the Veertak family, used her advanced age like a battering ram to commit the otherwise unforgivable act of interrupting one of the other family heads. Almost as ancient as her husband, she nevertheless had one of the sharpest minds that Elen-ai had ever come across.

"Are you proposing that we pauper ourselves to pay those who teach your people to read and count, Karan?"

"Well, not exactly," Karan said, but she was again interrupted, this time by the woman to her right, Arlena Aadran. Another frighteningly competent woman, her family were the Taks' traditional ally.

"That's not what she meant, Valena, and you know it."

Not easily goaded, Valena stared down the Aadran matriarch. "What exactly did she mean then, Arlena?"

To Elen-ai's dismay, Gidyon spoke before anyone else could. She had been looking forward to an escalation between the three women. Her money would have remained on Valena, and it would have been very entertaining to watch the old woman put the Taks and Aadrans in their place, especially given how accustomed they were to getting their way through combining their wealth and power.

"The benefits of having people able to read and count have been well established. I think all of the families here have profited from their people's knowledge with sums. To name one example, being able to make an inventory of any commodity means you can keep track of your livestock, or grain, or ceramics not only when they are sold, but wherever they are. My great-grandmother's edict regarding the education of our people was a good one and there is no reason to remove it. The Veertak scholars are the best positioned to instruct teachers for all the families. As it stands, no alternative funding method seems viable. I think perhaps it is best if the existing way remains: all families will pay a set sum to the Veertaks for the instruction of teachers."

At this, Halen cleared his throat ever so gently.

"Something to add, my lord Katan?" Gidyon asked politely.

"Oh my King, it is nothing," Halen demurred.

"I welcome any contribution from those whose longer lives than mine may offer some unknown experience." Gidyon's courtesy masked that he was throwing words at Halen that the man had once said to him. Elen-ai swallowed a smile.

"Well, if you insist, then. I just wonder whether, given that the Veertaks themselves pay nothing for the training of teachers, if it wouldn't seem to the uneducated observer as though you were displaying a certain favouritism toward them?" The ingratiating demeanour with which Halen suggested Gidyon was playing favourites had Elen-ai all but reaching for the many blades concealed about her person. It was undeniably true that the Veertaks were the closest to Gidyon of all the families. It was also undeniably true that the Veertaks had never demonstrated a significant desire to expand their power, merely an impulse to protect what power they already had, as well as the knowledge that resided within their estate. As scholars, they controlled the Second Country's institutions of knowledge. All members of the Veertak family were bookish to some extent, less concerned with politics and power than the acquisition of knowledge. Varl and Valena were unquestionably two of the most formidable scholars of the time. Although, they could be as skilled at political games as anyone else in that Council room, if the need arose.

Gidyon might have pressed his lips together in rage, or he may simply have been musing on Halen's words. Elen-ai knew it was the former but nobody else would have.

"My lord Halen, you are very kind to be so concerned with perceptions of my position. I am so fortunate to know someone is so interested in my welfare. I will certainly weigh your words carefully, but I would not want to make too hasty a decision. For now, I think things should stay the way they are."

A muscle tensed in Halen's neck. It really must have galled him to be verbally outmanoeuvred by a boy young enough to be his grandson, Elen-ai thought. She delighted in that fact. The small victories were just as important to relish as the important ones, she told herself.

The meeting dragged on. Petty issues were raised and resolved, and everybody vied for just a little more power, to prove how much more important they were than anyone else in the room. Even the Veertaks, who Elen-ai adored, at times were more competitive than was strictly necessary. But perhaps that was her view as an outsider. Nobody else seemed to think the subtle assertions of authority or wealth or cleverness were unusual. Elen-ai realised how commonplace and relatively minor this sniping was because she saw how the room's occupants reacted when the true power move of the afternoon took place.

The weak afternoon light was valiantly trying to illuminate the room and Elen-ai was preoccupied with the desperate hope that the talks might soon draw to a close when Julyana Bertak shifted her enormous bulk, making the chair creak ominously, and spoke. "My King, what is this about reforms to the judicial system?"

Everybody stilled. Halen couldn't resist a smile of smug satisfaction. Elen-ai thought it stupid that he would reveal the Bertaks were so closely allied with him, but perhaps that was in itself a certain show of power on his part.

Julyana Bertak was not by any description a good looking woman. Perhaps once she had been, but any attractiveness had been lost under a mound of fat and years of snide superiority that had distorted her features. The only remotely lovely thing about her appearance was an unexpectedly delicate nose, but that only served to emphasise the ugly vastness that was the rest of her. Perhaps her physical enormity was her inner twistedness made manifest. Certainly, Elen-ai knew a number of people whose generous girth was not accompanied by such a foul personality. Julyana had received Gidyon and Elen-ai during their spring travels in a manner that was unpardonably rude. Upon their departure, Elen-ai had offered Gidyon her skills as an assassin to exact vengeance upon the woman. To her regret, he had declined. It was an offer that she resolved to remind him about once this infernal meeting was over.

"What do you mean, Julyana?" Gidyon asked. It was the first time that he had not addressed someone by their title, indicating she had crossed a line. Arlena Aadran straightened; the imposing woman's gaze was darting between Gidyon and Julyana with an almost predatory focus.

"Well, my King, the manner in which you plan to separate the different types of cases to be heard, and the changes you propose to the local magistrates are very ambitious," Julyana said. Her tone was so sweet that it could only be interpreted as false pleasantness.

Elen-ai wondered if the roll of flesh that bulged over Julyana's collar would impede the progress of a blade. As far as she was concerned, Julyana would make an exemplary test subject for that question.

"But they're good changes," Gidyon protested. "As it stands, more often than not, the challenge to a decision by a local magistrate costs lowborn more than they would stand to win or regain. And the courts in Herran have weeks of waiting time to hear cases due to the lack of differentiation."

"That may be, but people can only take so much change and you are imposing a lot of it," Halen interjected gently.

As much as Elen-ai hated to admit it, the odious man had a point. Gidyon evidently recognised that fact, too. After a very unpleasant moment of silence, he said, "Once again, my lord Katan, you have given me something to think about. Thank you for bringing this to my attention, lady Bertak, lord Katan. I would still like to implement the changes, but perhaps over a longer period of time, and only once I have considered suggestions from all of you, of course."

And there Elen-ai saw the brilliance of how Halen had played the meeting. His comment about the Veertaks had pointed out that Gidyon possibly was closer to one family than the others – breaking the monarch's requirement of impartiality – but it had been made in such an obvious way that Gidyon would dismiss it and the accompanying request to reconsider his stance on the matter of funding for teachers. But had Gidyon rejected his second, far more reasonable point, in support of another family too, Halen could have plausibly claimed that Gidyon was being a pigheaded child who would not listen to wisdom when it was offered to him and was ignoring anything that Halen said because of the well known – if not openly discussed – acrimony between Gidyon and the Katan family. There had been no choice but for Gidyon to heed Halen's suggestion.

The meeting was finally concluded about an hour after Halen's victory. The attendees left to prepare for that evening's feast to celebrate the conclusion of the Winter Council of Families. Elen-ai fell into step with Gidyon as he made his way back to his rooms. Finally alone, he allowed his frustration to show.

"That was stupid of me," he said quietly.

"Don't feel bad about it." Elen-ai valiantly tried to console him.

"I should have known that he had something else planned. Now he looks like he can best me. Which he can."

"So best him next time," she suggested.

"No. I have to best him every time," the King snapped. "This is not about who wins the best of three. This is about whether or not I am his monarch, whether he kneels to my authority. He cannot do that some of the time. He has to do that all of the time."

There was no response to that, really. "I'm sorry," Elen-ai said eventually.

"I am sorry, too. It is wrong of me to take my anger out on you," he said with a sigh.

"I'm here to help you. If being the target for anger you can't express elsewhere helps, I suppose I can manage that," she said.

They reached Gidyon's rooms. He nodded a greeting to the guards outside his door who stood to attention at his approach. Shadows from the enormous fire in his sitting room danced across the small mountain of papers had been placed neatly on his desk. At the sight of it, Gidyon groaned. "Two hours until dinner commences and I am going to be spending them reading."

"Anything I can do to help?" Elen-ai asked.

"Do you want the throne?" Gidyon offered in jest as he used a taper to light the candle sconces above his desk.

"I think I'll pass on that one," she muttered. "Don't want to take all the fun away from you."

Gidyon laughed. A genuine laugh this time.

"You know that offer still stands for me to take care of Julyana Bertak, by the way," Elen-ai added. "At least Halen has the stomach to try and take you on directly. She's just wallowing around with whoever she thinks will give her the most power."

Gidyon made an amused sound as he read the first paper. "Don't tempt me," he said distractedly.

"I was trying to figure out if her bulk would act as a sort of shield," Elen-ai commented conversationally.

Gidyon looked up, amusement written in the arch of his eyebrows and set of his lips. "I dare you to say that to her tonight."

"If I do it, will you give me her lands?"

"You would almost certainly do a better job of managing them than her. Divine One, she's a right terror."

"How do you think her husband faced the prospect of procreating with her? Carefully?" Her lips twitched at the thought of Julyana's slender husband approaching her bed with timidity if not outright fear for his life.

Gidyon tried and failed to look disapproving. "There are a great many things about her to mock other than her size," he commented.

She threw herself onto the couch with a sigh and propped her feet on one of its high sides. "Yes, but I hate her so much, that I don't feel she deserves my effort when it comes to insulting her."

Gidyon glanced at her, evidently giving up on his point. "Shouldn't you be doing something assassin-y?"

"I'm too tired after that boring meeting." She gave an exaggerated yawn.

"Here I was thinking the life of an assassin was all discipline and rigidity," Gidyon muttered, lowering his eyes back to the document in his hands.

"Nope, I think you were mistaking it for your life," Elen-ai told him cheerfully.

Making a noise of disgust, Gidyon paced as he read.

"What's this?" She plucked several drawings from the table in front of the couch. "Fancy." The pages were of vellum, normally reserved for important or official documents, rather than the paper pulp or cloth scraps that were used to make pages of lesser quality.

"Oh, they're proposed drawings for a new wing to the Palace," Gidyon said distractedly.

"Another wing? The Palace has so many wings that I can't remember them all."

"Apparently it's the thing to do when you want to be impressive. Build something," Gidyon said.

"Yes, but where are you going to build it?"

"Mm, it is a problem. I was thinking that I would tear down an existing wing. Maybe this one."

"But there's nothing wrong with this one," Elen-ai protested.

"I have been in these rooms since I was ten. I think it is time for a change."

"So pick one of the other five hundred rooms that nobody sleeps in."

"I really think we should rebuild this wing. It is very old."

"So? There's still nothing wrong with it. It's a perfectly good wing." Elen-ai held up two of the drawings side by side. Both designs certainly looked grand.

"Nonsense." Gidyon's tone was condescending. "Apparently the foundations of the wing are in need of modifications. And haven't you noticed that the corridors here are tiled, not painted? It's so outdated. Anyone who sees it will think that we cannot afford to stay up to date. As silly as it sounds, these sorts of perceptions do matter."

"So fix the foundations and slap a few paintings in the corridors. You don't need to tear down the whole thing." Elen-ai couldn't understand why Gidyon was so adamant about this.

"We already have one room in the Divine-cursed wing that can't be used." It wasn't quite an exclamation, but Elen-ai heard the slight edge of distress in Gidyon's tone and immediately understood her error. Gidyon's mother had been killed only a few rooms away. Nobody had entered the chambers since her funeral. It seemed the worst form of sacrilege to disturb the site of such a gruesome and unnatural crime. It was little wonder that

Gidyon wanted to tear down the wing in which his mother had died before his eyes.

"I like this design with the curly bits on top." There was nothing else Elen-ai could say. Unless he specifically referenced Queen Latana, she never discussed the matter with him. She did not ask anything further about the Queen's murder. She knew Gidyon wished to speak no more of the subject.

"Curly bits, really?"

"As well you know, I am neither a designer nor mathematician," Elen-ai pointed out.

"I will keep in mind your preference for the curly bits." Gidyon smirked at the term, then returned to his reading.

Elen-ai rested her head against the couch's arm. As she reposed, she thought back to the meeting. Halen's play concerned her more than she had let on to Gidyon. While the man might have been contemptible, he was also clever, and he had his sights set very obviously on the Palace. He was even clever enough to use the fact that he wasn't particularly well liked to his advantage. That was troubling. She ruminated on what she had learned in the Family's home. The fact that he was buying himself an army was worrying, especially given the belligerence he had demonstrated in the Council. While every family was expanding the size of their household guard under a variety of pretences, this was something else entirely.

When she was certain he wasn't looking at her, Elen-ai sneaked a glance at Gidyon. He seemed to have shrugged off the anger at Halen's behaviour and the anger at himself for falling into the man's trap, but she knew that he was readying himself for the evening's social activities and the traps Halen may have set for him there.

FOUR

Of all the things about the royal life that Elen-ai loathed – and there were many – she despised the social events the most. Very rarely were there any truly inconspicuous places for her to unobtrusively skulk, and inevitably someone would seek her out. Since Gidyon had announced that he would marry a lowborn woman from Herran to ensure that any child of his would be as free from political obligation as any of the Second Country's heirs were supposed to be, the world had simply assumed she was the King's lover, currently being groomed to marry him. That meant that at social functions, she was viewed as a potentially sympathetic and useful ear. She was regularly accosted by any number of people with an ingratiating smile etched into their faces, and a request that she appreciate the importance of something near and dear to their heart swiftly following their introduction. This torment was compounded by the fact that she was inevitably forced to wear some ridiculous garment or another. Gidyon had yet to coerce her into wearing a skirt or dress, but he had bet her if he could convince Silius to dance at the upcoming midwinter festival, she would have to wear a skirt to the next social occasion. While she was confident Gidyon would not be successful, she nevertheless feared he may miraculously accomplish the impossible. Elen-ai might have been an assassin of the Family, trained in the art of being invisible, of winning any fight in which she might find herself, but the prospect of being put into a dress left her terrified.

Tonight she wore a dark green tunic over a pair of grey trousers. Gidyon really hadn't been joking about a new wardrobe for her, as Elen-ai had ruefully discovered. The material was so fine and soft that she imagined the value of her clothes would easily buy at least one of the houses in the lowborn district outright. The thin fabric and beautiful cut of the garments made them totally impractical and as such, something she would never have chosen for herself. However, as Gidyon had pointed out when they had chosen which clothes would become part of her new Court-appropriate wardrobe (he had actually taken time out of his schedule to inflict this small torment upon her), if she didn't have fine clothes she would look totally out of place. And that would raise further questions about who and what she was. Adding to tonight's frustration, one of the Palace tailors, skilled in everything from repairing a torn garment at the last minute to the artistry of makeup and coiffure, had tried to do things to her face and hair as she had prepared. Elen-ai had restrained her impulse to pull one of the blades concealed on her person and brandish at him and settled for swearing at him until the man had fled in terror.

The evening began with two fencing champions duelling for the enjoyment of the gathered families. Men and women across the Second Country competed in arenas every night for the amusement of high and low born alike. The Seven Families even sponsored certain fighters, taking a percentage of any winnings – and glory – that their swords might collect. Elen-ai herself almost never went to the arenas. She had never found much point in fighting for the entertainment of others. Yet she had no choice but to watch tonight's match. To add to her discomfort, Elen-ai ended up sitting next to Halen, whether by chance or his design, she couldn't tell. She made a valiant effort to watch the match and maintain an internal commentary on the silliness of such a functional skill being made into a spectacle so she could ignore the smugness that radiated from the man. He was sucking on the type of fruit lozenge often favoured as a means to sweeten the breath. Elen-ai could hear it clinking against his teeth.

"You know, lady Elen-ai, some say the art of swordcraft is much like the intrigue of politics." He spoke conversationally, but Elen-ai knew he was leading to some point.

"My lord Katan, surely politics is far more deadly than swordcraft," she replied, struggling to keep the venom from her tone.

Halen chuckled softly. The clash of metal rang across the room as the competitors engaged. "My lady, perhaps you should consider the merits of my analogy. Look at how the opponents size each other up before truly attacking. Even when they do engage, almost in every exchange neither swordsperson is injured. They retreat, regather and then wait for the next engagement. The fighter who can understand the rhythm of the other the best will see a weakness, and then practice and patience will give them the necessary edge to snatch victory."

Elen-ai looked away from the fight so that she could see him properly. Halen's face was flushed with some form of excitement. The light from the torches flickered across his features, making him appear alternately wreathed in shadow or bathed in harsh light. She thought about what a blade would feel like slipping into the delicate flesh of his neck.

"Well, my lord, when you put it that way, I see the persuasiveness of such a perspective," she said.

His smile was like a curved blade.

"Then again, others may simply interpret such a thoughtful analysis as someone attempting to draw a parallel when none exists in an attempt to sound unnecessarily dramatic," she added. If she wasn't to have the pleasure of killing this man, she would at least enjoy the slight puckering of his lips as he heard her insult. It was a truly exquisite feeling.

"You know, lady Elen-ai, you remain a mystery. Your origins, and why our King seems to trust you so much, have yet to be revealed to me." His abrupt change of subject was either because he had been stung by her insult, or because this was the real reason for striking up a conversation. She suspected the latter.

"There are a great many mysteries in this world of ours, my lord," Elen-ai responded coyly.

"I wonder how the people of our country would feel if they knew how close you were to him," he murmured.

"I imagine safer than they would with an inexperienced girl-child on the throne," she replied.

Halen laughed quietly. The sweet smell of his fruit lozenge wafted across the space between them. "An attack rather than a parry. I suspect my little comparison may have merit after all."

The blade on her left arm was so slender that she could have slipped it into the flesh of his side without anyone noticing. But she held the impulse in check. "The only problem with your analogy, my lord, is that it assumes both contestants will abide by the rules. In such a situation, I would likely throw a punch or kick to gain the upper hand. I can't help but feel you may be overtaken by a similar urge," she said. "Excuse me, I think we've missed the winning exchange," she added before he could respond.

Indeed, a round of applause filled the room as the young woman, panting heavily, held her blade aloft and bowed low to Gidyon.

"It seems tonight's loser may lose more than the match," Halen observed, gesturing to the defeated swordsman who was bleeding heavily from a wound in his chest.

"It seems a waste," Elen-ai commented as attendants ran from their place waiting at the side of the court and tried to staunch the bleeding.

"It is an unfortunate possibility when one plays such games," Halen replied over the applause.

Dinner was served immediately following the conclusion of the match. It seemed a callously gruesome thing to do, given the likely loss of the loser's life, but Elen-ai was grateful for any opportunity to get away from Halen. She feared her resolve to not stab him may falter. To her immense relief, Elen-ai was seated next to Varl Veertak. Halen was two to Gidyon's right, far away from Elen-ai. She had seen his granddaughter and would-be queen, Serenah, earlier in the evening, but the girl was so uninspiring that unless one was looking directly at her, it was easy to not see her.

"And what did you think of the sword fight, my dear?" Varl asked. He and his wife were the only two family leaders to know she was a member of the Family. Valena had discerned it almost immediately upon meeting Elen-ai, but they both had promised to not speak of it to anyone.

"Show fighting. If either were in a real fight they wouldn't have lasted a minute," Elen-ai replied around a mouthful of food. The food, as always exquisite, was served on delicate Katan plates. Each plate alone was worth a fortune. It was unfortunate that such a necessary display of wealth and status came from the family of the man who would remove that power and wealth from Gidyon if he got the opportunity.

Varl chuckled. "I do regret I'll never see you with a blade in your hand," he admitted in an undertone. "I've heard that skills like yours are unforgettable to witness," he added, avoiding any overt reference to her origin.

Elen-ai smiled and shook her head. The tiny man's thirst for knowledge was endearing. In his youth it would have been terrifying. "If you ever do get a chance to witness such a thing, my lord – Varl," she corrected herself when he made a noise of protest, "I'm not sure it will be an opportune moment to appreciate such a spectacle. My people aren't particularly interested in fighting for the amusement of others." Elen-ai pictured the triumphant face of the winner. By the look of her, the woman had been lowborn, which gave Elen-ai a small measure of solace. Many champion swordfighters came from families of people with at least some power. The whole exercise still seemed a terrific waste to her, though.

Varl shook his head, fluffy white hair quivering with the movement. Elen-ai saw his attention fall on Wenden Rasatan. Once possessing a reputation for being domineering and forceful, since his son's regicide and death, and the apparent suicide of his wife upon hearing of her son's act, Wenden had become a spectre of that image. To what extent he had been encouraged to present a blusterous persona by his cruel wife, Elen-ai was uncertain. Since the unconscionable crime of his son, though, trade with the Rasatan family, whose primary source of income came from fish in the estuary within their lands, had become a dirty task, undertaken only in the barest minimum.

"Poor man," Varl said softly.

Elen-ai did not know what to say. Wenden had said practically nothing in the Council, for the most part simply looking down at the table. Nobody was particularly surprised. Not only was the Rasatan family fortune being eroded by the diminished trade, but perhaps more crucially, the family's reputation was irreparably shattered.

"Do you think the Rasatan family will survive?" Uncertain how to tactfully refer to Erek's regicide, Elen-ai avoided mentioning it explicitly.

Varl considered her question with a slight tilt to his head. "I honestly don't know. It would be curious to see what happens to the land if the Rasatans were unable to pay the taxes on it, or be a sufficient political force to retain power."

It was with slight discomfort that Elen-ai realised the Veertak estate bordered the Rasatan lands. The Veertaks were in a position to make significant territorial and power gains if indeed the Rasatan family did fall. She wondered if Varl's interest in the prospect was born of such a realisation. As much as she adored the old scholar, he was still one of the Seven Families, and they were all ultimately invested in securing their own power.

Dinner finished and the plates cleared with a flurry of efficient servants. Guests were free to stand up from the long table and mingle, dance, or gossip. She excused herself and stood. Lively music started playing as she walked across the grand dining hall. Kaine appeared in front of her as though from thin air. His boyish good looks were emphasised by some clever artist's pattern on his face, Elen-ai could not help but notice.

"Lady Elen-ai." An ironic smile settled briefly on his lips.

"Kaine." She refused to ask him what he wanted.

"You captivate my eye, as always. Perhaps you would care to dance?" He held a glass goblet – the material from which it was made another marker of power and wealth – aloft as he spoke, as though he was toasting the suggestion they dance together.

"I might decline," Elen-ai said. She wondered if he was intoxicated.

"A shame." He gave her a look that seemed to linger, or perhaps it was her desire to be out of the room's centre that made it feel protracted.

"One day, perhaps, I'll get a yes from you." He bowed slightly and winked at her with his bright golden gaze. He suddenly looked completely sober, and Elen-ai found herself fighting a smile at his charm.

Focusing her gaze on the check pattern of the tiles so that nobody else tried to invite her to dance, she made her way toward Gidyon. As she neared the King, she paused once more to speak with the emissary from the Third Country, Freyanna Kuch, known simply to her as Freya.

"Are you well, Elen-ai?" Freya asked, a smile touching her face.

Elen-ai gave a little sigh that caused the other woman to laugh. "It's a bit like that, isn't it?" Freya said kindly.

"Do you have anything like this in the Third Country?" Elen-ai gestured to the room full of people adorned with finery and ulterior motives.

The Councilwoman shook her head, her dark mass of hair swinging ever so slightly from side to side. "The Council members are not born into their positions. And wealth and prestige is not really maintained within a few families like it is with your Seven Families," she explained.

"I wish I lived somewhere like that," Elen-ai muttered.

"It has its own problems," Freya noted. She was certainly correct. She had been a part of the religious Pious community who had overthrown the Kade governance, who themselves had overthrown the previous regime several years earlier. The Third Country was more like a city-state than a country, in the middle of nowhere but on the way to everywhere, so the political turmoil had been of interest to many. The woman, who Elen-ai considered a friend of sorts, was a legend amid the stories of that time. Rumours of her ability to heal with her mere mind were woven into the mythology that surrounded her. The fact that those rumours were correct – much like the skills of the Family, Freya had capabilities beyond many others – was in some ways incidental to what Freya represented. Not that those skills were useless; Freya had healed Gidyon in the spring when Erek Rasatan had orchestrated an attempt on his life and nearly succeeded.

"I still think I'd prefer a different set of problems sometimes," Elen-ai said.

Freya gave her a sympathetic pat on the shoulder.

Elen-ai would have liked to linger and talk longer with the foreigner, but she felt she should check on Gidyon.

By the time she reached him, he had gotten to his feet, a polite smile on his face that gave no indication whether he was actually enjoying himself.

"Are you all right?" he asked her, a slight frown of concern flashing across his face. Her expression must have been more troubled than she realised.

"Yes. I sometimes forget that everybody is here for their own benefit," she mumbled.

He gave her arm a light squeeze. Most would dismiss the unusually intimate gesture as the King being foolish enough to parade his affection for her in front of anyone who cared to look. She appreciated the comfort he sought to offer.

"I sometimes forget that it is not like this for everybody," he told her softly.

She gave a tiny shrug. "In a way I guess it is, but the stakes here are so much higher."

"I am sorry," he said. "If it helps, you have been quite magnificent. You are quite magnificent."

His sincerity touched her. Coming from him, the compliment meant a great deal.

"My King," she teased, smiling despite the profound sadness that had made its way into her heart at the realisation that Gidyon inhabited a world in which even the sweet Varl worked to fulfil his own purpose. To anyone who did not know, she and the King must have looked like a couple caught amid the throes of adoration for one another. In some ways, that was correct.

"Would you care to step outside for a little while? I wish to speak with the dear Rania Harete and I would very much like an escort." The request was an unexpected one.

Elen-ai raised her eyebrows. The daughter of the Harete family had been pushed by her parents to try to seduce Gidyon when they had visited them. Only Gidyon, Elen-ai, and Rania knew that she had very nearly succeeded; Elen-ai had found them before anything serious had transpired. Gidyon's fury upon learning that Rania was trying to better her family's position still made Elen-ai shiver. With a terrifying calmness he had outlined every action he would take to ruin Rania's family if what had transpired between them ever came out. Elen-ai had no doubt that he would fulfil his word.

"You want to talk to Rania?"

Gidyon deliberately ignored Elen-ai's surprise. "Yes, she may be of some use."

"As you command, my King," she said, causing him to snort in amusement.

She met him and Rania by the door to the garden outside the dining hall. In the summer, flower beds were overflowing with beautiful displays that guests could look out on as the light lingered long into the evening. Of course, the high bushes and trees also made the garden perfect for a discreet moment away from the eyes of those in the hall. Rania had her left arm hooked through Gidyon's right, a look of disconcerted unease on her face. Her long tresses hung free in her preferred style, swirling around her blue dress. Naturally pretty, someone had done something to her face that meant someone who had never seen her before might think her beautiful.

The King and Rania strolled through the garden, Elen-ai keeping a polite distance behind them so that Gidyon and Rania could converse naturally. It would have been almost possible for Gidyon and Rania to forget she was there. Almost.

"And what have you been reading of late?" Gidyon sounded as though he had never been more interested in anything than what her answer would be.

"Oh, nothing that interesting, your Majesty," she replied hesitantly.

"Come now, there's no such thing as an uninteresting book," he cajoled.

"Well, I'm reading the most recent book by Har-ai of Herran," she admitted.

Gidyon let out a warm laugh. Har-ai of Herran was an author whose fiction was very popular, if not a little puerile at times. Elen-ai had chanced to read one or two volumes herself. The stories had been commendably engaging.

"There is no shame in reading Har-ai of Herran. I wish I had the opportunity to read for enjoyment," Gidyon told Rania kindly.

"You don't have any time now?" Rania asked, seemingly encouraged by Gidyon's warm demeanour.

"Sadly, no. Being the king is a time-consuming business, Rania," he said. "And your parents, they are well? I was saddened that Janyce was not in attendance at the Council."

"It's very kind of you to say. My parents are very well. Mother is still recovering, though. The baby's birth was a very difficult one," she said.

"Mm, I heard," Gidyon replied.

Elen-ai was sceptical about the truth behind Rania's claim. The acrimony between Janyce and Timet was clear for anyone to see. She had even eavesdropped upon a violent argument between the two of them in which they had hurled the most vicious insults at one another. If she had been betting, she would have put her money on the fact that the birth of their most recent child was a convenient excuse for Janyce to seclude herself, away from her husband and the family into which she had married and had been made to feel she did not belong.

"Are you well, my King?" Rania asked after they'd taken a few steps in silence.

Gidyon took a moment to reply. "My health is perfect, if that is what you were asking," he said slowly. Then he took a breath and continued. "However, the fact that some individuals – and I am sure you know who they are – seek to take the throne from me leaves me disquieted."

Rania's body stiffened, almost as though she was waiting for Gidyon to turn and hit her. While Elen-ai didn't know exactly what Gidyon had planned, she knew that something perhaps worse than a mere blow was about to follow. It surprised her that she felt a stab of pity for the girl.

Gidyon stopped and pulled Rania to a halt. "Rania, have you heard any talk in your home of a plot against me?"

"Surely nobody would dare," the girl said breathlessly, as though shocked by the mere prospect. Her pretence of surprise was not convincing.

"Do you remember that evening at your home, Rania?" Gidyon's voice was suddenly quiet. He did not need to specify to which evening he was referring.

She nodded.

"Have you heard of any talk in your home that may suggest your family will move against me?" Gidyon grasped Rania's arm, his fingers digging in.

"Your Majesty, my arm—" Rania said, fear choking her voice.

"Your arm is the least of your concerns if you do not answer me truthfully, Rania." Gidyon's voice remained soft. He didn't need to raise it. "Now answer my question, please."

"I don't know." The beauty loaned by the artistry on her face was tarnished by the way her features crumpled with fear.

"Rania, if you are lying to me, I will destroy you and everything and everyone you care about." Gidyon's voice was quite even.

Fear gave way to outright terror and Rania made the tiniest movement to jerk her arm out of his grasp.

"You are right to be scared. Even if the throne is taken from me, if I find out that you have misled me, I will ensure that your family is ruined. That is a promise, Rania." He was clutching her arm so tightly that Elen-ai was sure he would leave bruises.

"I know of no plans, I swear before the Divine One," Rania gasped.

Gidyon held onto her a moment longer, staring into her face. How he could see anything by the feeble light cast by the yellow moon and the intermittent braziers throughout the garden, Elen-ai had no idea. He did not have the skills of the Family to provide clear sight in the dark. Yet it appeared as though he was seeing through to Rania's very mind. Finally, he released her arm with a slight sigh. "Go inside, Rania." He sounded tired, even fed-up. "And do not forget my promise."

She stayed where she was for a moment, then walked swiftly back toward the Palace, not even appearing to notice Elen-ai as she passed the assassin.

Elen-ai joined Gidyon. "Was it really necessary to be that hard?"

He looked at her in surprise. "Maybe not," he admitted.

"Is this because you didn't realise she was only pretending to be interested in you?" Elen-ai had no compunction about asking such a brutal question. She felt he deserved it a little bit.

With the skills of the Family, Elen-ai was able to see his face clearly. The slight tension in his jaw gave away the fact that she was right.

"I learned something," he said, ignoring her point. She decided to let it slide. She couldn't expect him to be perfect in his conduct and self-restraint all the time.

"Oh?"

"The Haretes are likely to move against me if it comes to siding with me or the Katans." Gidyon tried to sound nonchalant, but he couldn't quite manage it. Smugness warred with tension in his voice.

"You discerned all that?" Elen-ai didn't bother to hide her scepticism. It wasn't as though he could see her raised eyebrows, anyway.

Gidyon snorted in a most unregal manner. "I have heard rumours from our spies in their household about some of the conversations occurring between members of the Harete family. Besides, as much as he may hate her, Timet is married to a Katan. That sort of marriage does not occur for fun. There is a tie between the two families that he cannot deny out of hand."

"It almost feels as though Halen's been planning this for a long time," Elen-ai commented.

Gidyon exhaled, his breath a long stream in the cold night air. "It certainly feels like it, doesn't it?"

FIVE

It was a relief when the families left Herran the next day. Even though they had all stayed in their city residences, simply knowing how close the lot of them were to her left Elen-ai with a somewhat unpleasant taste in her mouth.

With Gidyon taking the morning to meet one of his tutors, Elen-ai roamed the Palace, feeling slightly like a caged animal.

She went to the stables to see the kittanae. Fascinated by the giant cats, she went there as often as she could. At her approach, two of the five beasts raised their heads to regard her with the natural insolence of all felines. Having regarded her with sufficient hauteur, the two heads were lowered, and Elen-ai approached the animals, all curled up in a tangle in their pen. She often came here simply to regard the animals. Knowing her by now, they permitted her to vault lightly into their stall and place her hands gently on them.

Kittanae were owned only by the most wealthy of individuals. They were notoriously difficult to find in the wild, and often rejected anyone who tried to train them whom they deemed unworthy of their affections. They were highly valued, though: if they consented to bear people, they could cover the same distance as the Fourth Country's most popular beast of burden, the hearat, in less than half the time. Elen-ai had been fortunate enough to see kittanae a few times when slipping through the homes of the wealthy on a contract, but she had never ridden one. Most people never even got the chance to see them up close.

Elen-ai stepped lightly into the pen and allowed her hand to sink into a cat's silky coat, marvelling at the softness of the fur. The russet-furred animal purred its appreciation as she stroked it. She could not help but smile as she moved around the animals, admiring the different colours of their coats, or the tenderness of the manner in which they curled together. She would deny ever thinking it if directly asked, but she had to acknowledge that there were some benefits to living in the Palace.

Following a whim, when she left the stables some time later, she made her way into the library. She had only taken a few steps into the room where she almost stumbled over Kaine sitting cross-legged on the floor. He was surrounded by a mountain of books, far too many to fit on any of the library's reading desks.

He brushed the curls out of his eyes as he looked up at her, then smiled mischievously. "Ah, our resident assassin."

Uncertain if it was a comment or an insult, Elen-ai walked forward so that she was standing directly in front of him. To look at her, he had to crane his neck. It might have been slightly petty of her, but she took her enjoyment where she could find it. "What are you doing?" she asked.

"Building a fortress." His response was immediate and deadpan.

"You'll need a few more books." She glanced down at the titles of the considerable stack in front of him. All of them were legal texts of some form or another. "Researching Halen's – sorry, Serenah's – viability to claim the throne?"

He laughed at her biting joke with a lack of restraint that suggested his initial greeting had not been intended as an insult after all. "Quite correct," he said once he had regained control of himself. "Now if only I could prove that Halen would put Serenah on the throne as his puppet, then we may have a way to completely disqualify her."

After hesitating for a moment, Elen-ai sat down, sinking to the richly patterned carpet in one fluid motion.

"Divine One, sometimes I forget what exactly you do, and then I see how you move like that." Kaine shook his head in amazement.

"I just sat down." Elen-ai protested, awkwardly remembering the way he had complimented her on the evening of the feast.

He shook his head. "You didn't 'just sit down'. The rest of us lumber to the ground like a falling tree, but you gracefully sink down."

She laughed. "If you did the exercises I do every day, you probably would fall less like a tree and more like a feather too."

"But then who would read all this?" He made an exaggerated gesture to the piles of books surrounding him.

Elen-ai leaned forward to pick up the closest one, the motion bringing her close to Kaine. He grinned mischievously. Kaine was the youngest of Gidyon's uncles, and the most handsome. Not for the first time, Elen-ai wondered whether or not any of Gidyon's uncles had lovers. She knew that if they wanted to marry and have children, they had to renounce the name of the Royal Family and leave the Palace, but she imagined that the convention when it came to taking a lover was less rigid. The image of Kaine winking came back to her.

"You smell of cat," he said.

"I've just come from the stables," Elen-ai said, feeling uncharacteristically self-conscious.

"Admiring the kittanae?"

She nodded.

"Do you like them?" His pride in them was obvious and merited. The Palace beasts were in obviously superb condition.

"They're magnificent," Elen-ai said, the words almost falling over themselves as they left her lips. She became uncomfortably aware of the unusual effusiveness with which she spoke and dropped her gaze to the book she had plucked at random from Kaine's small mountain of books. "*Conventions of Legal Heritage,* volume one of fourteen!" The last word became an exclamation of horror at the prospect that thirteen more books of such dull material had been produced by some poor person who likely considered the collection their masterpiece.

"It's my favourite bedtime reading," Kaine told her seriously, breaking into that mischievous grin again at the last moment.

"Oh, mine too," Elen-ai said.

He laughed. "Divinity, this is the most boring task I could possibly think of. Why did I volunteer to do this?" He threw his hands up in the air, casting around at the books that surrounded him.

"I have no idea what notion overtook you," Elen-ai told him. "Don't you have a life of your own?" Her earlier thought prompted the question and she asked it before realising perhaps it was too personal.

"The uncles of the queen – or king, I suppose – live in service of the Second Country." The cadence made it clear he was reciting an oft-told maxim. Despite her worry, he did not seem at all offended.

"And in the three minutes of each day when you aren't living in service of the Second Country?" Elen-ai prompted.

His face went blank for a moment, either concealing a thought or trying to comprehend the idea. "All I have ever been taught to do is to serve the throne. No part of my life is not affected by that."

"Don't you ever want to do something else?" Elen-ai persisted.

"Why, did you have something in mind?" The gentle teasing in his tone was at once deflection and flirtatious invitation. Elen-ai had to admit, the invitation was a tempting one. Kaine looked unfairly good, especially considering he was sitting on the floor, surrounded by the world's most boring books.

"It's your life." Elen-ai held up her hands, fingers spread wide.

He reached forward and captured one of her hands in his. Dangerous, given what she could do with her hands if she so chose. "You are certainly interesting to have around, Elen-ai," he said, kissing her hand.

"What's that supposed to mean?" Her skin vibrated with phantom tingles where his lips had brushed. She told herself to cease being foolish.

"Exactly that," he told her.

From somewhere within the library, a bell marked the hour. According to history, that on a day of the Council of Families several generations ago, a queen had been so engrossed in a book that she had completely lost track of time. The heads of the Seven Families had been forced to wait for several hours, unwilling to leave their seats in case they might be absent when she arrived. While nobody had disgraced themselves at the Council table, almost all requested that they briefly take their leave of her to relieve themselves as soon as she had arrived. This caused more upset as nobody wanted a mass exodus that left the queen alone and might inadvertently cause the perception that they were in some way colluding to offend her. After that hilarious but uncomfortable incident, a bell was installed in the library so that people did not lose themselves in the pages of whatever they were reading. Not that Kaine's choice of reading matter seemed to be in danger of doing such a thing to anyone.

"Gidyon's lessons should be done by now, I'll go and find him," Elen-ai said, rising swiftly to her feet.

"See? Ridiculous." Kaine gestured up and down at her.

Shaking her head at him, although feeling nonetheless replete with flattery, she left the library and made her way to the room where Gidyon had told her to find him. She knocked on the door then immediately entered, assuming he would be alone. He was not.

The priestess of the Divine One who chanted over his kneeling form was the last person Elen-ai expected to see with Gidyon. The woman's raised hands glowed softly in the dim room as she spoke the final words of the prayer of light.

Elen-ai closed the door behind her and leaned against the wall. The priestess had her back to the door so she may not have noticed Elen-ai's entry. Gidyon, despite not having acknowledged her, almost certainly would have.

As someone whose path was dictated by the Shadow God, it was strange for Elen-ai to be around the rituals associated with a different god, especially a god that few people followed with any true devotion. She observed the glow around the woman's hands with cool curiosity, realising that the priests and priestesses of the Divine One, it appeared, had their own memory of the forgotten skills. That was not something the Family knew, as far as she was aware. The next time she went to the home, she would tell them. The priestess' hands glowed a little brighter, then she lowered them completely. "The light grows bright within you," she told Gidyon.

The King nodded solemnly. "You do me a great honour, priestess," he replied. "Until next time."

The priestess gave him a stern smile and turned to leave. She gave a sharp intake of breath when she saw Elen-ai, then turned back to Gidyon as though to say something about Elen-ai's presence. But she seemed to think the better of it and simply left the room, staying as far from Elen-ai as she could.

"That was odd," Gidyon commented, frowning.

"I'll say. What are you doing with a priestess?"

"I was actually talking about her reaction to you."

"Her reaction to me? It was hardly odd. I follow the Shadow God. She is an agent of the Divine One. The Divine One brings the sun, which is the opposite of shadow, if you hadn't noticed. I would have been surprised had she not reacted to me, really, especially with..." She trailed off, unwilling to note that people were turning to the Divine One in their uncertainty over a man being on the throne.

"Especially with people rediscovering their faith in the Divine One as uncertainty increases over the throne being held by a man?" Gidyon finished the sentence for her. He continued into her silence. "I'm not blind, Elen-ai. I know the hearts of my people, even if what I see I would rather not be there. Besides, you and I both know the power that faith can have." He absently rubbed his stomach where he had been gored in the attack on his life. Freya's ability to heal him was the result of her faith in her deity – the Goddess. It was the same when it came to Elen-ai's own skills. "What faith can do is quite amazing. We barely understand it."

"How long have you been reading about what faith can bestow?" Elen-ai wondered how Gidyon had managed to hide this interest from her.

"Since the attack," he said. "I never realised you were so devout, by the way."

"Oh?" Elen-ai went over to a chair and flung herself into it.

"To be bestowed with the gifts of the gods one must not only believe, but believe with a deep conviction," Gidyon said.

"I am aware," she said dryly. Only members of the Family who had profound belief were allowed to be assassins. Her instruction about the Shadow God had begun at the same time as her combat training, before she could even walk properly. "I still didn't realise you were particularly devout," she persisted, mildly uncomfortable with the subject of her faith.

"Of course I am." He sounded surprised that she didn't know.

"You've never talked about it, though."

"Conviction does not need to be shouted for everybody to hear in order to exist," he replied.

She shrugged, discomfort and uncertainty robbing her of an immediate response. She wondered how often he conferred with the priestess of the Divine One, and why she had not discovered it sooner. "I just didn't think that you thought much about the Divine One, or the gods. Faith isn't for everyone."

Gidyon gave a small laugh and came to sit next to her. He looked tired. He always looked tired. The bright blue of his eyes practically jumped out from the shadows on his face. Perhaps he had lost weight; he looked a little gaunt.

"Elen-ai, I have to have faith," he said softly, clasping his hands together and resting his forearms on his knees.

"Nobody has to have faith," she countered.

"I do. When the modern state of the Second Country was formed at the conclusion of the great wars, it was decided that no man should be entrusted with the throne. So the land was divided among the eight strongest warriors, with the strongest of them, Latana the First, being given the throne, and that is the way things have been for centuries."

Elen-ai nodded when he paused for breath. Every child was taught this alongside their numbers and letters.

Gidyon continued. "As time progressed, the regard in which men were held waned, then grew again. As you know, there was even a time when no man was permitted to hold property. And now we have me. The first man on the throne. Perhaps the only man to ever take the throne if I do not do the best I possibly can. Elen-ai, I cannot believe that I am here due to some accident. I have to believe that I am part of something bigger, something greater than myself. I cannot think that I am here on my own for no real reason."

The intensity of Gidyon's gaze was like the point of a knife. His knuckles were white from the strength with which he gripped his hands together. "I have to be a part of some greater plan," he concluded softly, almost more to himself than to her.

For a moment, silence stretched between them.

"And that's what you honestly believe?" she asked.

As with any question of weight, Gidyon did not answer immediately, choosing the correct words for his response. "I do not think that I have a choice except to believe it."

She scrutinised him, the handsome face, his blue eyes, the way his broad shoulders were set with such tension. The fact that he was driven to overcome fatigue and uncertainty through sheer willpower had not escaped her. He certainly shouldn't have been able to possess the energy that he did with the meagre sleep he got each evening. Now she saw how desperately he was clinging to the belief that he had just confessed to her. It wasn't just that he believed he had some divine part to play. He needed to believe it in order to keep going, to keep fighting.

"Do you want glory in the name of the Divine One?" Elen-ai asked.

It gave her some comfort that again, Gidyon did not answer immediately. "I just want to know that my life, what I am, what I did, that it meant something more."

It was a good answer. "And where does being allied with one who follows the Shadow God fit in with being an agent of the Divine One?" Knowing how Gidyon felt, she could not dismiss the priestess's reaction to her with simple amusement.

Gidyon gave her a look of incomprehension. "You are my friend," he said, as though it were the most obvious thing in the world.

She thought about arguing with him, about pressing the point that he was unable – or unwilling – to see, but she thought better of it. He did not need yet another worry on his shoulders. So instead, she gave him what he did need: levity. "And have you found divine enlightenment, yet?" She forced a teasing note into her voice.

"Oh yes, just last week the world and all its mysteries were revealed unto me," Gidyon said. "That's why the priestess was blessing me just then, and why I was still receiving religious instruction from her."

"You might have been instructing her," she said innocently. "The ways of the Divine One and its followers are a mystery to me."

"Perhaps you could do with a bit of religious instruction yourself," Gidyon said, his tone prim, leaning back. His shoulders had lost their tightness and his face looked a little less pinched.

"You wound me, my King." Elen-ai put a hand to her chest, recoiling with mocking exaggeration.

"You should remember that I have this power to wound you, my assassin," he said, his mask of seriousness marred by the fact that the lines around his eyes were, for at least that moment, crinkled with amusement rather than worry.

"My life is yours to do with what you will, your Majesty. Wound me, maim me, kill me, I am but your loyal subject." Elen-ai bowed her head, the very portrait of a subjugated servant.

Gidyon snorted. "Unless you disagree with me," he said. "Come on, you can be my loyal servant in the petition hall." He rose to his feet, straightening his jacket as he did.

Elen-ai shadowed his movement, albeit without the perfunctory straightening of her clothes. Nobody would really look at her, or care if her clothes were slightly rumpled. As ever, she would stand in a shadowed part of the hall and watch almost completely unnoticed, as those petitioners who had been granted an audience with Gidyon would speak to him of their grievances and he would listen with a completely genuine sincerity. From the petitions that he heard, he would often make notes to which he would refer back when later considering other matters of state. Gidyon was a ruler who did care, and for that, Elen-ai would follow him to the end of the world.

She and Gidyon walked through the Palace, both hunched slightly against the chill that seeped through the walls.

"I wish your Divine One would warm the day up," she said.

Gidyon laughed. "Somehow I suspect it does not work quite like that."

"Seems to me it should," Elen-ai grumbled.

The King laughed again, the sound echoing in the tiled corridor. "Next time I'm praying, I will be sure to throw that request in for you."

The ease of the exchange between them went some way to wearing away at the tension that had knotted in Elen-ai's stomach. It was perfectly understandable for Gidyon to have faith, to be faithful, and to find meaning in faith. Many did, even though until recently it was not a widely practised part of life in the Second Country. But the fact remained that she was not an agent of his god. She worshipped the shadows as he worshipped the sun. Perhaps she was being silly. She tried to allay her concern by telling herself that some of Gidyon's tension was seeping through to her. However, she couldn't quite shake the sense that something of a fundamental difference between the two of them had been pointed out. Now that she knew it was there, she couldn't dismiss it from her mind.

They reached the petition room. Gidyon turned to her, the intimate smile of a private joke on his face. "Maybe if I work hard enough people will think the sun shines from my arse. I keep trying to make it happen, but it never does."

With that crass joke, the thoughts that were chasing themselves around Elen-ai's head fled as she struggled to keep her composure. "Only if they know you like I do."

SIX

When he had been just the son of the queen, not her heir - certainly not the king - every week Gidyon would go to the great market of Herran. There, food was laid out with care and carelessness, people were harangued by stall owners promising their wares were the best, and deals flowed like water. The marketplace truly was a spectacle of life in the Second Country at its most vivid. But Elen-ai thought it was the docks that were the true heart of Herran. Far removed from the ordered quiet of the Palace, the docks offered a jumble of sounds, smells and people which tumbled over each other in a chaotic sort of order. The excitement of travel and exoticisms created an intoxicating atmosphere that could not be found in any other part of the city. Not the fencing arenas, not the market, not the beautiful district of the high-born nestled underneath the Palace walls. Crates were unloaded and loaded under the supervision of beady-eyed traders who screamed orders or encouragement to the workers straining underneath the weight of whatever goods were contained within the boxes. Deals were quickly made between individuals who shook hands and slipped away, both parties feeling as though they had netted a bargain. And on beautiful days, the water glistened. Even today, despite the stone-grey sky, the docks were vibrant. One could hear half a dozen dialects while walking only a few paces. There was even a ship in the harbour from the notoriously xenophobic First Country, a relatively uncommon sight. The only known way to get to the First Country was by a treacherous channel, so one of the few places on the Godskissed Continent outside the First Country to see its inhabitants was at a port. Even then, few came ashore. To her chagrin, the vessel was too far out for Elen-ai to make out any clear details of the people on deck.

Of course, a place where so many people congregated also meant that crime flourished, but Elen-ai knew how to avoid trouble. She ignored the offers of the women and men selling their bodies, and dodged the girls chasing each other through the chaos, who would slip a hand into the pockets of anyone they passed quick as a breath, and stopped at the berth she sought. A relatively small but sleek-looking ship from the Fourth Country was docked there, gangplanks down crates in the process of being unloaded by men whose every scrap of skin was covered from sight. Several carts were waiting to receive the crates. From a glance, Elen-ai thought that the crates were filled with spices, but she was not close enough to verify her guess.

An entrepreneurial individual had set up a food cart close to the wharf and was conducting a roaring trade. Perhaps she had been in the Palace too long, for Elen-ai shuddered to imagine what meat the man was cooking over the brazier which belched black smoke into the cold air. Cats, the smaller cousins of the kittanae, prowled around with an equal mixture of haughtiness and hopefulness. There seemed enough of them to dispel Elen-ai's concern that they were the filling of the street vendor's food.

She had to admit, it did smell delicious. After a moment of contemplation, she joined the line where the order of arrival only loosely dictated the order in which they were served, and held up two fingers. The man deftly flicked the just-cooked meat filling into waiting parcels of thin pastry and handed them to her. Taking a bite from one of the little parcels, Elen-ai grunted in satisfaction. To say that the food within the Palace was divine was no understatement, but there was something peculiarly reassuring about the taste of the type of food she had eaten her whole life, even if its contents were dubious. But that too, was part of the familiarity.

When she'd finished the first parcel, she ambled over to the wharf where a beautiful woman supervised the unloading of the ship's cargo with a beady eye. The woman barely regarded her as Elen-ai came to stand beside her. Wordlessly, she held out the second parcel of food.

"You can't bribe me with that dubious offering." The trader's voice was heavily accented, her vowels drawn out to the point that they were almost unrecognisable. But she took the proffered food and bit into it, her red-painted lips parting to allow sharp, white teeth to sink into the unidentified meat.

"How have you been, Ziziana?" Elen-ai asked.

"The wind was not fair on our journey, your boy-king has made the market unacceptably volatile, and my favourite *elui* has issues with his ... performance."

"All grave problems," Elen-ai responded solemnly.

"The worst of course being Hanan." Ziziana was perfectly serious. In the time that Elen-ai had known the formidable trader, she had often grumbled about her slave-husbands.

"Of course," Elen-ai said.

Ziziana barked out a command to her slave-husbands in the language of the Fourth Country. Although Elen-ai knew only a handful of phrases, the sharpness of Ziziana's voice was clear enough to understand. The men did not reply – to do so would have been an unforgivable breach of their station – but their pace slowed and they appeared to take more care with their burdens. Custom demanded that men of the Fourth Country, other than those who were in the midst of fighting, cover themselves from head to toe so that only the merest amount of skin was visible. From time to time, the movements of the men under the ownership of Ziziana would reveal the suggestion of their form – the broadness of the shoulder here, or the curve of a hip there – but for the most part, they were simply cloth-covered pillars undulating with human-like movement. Elen-ai always found the Fourth Country's practice of veiling men profoundly odd, even off-putting. Many of the Fourth Country's customs perplexed her, though.

"Look at them," Ziziana said to Elen-ai, a patronising affection in her voice. "They'd be utterly hopeless without a firm guiding hand."

"Yes, where on earth would they be without you?" Elen-ai's sarcasm turned the trader's head.

"You seem unusually serious, my dear. You know, a cohort of *elui* would do you the world of good. Your every whim would be taken care of, emotionally, spiritually..." her voice dropped to a seductive bass, "...sexually."

Personally, Elen-ai did not see the appeal of having several husbands who were bound to her by a slave contract. "Maybe when I grow old and tired of this life," she replied lightly.

Ziziana cackled, the bangles on her arms jangling as she gestured effusively. "You really don't know what you're missing. All of my husbands are from the finest families."

The assassin shook her head, amused. "I was wondering if you could help me with something."

Her comment elicited a theatrical sigh. "Darling Elen-ai. You never want to see me simply because I'm in your lovely city. Always it's because you want some thing or the other from me."

"Now don't be like that, Zizi," Elen-ai protested. "You know that the Family loves you for your wonderful wares."

"Don't flatter me with business talk – it's cheap." Ziziana mock-pouted.

"Must I buy you more food?"

The woman wiped invisible crumbs from her fingers. "I'm not sure my stomach could take it. All right, what do you want to know?"

"Halen Katan," Elen-ai said.

Ziziana made a derisive noise in her throat. "He certainly pays well," Ziziana said, a dismissive slant in her voice. "Ridiculous man. Now there's someone who should cover himself. Then nobody would see that unfortunate bald spot."

Elen-ai almost choked as unexpected laughter took hold of her.

Once she had recovered, she asked, "So you've traded with him?"

Ziziana blinked deliberately. "On occasion."

"May I ask the nature of your exchange?" She worded the question carefully so as not to offend Ziziana. The people of the Fourth Country were a proud lot.

"It sounds as though you already have some suspicion of what items changed hands." Amusement gave the woman a little, full smile. "I'm not much use to you. As you know I normally travel by boat, here and to the First Country. Especially given the current issues that plague my home country, I increasingly prefer to avoid land routes. Ship is much safer, if not a more expensive way to travel." A dismissive wave of her hand accompanied the comment. Elen-ai suspected that the woman was covering a deeper sadness at seeing her country wracked by constant infighting. Ziziana was a handsome woman, her features strong, her skin smooth. She was also a rich woman, hailing from one of the Fourth Country's most powerful families. As a trader, she was somewhat insulated from the instability that plagued her home. But given the fractured nature of power in the Fourth Country where a family could be invaded by another and lose their power in the blink of an eye, she lived with the knowledge that her power and wealth were only as secure as she could make them with trade and guile. It seemed an impossible way to live, to Elen-ai's mind.

"Don't your *elui* dislike being covered?" Elen-ai asked after watching one of the men stumble.

Ziziana shook her head. "For them, to be without their robes would be as though they were naked."

"Why veil them, though?" Elen-ai persisted.

She received a blank look. "Men are little better than animals, my love. They must be restrained, for their own good, as well as ours. Surely you know that."

Elen-ai said nothing, not knowing how she should respond. "So what sort of weapons is Halen buying?" she asked, diverting the conversation away from the awkwardness she felt at Ziziana's prejudice.

"Oh, anything and everything. Whatever I could get my hands on, he bought."

"And you never thought to ask why?" Elen-ai couldn't help but sound a little frustrated. The woman's lack of concern about Halen's purpose for wanting a significant number of weapons seemed irresponsible.

"Now, now," Ziziana cautioned. "I'm not bound to your king." Her lip curled at the word, making it perfectly clear what she thought of a man on the throne. "I have to make an honest living. I have husbands to support."

"You're right," Elen-ai relented, knowing she had overstepped.

"Hm." Ziziana's red lips pressed together.

"I had better be off." It was clear that no further information would come. "Take care, Zizi," Elen-ai said, turning to leave.

"You too, Elen-ai. Are you all right?" The question was oddly gentle, coming from the formidable woman.

Elen-ai turned back. "Of course. Why do you ask?"

Ziziana tilted her head slightly and scrutinised Elen-ai before she spoke. "You seem different to when last I saw you. Worried, perhaps? No," she answered her own question. "Well, yes, worried, but also ... different."

Elen-ai gave her a bemused look. "I'm the same as I always was."

"Maybe I have too many things on my mind." Ziziana's shrug was an elegant dismissal.

"Like I said, take care." Elen-ai gave her a brief smile before leaving the dock and its bustle behind her.

She hadn't realised how cold it had been on the docks out in in the wind that had blown in straight from the sea until she returned to the meagre cover offered by the buildings which ringed the docks. Those structures housed a variety of places where one could buy food, a drink, somewhere to stay and a warm body to offer companionship, and shops to restock the essential items – at a price which reflected the convenience of acquiring the items so conveniently close to the docks, of course. Some of those operations were even properly licenced, too. For a moment, she stood in the cobblestone alley between two buildings as she considered the fastest way back to the warmth of the Palace. A ripple of air at her side told her that a member of the Family had appeared next to her.

"Mari-am." She smiled as she turned to face her Sister. Mari-am was her favourite Sister. In their younger years they had done absolutely everything together, much to the amusement of their Mothers and Fathers. That closeness had remained as the two girls had become women, although, for the past few years, Mari-am had sought contracts in other lands, often leaving the Second Country for months at a time.

"Elen-ai." Her sister returned the greeting with a taciturn demeanour.

"How are things at home?" Elen-ai asked.

"As ever," came the reply. "Have you learned anything the Mothers and Fathers may deem of interest?"

"Is that the only reason you came?" Elen-ai could not help but feel slightly disappointed. A bloom of joy had spread through her at seeing her Sister. She missed home, and the sight of Mari-am made the ache of feeling out of place in the Palace, slightly less acute.

"I am a loyal child of the Family, simply undertaking their bidding." Her comment sounded like it could have been a rebuke.

"We are both loyal children of the Family, Mari-am. I returned to the Palace at their behest." Elen-ai hated the defensiveness in her tone. She had done nothing she should feel the need to defend.

"Of course."

"I just spoke with a trader from the Fourth Country. Halen Katan is buying weapons from anyone there who is willing to sell them to him. He also challenged Gidyon in front of the Council."

"Things do not look good for the boy-king," Mari-am commented.

"Well, when everybody's arming his enemy with no concern for what that may bring, of course they don't," Elen-ai said.

"You are too involved, Elen-ai." Mari-am made no effort to hide her disapproval.

There was no good reply that Elen-ai could give. She could not deny Mari-am's accusation. "I didn't realise you were such a traditionalist," she said instead.

"The Family's neutrality is everything, Elen-ai. Everything. For one of our own to be a part of the power games played by the Seven Families and the throne is…" Mari-am trailed off with a shake of her head in place of an end to the sentence.

"The Family is as old as the Second Country," Elen-ai retorted, a defensive anger uncurling inside her. "For as long as it has existed, so have we. The Family was founded alongside the Second Country. Or have you forgotten your lessons?"

"What's your point?" Mari-am folded her arms across her chest.

"We have always been involved in the power games of the Second Country, but we've merely done the bidding of whoever happens to be able to pay." Elen-ai fought to keep her growing anger out of her voice.

"Are you doubting your place in the Family?" There was a challenge there, a note of disgust, even.

"I want to come home. I can't yet, though." Elen-ai wished she could explain to her Sister what was occurring inside her head. She wished she could show her the conflict she felt. The Family's neutrality was a cornerstone of its identity and its place within the Second Country, and it was true that she had cast that neutrality aside in her fealty to Gidyon. But she would not have gone back to the Palace had the Mothers and Fathers forbidden it.

Mari-am snorted. "You can come home whenever you want."

"We don't live in ordinary times, Mari-am. Perhaps you've been away from home too long to realise what's going on. Do you think Halen and his ilk on the throne would be good for anyone? For us?" Elen-ai took a step toward her Sister, looming over her by half a head.

Mari-am gave an angry laugh. "There's a delightful irony in you telling me that I've been away too long."

"Do you speak for all the Family or just for yourself?" Elen-ai snapped out the question, tired of being made to feel as though she should be ashamed.

Her sister's lips pursed. "There are many at home who view your actions with some consternation. You put us at risk, Elen-ai."

"Nobody outside the Royal Family knows I'm a member of the Family." Elen-ai chose to overlook Varl and Valena's knowledge of who she was. They were close enough to the Royal Family for the sake of this argument.

"Ah yes, you're the King's mysterious lover."

Something in Mari-am's tone made Elen-ai pause. "You think he and I are actually lovers?"

"You speak about him as though you're blinded by lust for him."

For a moment, Elen-ai was speechless, her mouth hanging open. "That's a disgusting thought," she thundered.

"You don't need to tell me that. A man on the throne. You'd be tainted." Mari-am's lip curled with distaste.

"Did you come here just to pass judgment on things of which you know nothing?" Elen-ai had heard enough. Anger, now free from its restraints, crackled around her body.

"You're very defensive." Mari-am's calm only served to infuriate Elen-ai further.

"You're very blind," Elen-ai retorted. "Please deliver my information to the Mothers and Fathers."

Without waiting for a response, she stomped off, rage and hurt pulsing under her skin. The cold swirled around her, but she didn't notice it. She moved through the streets quickly, trying to leave her hurt behind. She did not want to think about Mari-am's words, the accusation, the rejection. If she were calmer, she might have come to the conclusion that Mari-am herself might be feeling hurt, believing Elen-ai had left the Family for the King. But her own turbulent emotions left no room for such charity.

The narrow streets with their jumble of shops promising a variety of wares - some reasonable, some enticing only to the naive - passed by in a blur. Elen-ai dodged carts, people, stray animals, as she made her way to the upper areas of the city. She did not even see the shrines that she passed, despite the fact that she normally made a point of counting them. She was completely lost in her focus on simply getting to the Palace and leaving Mari-am's cruel words outside its walls.

Tiny buildings that housed up to four families as well as shops gave way to houses for one family, then to the grand residences of the city's rich. But Elen-ai barely noticed. When the streets emptied of people, as they did in the most luxurious parts of the city, Elen-ai broke into a sprint, craving the release and distraction of movement. She moved almost too fast to see. A part of Elen-ai wished she had hit Mari-am, but she knew her Sister would likely have dodged the blow and received only the satisfaction of knowing she had upset Elen-ai.

She reached the section of Palace wall she knew to be on the least inhabited street and, after a cursory glance around, Elen-ai flung herself at the wall, scaling its massive height with ease. Once she was over the top and in one of the Palace's gardens, she stopped for a moment, her breath only slightly heavier than usual. She looked back up at the wall. Nobody other than a member of the Family would have been able to do what she had just done. The wall was far too smooth and far too high.

"Always a member of the Family," she muttered, feeling the hard edges of her shock and hurt slide down her throat and into her chest. Then she walked into the Palace to tell Gidyon what she had learned from Ziziana.

SEVEN

Following her exchange with Mari-am, Elen-ai spent several days in a very poor mood. Gidyon was busier than ever upon learning that Halen Katan had been buying weapons, and while Elen-ai could give him the benefit of her extensive knowledge on any weapon in existence, she could not tell him how to stop such trading. He exchanged several communications with the Lord Protector of the Fourth Country, sent by messenger birds for speed. Before each reply, Gidyon spent hours on end in consultation with his uncles on how exactly he should word his messages. They could all read and write the language of the Fourth Country, although Kaine apparently was the most proficient when it came to speaking it, which was why he had been chosen as an emissary to them the year before.

Unfortunately, Elen-ai could not offer any counsel on how to most diplomatically word a letter, so she was left to roam the Palace with a certain aimlessness. She could have gone down into Herran, perhaps even consulted with the Family, but following her altercation with Mari-am, she was distinctly disinclined to do that.

One midmorning, as Gidyon composed another letter to the Lord Protector, Elen-ai curled herself up in one of the library's chairs and immersed herself in Har-ai of Herran's latest tale. Ever since Rania had mentioned the author, Elen-ai had been overtaken by a hankering to read more. This story was particularly gripping – a tale about a merchant boy erroneously accused of stealing a cargo of precious gems. She was reasonably certain she had discerned who the true culprit was, but enough doubt was left in her mind that she was pulled inexorably on to the story's conclusion.

Kaine strolled in. She barely registered his entrance, so enthralled was she in the book. He stood directly in front of her and bent down to see what she was reading. She ignored him. But. at his surprised chuckle, she felt it necessary to put the book aside.

"I honestly would never have expected lady Elen-ai, fierce assassin, to be absolutely absorbed by Har-ai of Herran," he said, his voice full of amusement.

"I do things other than stab people, you know," Elen-ai responded peevishly. She had endured a similar conversation when she had tried to discuss poetry with Gidyon the previous year.

"The fault is mine for being ignorant," Kaine said, his golden eyes dancing with laughter. He remained leaning down, his face close to hers.

"Shouldn't you be helping Gidyon?" Elen-ai asked.

He shrugged. "If you truly want to distinguish between the slightest nuances of two written words, Silius is your man. I'm better at charming people with my tongue." The laughter in his eyes turned wicked at the double entendre.

Unable to resist smiling in reply, Elen-ai leaned forward. "Has it ever occurred to you that you aren't as good as you think?"

Kaine's smile broadened. She almost lost herself in his golden gaze. Just as with his late sister, when he properly looked at a person, it felt as though they were falling into the very depths of his being.

"Perhaps one day I'll be fortunate enough to have you arbitrate on the matter," he told her in a voice so nakedly seductive that an unstoppable thrill ran along Elen-ai's skin.

Sadly, that exchange was the only notable moment in the lead-up to the midwinter festival of the Second Country, and Elen-ai had struggled to put thoughts of her confrontation with Mari-am from her mind.

Traditionally, the celebration of midwinter – the shortest day in the year – took place in the streets of Herran. Unlike on other days of celebration throughout the year, queens by custom would participate in the festivities alongside any of the city folk who wished to join her. Gidyon had been warned of the danger he may face in taking to the street due to the danger posed by the myriad of overhanging roofs, entrances and exits, and shadowed doorways. But he ignored the risk of attack, adamant he would take to the streets like the queens before him to celebrate. Lowborn who wished to celebrate with the king mingled alongside the Royal Family and the Palace servants, laughing, joking, sneaking a glance at their king. The celebration was the people's bid to prove to the Divine One that they had not forsaken the sun during the short winter days. As excuses for a festival went, it was quite a good one to Elen-ai's mind, even if she was not a devoted follower of the Divine One. She had always joyfully participated in the carousing. One of the contracts she was most proud of she had conducted under the cover of the midwinter festivities, slipping a poison into the woman's drink and gently escorting her toward the water so that it looked as though she had stumbled into the water thanks to the befuddling effects of too much ale. After she had ensured the woman's demise, Elen-ai had returned to the festivities with the satisfaction of a job well done, making that year's festival even more enjoyable. So Elen-ai allowed herself to be dressed in garb of deep crimson rather than the muted tones she preferred, and accompanied Gidyon to the street upon which the king's celebrations were to take place.

The wide street was lit by a long line of tall braziers, and at one end, an enormous fire over which several meals were being prepared. Elen-ai felt sorry for the guards who were ensuring that not too many people came into the street where their ruler celebrated, but they were being well compensated for the duty, and the ambience over Herran was one where even someone who was working felt a certain lightness in the task. The midwinter festival was a time of joy and merriment that nobody could properly escape, regardless of the cold weather. One year, it was said, the festivities were held despite the presence of a terrible storm. The legend surrounding that story also said that the following year brought unprecedented prosperity for the Second Country.

As more and more people came into the grand road leading to the Palace gates, music began to sound, and revellers began to dance. Elen-ai suddenly found herself face to face with an unfairly handsome Kaine.

"Would you care to dance?"

His customary mischievous grin almost split his face from ear to ear. He wore clothes of flaming red and orange that offset the liquid gold of his eyes, which had been further accented by the dark blue pigment set around them. He looked very good.

When Elen-ai hesitated, his smile widened. He leaned in close to her and whispered, "I didn't realise assassins didn't dance."

"I can dance perfectly well," Elen-ai snapped, slapping her hand into his proffered palm.

He laughed as he led her to the ring of dancers.

To her right, Gidyon gently swung around a girl who could not have been more than twelve. She looked caught between delight and amazement that her king was dancing with her.

Elen-ai lost sight of the King and his partner as Kaine twirled her around and around, completely sure of himself as he moved to the music.

"You dance well," she told him.

"And you aren't even slightly out of breath," he protested.

She laughed, tipping her head back as they whirled around, looking up at the night sky as it turned end over end before her eyes. "Does that really surprise you?" she asked once he had pulled her back upright and she was staring into his beautiful eyes once more.

"No." He laughed again, pulling her even closer. She could have resisted. She could have had him lying on the ground, winded and with a broken arm. There was something endearing about the fact that he too knew that, and yet he still pulled her to him.

"I heard about your bet with Gidyon," Kaine said in her ear. She was most aware of the way his lips brushed against her as he spoke.

"About Silius dancing?"

He nodded, moving his hands to her waist. He might not have been as physically fit as her, but he did dance very well.

"Gidyon swears he'll goad Silius into dancing with someone tonight. I think he said something about finding the prettiest lady," Elen-ai said. "I must admit, Gidyon does have a way of convincing people. I'm a touch worried."

Amusement seized hold of Kaine's features. "You needn't be, unless Gidyon finds the prettiest man here to entice Sil to dance."

Shock almost had Elen-ai missing a step. She thought of the prim and proper Silius, his slightly balding head, the cheekbones so high that they had doomed him to a haughty air. His austere demeanour did not seem to fit with the other men she knew who slept with one another. Of course, the men who sold their bodies were always overt with their sexuality. The sensuousness with which they carried themselves made it easy to envisage them yielding to the touch of another man. The men of the Family who preferred men were simply quite comfortable and natural with that part of themselves. But Silius with his reserve and somewhat dowdy manner just seemed so incongruous with the idea of ever taking someone to his bed, man or woman.

As he watched her contemplate this new piece of information, Kaine grinned wickedly.

"Gidyon doesn't know?" Elen-ai asked, her lips close to his ear as another song commenced.

Kaine shook his head, his hair brushing against Elen-ai's cheek. "I don't think it's ever occurred to him," he yelled over a sudden crescendo in the music.

As the song became even faster, conversation became impossible, and they danced for several more before Kaine relented with a wry grin. "I admit, I'm weak. I must rest," he told her, panting slightly.

"I was just getting warmed up, too," Elen-ai said. She was disappointed. Dancing with Kaine had been fun. He was lively, and she was willing to admit that being so close to him offered a certain thrill.

Gidyon appeared by Elen-ai's side. "Uncle, are you getting old?" He put his hands on his hips. Like Kaine, Gidyon was dressed in reds and oranges. Most of the people were, the burnt scarlet and yellow hues and of their garb chosen to emulate the sun. His blue eyes shone in the light cast by the braziers, emphasised by the black swirls that had been carefully painted around them.

Kaine mouthed an obscenity at his nephew that had both Gidyon and Elen-ai giggling.

"I bet I can outlast him – and I've been dancing already," Gidyon said.

"Are you sure about making more bets? I've heard on good authority that the likelihood of Silius dancing is very low," Elen-ai challenged.

Gidyon grabbed Elen-ai's hand and pulled her into the stream of dancers. "Trust me, Sil will dance before the night is over."

Giving up the argument, Elen-ai instead set a tormenting pace for Gidyon. However, as the King always managed to find time among his many duties to practise fighting under Elen-ai's tuition every day, so he managed to keep pace with her now. Gidyon danced with a light-footed grace, his movements curiously beautiful. It was a pleasure to dance with him, and in the time that they danced he was not her king, she was not his assassin. They were simply friends dancing together.

As the final song before the evening's second feast commenced, Gidyon dared her with a smirk to dance as fast as possible. Never one to resist a challenge, Elen-ai moved faster and faster, the King matching her step for step. Finally, he faltered, no match for an assassin's quick feet, and Elen-ai caught him, the two of them collapsing into peals of laughter at the ridiculousness of their game. The pair were applauded by the other revellers and rewarded for the spectacle they had provided by being handed the first plates piled high with food. She wandered away from Gidyon, contentedly chewing on a wing of karrabal – a bird which was famed for its deliciousness. It had been cooked to perfection.

"To one who didn't know, you and Gidyon look very much in love." Nikalus' voice came from beside her elbow. It was unclear whether he was amused or disapproving.

Her mouth full of food, Elen-ai simply looked at him.

"It was not intended to be a disapproving comment," he said.

She shrugged, wiping her mouth with the back of her hand. He cringed at her lack of decorum. She delighted in it. "Gid and I are friends," she said simply, unsure what else she should say.

"I know that. He," he hesitated, "he trusts you. He can confide in you. It is good that he has a friend."

"I'll always be here for him." She found herself curiously touched by the comment.

"Hmm." He did not elaborate further on whatever the noise was supposed to mean. "The rumours about you two will continue to spread. It is good. Nobody will suspect the truth." His last words were spoken so softly that nobody else could possibly overhear.

"Can't have anyone knowing the truth, can we?" She swayed her hips at him suggestively.

At that moment, Kaine appeared by his brother's side. "Are you bothering Elen-ai?"

"Don't be ridiculous, Kaine," Nikalus snapped, although there was no bite behind his words.

"Come. Drink. Be merry. Once the music begins again, I believe I have recovered myself for another bout of the exquisite torment that is trying to keep step with you, if you'll indulge me, Elen-ai?" Kaine said.

She couldn't help but smile. "Are you sure I won't tire you out?"

"Almost certainly you will, but who in their right mind would resist an opportunity to dance with you?"

The music and firelight did cast a certain spell that anybody would struggle to resist, but she made a point of considering his offer.

"Oh, come on," Kaine pleaded, holding his hand out. "Tell me you don't want to."

She did consider refusing him. Truth was, she wanted to dance with him far too much. She made him wait until she had finished every morsel on her plate, then she handed the simple wooden item – no Katan finery tonight – to a waiting servant.

She had finished eating just in time. Music began to sound through the street once more, and Kaine took her hand in his, pulling her into a dance. His body was far closer to hers than was decent. However, tonight was midwinter festival. What was or wasn't proper was discarded in the face of the wine and food and the spirit of revelry that overtook the city on this night. Kaine's grip on her arm tightened suddenly. Her heart froze as she feared an assailant had appeared to threaten Gidyon.

"Divine One, how did he do it?" He shouted the question in her ear, incredulity across his face.

She turned to where Kaine was looking. There, his arms linked with a girl on his right and a slightly portly man on his left, Silius performed a surprisingly adept two-step dance with exuberant abandon. Elen-ai stared at the spectacle, aware of Gidyon in the background with a grin that showed all of his teeth.

Elen-ai excused herself and marched over to the King. "How?"

His grin widened, if that was possible. "The how is unimportant."

"Don't give me that rubbish. How did you do it?" Elen-ai gestured wildly toward the now twirling Silius. He practically bounced, bringing his knees up high with every step.

"I fastened a few cups of wine upon him," Gidyon admitted.

"You cheated!" Elen-ai accused.

"You bet I couldn't do it. You never said you bet that I couldn't do it without getting him drunk," Gidyon pointed out.

Elen-ai waved her hands at him in ire, but did not actually have a sufficient riposte.

"I'll send the tailor to you," Gidyon said, gloating.

"I hate you," Elen-ai told him vehemently.

"I still won."

"I definitely hate you." Elen-ai stalked back to Kaine.

"Happy midwinter," Gidyon yelled at her retreating back.

She seriously considered making an obscene gesture at him, but she suspected it might shock people too much to see her treating their king with such irreverence. She resolved to do it in private the next chance she got.

"I personally look forward to seeing you in skirts," Kaine told her.

"You do know where I come from and what I could do to you?" Elen-ai asked, pursing her lips in an exaggerated pout.

Far from inspiring fear in him, he laughed and drew her to him once more. "Our poor beleaguered assassin," he murmured in her ear, one hand caressing the small of her back.

The music stopped to rapturous applause. Everybody settled them-selves on blankets or chairs as new musicians replaced their colleagues who had admirably kept such a lively pace for so long. Kaine let go of Elen-ai's hand and they stood together, watching as the new musicians set up their instruments. She was once more disappointed that she was no longer enjoy-ing the thrill of being so close to Kaine, but this part of the evening, just like the break for feasting, was part of tradition. Over the momentary hush, Gidyon called out to his uncle. "Kaine, will you sing?"

"You flatter me, my King," Kaine called back.

Gidyon addressed the crowd, an easy, charming smile on his face. "My uncle Kaine has the finest voice I've ever had the good fortune to hear. I would love to share this with you all."

The street echoed with cheers and claps of encouragement.

"Go on," Elen-ai told Kaine, nudging him in the ribs.

"He knows I'll do it. But I can't capitulate too quickly. He has to think that he can't get everything he wants. You failed on your end," he told her in an undertone.

"I will stab you," Elen-ai threatened.

"Do you solve all your problems with violence?" he muttered as the calls for him to sing continued.

"Not all."

He laughed as he strode to his nephew's side. "As you command, my King." He bowed in a gently mocking manner.

"I only ask," Gidyon protested, making an exaggerated face of weariness, much to the audience's delight.

Kaine had a beautiful voice. Sonorous and pure, his first choice of song was a ballad about a man who sets out to find riches to make his mother happy. By pure chance, Kaine had chosen one of Elen-ai's favourite songs. The story ended with the man coming home poor and his mother, who was very old by that point, telling him that all she needed to be happy was her child near to her. It was far sadder than many of the other songs popular in the Second Country, but the composer had skilfully blended a beautiful melody with well-chosen words to make it linger in the minds of those who listened to it even once. Kaine's rendition was particularly moving. He was either a naturally talented singer, or someone had given him superb instruction. In addition to a beautiful voice, he knew how to sing with meaning, holding certain notes for a fraction of a second longer than strictly necessary, wrapping sorrow and bittersweet heartbreak around them. The song's conclusion was greeted with a cheer of approval from the audience and shouts for more. Clearly enjoying the attention, Kaine chose a love song. For the entirety of the song, he looked directly at Elen-ai. She appreciated his bold interest. It was a refreshing change from the allusions and layered meanings that characterised exchanges in the world of the highborn.

Kaine sang five more songs, the final one a bawdy tavern song that everybody cheerfully joined him in singing. Elen-ai sang too, swept along by the excitement of the gathered crowd.

As was the custom, the carousing lasted until the first rays of dawn began to peek across the horizon. A ragged cheer went up from the (mostly inebriated) crowd when the golden glow became apparent. At this signal, people began to leave the street that had for that evening, offered them food, dancing, music, and merriment. For the rest of the day, they would sleep, or at the very least rest, enjoying one of few days within the year that could truly be filled with nothing other than nursing the effect of too many drinks. Elen-ai walked slowly back up the hill to the Palace with Kaine, two guards following them. How he had contrived to leave with her, she did not know, but she did not protest. Their pleasantly fatigued strides brought them to gently brush against each other. There was a certain enjoyment to be found in the inadvertent yet deliberate contact. Kaine smelled of alcohol and wood smoke and sweat, and it was a curiously intoxicating combination. When they went inside the Palace and he pulled her to him and suggested they go to his room, she agreed.

EIGHT

Afternoon sunlight came in through the windows of Kaine's bedroom, falling onto Elen-ai's skin. With the heat of the room's fire and gently smoking braziers, the sun almost felt warm. Beside her, Kaine ran a curious hand along her body, making an inventory of the scars she had collected.

"This is the twenty-fourth and I'm only up to your waist," he said, lightly brushing a fingertip over the offending mark.

She shook her head at his dedication to the task. "I've spent my whole life around blades and fighting, what do you expect?"

"I honestly don't know," Kaine admitted, moving his hand to the small of Elen-ai's back and running it up and down her spine. She arched her back in pleasure at the sensation of his fingertips on her skin. "I've never been with an assassin before." His hand moved up to her shoulders.

"You've given up counting?" she enquired, turning to look at him.

"Too many to count," Kaine declared, placing kisses along the wake of his hands. His lips felt good on her skin. Coming to his bed had been a good decision.

She rolled from her stomach to her side and he lay back down on the bed, his hand coming to rest on her waist.

Kaine looked very appealing like this: mussed up, tired, naked. "You're very charming like this."

"And I'm not always?"

She leaned forward to kiss him. He eagerly kissed her in return, slipping his hand down the slope of her back to pull her against him. As she pulled away from him, her glance fell over his shoulder to the table by the bedside.

"Oh!" She scrambled to her knees, eliciting a groan of dismay at her departure. She reached over him and retrieved the object that had caught her interest.

"Conventions of Legal Heritage, volume one. It really is bedtime reading for you."

He sat up and took the book from her. "It is a sad truth that I take books with me to bed more frequently than beautiful women."

"Do you take women to your bed regularly?" She feigned haughtiness, putting her hands on her hips.

"Not often enough," came the mournful reply.

She rolled her eyes. A sense of possessiveness when it came to her lovers had never been something with which she had ever struggled. Yet a tiny thorn of competitiveness pricked her side. Kaine would have been discreet, yet she was certain he would have had his share of people in his bed.

"You know, you're quite energetic," she told Kaine, the condescension of the comment causing him to huff, and her to laugh.

"Are you trying to goad me into something, Elen-ai?" he challenged. The point was somewhat lost as his eyes roamed hungrily over her naked body.

Darkness was falling when Elen-ai raised her head, fighting the pleasant drowsiness that had settled over her. Kaine lay beside her, resting his head against her arm.

"I should go," Elen-ai said.

"Mm." Kaine's sound of protest was tinged with fatigue. Neither of them had slept since the night before the midwinter festival. Elen-ai at least had been trained to require very little sleep.

"I should go," she repeated. "I'm sure Gidyon will be awake and doing something dull like reading a petition or a report, or studying shipbuilding to better inform how to redesign the harbour."

"And? Let him. It's the day after midwinter, nobody should do work, let alone anything as impossibly dull as any of those things." Kaine turned so that his face was pressed directly against Elen-ai's arm, muffling his words. The offhanded manner with which he spoke about the tasks of rule belied the sincerity with which Elen-ai knew he took his role as Gidyon's adviser.

"Still, I should go," Elen-ai said.

Kaine groaned. "I can't believe you're thinking about my nephew when you're in my bed. Naked."

"I live and die by the wishes of the king," Elen-ai responded glibly, eliciting another groan from him. She laughed as he moved his head to bury it in his own arms. "Not liking your duties, my lord adviser?"

"Being adviser to my sister was much easier than being adviser to Gidyon," Kaine lamented, raising his head.

"Well, nobody ever thought they would see a king in the Second Country."

"There's a good reason for that."

Something in his tone caused Elen-ai to raise herself up so that she could look at him properly. "What do you mean?"

Kaine's reluctance to answer was obvious. "I just ... men shouldn't be on the throne."

"Why?"

"Men have less suitable temperaments to rule. Think about the fact that the jails to Herran's west are filled with men who have beaten their women, or each other, or who have raped someone weaker than them. Women just don't do that sort of thing."

"How are you so certain?" Elen-ai asked.

"Like I said, look at who we imprison. It's only exceptional cases where we lock up women. Think about Meg-am the murderess. She was imprisoned six years ago for killing fifteen people with a blunt axe. Since her trial, maybe one or two other women have been jailed, whereas I can't count the number of men who have been locked up for violent crimes."

"Just because most women are not always as strong as a man doesn't mean that they can't or won't also be violent, or dangerous, or of poor temperament," Elen-ai countered. "I've seen women order a killing just as easily, if not more coldly, than any man."

His disagreement was apparent on his face. "Women might be cold, they may be capable of poor impulses or even violence, but they're just more temperate, more naturally suited to finding reason and rationality," he said.

"Surely that's just taught."

"Of course it's taught. But it comes more naturally to women. Sil, Nik, and I had years and years of lessons to teach us to be rational and logical, even in the heat of argument."

"So you've never wondered whether you would be a good king?" Elen-ai asked.

"I would never presume to think it appropriate for me to sit on the throne," Kaine said. "I mean, I love my nephew, but the second he's anywhere near the throne, we're facing down a war. When a woman sat on the throne, there was never even the suggestion of any divide within the country serious enough to lead to war."

"But that's just Halen Katan," she protested.

"Exactly. Another man. The Second Country should have a woman on the throne to counter that sort of tendency."

"So what do you think about Gidyon then?"

"I think him being on the throne is an accident of my sister's inability to bear a girl. He should not be on the throne, but he is, and given that he is, he's doing a magnificent job. But he still shouldn't be on the throne."

His conviction surprised her. Kaine's light-hearted preference for mischief suggested not much overly bothered him. The fact he was so certain about the flaws of his own gender belied that levity.

"Surely you agree with me?" he asked.

She opened her mouth to disagree but found that he wasn't entirely wrong. When Latana had first told her about the decision to make Gidyon her heir, Elen-ai had been furious. She had thought the decision a terrible one, and the prospect of a man on the throne nothing short of blasphemous. Her reaction hadn't simply been informed by a natural preference for tradition. It was the thought that a man would be on the throne rather than the moderate, cool, calm competence of the unbroken line of queens who had safely guided the Second Country through generations of prosperity and security.

Kaine knew he had made his point. "It's all an exercise in rhetoric for the most part, really," Kaine said. "We have to deal with the circumstances in which we find ourselves, and right now, the circumstances are that Latana is dead and Gidyon is on the throne." He took one of Elen-ai's hands in his and kissed it firmly, indicating he felt no ill will over their disagreement.

"Do you miss her?" Kaine had been on a diplomatic journey to the Fourth Country when the queen had been murdered. The message informing him of Latana's death wouldn't have even reached him by the time the funeral service was held in Herran. Elen-ai had always felt sorry for him, that he had never been given the opportunity to say goodbye.

Kaine shook his head slightly in thought. "She wasn't just my queen, she was my big sister. I still can't believe that she's gone. Reading on a page what happened just doesn't feel real."

"I'm sorry, I shouldn't have asked." Despite his honest answer, she felt as though she had pried beyond what was reasonable. And she knew what Kaine did not: Gidyon was the product of a relationship that broke the sacred rules of impartiality. In some ways Kaine was lucky that his memory of Latana was not marred by that knowledge as it was for Gidyon.

"No, it's fine. You understand better than most people." He squeezed the hand he still held in emphasis.

"I really should go." She slipped out of his bed, her skin prickling at the chill in the air that the braziers could not entirely dispel. She cast about for her clothes.

Kaine watched her with undisguised appreciation. She tugged her tunic over her head. As she checked her blades were all properly in place, she wondered whether coming to his bed had been a mistake. At the time, when she had been caught up in desire and slight drunkenness on the spirit and the atmosphere of the festival, it had seemed a good idea, but now she wondered what exactly it was that he wanted from her.

Kaine took a breath to say something then apparently reconsidered, the hesitation lingering on his still-parted lips.

"Yes?" Elen-ai paused midway through buttoning up her trousers.

"This doesn't have to happen again, if you don't want it to," Kaine said, waving his hand at the tousled bed. "I mean, I enjoyed today, but you understand that as adviser to Gidyon..." He paused, seemingly at a loss for words – the first time Elen-ai had ever seen him as such.

The uncertainty of the unflappable Kaine made Elen-ai smile. She strode over and leaned down to kiss him, long and sweet. His hands made their way up to her waist, pulling her back toward him, and for a moment she contemplated surrendering to his suggestion.

"I'm sure we'll figure something out," she told him before she left.

On her way to Gidyon's rooms, Elen-ai ran into Freya. The Councilwoman's face looked comically small amid the scarves, throws and handmuff piled around her frame.

"I know I look ridiculous," the older woman admitted. "It's so Goddess-cursed cold here. Oranis is always reasonably warm."

"It does seem as though you could get lost in there," Elen-ai said, stifling a laugh.

"I cannot wait until we get back home. All I ever wear on my feet in Oranis is sandals." The wistful note in her tone was unmistakable.

"You aren't leaving us, are you?" Elen-ai was saddened by the prospect. She liked the foreigner very much.

"Sadly, yes. More than time we went home. We stayed far longer than we expected, but establishing the treaty with the Fourth Country to get some guarantee that our people will be safe took longer than any of us expected due to the Queen's death. Honestly, we should have left weeks ago, but we stayed especially for the midwinter festival. It reminded me of the festivals of dance back home."

"Did you enjoy it?"

"Oh, very much. And by the looks of it, you did, too." The knowing twinkle in Freya's eye indicated she was quite aware of what had transpired between Elen-ai and Kaine.

Not knowing how she should reply, Elen-ai dropped her gaze to her feet, eliciting a laugh in response. "I will miss you," she said truthfully, ignoring the subject of with whom, or how, she had spent the day.

"And I you. I have enjoyed the time I have spent with you, Elen-ai. But I think it is time to go home."

"The Palace is beautiful, but there is nothing quite like home," Elen-ai agreed.

The comment earned her a look of surprise. "I thought you had left the Family," Freya said. She too knew of Elen-ai's origins.

Elen-ai shook her head. "I suppose you could say I'm on loan to Gidyon."

"Perhaps I'm wrong, but I thought the Family was politically neutral."

"We are. That's why I'm not here as a member the Family," Elen-ai explained. She uncomfortably remembered her argument with Mari-am. It had been the first day she had not been preoccupied with it, until that moment.

"Ah." The Councilwoman clearly did not understand. "Well, wherever ends up being home for you, I hope you get there soon."

"Thank you, Freya." Elen-ai moved on to find Gidyon.

The King was in his private rooms, writing. The document looked long and was almost certainly boring. He glanced up as Elen-ai came in. "I was wondering what time I'd see you."

"I was taking some rest, like you should have been doing," she said, walking over to peer over his shoulder.

"Is that what you want to call it?" Amusement flashed through his bright blue eyes as he glanced up at her.

"I have no idea what you're talking about. Have you eaten today?" She adopted a haughty tone that almost completely failed to be effective.

"I think you and Kaine will be good for one another," he said, ignoring her question.

"Um." Elen-ai had no idea what she could or should say in response.

"Oh please, I have seen the looks he has been throwing your way, not to mention the way you two were with each other last night. And you are wearing the same clothes as last night, too."

She hadn't thought about her clothes. On reflection, she probably should have taken the time to change. She saw no point in trying to pretend. "Are you certain it doesn't bother you?"

He made a nonchalant gesture. "Provided you do not start doing anything where I can see, I have other things to find far more upsetting."

She didn't bother repeating the question. If Gidyon said he was fine with it, he was fine with it. "What about you? Did you find a willing woman to take your innocence last night?" she asked, knowing full well that he hadn't. Gidyon had never said it, but she knew that he was afraid of caring romantically for someone after the trouble he'd had with Rania Harete.

At this, Gidyon spared her a withering look. "Like I said, I have more important things on my mind."

"Not many boys your age would say that," she commented, the teasing tone still in her voice.

"How many of them are the unwanted king of a country?" Gidyon asked distractedly.

"Good point. Tell me, do you think men have a more violent temperament than women?"

Gidyon continued his writing, suggesting that whatever he was doing, it was of reasonable importance. Or he didn't want to lose his train of thought.

"It is not really a debate I have given a great amount of thought to. Why? What do you think?"

"I don't know what I think."

"You really are a terrible liar. You will not hurt my feelings if you say you think men are less suited to rule, you know."

"You say that now," Elen-ai cautioned.

"Yes, I do. I happen to think I am well suited to rule and I happen to be a man, as many people have noticed. I do not have a choice, anyway. I have to be well suited to rule. And regardless of your thoughts on the male temperament, you support me, so clearly the question is a theoretical one."

"You could indulge me in a little roundabout conversation."

"I indulged you last night with all the dancing and merriment," Gidyon said, not looking up from the page.

"What are you doing anyway?" Elen-ai asked.

"I am writing, Elen-ai. Honestly, all these skills of observation the Family supposedly have seem to be just a myth."

She had to fight not to laugh at his facetious tone. "I did indeed notice that you weren't dancing on the tabletop, Gidyon. I was wondering what exactly you were writing."

His serious demeanour returned. "I am writing a letter to Kar-am of Atak. She is the leading expert on warfare theory, and I have been receiving quite the education from her by correspondence."

"Do you really think that you need to know this stuff?" Elen-ai asked.

From her vantage, she could see Gidyon arch his eyebrow. "Would you rather I find out I need to know it and do not?"

As was often the case, Gidyon had a point.

"Do you need me to do anything?"

"What, you want me to give you something to do? Surely you could just go and enjoy not having to do anything. I am sure Kaine will be still in his room."

Ignoring the attempt to rile her, Elen-ai sighed slightly. "Yes, but I knew you would be working, and I didn't want you to be working alone."

Gidyon looked up at her with his full attention. "You know, Elen-ai, I could say that I have been fortunate in a number of aspects. But I think that your friendship is the thing in which I have been the most fortunate. You are a wonderful friend." He smiled.

Elen-ai made a noise of dismissal to dispel the weight of the emotion. "Just give me something to do," she said brusquely to hide how deeply touched she was.

He directed her to a stack of petitions, telling her to put aside the ones that she thought were of importance. Happily, she began, bored by the task reasonably quickly but nevertheless willing to do it so that Gidyon had one less thing to complete.

The letter from Halen arrived an hour later.

NINE

"I really hate to admit how clever Halen has been about this," Gidyon said after he had finished reading the letter for the umpteenth time. He had not sat down since down since he had first stood to take the missive. His unceasing pacing of the room as he read and re-read the letter had Elen-ai on the verge of snapping at him to sit down.

"Don't. Give the credit for his cleverness to someone else," Elen-ai suggested, drawing an embattled laugh from her king.

Gidyon glared at the offending document before he finally put it down. "You know, doing this the day after midwinter was just mean."

"He's just a mean man with pretensions of importance," she said scathingly.

"Yes. Well, he just declared that Serenah is the rightful claimant to the throne and demanded that I recognise it. I am not exactly sure that I would have expected anything less from him," Gidyon said. Fatigue hung heavily in his voice.

"Does he honestly expect you to abdicate?" She still hadn't got over her incredulity at the man's boldness.

"Of course not. That is not how the game is played, Elen-ai."

"The game is stupid." Elen-ai put one foot after the other on the low table, which was probably worth more than she could have earned for the Family in an average year.

Gidyon sighed. "I do not necessarily disagree with you, but unfortunately this is how things are done."

"I think you should throw him in jail," Elen-ai suggested unhelpfully. "And while you're at it, Julyana Bertak could join him."

"While the prospect of Halen in a jail full of murderers, thieves, and rapists does fill me with a sense of childish glee, do you not think that people may feel he has a legitimate case against me if that is my immediate response to this?" Gidyon picked the letter up once more and waved it at her, as though she needed some kind of reminder of its contents.

Elen-ai grunted.

Gidyon sighed and threw the page back down on the table near Elen-ai's foot. He sat beside her with a thud.

"Are you all right?"

He threw his hands up. "My mother was killed by the man who might have been my father. Nobody wants me on the throne because of something I cannot help, Sil keeps telling me I need to find a wife, and now Halen is suggesting that my younger cousin who is clearly ill-versed in matters of state should rule instead of me. But aside from all of that, I'm fine."

"Speaking of fathers, have you spoken with Zekken?" Elen-ai asked. "The Aadran family may be able to assist if you approach him."

Gidyon made a derisive noise and shook his head. "I want nothing to do with him. Besides, if the relationship between him and mother is discovered, I would be finished. It is best if I do not speak to him."

Recognising that he had a point, she did not push him further. "Fair enough."

"You know, I am so angry with mother for leaving us in this incredible mess," he confessed.

Elen-ai did not respond. Gidyon rarely spoke of those feelings. She figured it was best to simply let him talk at his own pace.

"If she had not carried on with Zekken, Erek would not have killed her, and she would still be here to ensure my claim to the throne was secure before I had to actually take the throne."

"You can't know that Erek wouldn't have killed her. He was infatuated with her, and he wasn't well. Infatuation and instability are rarely an ideal mix. If not that night, perhaps at some other time in some other way," Elen-ai said gently. "He'd already tried it once before." She reminded him of Erek's first attempt on both Gidyon and Latana's lives with a pointed glance at where his stomach had been gored.

"You're trying to make me feel better," Gidyon said.

"Is it working?"

"No."

They both chuckled. Silence descended for a moment.

"I am so angry with her," he said again.

"She did love you," Elen-ai said. "She wanted so badly to protect you from her mistakes. It was why she hired me." Elen-ai remembered the calculated way the Queen had let her self-control slip in that first meeting, revealing the depth of her love and fear for her son. At the time, it had felt profane to witness the emotions of a monarch, but also curiously intimate, and had in no small way pushed Elen-ai toward accepting the contract despite her revulsion at the prospect of a man on the throne.

"I know. But it does not change that she died with me angry with her," he said, his voice dropping low with the admission.

"Death is rarely neatly tied up," Elen-ai said.

"Is that your professional experience speaking?"

"Yes and no. I've often heard a great many meaningless or angry words which are unknowingly the last ones spoken to a loved one. Some of them have even been mine. You are not unique in this."

"Does it ever bother you that you took away that proper last goodbye for so many people?" Unlike in the past, Gidyon asked about her trade with no judgment; now he simply sounded curious.

"Not really. It was their time. And there's no guarantee that anyone will have the opportunity to say the right goodbye to their loved ones – if such a thing as the right goodbye even exists."

The King was silent, his forehead furrowed for a moment as he considered what she had said. "I miss her, you know." The admission was laced with pain.

"Of course you do. She was your mother." Elen-ai put her hand on his knee.

"I do not want to be angry with her, you know. I'm scared I will never stop being angry with her for that stupid, awful choice."

"I don't know if you will or won't." She didn't like not being able to offer him certainty, but she would not lie to him to make him feel better.

"She should be here, fixing this. She always knew what to do in response to this sort of thing. She would have known how to outmanoeuvre Halen." His hands fisted in his lap. "Divine One, she would already have had a plan by now."

Elen-ai said nothing, knowing that there was no way for her to salve this particular wound. Gidyon's grief was still too raw to be eased by a kind word or platitude. Instead, she gently squeezed his knee in a poor offering of comfort. "We might not have your mother, but we'll come up with something."

He sighed. "I know. I must say, though, I do not look forward to breaking the news to my uncles at supper tonight."

Supper, a light meal in deference to the excessive quantity of food that had been consumed the previous evening and the slumber that had taken up most of the day, took place only a little later. Elen-ai, after changing into fresh clothes, accompanied Gidyon into the intimate dining room where he usually dined with his uncles. Silius was already there, in conversation with Councillors Freya and Ashtyn from the Third Country. While everybody always looked tired the day after midwinter festival, Silius had somehow contrived to look as immaculate as ever. If Elen-ai hadn't witnessed his dancing with her own eyes, she never would have believed it had occurred. It was almost worth losing her bet with Gidyon to have seen it.

At Gidyon's entrance, Silius, Freya, and Ashtyn rose. He waved them to sit back down and took his seat with minimal ceremony. Only a few moments later, Kaine strode in. His gaze slid to Elen-ai immediately. Their eyes met across the room. Both smiled.

Gidyon, evidently seeing this, cleared his throat and rolled his eyes with the briefest of movements at Elen-ai. "Is Nik joining us?"

"I wouldn't count on it." Kaine chuckled as he slipped into his seat, then elaborated for the Councillors and Elen-ai: "He always overindulges at midwinter and is in a right state the next day. He's learned that it's easiest if he just stays in bed all day."

"I can see why one might be tempted to overindulge." Ashtyn leaned forward, his green eyes glittering in the light from the torches on the wall. "The festival was quite wonderful."

"We are so glad that you decided to stay for it." Gidyon's smile made it seem as though there could be nothing else bothering him. Elen-ai couldn't understand how he managed it.

Servants converged on the table with plates – Katan plates, of course – of food.

While they were perhaps a little overly formal to her mind, Elen-ai had come to quite like the dinners at the Palace. When not in service of some grand occasion, or to entertain some guest or another, the candid discussions among the family members was quite enjoyable to be a part of. It reminded her of home.

"Well, you both witnessed a never-before-seen feat," Kaine told the Councillors.

"Oh?" Freya's mouth quirked in anticipation of whatever he was about to say. Despite the deep love she and Ashtyn shared, it seemed she, too, was not immune to Kaine's charm.

"You witnessed Sil dancing." Kaine chuckled gleefully. His elder brother glared at him balefully.

"Oh!" Gidyon punctuated the exclamation by clapping his hands, inadvertently claiming the attention of the room. "I will have to determine the best occasion for Elen-ai to debut her skirt."

"They made a bet about whether or not you would dance, Sil. Elen-ai lost," Kaine explained.

Silius glared first at Elen-ai then at his nephew. In reply, Gidyon smiled back sweetly. Both Councillors were obvious in their fight against laughter.

"I'm sure you will choose the least convenient time for me to be paraded around looking ridiculous." Elen-ai couldn't resist pouting. The thought of anybody seeing her in skirts, let alone a room full of people, was horrifying.

"Nonsense, Elen-ai. I would never have someone associated so closely with me looking ridiculous," Gidyon said with a wicked grin.

"Just for that, I hope Serenah takes the throne and bans the wearing of skirts," Elen-ai informed him haughtily.

Gidyon simply laughed at her response. It was a light exchange that for one moment made it possible to forget Halen's letter, and the very real threat that it promised.

Once dinner was over and the Councillors had excused themselves, Gidyon broached the subject of the letter. There was something heartbreaking about seeing weariness and resignation replace the humour on the faces of his uncles. Even Silius, despite his ire at the wager on his dancing, had seemed relaxed for once.

After the moment of shocked silence following Gidyon's announcement, Kaine cursed extensively. Gidyon said nothing, merely watching his two uncles.

"Well, obviously we need to have a response to this within a legal framework," Silius said from above steepled fingers.

"I've read just about every legal book in the Second Country," Kaine said. "The Veertaks were kind enough to send me a small mountain of them several weeks ago." Kaine threw a tired smile at Elen-ai over their shared joke about his bedtime reading material. "I imagine I would be able to start drafting something."

"Should I get Nik?" Silius offered.

Gidyon made a noncommittal gesture.

As the conversation continued, Elen-ai rose silently from the table, her departure almost unnoticed. There was little she could contribute to the discussion among the members of the Royal Family. But there was something she could do instead.

She detoured by her rooms to pick up warmer outer clothes before she exited the Palace. Herran, the evening after the midwinter festival, was quiet. Its inhabitants were still recovering from the previous evening's revelry. The near emptiness of the streets was disconcerting. Elen-ai was accustomed to the city resonating with the sounds of life at any time of day or night. Walking through the empty streets in the cold night air was quite eerie, and Elen-ai hurried to the Family's home. On a whim, she chose one of the roof entrances, and scaled the building with practised ease. She enjoyed using her skills. For the briefest moment, it took the worry from her mind. The warmth of the home enveloped her as soon as she stepped inside. After the cold stone walls of the Palace, it was blissful. A Mother appeared by her side almost instantly.

"Was I so loud?" Elen-ai asked. She didn't think that she had been at all perceptible in her entrance.

"Are you worried that you are losing the finesse of the Family?" A slightly sardonic smile kissed her Mother's lips. Evidently she did not view Elen-ai's presence in the Palace with favour.

"I have news, if you will hear it," Elen-ai replied in an even voice rather than the snapped response she instinctively wished to give.

Without any word of acknowledgment, her Mother led Elen-ai through the house. Even if she might disapprove of Elen-ai's open support for Gidyon, Elen-ai was still a daughter of the Family. Whatever information she brought would not be heard standing in an entranceway.

In a small room, Elen-ai's Mother poured tea that had been left on a low table ahead of their entrance by unseen hands. The Family had no fine Katan ceramics, nor did they have any of the achingly beautiful but outrageously expensive glass tumblers of the Palace. Instead, she was handed a simple clay cup, which itself was a luxury. Many drank from crudely carved wooden vessels.

As she sat on the floor, Elen-ai wondered if this room had been chosen on purpose. Was the absence of any furniture other than the table a silent jibe, suggesting that she was growing soft in the Palace surrounded by finery and luxury? She told herself not to be paranoid. Perhaps she had grown too accustomed to Palace life, seeing political messages in even the most mundane things. She looked down at the still water of her tea as she raised the cup to her lips. When she had been very young, she had been required to drink tea without creating any trace of the cup's passage from table to mouth on the water's surface. It had been a difficult task to master and the hours she had spent practising it were still burned into her memory. Now, she didn't have to even think about it. Whenever she lifted any vessel to her lips, whatever was in it remained as still as if it was not moving at all.

"Now. Your news." Her Mother sipped the tea, the picture of composed serenity.

"Halen Katan has officially requested that Gidyon recognise his granddaughter's legal claim to the throne and abdicate immediately."

Her mother offered no reaction.

"You seem perturbed by this," her Mother commented after she had taken another sip.

"The girl has neither claim nor aptitude to rule," Elen-ai replied.

"What does it concern the Family if some incompetent girl sits on the throne? It is not our way to hold an opinion on the politics of the Second Country."

"Unless the politics of the Second Country endanger the Family," Elem-ai noted.

"And how might an unseasoned girl be a danger to the Family, exactly?"

"She has too many ties to the Katan family. Not enough people would accept her on the throne. Civil war could come to the Queendom. If it reaches the streets of Herran, who knows what damage could be wrought. Our children who are not of an age to defend themselves may be placed in harm's way." One of the main reasons that Elen-ai had been sent back to the Palace was so she could alert the Family to any possibility of warfare so that they could move their children to safety well ahead of time. The Family would always protect its own.

"Very true. While unsurprising, Halen Katan's move is an unfortunate one indeed." The Mother sipped her tea calmly, as though they were not discussing the possibility of a terrible and destructive civil war.

"We should—" Elen-ai began.

"We should do nothing other than protect ourselves," her Mother interrupted firmly, the first suggestion of emotion in her voice.

"But surely we protect our own better if we can affect the outcome of such a struggle," Elen-ai said.

Her Mother raised an eyebrow. "You do not speak as though you are a member of the Family, Elen-ai." There was definitely the edge of a rebuke in her comment now.

"I am a loyal Daughter of the Family, my Mother, but that loyalty does not mean that I do not question, do not disagree," Elen-ai countered. She paused, expecting a rebuke or retort, but when she met only silence, she continued. "I know that you may think I have misstepped in becoming close to the King, but that does not make my thoughts any less valid. We find ourselves in times when precedent and history have already been overturned. If there is sufficient threat to the stability of the Queendom then perhaps the Family may find neutrality is not possible to maintain. I think neutrality is a fine position to hold, but perhaps not in all matters, when the consequences are so..." She trailed off under the severe gaze of her Mother, worried she might have overstepped her place.

For what seemed like an eternity, there was silence in the room. Elen-ai sipped her tea to disguise her uncertainty. Finally, her Mother spoke. "You have raised a good point, my Daughter. I cannot say that it will lead us into battle on behalf of the boy-king, but it certainly is something that we must consider."

Relief flooded Elen-ai's body. She hadn't realised how afraid she had been of the response to her words. "All I ask is that the perspective which my place within the Palace may offer be heard."

Elen-ai hadn't long left the home when she came across two people huddled in a doorway. The sound of their hammering practically assaulted her ears in the deserted streets. The unusualness of someone out on the streets after midwinter, let alone someone doing any form of work, prickled along her senses. She took a few steps toward the pair. Despite the meagre illumination only offered by light spilling through the windows of surrounding buildings, she could easily see them thanks to the skills of the Family. One of the people was nailing a notice into the timber door.

Elen-ai's first thought was that it was an eviction notice, but to deliver such news on the evening after midwinter, particularly a bitterly cold one such as this, was unlikely. Plus, like many of the houses in Herran, it was built from a mix of timber and wood, the reasonably solid construction and well-painted shutters suggesting that it was a successful store. She reflexively pulled the shadows around her, further concealing herself from view. Within a moment, the pair moved on. One held a large stack of pages. Truly troubled, Elen-ai went over to read the notice.

What she saw had her biting back a yell of anger.

She ripped the notice down and ran to the Palace, straight to Gidyon's rooms by the shortest route: the wall. As she had known he would be, he was still at work. Two huge stacks of paper were placed on either side of him. He did not seem particularly surprised when she unlatched the window and climbed through it.

"I always enjoy the new and exciting ways you come to see me, Elen-ai," he said, barely looking up as he placed a page onto the pile to his right.

"Halen is putting up announcements that he's demanded you recognise Serenah's legal claim to the throne." The words all but tumbled over each other as they left Elen-ai's lips. She held out the crumpled notice for him to see.

Gidyon stared at her for a second, his blue eyes flat. "Of course he is."

"He really is a right bastard," Elen-ai said.

"Well, we cannot send out people to try to tear them down. It will simply look as though I am afraid the claim is valid. I will have to respond."

"Try to get some sleep tonight," Elen-ai suggested, knowing that he almost certainly wouldn't.

"I will try. Thank you, Elen-ai. We are lucky you happened upon this now." Already, his mind was working on what he would do. Elen-ai could see it in the way his eyes no longer were quite focusing on her. There was no point in staying. She had no suggestion on how he should respond other than poisoning the entire Katan family. Despite how desperately she would have loved to undertake such a task, she knew her suggestion would not be taken up.

Figuring that her exit from Gidyon's rooms would perturb the guards outside given they hadn't seen her go in, Elen-ai went back out the window, easily moving around the outside of the Palace. She was halfway to her own rooms when she changed her mind.

The light still burned in Kaine's room, too. He looked up from the book he was reading in bed as she came through his window. Despite his surprise at her entrance, he remained reasonably composed. "What are you doing here?"

"I went to inform the Family of Halen's letter," she said.

"Thank you for telling me?" His confusion was dulled by the slight smile that touched his lips.

"Well, my bed will be cold. But you're already in yours." She closed the window and stepped toward the bed. She probably should have told him about the proclamations that Halen had put around Herran, but she selfishly wanted just a few more hours where she could forget about the actions of such a greedy, callous man.

The hint of a smile broadened into an outright grin as he put the book aside.

TEN

"Well, one thing I have to say for him, Halen has played this masterfully," Gidyon admitted a few days later, striding into the council chamber whose walls were papered with more maps, charts, and notes than ever. The room had been transformed into a space of political war council, inhabited almost constantly by some combination of Gidyon, Elen-ai, Silius, Nikalus, and Kaine. From within the room, they had coordinated the sending and receiving of messages across the Second Country, mapping out the political terrain as news from spies in the seven households and across the Second Country reached them. So far, the Veertaks had unequivocally declared their support for Gidyon, while the Bertaks had declared their support for Serenah. The remaining five families had failed to declare, although the Tak and Aardan were almost certainly going to release a declaration of neutrality within the coming days. That left the Rasatan and Harete families as the deciding factors. That was not a prospect with which Elen-ai felt comfortable, especially as Gidyon's exchange with Rania had led him to believe that her family would renege on their promise to support him.

"I think things are almost certainly going to come to a battle," Gidyon continued.

"Of the wits?" Elen-ai asked hopefully.

"If that is what eventuates, obviously we should send you in, Elen-ai."

The levity of the exchange poorly concealed the deep dismay they both felt over the fact that all of Gidyon's efforts to delegitimise Halen's actions had failed.

"What has happened now?" Kaine asked.

Gidyon strode over to the table where food and drinks had been placed hours before and picked up a small bread loaf. While Elen-ai thought to herself that he probably could be eating something slightly less stale, she was nevertheless glad that he was eating anything at all. Besides, the fine flour with which Palace bread was made was probably better stale than the coarse stuff used to make breads in the lowborn areas. He chewed as he composed his response, looking with slight disdain at the roll in his hand as he registered that it was far from fresh. With a shrug, he swallowed and took another bite. "It seems that, even though I did not enact the full reforms I wanted to thanks to the Council's objection, the minor change I made to how Herran's judges operate has been raised as evidence of tampering with the legal system."

"But that's nonsense," Silius exclaimed. He stood up, stepping around a precarious stack of books that Kaine had placed there the day before and ordered nobody touch, and looked at one of the pages Gidyon obligingly pulled from a pile with his free hand. So much communication had flooded in and out of the palace that Elen-ai couldn't understand how Gidyon kept track of one particular page.

"How many lowborn know enough about the legal system to know that what Halen's saying is nonsense, though?" Nikalus pointed out to his older brother. "Consider all they will take from such a claim: the King has tampered with the law to serve his own ends."

"Anyway," Gidyon said, cutting across his uncles' exchange. "Apparently the legal response that we spent so many sleepless nights crafting is invalid because of the tampering with the legal system that I have apparently conducted." He did a magnificent job of concealing his frustration with the futile effort that had been expended, but Elen-ai could see it in the clench of his jaw, nevertheless.

"I could have done so many better things with those nights," Kaine grumbled. He threw a glance at Elen-ai who quickly looked down to hide her smile. Regardless of how little sleep either of them had got, she had managed to make her way to Kaine's bed every night. She had only ever slept beside someone for several consecutive nights once before, and that had been so that she could get close to a contract. The woman had been an acceptable bedmate, but she had snored, which irritated Elen-ai. Fortunately, Kaine did not snore.

"All of us could have," Gidyon said, either ignoring or missing the implication behind Kaine's comment.

"Anyway, with this new accusation, he has an excuse to march against Herran and take it by force."

"The people of Herran will never stand to have the city taken by one of the Seven Families – especially not one that seizes it with an army," Elen-ai's response was a kneejerk comment. The idea that one of the Families might try to claim Herran as their own was repulsive to anyone who had been born in the city. The importance of the families being kept at a safe distance from the crown was taught to all children of Herran. It was vital to the security and stability of the country.

"If the streets are overrun, they may have no choice but to yield to him," Gidyon replied grimly.

"And Halen has the knowledge of warfare and combat to take Herran?" Kaine asked.

"At this stage, I honestly would not be surprised if he had been studying warfare for years." Gidyon sounded tired. "But superior numbers alone may make up for any lack of finesse on his part in any case."

"You know, I really don't like him," Nikalus said conversationally.

The unexpected sarcasm caused everybody in the room to chuckle, even Silius. It was a welcome relief from the imminent prospect of war tearing the Second Country apart. Almost immediately, however, sobriety returned to the room.

"We need to ask the Veertaks if they are willing to send troops to our aid," Gidyon said as he went over to stand in front of the map of Herran pinned to a wall.

"Even if they do agree, they don't have a large number of trained fighters who they could send to us," Silius replied. It seemed his information network rivalled even the Family; they hadn't been able to give Elen-ai any idea of how many trained fighters the Veertak family actually had in their employ. She tucked both the knowledge of Silius' spies and the number of Veertak fighters away in her mind to report back to the Family.

"And the Royal Guard is how many people?" Gidyon asked.

"A few hundred strong," Nikalus answered.

Gidyon turned to Elen-ai. "Do you think we could ask the people of Herran for help?"

She considered the question, standing and pouring herself a drink to give herself time to think. "I think some people would be willing to fight for the city. The Katan are not well loved by the lowborn of Herran. Some – those for whom the prospect of a man on the throne is still too much to bear – may actually march themselves over to Halen, although I think most will simply stay in their homes and hope that whatever strife occurs does not touch them."

"Some is better than none, though," Gidyon said.

"Yes, but how do you propose we use them? Give them a sword and point them at Halen and his forces?" Silius asked, his nose wrinkling in disdain at the idea.

"I'd put them in drills with the Royal Guard as soon as possible," Elen-ai suggested, unsure if Silius' question was even directed at her. "And I wouldn't give them swords. Spears, perhaps, may be easier for them to use." The image of a group of people who had never held a sword before swinging them wildly was a horrifying prospect.

"The Royal Guard exists to protect the Palace, not to train people off the street," Nikalus protested.

"The Royal Guard won't be able to protect the Palace if Herran is overtaken by Katan fighters. Besides, who else would you have train the city's lowborn to fight for us?" Kaine said.

"I think Nik has a point, Kaine," Silius said. "You can't disrupt the daily routine of the Royal Guard. It is important that it doesn't look as though we are panicking. Perception of Gidyon's control may be just as important as our ability to defeat Katan forces on a battlefield, if not more so. There is more than one battle going on here."

"Let those who are willing to fight for us train with the Palace Guard." Gidyon's decision halted the disagreement between his uncles and Elen-ai. "And maybe see if any of Herran's duelling competitors would be willing to join our people, as well. They at least will be able to use a sword. Nik, would you make the arrangements?"

Nikalus shot a glare at Kaine before stalking from the room, punctuating his irritation with a toss of his blond hair.

"Should I have worded my decision more nicely?" Gidyon wondered aloud once Nikalus had left. Concern flitted across his features.

"He'll be fine," Silius reassured him. "We're family. You don't have to worry about politics or diplomacy with us. Even if we disagree privately, we will all always support you in public. And we will do everything possible to make sure you win this."

Even though Elen-ai did not always find Silius to be the most palatable company – he was a bit too pompous and too severe – in moments when he spoke with such quiet effusiveness and loyalty, she could not find someone she respected more. She had seen Silius' unwavering loyalty to Gidyon in enormous amounts over the days since Halen's ultimatum had arrived. And she had seen how Gidyon in turn drew strength from the support of not simply Silius, but all his uncles. If the bonds of family alone were sufficient to guarantee victory, the Royal Family would win any challenge.

"Sil is right, Gid," Kaine said. "We're in this together."

Gidyon sighed, his shoulders slumping as he let go of his rigid self-control for a moment. He ran a hand through the spun gold of his hair and sat down for the first time since he had entered the room.

The door slammed open and Nikalus re-entered, a letter in his hand. "I'm sorry, Gid," he said, his face grave. Any trace of his frustration at his nephew's disagreement with him had vanished.

Gidyon's face fell even further. He took the linen page from Nikalus. He read it twice then hurled it to the floor. He stood, completely rigid, then quietly said, "I need a moment," before striding from the room.

"The Harete family has declared for the Katan claim," Nikalus explained to the perplexed Elen-ai, Silius, and Kaine.

"Janyce is Halen's niece, it's not entirely surprising," Kaine pointed out as he gave a worried glance toward the door through which Gidyon had left.

"But she and the rest of the Harete family despise one another," Silius said.

"Perhaps being situated between the Katan and Bertak lands might have been a compelling reason to throw their lot in with them," Nikalus suggested.

Elen-ai walked over to the map, looking at the way the Harete forest was bordered by the clay-rich soil of the Katan lands and the mountainous Bertak estate. The dense forest would likely make assaulting the Harete family with outright force difficult, if not impossible. But there were many threats that could be levelled against them other than direct attack. If the Bertak and Katan forces blockaded the forest, then the Harete family would be cut off from the outside world, unable to export the timber from which they made their fortune, and unable to bring in any supplies. The threat alone of such action might be enough to foster the allegiance of the Haretes. That certainly was what Elen-ai would do in Halen's position. She shook her head. She was starting to think like a warmonger, not an assassin.

"Are we certain that they will all march on Herran?" she asked.

"I would be surprised if they didn't," Nikalus answered. He sounded so worn down.

"He always knew it would come to this, didn't he?" Elen-ai said.

The war maps, the correspondence with the military expert, the plans within plans. Gidyon had known all along that this was going to be the out-come of his power struggle with Halen, and he had been preparing for it even as he tried to avert it. The weight of trying to prevent a war on the shoulders of a seventeen-year-old boy seemed criminally unfair. Elen-ai hated Halen not only because of his greed for power and delusions of grandeur, but also for what he was doing to her friend. She could go without sleep, she could use any weapon put in her hands and improvise several more, she could taste the most subtle of poisons, she could weave the shadows about her so that no-body could see her. But she was as hopeless and helpless as she had ever been in that moment. There was nothing that she could do to help ease the burden that had been placed on Gidyon.

Gidyon's uncles were silent, perhaps having arrived at that conclusion before her. She turned from the map to look at the three men, varying ex-pressions of dismay and concern drawn across their faces. She felt tears prick her eyes at the unfairness of the situation. "I'm going to check on Gid," she said, and left the room before anything else could be said.

The King was simply standing just a few paces down the cold corridor, staring out a window. The two guards outside the war room's door regarded him with uncertainty, but he did not appear to notice the scrutiny.

Elen-ai stood beside him. The guards shuffled back, giving them a measure of privacy. Gidyon said nothing, his attention focused on the garden below. An unpleasant wind buffeted the winter-blooming flowers, their ice-blue petals bringing no sense of warmth to the scene. That same wind forced its way through the cracks in the walls and windows. At least, Elen-ai reflect-ed as she waited for Gidyon to speak, shutters – what most buildings had, given the expense of glass – kept wind out completely, even if it also kept out light, too.

"Why won't they support me?" he asked in a low voice. The confused heartbreak on his face was devastating.

She delivered that brutal truth as gently as she could. "They don't believe in you, Gid."

"They don't believe in me?" he repeated, his incomprehension mingling with hurt.

"I know you, and I know you're a wonderful ruler. But most people haven't had the opportunity to see that. So all they see on the throne is the sort of person they've always been taught needs to be kept away from it – a man."

"I know all this." Gidyon waved his hand in a tired motion. "I just ... what do I need to do to change their minds?" He sounded so defeated. That terrified Elen-ai.

"Most people do want to believe in you, Gid," she said.

"So how do I give them something to believe in?"

"Defeat Halen, prove that this is your throne and you can – and will – hold it."

"Ah yes, I'll just do that, then." His mouth curved in an acerbic half-smile.

"I know." She chuckled.

"Sometimes this all seems so impossible, that there is no way for me to beat Halen," he admitted.

"If it helps," Elen-ai paused and put her hand on top of his where it rested on the sill. His skin was already cold. "I believe in you, Gidyon."

He tore his gaze from the garden and looked at her. The defeated look was gone from his face, replaced with his usual composed determination. "It does."

Gidyon strode back into the council room with renewed resolve, Elen-ai following him, his customary shadow.

"All right, what must we do to ensure we defeat Halen Katan?" he asked.

"I think we need to ask the Aadran and Tak families to support us," Nikalus suggested, as though Gidyon had never left.

The proposal was met with a sceptical look from the King, who had gone once more to regard the map on the wall.

"They have very little need to throw their lot in with anyone," Silius pointed out. "Their wealth is so significant and the alliance between their families so strong, that their position within the Second Country is quite secure, regardless of the outcome."

Gidyon turned, the beginnings of an idea written across his face. He pushed back the strands of hair that had fallen across his eyes and stared off into the distance. After he had turned the thought over in his mind sufficiently, he said, "I might have a way to push the Aadran family into feeling that supporting me is in their best interests." He looked at Elen-ai. She immediately understood his line of thought.

Even though almost nobody had known for certain about the relationship between Zekken Aadran and Queen Latana, Zekken had admitted to Elen-ai that his mother, the formidable Aadran matriarch, was aware that something illicit had existed between her son and her queen. When she had first learned this, Elen-ai had even entertained the suspicion that Arlena had been behind the first attack on Gidyon and Latana to ensure that her family would be protected. If anyone had uncovered the breach of the sacred neutrality between the throne and the Seven Families, both Latana and the Aadran family would have been utterly ruined. While it was a compelling motive to seek murder – indeed, the Family had been engaged for far more trivial reasons – Elen-ai had ultimately decided that Arlena was not the kind of woman to order an assassination that failed. She was, however, the kind of woman to go to great lengths to protect her family's reputation and position of power. Even the Taks, whose business and family were entwined with the Aadrans, would desert them if the truth came out. Perhaps Gidyon did in fact have something that might be used to prevail upon Arlena to persuade the Tak family that it was in the best interests of both clans to support him.

"What do you mean?" Silius did not hide either his confusion or the desperate hope in his voice.

"I think I may be able to convince Arlena to support us, and to persuade the Taks to support us, too," Gidyon said, refusing to elaborate, to his uncles' visible consternation. They did not know what his mother had done, and he would keep it that way.

"You'd need to get there quickly," Elen-ai said.

"And discreetly," he replied, an excited smile dawning on his face. It was the first time she had seen true hope in his face since Halen's letter had arrived.

"I assume we're thinking the same thing?" she confirmed, unable to hide a smile of her own. The idea of travelling once more with Gidyon across the Second Country, just the two of them, was lovely, despite the circumstances.

He nodded.

"Would we be riding kittanae?" Elen-ai asked, unable to keep the excitement from her voice. She often visited the wonderful beasts, but had never ridden on one. She was most keen to, although she would never have admitted that aloud.

"I am certain that we could arrange that."

She had to restrain herself from clapping in childish delight.

"Are you honestly suggesting just the two of you travel across the country to try to convince two families to lend their forces to ours? You can't be serious," Silius objected.

"It is the only way we will get there and back in time," Gidyon told his uncle. The expression on his face made it clear that the King had made up his mind.

Silius opened his mouth to object, then threw his hands up in resignation. "If this is what you want to do, you know I am unable to stop you. But this carries with it an incredible risk."

"If this is what Gid thinks is best, Sil, maybe it is what's best," Kaine said, his own reservations obvious in his expression, despite the support he voiced.

Silius relented with a nod, although the tight press of his lips spoke loudly of his disapproval.

They farewelled the Councillors from the Third Country later that day. The bitter wind had abated, leaving the chill to hang in the air. The air outside was like a knife, so still and so cold that it felt like it cut into Elen-ai's skin. Freya was almost lost to sight under the mountain of scarves and throws that engulfed her. Councilman Hart did not seem to struggle as much with the cold, but he too looked as though he would be happier when they reached the warmer climate of the Third Country.

From underneath the fur-lined hood that almost completely covered her face, Freya smiled at Elen-ai. She engulfed Elen-ai's hands in her own gloved ones. "I have greatly enjoyed getting to know you."

"And I you," Elen-ai told her. "Although, it's good you're leaving now, before things get worse."

"I will be praying that the Goddess watches over you and Gidyon," Freya replied. "He is a good king to your people. I wish we could stay and help."

"This is not your fight." Elen-ai smiled at the earnestness in Freya's voice. She really would miss her.

"When – not if – you prevail, will you come to the Third Country?" The Councilwoman looked hopeful.

"I've never been," Elen-ai admitted.

"Then you must come. As my guest," the other woman insisted.

Elen-ai relented with a laugh. "I promise I will visit you."

As she watched the two Councillors confer quietly with Gidyon, Elen-ai realised how sad she was that Freya was leaving. Freya had saved Gidyon's life, and she and Ashtyn were the only people outside the Family who actually understood the gifts of faith. But, as saddened as she was by their departure, Elen-ai knew that the foreigners should not be caught in the oncoming conflict. As she had said, this was not their fight.

"You should reach the border without much trouble, although I still worry," Gidyon said. "Are you sure that you do not wish to be escorted by Royal Guards?"

Elen-ai did not need to see Freya's face to know that the woman was smiling.

"I'm sure we'll be safe," Ashtyn said, amusement in his voice.

Elen-ai had seen Freya kill several attackers without laying a hand on them. Her formidable gift did not just heal but could also be used to kill. She was all the protection they might need.

"Be safe, King Gidyon. We will wait to hear news of your victory." Ashtyn's voice was formal and strong, carrying clearly across the still air of the courtyard. "Your hospitality and friendship will not be forgotten."

As the foreigners' carriage left the Palace courtyard, Nikalus murmured something in Gidyon's ear. The King strode over to Elen-ai.

"I am sorry that they are leaving," he told her softly.

"Me too," she replied.

He placed his hand on her shoulder. "If you are ready, we will set out for the Aadran estate tomorrow. The preparations have been made."

"Provided it doesn't rain, we should be able to make it in just over three days' hard riding."

"Thank you for coming with me, Elen-ai," he said.

"I'll always come with you, my King," she told him.

They stayed side by side in the knife-cold air, watching as the Councillors' carriage made its way down the hill until it turned a corner and was lost from sight.

ELEVEN

Light and heat from the fire blossomed across the ground. As was so often the case, the King was lost in his own thoughts, staring into the fire as its light flickered across his face. He drew the fur-lined cloak more tightly about him as a penetrating breeze whispered across the night. The heat of the combat training they had undertaken earlier had long since faded from her muscles, replaced by the slight ache caused be three days of hard riding. Elen-ai had been instructing Gidyon in the craft of fighting almost every day since the first time they had travelled across the Second Country. Gidyon had always stubbornly found time in his days to be given instruction by Elen-ai, even if it was late at night or early in the morning. Even out on the road, he refused to cease training, despite the weariness the hard travel visibly imposed upon him. Elen-ai had not protested when he insisted. He may be required to put those skills to use quite soon, and while her punishing instruction, building on top of his life of sword lessons, had made him a better than average fighter, she wanted to ensure he had every chance to win in a fight. That meant practice.

This was their third and final night of travel. The kittanae had been as magnificent as Elen-ai hoped they would be. Despite the trepidation which had engulfed her when she first approached them in the palace yard on the morning of their departure, the beast on which she rode – Hlevan – had purred when she stroked its coat, and docilely allowed her to mount it. The ground had flown by underneath the powerful gait of the animals over the days of travel. The curious motion of the animal's movements underneath her had at first been disorienting, but Elen-ai eventually accustomed herself to it. She could understand why the animals were so highly sought.

Fish slowly cooked in the coals of the fire. Occasionally, the flames danced with particular intensity, and the water in Lake Aadran would flash with the light. Mostly though, the lake made itself known in the gentle sound of the water lapping against the shore. Were it not for the pressing need to reach the Aadran house, and the deep chill of winter, the serenity of the night would have been quite absorbing.

Elen-ai broke the silence. "I think Kaine may know about Zekken."

Gidyon spared her only the most fleeting of glances. "What did he say to you?"

She thought back to the conversation that had occurred in his bed-chamber the evening before their departure.

It had been deliciously warm in his room. As they lay together, limbs heavy with sated drowsiness, Kaine had said, "Do you really think that Gidyon will be able to threaten Arlena into supporting him? She may consider the threat more easily resolved by joining forces with Halen."

The pleasant afterglow had sloughed off her at Kaine's inference he knew about Zekken and Latana's relationship.

Kaine must have seen the shock on her face. "So you do know. You really are blindly loyal to Gid, you know."

"I am not."

"What of his secrets don't you know?" Elen-ai couldn't tell if he was angry or simply curious.

"Does it bother you that I'm this close to him?"

"Do you want me to be jealous?"

Infuriated to have him question her relationship with Gidyon, she rolled out of the bed near-impossible speed. She did not want to play these games, especially not with Kaine. The hide-and-seek of discovering someone else's feelings or thoughts was tiring enough in every other part of the Court. Kaine's questions about her loyalty to Gidyon went too far. Her friendship with the King was not to be subject to the same scrutiny as everything else in the world of the Palace. She should have known better than to be indirect with someone who had grown up playing the games of the Court.

He reached after her. "Don't worry. I'll never speak of it. I only bring it up because I do wonder if Gid is taking the best course of action here."

After a second's hesitation, she had allowed him to pull her back onto the bed and close to him. He kissed her, his mouth was warm and sweet. He broke their kiss long enough to whisper in her ear. "Just come back in one piece."

"Elen-ai?"

Gidyon's voice, and the chill of the night air. brought her back to the present. The tingle the cold breeze left on her bare skin was not dissimilar to the way her skin felt underneath Kaine's fingertips. Gidyon was looking at her expectantly.

"He didn't say much. I just think he might know about Latana and Zekken."

Gidyon gave a long sigh. "I don't suppose it really matters. He would never speak of it. What unsettles me is the scope of the carelessness my mother seems to have demonstrated."

Elen-ai idly weaved shadows around her, flicking her outstretched forearms in and out of sight. "I think very few people were in a position to ever guess. Kaine was one of them. He is also quite perceptive about certain things – things like this. More so than Silius or Nikalus."

Gidyon's gaze fell to her arms. "You like him."

She pulled the shadows up to her shoulders. "I suppose I do," she admitted.

"Am I correct in remembering that anyone in the Family who wants to marry and have children must leave the Family?"

"I don't want to marry and bear children." Her response was a reflexive one. "And I don't really think Kaine does either," she added thoughtfully.

"That was not what I meant," Gidyon said.

Elen-ai slipped the shadows over her completely so that she vanished from sight.

"Sorry, I do not mean to make things awkward," Gidyon said, perhaps worrying that he had pried too far and her disappearance from sight was her way of saying as much. "I am glad that you and Kaine have each other – for as long or as little as that may last. You are both very dear to me."

"And we would both do anything for you," Elen-ai reappeared into view to tell him, before flickering back out of sight.

The King shook his head as though trying to clear it as he looked at Elen-ai, or rather, the blank space where she sat. "I beg that you stop that. I am getting a spectacular headache watching you. Just decide if I can see you or not."

Elen-ai tightened the weave of the shadows around her. When she spoke, her voice would have seemed disembodied to Gidyon. "Better?"

"Oh, much." The dry sarcasm in his voice made Elen-ai chuckle.

"How do you do that, anyway?" he asked.

Elen-ai slipped the shadows down to her neck. Her head floated seemingly out of nowhere. "I just find the shadows and give them, well, a bit of a tug."

"A bit of a tug?" Gidyon made no effort to hide his incredulous amusement.

"I don't know how to describe it," Elen-ai said. "I just find the shadows near me and pull them over me."

"Do you have to think about your god when you do it?" The light of the fire turned Gidyon's blue eyes orange-yellow.

"I never have to think about the Shadow God," Elen-ai replied. "My faith is always just there." She made a gesture with her hand to emphasise the comment, but realised that she was still shielding it from view.

"But do you draw on that faith?" Gidyon asked.

"I've never really thought about it. My belief in the Shadow God has always been there. I've always been certain. I don't know what it would feel like to not have faith."

Gidyon held his hands out in front of him. A slight frown crossed his face, then the darkness around his splayed fingers receded as his hands began to glow ever so slightly. It was similar to what Elen-ai had seen around the priestess of the Divine One's hands when she had inadvertently intruded into Gidyon's religious instruction. But something about seeing the light at the King's fingertips scared her. No ruler had commanded the light of the sun. To summon light was the stuff of legends, from a time when gods and humans had walked hand in hand. For Gidyon to have true faith and be able to harness the power of the Divine One's light was as unprecedented in the Second Country as a man on the throne.

Elen-ai told herself to stop being foolish. If she was going to think that way, she was just as much a figure of legend as Gidyon. Her playing with shadows would have terrified any casual observer. If anyone were ever to witness that, she would be just as quickly relegated to a figure from legend as Gidyon would – just like Freya from the Second Country, who could heal and kill with a thought. It was simply disconcerting to see Gidyon's faith manifest so clearly. He had kept his piety hidden, and as such, his ability to command light was unexpected. Shadows were different. They were everywhere, easily found and easily moulded. To manipulate shadows seemed to her far less awe inspiring than summoning light in the middle of the night.

"How long have you been able to do that?" she asked. She loosened her grip on the shadows as she looked intently at the light in Gidyon's hands. They fell away and the rest of her reappeared to sight.

He shrugged, his eyes still on the yellow-bright light surrounding his fingertips. "Always, I think. But for a long time I never paid it much attention. When I was little, I thought everyone could do it, and then I thought that it was just my imagination."

"So when you realised that Freya had healed you—"

"I knew that I had not been imagining things," Gidyon said.

"How do you make the light appear?"

He made a little motion with his head that could have meant anything. "I do not really know how to explain it. Maybe I just find the light and give it a little tug." He turned to look at her, a cheeky smile on his face.

"Just because you're the king and able to summon light, doesn't mean you can be smug about it. Can you do anything else with the light?"

In reply he turned his hand to face up. The light slipped down from his fingertips to form a glowing sphere that rested in his palm. The shadows it cast clashed with those from the fire. Then Gidyon closed his hand and the light went out.

"It is not as though I could ever do anything with it," Gidyon said, the faintest suggestion of disappointment in his voice. "It would scare people far too much."

Elen-ai agreed with him, but did not say as much. She thought it might hurt him to hear that opinion corroborated.

They remained silent for a while, each preoccupied with their own thoughts.

"What are you thinking?" he asked, eventually.

"How do you plan to deal with Zekken?" She finally asked the question had been with her since they left Herran.

She glanced at him.

He was pressing his lips together in thought. "I do not know," he admitted finally.

"He might be able to persuade Arlena to support you if she refuses," Elen-ai said.

"I know," he replied. "I have been wondering whether or not I should appeal to her through him. I do not know that I want to owe him a favour, though."

"Do you really think he'd call that favour in?" she asked.

"Not really. But I do not want to owe him anything."

"And if that's what it takes to secure your crown?"

Gidyon sighed. The sound carried the weight of his anger at his mother and Zekken. "Then I will do it."

Elen-ai reached across the space between them and placed a hand on his shoulder. It was all the comfort she could offer him.

"You know, I have never actually spoken with him about it. Any of it," Gidyon said.

Of course Elen-ai knew, but she also knew that it was his way of telling her that he wanted to discuss this matter. "Do you want to?"

"Not really. It would be too dangerous. Besides, he might not even be my father." Gidyon reached to examine the progress of the fish.

Elen-ai didn't point out that having Zekken as a father was probably preferable to being Erek's son. While Zekken had conducted a dangerous illicit love affair with Latana for years, at least he hadn't stabbed her before Gidyon's eyes.

"I think the fish is ready," Gidyon said before Elen-ai could say anything else. Deftly, he flicked the fish from the coals.

"I still can't believe you know how to fish," Elen-ai muttered as she watched him.

Gidyon declined to respond to her comment, skewering the fish and handing one to her. The flesh practically fell off the bones. Steam from the fish rose into the cold night air. The meal was plain but satisfying, and the fact that the fish was so hot it all but burned her mouth was a welcome warmth.

"Seriously, where did you learn to catch and cook fish?" Elen-ai asked as she waited for a piece to cool. She threw the tail across to the kittanae who were curled together nearby. They raised their heads with intelligent interest and fought gently over the scrap.

Gidyon gave a smug smile. "The Herran market," he told her. Until his mother's death, Gidyon had gone to the markets in Herran every week. Elen-ai had accompanied him once. She had seen for herself that he had friends there. It wasn't unsurprising to think that one of them might have taught him to fish.

"Surely there wouldn't be that many fish in Herran's harbour," Elen-ai said between bites. "Too many boats, and too many people fishing."

"There weren't," Gidyon replied. "That is what made it tricky."

"Did you even ever catch any fish?" Elen-ai asked.

"Of course I did." She could hear the smugness in his voice.

"Outrageous," she muttered. "Do you miss going there?"

It was a silly question. Gidyon had passionately argued with his mother that he should be allowed to continue visiting the market, even when Latana feared there was a threat against his life. Of course he was going to miss that weekly outing, along with many other parts of his old life.

"Often."

"Why don't you go there, then?"

Gidyon scratched the bridge of his nose. "I am their king. Not their prince, not the son of the queen. I rule them. I cannot walk among them like I am one of them." The sadness in his voice was unmissable, as was the certainty that signalled the decision was a final one.

Despite the fact that she knew he was the king, that he ruled the Second Country, Elen-ai had never truly felt what exactly that meant until that moment. She looked out beyond the fire. Here, as with the Tak lands, the Aadran estate was flat plains. The lake was a smooth sheet of water that had settled itself into a dip in the endless fields of grain. Mist had risen from the land and was now brushing the lake's surface. The ephemeral conglomeration which could have been mistaken for smoke, were it not so far away from the fire, moved across the surface of the water with an imperceptible slowness. It seemed so preposterous that she was sitting here in the biting chill of winter, looking at this sight beside her king. Gidyon was her friend. She had seen him cry, rage, struggle with who he was, and other people's perceptions of who he was. But he was not simply that friend, but also her ruler, and the ruler of everybody within the Second Country. Try as she might, Elen-ai couldn't quite touch that reality even as she comprehended it.

They lapsed back into silence as they ate the fish, the crackle of the fire and the almost inaudible lapping of the lake's waves enough sound for them. The quietude of the open land was so distant from the palace and the constant noise of some activity being undertaken.

After Gidyon had finished his fish and thrown the bones across to the kittanae, he spoke. "Elen-ai?"

"Yes?"

"When will you go back to the Family?" Asking the question, he certainly didn't sound like a self-assured king who knew too well the need to separate himself from his people. He sounded like an uncertain young man.

"I don't know," she admitted.

"But you miss your home."

"I do," she said cautiously. "But I also like being by your side."

"If – when – you go back to the Family, will we still be friends?" There was a childish quality to the question that tugged at Elen-ai's heart.

"Of course we will, Gid." But even as she reassured him, she wondered if that would be true. Assassins and kings did not inhabit each other's worlds, and there were many good reasons for that.

He scrutinised her face for a moment. "I gave you up once. I do not want to do it again." He didn't say it with a great flourish or any significant emotion. It was simply the quiet, emphatic statement of a truth that had curled itself around his heart.

"Gid, I promise that I will do everything I can to ensure that we are still friends."

The ground rustled as Gidyon lifted himself up to kneel, turning to face Elen-ai properly. "I swear before the Divine One that you, Elen-ai of the Family and Shadow God, are my friend, and that friendship is something I will never deny or turn away from."

Profoundly touched, Elen-ai reached across to take his hands. "I swear before the Shadow God, that you Gidyon, my King, are my friend and always will be. I swear that I will never forsake you, nor will I leave you." She offered the vow without even thinking.

His hands tightened around hers, the flickering fire casting light and shadow across their linked forms before he let go.

"It might be silly, but that made me feel better," he admitted.

"Don't think that, Gid," Elen-ai said. She too felt a slight relief. Breaking a vow to a god was not something one could do lightly, especially not when the two people making their oaths had genuine faith. The fact that she and Gidyon had vowed their friendship before their gods somehow made her feel that she and he were now bonded inextricably, that nothing could keep them separate, even if the worlds of an assassin and king were not supposed to meet.

When they were ready to sleep, practically smothered in the furs and blankets that barely kept the cold of the night at bay, the concern that Kaine had managed to instil in her returned. Gidyon was taking the first watch, still seated and facing the fire. Elen-ai had, as she always did, offered to take the watch for the whole evening, but he had refused, as he always had. From her cocoon of tentative warmth, Elen-ai looked at the dark mound that was Gidyon and worried what would happen if Arlena turned on them or failed to support them, despite any promise of ruin with which Gidyon might threaten her.

"Gidyon, how do you know that this plan to get Aadran support will work?" she asked so softly that her voice might have been lost amid the fire's crackle.

He didn't turn around but stayed looking into the fire, but in his reply she could hear his smile. "I have faith," he told her.

TWELVE

The Aadran family home was as imposing as its matriarch. It rose up from the flatlands as they approached. Here was wealth cultivated over generations. The simple elegance of the house's design, visible even from far away, spoke to the absence of need to add any unnecessary flourishes to prove how much power or status the Aadrans had. Despite the suggestion of rain hinted in the smudge of clouds that hovered on the horizon, crisp winter sun had shone on Elen-ai and Gidyon's morning. That sun now shone on the Aadran home, glinting off the building's many windows.

The current inhabitants of the Aadran residence in Herran, servants and one or two minor family members, had been notified of Gidyon and Elen-ai's impending arrival. They had in turn sent this information on to the Aadran estate by messenger birds. Messages that were trivial – or so time-sensitive that the threat of interception was secondary – were sent among the powerful families of the Second Country by birds. It had been a concern that Zekken may learn of Elen-ai and Gidyon's travel to the Aadran estate and attempt to apprehend the king, but it was a risk they had decided was worth taking. Consequently, a line of people was waiting for the royal visitors in the neatly maintained yard. Elen-ai wondered whether they had been standing there all morning or if someone had spied their approach across the flat land. For her own amusement, she hoped that it was the former.

Arlena headed the line of welcomers. Unusually, Zekken was not by her side. It would not be surprising to learn that she had banished her son and right hand from this particular welcome. As ever, she stood perfectly straight, dressed immaculately in a blood-red tunic and white trousers, hands clasped loosely in front of her.

Gidyon dismounted and handed the reins of the kittanae to a servant who had come forward expectantly. "Lady Aadran." His voice was clear and carried across the manicured yard. "There was no need to go to all this trouble for us."

In reply, Arlena bowed before her king, her servants following suit. Elen-ai stood awkwardly next to Gidyon. She was not required to bow in such circumstances, Gidyon had made that clear. But she still felt silly standing next to Gidyon as everybody bowed to him.

"It is a great honour to be visited by our ruler. No effort is too small," Arlena said once she had straightened. "You must have ridden hard to get here in only three days, even on kittanae. Can we offer you refreshment, or the opportunity to bathe?"

"A bath would be most welcome, Lady Aadran," Gidyon said, allowing her to lead them into the house. As they passed through the grand arch of the doorway, Elen-ai suppressed a gasp. The entrance hall was drenched in quiet opulence. While it didn't quite match the beauty or impressive scale of the Palace's entranceway, the polished stone, rich carpets, and the friezes on the wall painted by the hand of an undisputed master, created a light-filled, spectacular space that had done to Elen-ai exactly what it was designed to impress.

"Welcome to our home," Arlena said, the sweep of her hand drawing the eye to the two staircases that curved away from each other. Between those staircases was the centrepiece of the magnificent entrance: a beautiful shrine to the Divine One. Elen-ai suspected the shrine was a relatively new installation in response to the religious fervour sweeping across the Second Country. However, it fitted the space perfectly. The gold that coated the sun symbol caught the morning rays shining through the tall windows. The carved iconography that surrounded the sun depicted to the most exquisite detail the faces of the figures who were looking in rapture at the glory of the sun.

"I've never had the good fortune to visit your home, Lady Aadran, but I must confess, it is truly magnificent." Gidyon craned his head to look at the high ceiling – painted with an image of a softly clouded blue sky, like the entrance hall of the Palace.

Arlena gave the barest suggestion of a smile. "You are too kind, my lord. Although this is but a small part of the building."

He returned his gaze to their host. "I look forward to seeing the rest of it, given what I have seen so far."

"And you, lady Elen-ai, what do you think of our home?" An almost imperceptible challenge edged Arlena's voice. Clearly, the Aadran matriarch was well aware what Gidyon had come to ask of her and was going to make them work for everything she might give them.

Elen-ai had in fact been in the Aadran family home on a few occasions, each time under a contract for the Family. Once she had hidden herself in an airing closet on the second storey for two days. From her hiding place, she had listened to the comings and goings of the household, sneaking out only in the middle of the night when the household was asleep to steal food and relieve herself. But despite the time that she had spent here – unnoticed even by her victims as she ended their lives – she had never even glanced at the entrance hall.

"I could not have anticipated how truly beautiful your home is, lady Aadran," she said honestly. "Why, some may say that it even comes close to rivalling the Palace."

Pleased with her own slight jibe, Elen-ai noticed the stern woman's eyes flash ever so slightly. "Gal-an will show you to the rooms we have prepared for you."

They were led up one of the staircases and along several corridors by the servant, who had leapt forward at his mistress' command. The door at which they stopped was an ornate piece of work, painted with an idyllic scene of a field in summer. Before Elen-ai could look too closely at it, Gal-an opened it to reveal one of the most sumptuous rooms Elen-ai had ever seen outside the Palace.

If Elen-ai hadn't known that the Aadran household had only been given three days' notice to prepare the rooms, she never would have thought it. The painted scenes adorning the walls gleamed with a lustre that made them look new. Even the furniture looked as though it had only just been finished, so immaculate was each piece. A fire burned merrily in the fireplace, and from the look of it, had been doing so since at least the early hours of the morning. Katan-made vases nestled in various corners, filled with an assortment of fresh and dried flowers. Normally, that many flowers in winter would have been spectacular on their own, but the fact that the Aadran household had so many Katan vases to simply spread about a room entirely overshadowed the display of wealth and resources that the flowers represented. Katan vases were singularly rare, as most of the clay workers in the Katan pottery houses specialised in bowls or plates. The clay of the Katan estate, despite producing spectacular pieces of crockery, was incredibly difficult to work. Years of training was required to produce a plate of good quality, let alone the delicate and wafer-thin plates that Elen-ai had seen at only the wealthiest of tables. The depth of skill required to craft a vase with the temperamental material was almost virtuosic.

"You have done a magnificent job. I already feel at home." Gidyon's voice was warm as he addressed the servant.

The man regarded Gidyon with a wary amazement. Clearly, he was uncertain about this boy-king, but that uncertainty warred with the astonishment at being given a compliment by his ruler. "We drew baths for you both," he eventually settled on, showing Gidyon and Elen-ai into a bathing chamber that held two huge stone tubs of steaming water. Unseen servants must have scurried only just ahead of them to fill the baths. The two small packs Elen-ai and Gidyon had brought with them had been placed at the foot of a massive bed. They looked utterly out of place in the magnificent room due to its modest size and lack of adornment.

"Thank you," Gidyon said, dismissing the man with the simple inflection of his tone even as he thanked him. It was a trick Elen-ai had seen his mother use when she had first been brought before Queen Latana. It was no less authoritative now than it had been then.

The servant bowed and left the room, enough control instilled in him not to scurry away from the male ruler and his inscrutable companion.

"The Royal suite," Gidyon murmured, perhaps more to himself than to Elen-ai. He turned in a slow circle to observe the fastidiously beautiful surroundings.

"Did they really get all of this ready in only three days?" Elen-ai asked.

"Queens do not often visit the Families, but just in case they do, all of the Families have a room specially prepared for the possibility. The rooms are reserved only for the use of the ruler – it is why we did not stay in any of them last year. Most of the furniture in here has only been used a few times and stays covered when the room is unoccupied. I would assume that they brought in an extra tub for us, though," Gidyon explained as he took off his outermost coat.

Elen-ai thought it was supremely wasteful to have an opulent room that cost more money than she could possibly comprehend almost always empty, but she had long since learned that the lives of those born into wealth and power were by their nature wasteful. She waited in the achingly beautiful room while Gidyon bathed first.

He was quickly out of the bath and Elen-ai slipped into the water of her own tub, grateful that she was out of the clothes coated with mud from the hard, long ride. The water was warm and scented lightly with something that smelled, impossibly, of berries.

"You know they would have given us servants to help us bathe if we had requested it," Gidyon called to her from one of the other rooms. He sounded amused.

Elen-ai dutifully soaped her hair, scraping her fingernails across her scalp to dislodge the grit and grease that had settled there. "That would have been off-putting," she called back.

"What, you mean you do not want people to scrub you down?"

"Normally I wouldn't want to do anything without the assistance of at least one servant," she said sarcastically as she heaved herself out of the tub. Even despite the warmth of the fire, after the heat of the water, her skin prickled once exposed to the cooler air.

"Ah yes, Elen-ai, your hidden preference for luxury and attendance." Gidyon threw her an amused look as she retrieved some clothes from her pack, a towel wrapped firmly around herself.

She dressed quickly, ensuring that her blades were all properly secured underneath her clothes, and turned her attention to her hair. It had grown longer than the short crop she favoured. Water had gathered on the bottoms of the strands, making the back of her neck unpleasantly cold. As she furiously towelled her hair dry, Gidyon shoved a brush in her face.

"What's that?" she asked suspiciously.

"Yet again, your brilliant and honed skills of observation make themselves known," he told her. "A hairbrush."

"Yes, obviously. What's that doing here?" She recoiled from him and it.

"Well, I thought you might like to brush your hair," he said patiently.

She glared at him for a moment, then snatched the brush from his hand.

"You do know how to use it, don't you?" Gidyon asked.

Her response was to turn away from him, struggling with a tangled snarl that had somehow managed to wind itself into her hair.

"Do you really think that Arlena believes we're lovers?" Elen-ai asked, knowing that Gidyon found the assumption many had made about them awkward. Sure enough, when she turned back to look at him, he had an expression of painful discomfort on his face. It was a delightfully petty revenge for making her brush her hair.

"I would imagine there is some doubt, given you are now being called my – what are we calling you now?"

"I think adviser. I must say, I'm surprised people haven't taken more issue with the idea that I'm your lover," she said, taking delicious glee in placing emphasis on the last word.

"You are not from one of the Seven Families; that is all that concerns people right now." He shrugged, trying to look as though he wasn't bothered at all by the word 'lover'.

She completed her coiffure and threw the brush down on the bed, relieved that she was finished with the pointless preening. "All right, I'm ready. Let's go and blackmail Arlena."

The room in which Arlena received them was as spectacular as the other areas of the house they had seen. Arlena was standing by an enormous window, looking out at the sea of yellow-green winter grain that began at the end of the house's boundary and stretched as far as the eye could see. It was a magnificent sight. Once more, the fact she was alone rather than accompanied by Zekken, or indeed any member of her family, was striking. Despite her solitude, her presence more than filled the room.

Arlena bowed low at their arrival. Even if she had declined to support Gidyon's claim to the throne, she still recognised him as her ruler. That was something, at least.

"The Royal suite is truly beautiful, Arlena," Gidyon said by way of greeting.

"It humbles me to hear you say that, your Majesty," she said, perhaps a sardonic note to her voice.

"May we speak privately?" Gidyon asked. Making the request was a courtesy he did not have to extend to Arlena. Gidyon could simply have ordered that they speak without the presence of the servants standing discreetly at the room's entrances.

Yet offering her that politeness was also a reminder of his authority. Arlena pursed her lips ever so slightly and nodded. At her gesture, the servants withdrew immediately, closing the doors behind them. No doubt, at least one or two ears were pressed against the doors – the Family knew well that servants were often the best sources of information.

"Would privately not also mean the exclusion of lady Elen-ai?" Arlena asked, one eyebrow arching as her gaze rested on Elen-ai's still-damp hair.

"No." Gidyon made no other offer or explanation, the single syllable firm and unmistakably final.

Arlena's other eyebrow joined its raised companion before both settled back in their normal place. Elen-ai knew these looks of surprise were deliberate. No member of the Seven Families allowed such obvious expressions to cross their faces unless they desired it. That Arlena had so openly displayed such an expression was her insubordination in response to Gidyon's assertion of his authority. Elen-ai supposed she couldn't blame her. If she had been an authoritative dowager, she too would have been rankled at being ordered about by a young man who seemed not to realise that his place in the world was not to take the throne or indeed to command those who were his elders, and most likely wiser than him, too.

"Very well then. May I be so blunt as to ask what brings you to our corner of the Queendom? I can only assume it is some purpose other than hearing the songs that our new resident minstrel has written." The understated sarcasm, in the world of the court, might as well have been an obscene gesture. Elen-ai made no attempt to stop her own eyebrows from ascending.

"Lady Aadran, I do not seek to create any pretence. You are well aware that the Katan family has challenged my claim to the throne. You and I both know that my cousin, Serenah, is not suited to rule, nor is her grandfather. Despite what he may think of his own capabilities." Gidyon took a step toward Arlena, who remained by the window, her face impassive.

"Even if I did believe that about your cousin, if Halen's ploy is successful and you are deposed, that still leaves his granddaughter on the throne," she pointed out coolly.

"And the way of the Second Country would be utterly disrupted. How would Serenah rule impartially? Surely she would be inclined to favour those who marched for her. The Bertak and Harete families would almost certainly be given whatever they asked. How might that erode the Aadran family fortunes?"

"Certainly, you make a compelling argument for throwing the weight of the Aadran family behind Halen and his quest to take the throne from you." Arlena smiled tightly.

Gidyon's face closed, an unsettling stillness falling across his features that a moment before had been quite imploring. "I know you find him and his methods distasteful."

"That is ultimately irrelevant when I am forced to consider what is best for my family. Sometimes we must do unpleasant things to protect those we love." Arlena's hand turned briefly upward in a gesture to emphasise the comment.

"Or for those who bear your blood?" Gidyon asked softly.

The stiffening in Arlena's already perfectly straight posture was only noticeable to one who was watching with intense scrutiny. Elen-ai found herself holding her breath, worried that Gidyon had shown his hand too early. It was only possible that Arlena might have been Gidyon's grandmother, but it was such a direct reference to the utter social ruin she faced if her son's relationship with Gidyon's mother ever became publicly known, that the threat was a brutal one indeed.

Arlena inhaled, the sound loud in the absolute quiet of the room. "So you want me to support you? Send my people to die for someone who should not be our ruler? The way I see things, neither you nor Serenah deserve to sit on the throne. Perhaps the best thing would be to let you both fight it out and then deal with whatever undesirable outcome arises." She made no attempt to hide the derision or tight anger in her voice. This was not a woman who liked to be threatened. "The Aadran family will always survive. We have wealth, we have power, we have our own people trained to defend our lands. What obligation is actually incumbent upon us if your mother decided that instead of bearing a girl, she would simply put a man on the throne and in so doing threaten the stability of the Queendom?"

Instead of answering her question, Gidyon walked slowly across the room to examine one of the paintings. Following him with her gaze, Elen-ai noticed that the figures in it were members of the Aadran family. Arlena too watched Gidyon, anger making her features pinched.

"Where is Zekken?" Gidyon asked quietly. "Normally in such a meeting, he would be by your side, as Elen-ai is by mine."

"I am the head of the Aadran family," Arlena snapped, her reserve gone. "It is ultimately my decision whether or not we support you, my King."

From where she stood, Elen-ai could see Gidyon's slight smile. Getting Arlena to lose her composure was no mean feat and it had now given Gidyon the upper hand he had been worried he would not attain.

Arlena's anger at herself for losing her control was obvious in the slight flare to her nostrils and clench of her hands. She too knew that she had just given Gidyon the leverage he had been seeking. Now was the time for Gidyon to go in for the kill, to turn that lack of restraint against her. Elen-ai felt herself tense in anticipation. Verbal exchanges such as this one had a curious and beautiful similarity to a physical fight. However, like any good fighter, Gidyon did exactly what Elen-ai would never have expected.

"Arlena. I am asking for your help. Please." His voice was so gentle, so imploring. Where Elen-ai would have gone in for the kill, he threw away his advantage to place himself once more at the matriarch's mercy.

Elen-ai looked to the woman. Arlena made no effort to hide her surprise. Or perhaps her surprise was so powerful that she could not conceal it. "Why should I risk the lives of Aadran women and men to keep you on the throne? You are a man, and your very existence brings with it," she hesitated so that she could find the correct word, "complications."

Gidyon turned to face her. "I might not be the right sex but I do want to do the best by my people. All my people."

Elen-ai sensed an unspoken understanding flash between the two powerful people. At that exact moment, they certainly looked as though they could be related, although she could not say if that similarity came from the fact that both of them understood the burdens of power and leadership in a way that loaned them a certain likeness, or because of shared blood.

"There is the faintest possibility that I might have been wrong about you," Arlena admitted. "Maybe we should talk at greater length." She motioned to the chairs. Gidyon took one of them. Elen-ai remained standing, her presence almost forgotten. Exactly the way she preferred.

Gidyon and Arlena had been talking quietly for almost ten minutes when a knock sounded at the door.

"My apologies. They should know we are not to be disturbed," Arlena said, vexation crossing her face. She raised her voice. "Yes?"

The door was opened by a cautious-looking servant, evidently aware that she was breaching her employer's strict instructions. "I'm terribly sorry to interrupt, my lady," she began, the slight tremor in her voice betraying her fear at the prospect of invoking Arlena's displeasure. "A bird has come with a message for you marked urgent."

Arlena sighed and held out her hand. The servant scurried across the room and placed the paper in the matriarch's outstretched hand. Arlena excused herself to the king, who made a gesture that indicated she should not worry, and she quickly scanned the paper. Her lips pursed as she read its contents, and she looked as though someone had whispered a series of particularly vulgar profanities in her ear.

Halen Katan was marching on Herran.

THIRTEEN

The debate between Gidyon and Elen-ai was furious. Arlena had graciously offered them a few moments to privately discuss the news of Halen's decision to try to take the capital by force.

"I'm not leaving you," Elen-ai insisted for perhaps the fourth time.

"You must. What if for some reason word does not reach my uncles of what is coming toward them?" Gidyon asked. In the face of her stubbornness, he was infuriatingly rational. Although, she could see the tension at this news underneath the calm logic that he was pushing onto her.

"Of course they'll know. How could they fail to have word passed to them of a Shadow-cursed army marching across the countryside?" She swung her arms wildly as if to emphasise how difficult it would be to overlook an army.

"I need you to go and help them, and I need to stay here and secure the assistance of the Aadran and Tak families," Gidyon said. The calmness with which he spoke seemed to belie the fact that now at least, the threat against him was real, and very much imminent. She had no idea how he was so calm.

"I can't leave you here on your own," Elen-ai said stubbornly. She crossed her arms in front of her chest and tried to stare down her friend and king.

"Elen-ai, I have already lost if I fail to secure Aadran and Tak help. Without them, my life is forfeit." Gidyon stood before the window, in almost the same position that Arlena had been when they had first entered. The clouds Elen-ai had earlier thought would cross the skies and pour rain down upon them had remained on the horizon. With his features cast into shadow by the brightness of the day outside, it was hard to see the nuances of Gidyon's expression. She wondered if Gidyon had moved to the window for that exact reason.

"I won't leave you," Elen-ai said.

"I can order you to go." His voice was low but he may as well have shouted at her.

"I'll ignore it," she said defiantly.

"And you will then be disobeying the direct order of your king." Suddenly, the authority that Elen-ai had seen Gidyon use on others to bend them to his will had been turned on her.

She held his gaze for a moment, only able to properly see the intense blue of his eyes. Unable to stare him down, she dropped her eyes, looking instead at the beautiful red threads of the carpet. "As you wish, my King."

Even though Gidyon had been right to point it out, Elen-ai still couldn't help but feel wounded that he had, as her king, ordered her to go. As far as she was concerned, for most of the time he was her friend first and king second. Except when things like this happened. She wasn't even angry, just filled with a vague sense of sadness that he had chosen to remind her of that now. Only half a room separated them, but it may as well have been half a world.

"Elen-ai, please. You will be faster on your own, and perhaps I will be faster on my own here, too," Gidyon said. He was pleading with her now, begging her not to hate him.

That horrified Elen-ai more than the fact that he had given her an order. Kings did not beg. The fact that he now humbled himself before her in such a fashion was terrifying. Something about that felt more wrong than anything she could have imagined, and she realised her error. She relented immediately. "Gidyon, I'm sorry. You're right, I'll go."

He stayed by the window for a moment longer, his features still washed out by the light as he looked at her. Then he nodded. He strode across the room to the door through which Arlena had exited several minutes previously. He opened it and came face to face with Zekken in a quiet but heated conference with Arlena.

Zekken had put on weight since Elen-ai had last seen him at Latana's funeral. He did not possess the strikingly good looks of Erek Rasatan, but the way he had carried himself had given him a certain charm that was quite disarming and endearing. Yet the grief-rounded face, and, more strikingly, the way his features seemed to have settled more naturally into an expression of dismay, had robbed him of that appeal. It was quite a shock to see such a dramatic change in his appearance.

Whatever conversation mother and son were having was cut short by Gidyon opening the door. The King and the man who believed himself to be Gidyon's father stared at one another in shocked silence.

Zekken spoke first. "Are you all right?" The words practically tumbled from his lips, desperate eagerness making him reach his arms out toward the King as if by touching him, he could assure himself of Gidyon's relative well-being.

Gidyon took an involuntary step back to evade Zekken's hands. Hurt at the rejection showed clearly on the man's face. Elen-ai almost shook her head. If he behaved like that in front of anybody else, talk was bound to occur.

Arlena all but pushed her son into the room and followed him, closing the door firmly behind her. "Really," she scolded Zekken.

Gidyon came to stand beside Elen-ai. He folded his arms across his chest in the same stance Elen-ai had taken only moments before and waited for either Arlena or Zekken to speak.

Zekken broke the silence, to his mother's obvious disapproval. "Are you going back to Herran?"

Gidyon took his time before answering, rocking back slightly onto his heels. "If I were, would I be accompanied by Aadran fighters?"

Zekken opened his mouth, then apparently reconsidered answering on his mother's behalf. It was the first sign of sense he had demonstrated. He looked to Arlena. If the woman had possessed skills of the Divine One, Elen-ai was certain she would have incinerated her own son in that moment. Fortunately for Zekken, it seemed Arlena was not as devout a believer as Gidyon.

"We have yet to arrive at any agreement," Arlena said. "But I must confess, Halen being so bold as to actually march on Herran has certainly changed things."

Elen-ai could sense Gidyon's relief. It mirrored her own. "I would greatly appreciate the opportunity to continue to speak with you on this matter. Elen-ai is heading back to the capital as soon as possible, given what we have just learned about the Katan movements. I assume we can continue our discussion about such matters after her departure?"

"Of course. If there is anything we can do to assist, just ask," Arlena said, the offer seemingly quite sincere.

Gidyon gave her a nod of thanks, then he and Elen-ai returned to the Royal suite to prepare for Elen-ai's departure.

As soon as they entered the rooms, Gidyon went to the desk by the window and began writing. Elen-ai exchanged her light formal tunic and soft trousers for a more durable and warmer outfit. She made sure all of her blades were securely transferred to the garments, double checking with a lifetime's training that they were sharp and ready for use.

A brisk rap on the door preceded Zekken's entrance. He did not wait for a response before coming into the room.

Gidyon immediately stood up, making no effort to temper the obvious fact that he did not want Zekken to be there. "What do you want?"

"I wanted to talk with you." Zekken sounded doggedly desperate. It was pitiful.

"We are busy." Gidyon turned toward the desk.

"I know, but I just—"

Gidyon whirled back toward the man. "What can you possibly say to me, Zekken?" His eyes were cold and hard.

"We used to be so close, Gid."

"That was before I found out why you wanted to be close to me," Gidyon snapped.

"That shouldn't remove all that came before," Zekken begged.

"It most certainly should," Gidyon said, unmoving, unreachable.

His harshness left Zekken silent for a moment, staring at the King with uncertain balefulness. "You know, I miss your mother every day. I loved her so much." His voice was a hoarse croak.

Gidyon's roar filled the room. "She was my mother, and you took that from me. Your stupid, reckless affair with her took that from me because now I have to live every day with the legacy of that, knowing that I cannot do one single thing wrong. And even then, if what you and she did ever comes to light, all of the Second Country will rise up against me. I can't miss her, I can't mourn for her, I have to live with the mistake she committed with you." The grief that he had carried with him, nursing quietly for months sat openly on his face. In the silence that followed his explosion, he continued. "I have nothing to say to you. Erek might have killed her, but you took my mother from me. I can't think of her now without thinking of why she died. And I can't think of her the same way because of that."

"I'm sorry." Zekken's eyes gleamed with tears.

"Get out," Gidyon told him. Elen-ai could see tiny tremors all along Gidyon's body.

"Gid, please let me know what I can do." Zekken stepped toward the boy he believed to be his son.

Elen-ai could stay silent for no longer. "Your king gave you an order." Her voice snapped across the room like a whip.

Zekken slowly turned his head to look at her. "I forgot you were here," he admitted, sounding dazed.

"Are you going to disobey an order from your king?" Elen-ai asked, clenching her hands into fists by her side, wanting to hit him for the distress he was causing Gidyon. She almost did, but she knew that was not what Gidyon would have wanted, so she bit down on her natural impulse.

Zekken blinked once, twice, then his head bowed. He cast one last look at Gidyon, then he left. With Zekken's departure, Gidyon sank down into his chair. He stared blankly ahead for a long, long moment, then the King of the Second Country put his head into his hands and wept.

"Would you like to talk about it?" Elen-ai asked him.

He did not raise his head. Perhaps he did not want her to see his tears. Instead, his voice was muffled through his fingers, the words coming between sobs. "There's nothing to say."

"Are you certain?" Elen-ai hovered near him uncertainly. Comforting people who were mired in the depths of grief was not her forte. She had normally departed long before it came time for grief. Eventually, she moved close to Gidyon and put a gentle hand on his shoulder. He leaned slightly into her touch, continuing to sob.

"I can kill him, if you'd like," she said, receiving a watery chuckle in reply.

He raised his head, offering Elen-ai a glimpse of his pale, tear-blotched face. "If that were how I dealt with all my problems, I think there would be very few people left in the Second Country," he said. He swallowed in an obvious effort to push back a fresh bout of tears.

"But those who'd be left would be very loyal to you," Elen-ai pointed out.

She was rewarded with a tenuous smile. The King took a breath, fighting valiantly to compose himself. "I am all right, Elen-ai," he tried in vain to reassure her.

Elen-ai raised her eyebrows, her most sceptical expression on her face.

"He took me by surprise more than anything. I honestly was not expecting him to be so," Gidyon paused and his eyes – reddened from crying – brightened afresh with tears, "so like that."

Her grip on his shoulder tightened. She understood what he meant. Something about Zekken's total prostration before Gidyon was deeply unsettling. It was as though Latana's death had seen the gentle warmth of Zekken's demeanour disappear, to be replaced with a man totally adrift from any composure. It had certainly been a shock to see the change in his appearance and demeanour, too.

"I can't even hate him. He is far too piteous for that," Gidyon said miserably.

"It's a lot easier to hate someone than see them as flawed," Elen-ai told him.

He nodded, his eyes fixed straight ahead, almost certainly not seeing any of the suite in front of him. Then he let out a shuddering breath, and while tears still threatened to breach his eyes, they did not fall any longer.

After his exchange with Zekken, Elen-ai wanted to leave Gidyon less than ever. It was not that she thought he was unable to cope on his own. Gidyon had more than proved his capabilities on a great many occasions. It was that she did not want him to be alone in the household of the man his mother had loved, surrounded with the reminder of his grief and anger. But before he had ordered her to go, he had asked her to go. Returning to Herran was the only thing that she could actually do for him, so she would do it.

"Should we send word to the kitchens and ask for supplies?" Elen-ai asked. She could offer him no more words of comfort. As he himself had said, there wasn't really anything further either of them could say that the other did not already know.

The blue of his eyes was made even more brilliant by the red that had been brought to them by his tears. "It's a good idea." His voice was hoarse. He said nothing further, seeming to lapse back into simply staring in front of him.

Elen-ai continued her preparations, summoning a servant and requesting that provisions be ready within the hour for her departure. There was more that she should have discussed with Gidyon – plans, contingencies, messages – but the King was silent, staring reflectively into his hands, and she did not wish to trouble him.

Elen-ai moved around the room silently, gathering the few things she needed. When she was six, the Mothers and Fathers had taught her how to have the lightest of touches, making her fingers sure, swift, and delicate. Clumsy hands were traitors, giving away those who could tread without even stirring the air. While stealing was something that was not encouraged unless absolutely necessary, the children of the Family were granted this one exception for the year while they perfected the skill of possessing nimble and deft fingers in the streets of Herran. After that time, anybody who was caught liberating anything that was not duly paid for in some way or another was punished by the Mothers and Fathers, often creatively. Elen-ai was especially glad for the skill now. She did not want to disturb Gidyon with any rude or unnecessary noise as she selected the items she would need for her journey back to Herran and packed them into her bag.

Finally, she was ready to leave. "Ah, Gid?" she said, reluctant to disrupt him.

He looked at her as though she had woken him from sleep.

"Time for me to go. Is there anything I need to take with me?"

"Yes, one moment." Obvious effort to focus creased his forehead. He finished the note he had been writing when Zekken had intruded, leaving splashes of ink on the page in his haste. "Give this to Sil."

Elen-ai stowed it away in her small pack. "Anything else?"

Gidyon gave a small laugh. She couldn't blame him. There was much they should have discussed, but they were out of time. She offered him a sardonic smile. "I know."

"Well, do try and be safe," Gidyon said.

"I'll always be the last person standing in a fight," Elen-ai reassured him. It was true. She was never concerned about her own safety in any confrontation that may arise. But not every threat was a knife that she could deflect, and not every battle was hers to fight. "Are you certain that you'll be fine here?"

Gidyon placed a hand on her arm. "What I am staying to do here is the sort of task, the sort of place, where I will always be fine," he promised. Of that, she had no doubt. Elen-ai had never met anybody who was as adept at navigating the nuances and trickeries of politics as Gidyon.

"When I secure the allegiance and support of the Tak and Aadran families, I will come to Herran as soon as I can with their people. We need to delay the Katan forces for as long as possible to give me the chance to arrive with reinforcements," Gidyon said. His voice grew stronger as he spoke, and the devastated young man who she had tried to comfort a few minutes ago had retreated in deference to the king.

Elen-ai nodded. "I'll make sure it happens," she promised.

"You do not seem particularly worried about the fact that I might fail here," Gidyon noted. He even managed to pull a real smile to his face. His humour reassured her.

Elen-ai pulled him into a hug, holding him as though she could lift all his troubles for just the briefest of moments. Then she released him and looked him straight in the eye. "I have faith" she told him. "In you."

FOURTEEN

Elen-ai pushed herself and her kittanae as far as they both would and could go. The only time of rest that she allowed herself was a little over an hour just before dawn to sleep, more for the giant feline than for herself. Alone, she focused completely on the experience of riding the kittanae. It was magnificent, striding across the land in easy loping bounds. Aside from Hlevan, her mount, who she found herself becoming more and more attached to with each hour that passed, the cold was Elen-ai's constant companion, pricking at her exposed face until the skin felt as smooth as polished stone.

Evening had well and truly fallen when she reached Herran, only two days after leaving Gidyon. She had seen no sign of Halen's army as she made her way across the Second Country, but that did not mean that he and his people were not advancing on the capital. The Aadran family had no reason to lie, and their network of informants was as good as any. The cheer that Elen-ai witnessed in the streets of Herran as she made her way to the Palace, the kittanae drawing stares from those she passed, seemed utterly incongruous with the urgency and worry that had settled in her stomach. A few optimistic stores were still open, the lights blazing invitingly inside, offering a refuge from the cold and dark. Chatter and laughter seeped from the taverns. Even the exclamations of wonder at the sight of the kittanae being ridden through the streets seemed utterly devoid of care. Under less worrying circumstances, she would have wanted to be within one of the taverns, not riding a beast of the highborn. Indeed, a part of her wished that someone else could worry about the advancing army, the safety of the throne and Herran, and the politics of those who cared nothing for others, and she could instead slip inside, hidden by the raucous sound of the lowborn relaxing at the end of the day. She pressed on, though, guiding the kittanae up the hill to the Palace, entering streets that were reserved for the wealthy. They did not gather in taverns like the city's lowborn but instead dined within their own walls. At the doorway of the Katan city residence, Elen-ai pulled the kittanae to a pause. Royal guards stood outside the front door. She had almost forgotten Gidyon's order that the household of the Katan city residence be placed under house arrest. The guards were totally impassive, and even with their presence, the house looked unchanged. The shrine still stood outside, the gold glinting in the light strewn by the lanterns and peeking through not-quite-covered windows. The urge to spit on the door was overwhelming, but Elen-ai did not wish to debase herself by sinking to the level of pettiness that Halen himself had exhibited. There was no way that she would ever give him the satisfaction of such an act.

Her face at the Palace gates was all that was required for her admittance. The guards – a double guard, she couldn't help but notice – lowered the weapons that had been raised at her approach.

The grand foyer was as cold as ever, illuminated by braziers in the walls that had been lit, even though nobody else would have been moving through the grand space that evening. The beauty of the entranceway was once again lost on Elen-ai as she ascertained from a servant that the King's advisers were to be found in the council room.

She made her way through the Palace at a swift walk. Even at such a pace, her footsteps made no sound on the corridors that normally echoed even the slightest sound. The few guards and servants she passed nodded greetings to her, worry stealing into their expressions as they saw the grim fretfulness on her own face.

The door to the council room was opened by the guards as she approached, and she strode into the warmth of the room with no fanfare other than the surprise at her unannounced arrival. The three brothers looked at her, the drawn and haggard lines on their faces confirming before she even asked that they too had heard of Halen's march upon Herran.

"Where's Gidyon?" Silius asked.

Elen-ai did not begrudge his lack of formalities. In his position she would have been just as blunt.

"In the Aadran lands," Elen-ai said. She held up a hand to forestall the objections that she knew would come. "He ordered me to come back. Here." She unslung her pack and drew from it the message Gidyon had written.

Silius took it wordlessly, his lips pursed in anger and worry at his nephew's decision to send away the protection that Elen-ai's presence by his side assured.

He turned away from Elen-ai as he read Gidyon's message. His head bowed slightly and his shoulders hunched as he paced past his brothers. Kaine mouthed a hello at Elen-ai, accompanying it with a tired smile. Within a minute, Silius finished reading, the linen page coming down to his side with a snap. "Well, it seems my nephew has some preparations for us to make in addition to the ones we have already implemented."

"Do you need me?" Elen-ai asked.

Silius shook his head. "Your particular set of skills cannot be put to use yet."

Elen-ai did not take the comment as a personal jibe. Once she might have, but she had been around Silius long enough to know that he was this way with everybody, especially when other, more pressing matters, like the imminent arrival of an army, were holding most of his attention.

"I'm going to go back into the city. I have something to attend to," Elen-ai told the brothers.

Nikalus' eyebrows rose at Elen-ai's announcement. "Will you return to the Palace?"

She nodded, but the three men were already turning back to confer with one another, trusting that whatever her business, it would be in service to Gidyon's cause. Kaine threw her a parting look and she gifted him with a smile before she left. It seemed a lifetime ago that once, all three men had distrusted her and objected to her presence in the Court.

Walking back through the Palace, Elen-ai could sense the agitation of the guards and servants. As she had rushed through to deliver Gidyon's message, she had simply thought her own nerves and worry were making her see what she was feeling in the faces of others. Now, she could feel the tension that was tightly bound around the Palace. Clues that spoke to the preparations underway were everywhere. More servants moved through the Palace than was normal for that time of night, and the distant clang of weapons suggested training was being conducted by the Royal Guard, again, not a usual occurrence at this hour. But what really unsettled Elen-ai was the atmosphere of uncertain anticipation in the great building.

Outside, the cold of the night had intensified during the short time she had been with the brothers. Or perhaps now that she had been given a small reprieve from the cold, she felt it even more keenly. Elen-ai drew her cloak more tightly about her and went back down the Palace hill and into the city. This time, she avoided the Katan house, despite the detour adding a few minutes to her journey. She did not want to be reminded of Halen or faced with the temptation of defacing his beautiful, expensive shrine.

The Family's home was as reassuring as ever: warm, dark, and with a slightly spicy scent that Elen-ai had never been able to identify as anything other than the familiar smell of her childhood. The Father who greeted her showed no surprise at her entrance. Elen-ai wondered yet again how her approach could possibly have been noticed, and how the Mothers and Fathers had chosen who to send to greet her. Those questions, however, were set aside in the face of the enormous request she was about to make.

"My Daughter." He greeted her with the impassive calm that she had always known in her Mothers and Fathers.

"Father." Elen-ai weathered his scrutiny.

"What purpose brings you to us, Elen-ai?"

"Halen Katan is marching on Herran," she said.

"We are aware. The youngest of our children have already been moved to where their safety is assured."

She did not spare the time to ask where that was. Instead, she pushed forward to what she had come to ask of the Family. "I believe the Family should fight for the King."

The serenity of the house cracked. Ears that were aware of the conversation with her Father were no longer passive listeners, but suddenly keenly interested in what was being said. Suddenly there was a tension in the house similar to the one that wound its way through the Palace.

Her Father's expression did not change, although perhaps his eyes became a little colder, his words a little more carefully chosen. "This is not something that I would ever presume to speak to, my Daughter."

She nearly crumbled then, feeling the horror and hostility of the very house at the blasphemy that she had proposed, but she held herself tall. "Then who can speak on the matter?"

For a moment she thought he might strike her for her insolence. After nearly a week of travel in the cold, with little opportunity for her to practise or train properly, Elen-ai had significant doubts about her ability to hold her own in a fight against any member of the Family. However, the moment passed and he wordlessly turned on his heel. She followed him through the house to its uppermost level with no small amount of relief.

The rooms to which she was being led were rarely frequented by the children of the Family. Here resided the Family's Grandparents, those who no longer wished to take on the day-to-day responsibilities of life within the Family. Elen-ai had only ever seen her Grandparents a few times in her life. Mostly, she had been offered glimpses of them watching as the children trained in weaponcraft or lessons. Only once had Elen-ai directly spoken with one of them, when she had been brought before them immediately prior to her first contract. She had been so full of youthful certainty in her capabilities, of the fact that her body, nubile with youth and years of training, was the Shadow God's most superior weapon. The Grandfather who had spoken for the circle of elders had looked her over once, then knocked her from her feet. Even now, she had no idea how he had managed it. She had never seen him move, but she had certainly felt the blow of his arm against her and the sting of humiliation that spread throughout her as she lay sprawled on the floor.

"You always know less than you think you do," he had told her kindly, heaving her to her feet with a gnarled hand that held strength not only from years of practice, but years of lessons learned and taught.

The fact that she was being brought before her Grandparents now did nothing to alleviate her sense that she was being brought before some tribunal to face a terrible judgment. Her Father knocked on the door, the slightest hesitation obvious before he raised his hand.

"Come in, my Son." The imperious voice held an authority that could not be missed. Its tone reminded Elen-ai of Gidyon, or Arlena Aadran.

Elen-ai and her Father entered the room, which was lit by the soft glow of candles rather than torches on the walls. Seven people sat in cross-legged conference. None of them gave any appearance of being particularly troubled by the intrusion into their space or the impending battle for control of the city and the Second Country. Their wizened frames would fool the casual observer into thinking they were harmless, but Elen-ai knew they were all deadly. Most Grandparents still took occasional contracts.

The quiet discussion across the semicircle of seemingly ancient people ceased as Elen-ai stepped into the room. She felt their gazes bore into her. Nobody stood, nor did anybody seem to be preparing themselves to act as spokesperson. Instead, she was forced to stand in front of them as they sat comfortably and appraised her.

The sound of the candles was louder than the breath of the nine people in the room, the warm flickering sound of the burning wicks was almost deafening in the space which was otherwise silent. Then a Grandmother spoke. Hair the colour of pure, pure snow hung about her face. It was uncharacteristically impractical for a member of the Family to have hair hang free like that.

"You would ask the Family to take a side in the forthcoming battle." There was no anger in her voice, no judgment, nothing at all.

"I would," Elen-ai replied.

A Grandfather said, "The Family does not involve itself in the affairs of those foolish enough to believe that power is best measured with weapons and riches." His head was completely hairless and his face was richly wrinkled.

"This is not a question of weapons and riches. It is a question of the Second Country – our country. If the Katan family takes the throne—"

The Grandmother who had first spoken cut her off. "Then the Family will still accept contracts, still train our children, still continue to exist. Those old families are not like us. They are not our concern." She dismissively waved a hand that resembled a gnarled tree root. Elen-ai had no doubt that the hand in question would still be able to extinguish life with frightening ease.

"With respect, Grandmothers, Grandfathers, the Family is as old as any of the powerful families of the Second Country," Elen-ai countered.

Another Grandmother leaned forward. Her hair was the colour of an angry sky, her eyes were a more vibrant blue than even Gidyon's. "It may be that we, like the old families, fought in the battles of the Godskissed Continent long ago, but those who formed the Family came together precisely because they did not wish to inhabit that world where such fighting continued.

They wanted the certainty that their skills could earn them enough to survive and protect their own. Nothing more."

"And that is a fine reason, but perhaps it is time for that tradition to be broken," Elen-ai said.

Another Grandfather said, "How do you, Elen-ai, come to us and suggest this when your own impartiality is so compromised? You call this boy-king a friend, you bed his uncle. You come asking the Family to risk itself and its children for your own cause."

Shame burned Elen-ai's cheeks. There was too much truth in the accusation for her to even try to deny it.

The Grandmother who spoke retained dark colour in her hair, perhaps could even have been mistaken for a younger woman but for the way her eyes gave away her years. "What have you to say for yourself, child?"

Elen-ai marshalled herself. She would not cry, or whisper out her excuses to these people. She was their Granddaughter, a child of the Family, and she was stronger than simply dissolving in the face of this barrage. She had every right to stand in front of them and speak her piece. "It is not wrong for a child of the Family to hold their own opinions and thoughts. I am a loyal Daughter. This is my home, and it always will be. But I have been inside the Palace, inside the world of the wealthy, and I think that the right thing to do is to support Gidyon against Halen and his allies." Her voice was clear and strong in the room. It seemed to carry through the entire home, heard by all who were straining to listen to what was being said in that uppermost part of the house.

"The right thing?" The Grandmother with the white hair who had first spoken sounded distinctly amused. "We are not so arrogant as to claim we know right from wrong. Those judgments are best left to the gods, my Granddaughter."

"That's a convenient excuse." The insolent words were out of her mouth before she could stop herself.

It sounded as though a hundred tiny breaths were suddenly drawn in. Elen-ai almost brought her hands up to cover her mouth as though to push her words back inside, but she stood resolute, her hands locked against her sides.

"Elen-ai. Not the most clever, most adept, or most deadly of our children. Who are you to tell us, your elders, your grandparents, how we should behave?" The bald Grandfather made no effort to disguise the threat or ire in his voice.

"I am just a child of the Family." Elen-ai met his gaze. She was afraid that she might crumble under the fire and iron she saw there.

"Isn't it time you run back to the Palace? Surely some errand needs to be run," he said. His voice was cold.

"I am a child of the Family. Not a servant of the Palace. I come to you as your Granddaughter, telling you that I think this is not the time for the Family's neutrality." Elen-ai clenched her jaw so tightly that she knew it would ache for days afterwards. Her gaze roved to each of the Grandparents. On their faces she saw no encouragement, no warmth, no expression at all. "Perhaps if that will not convince you, then consider this: the Katan family is not the Royal Family. Will our unwillingness to take a contract on the Royal Family extend to them? Even if it does, will Halen ever feel truly secure? How long until he seeks to hunt us down, to remove us as he is seeking to do to the Royal Family?

"Or if not that, how stable do you truly think the Second Country will be under his rule? He may be able to procure fighters to steal the throne, but he can't buy the hearts of the people. A man on the throne may be unpleasant, but a member of the Seven Families on the throne can only lead to more warfare. We believe in the balance that currently exists because it is safe for us. There is no guarantee of that under the rule of this foolish, bloodthirsty man." More than anything, Elen-ai wanted to turn on her heel and run from the gaze of the seven ancient assassins. The weight of their judgment was almost more than she could bear.

"We promise you nothing, Granddaughter. It is time you leave us," said the Grandmother with the snow broth hair in answer to her diatribe.

Elen-ai did not need to be told a second time. She left, only noticing then that the Father who had brought her in had at some point disappeared. Nobody guided her out, a fact for which she was immensely grateful. She did not think that she could survive the judgment of yet another member of the Family for her request that they fight on behalf of Gidyon.

Elen-ai slipped into Kaine's unoccupied room. The fire slumbering in the hearth warmed the space. Elen-ai gratefully discarded her cloak, content to simply be in the room even if he was not – even if he did not come back to his room that night at all. Taking the first moment of stillness that had been offered to her in days, she sat cross-legged on the bed and breathed deeply.

She prayed. Prayer had always brought her comfort. It had always been an opportunity for her to still her thoughts when they raced, to calm her heart when nothing else would settle it. The chant of worship to the Shadow God were the first words children of the Family were taught to speak. It was as familiar to her as breathing. When all else was uncertain, she had found certainty in her belief.

Yet now her prayer only sufficed to remove the edge from her raging emotions. She could sense the presence of the Shadow God across the veil separating immortals and humans, but today she could not lose herself in the awe of something larger and infinitely more complex than herself. Her preoccupation, her fear, her anger, were too great for her to clear her mind and truly pray.

Her eyes flew open at Kaine's entrance. He did not appear to be surprised to see her there. "It's Divine-cursed cold outside," he said by way of greeting.

"It'll likely be snowing in the Katan highlands. Maybe that's why he's so desperate to control the throne, to get away from the snows in winter," she replied.

To his credit, Kaine did smile, but the joke fell flat in the face of the Katan army's impending arrival.

The children of the Family had no need for fear. They lived with the certainty of their own survival. But she did not feel like a child of the Family at that moment. She felt like she was out of time, out of place, and out of home, buffeted by forces with which she had never held any interest in consorting.

She couldn't say exactly what she sought from Kaine, but she knew that she wanted him. He crossed the room and came to stand in front of her. The gold of his eyes blazed in the firelight as he looked at her. She could see his own fear meeting hers in the space between them.

"Are you all right?" he asked softly, reaching out to caress her cheek. The tenderness was unexpected. With the intrigue, and violence, and fear, Elen-ai had felt that there was no place in the world for any gentleness at that moment. It melted her.

Instead of answering the question she pulled him to her, crushing her lips against his. He tasted like spices and sweetness mixed together, a taste that was now exquisite in its familiarity. She had never considered how the thrill of discovering someone could be surpassed by the delight of knowing them. He sighed, his hands coming to delicately rest on her back. She wasn't all right – how could she be? But she would take whatever respite she could from the fear, uncertainty, and loneliness that had descended upon her as she had ridden away from Gidyon two days previously.

FIFTEEN

She was exercising in one of the courtyards when Kaine found her the next morning. A fine drizzle had set in just after dawn, and the clouds that covered the sky were the dirty grey that promised snow in higher areas of the country. He watched her cartwheeling her body end over end.

"What are you doing?" he asked after a while.

She halted her tumbling and sprang nimbly to her feet in front of him. The week of riding had not put her as out of shape as she had feared, a fact for which she was grateful. "Preparing to fight," she answered.

"Why?"

"Because I'm going to be fighting." She breathed deeply, not liking the slight catch to her breath. Despite her worst fears being unfounded, she was nevertheless less fit than she wanted to be.

"You should be in the back tents, calling orders with the rest of us," he said. Three tents were going to be placed on a slight hill near Herran that overlooked what would become the battlefield. From that vantage point, messages would be sent to the forces to adjust strategy as the battle unfolded.

Elen-ai sank into a deep stretch. She looked up at Kaine as she spoke. "I'll be more use to you if I'm fighting."

He opened his mouth to disagree, but Elen-ai drew the shadows around her so that she shimmered out of sight and circled around him faster than he could draw breath to put into speech. Her blade came to rest against his throat. She released him just as suddenly. A hand constricted around her heart when she saw the wary fear in his eyes. She hadn't meant to leave him afraid of her, but her worry and preoccupation had made her temper short, and she had chosen to make her point with blunt brutality.

"As you wish." He shrugged and left her to continue her training.

She glanced at his retreating back, but she found no room in her heart to nurture any worry over what she may have just done. This was how she kept the fear that was bubbling in her stomach at bay, by focusing on the ache of her body as she honed herself into the most sublime weapon she could possibly be. She glanced up at the sky, wondering if the rain would develop into a heavier storm. It didn't really matter. She would continue her practice even in a torrential downpour. Being able to negotiate slippery ground, or see through a sheet of water that seemed to hang from the sky, were things for which she had been trained. Fate did not always grant clear skies and perfect conditions and it was the responsibility of any member of the Family to turn such things to their advantage. This was what she knew. This was what she could do. Gentle words and sweet embraces were not of her world, and she could not use them to offer comfort to those around her. She could only offer the certainty of her blades and deadly skills.

When she went to Kaine's bed that night, neither of them spoke of what had transpired between them in the courtyard. She fleetingly wondered as his deft hands removed the strap on her arm that held some of her blades whether she was simply there to seek desperate, mindless comfort, and he to find that in her. But then he pulled her to him and scraped his teeth along her skin, and the delicious thrill danced its way along her skin. Her musings flew from her mind, chased away by need and desire and the desperation to forget even for a fleeting second, the worry that had descended upon her and re-fused to leave.

Two days after Elen-ai arrived back from the Aadran lands, the Veertak forces arrived. Even high in the palace, the charge of fear and anticipation that ran through Herran at the sight of the fighters marching toward the capi-tal, could be felt. Those from Herran who had agreed to fight for Gidyon had dutifully trained every morning in the flatlands outside the city – the only possible place a battle could take place – but there was something final and confronting about the mass of fighters from another family arriving. It meant that war had truly nestled itself in the heart of the Second Country.

Still no word had been heard from Gidyon. Elen-ai had never felt so united with the three royal advisers as she did in their shared concern for the King. The four stood just outside the grand entrance of the palace as the Veertak carriage drew up. Elen-ai's place within the Royal Family, while still a mystery, had been a constant for so long that nobody bothered to question it anymore. Those who might have found consternation in her presence were by now, mostly too preoccupied with the prospect of war to wonder about the origin of the King's ever-present, ever-silent adviser.

The Veertak army was camped on the outskirts of the city, its presence causing no small amount of consternation among the residents of Herran, by all reports. Even though the men and women in allegiance to the Veertak family were here to fight for Gidyon, there was an undeniable wrongness to their presence that gave the air an oily taste which lingered on the tongue.

The faces of the two ancient Veertak family leaders were grave. That solemnity made them look even older. They unabashedly held hands as they walked across the yard to the steps of the Palace, a curious note of tenderness amid of the horror of the bloodshed and nastiness that swirled around the Second Country.

"Silius, Nikalus, Kaine, Elen-ai. It is a shame that we meet again under these circumstances," Valena said. Her stoicism didn't quite succeed in concealing her uncertainty and anger.

"Valena, Varl. We truly cannot tell you how grateful the Royal Family is for your support." Silius' deep voice was unusually melodic in the cold stillness of the morning.

Varl offered them a tight smile. There was no need for him to say anything else. His disgust with the Katan actions had been sufficiently expressed on other occasions.

"Please, it's too cold out here, especially after your long journey. Let us continue our discussion inside," Silius suggested.

"That's most considerate of you," Valena told him. "We have also, at the King's request, brought with us one of our scholars, Kar-am." She gestured toward their carriage. At her motion, a woman who looked as though she was of an age with the two Veertaks came forward with a ponderous slowness. A lowborn as evidenced by her broken name, the woman wore clothes that were nowhere near as fine as the garments of the Veertak leaders. However, her back was just as straight as Valena's, and while she showed appropriate deference to the Veertaks in waiting until she was summoned, there was a clear degree of respect that the Veertaks felt for her.

"Welcome, Kar-am," Silius said.

The old scholar bowed low to them. "It is an honour." Her voice sounded like a tree branch being twisted in the wind. It set Elen-ai's teeth on edge.

The ensemble moved through the Palace in silence, the shuffle of feet echoing in the halls.

Once everyone was seated in the golden sitting room – the room in which Elen-ai had first met Latana – refreshments were brought and the real discussion began. Kar-am's tiny form reminded Elen-ai of the Family's Grandparents. While this woman did not seem as though she would be able to deal deadly blows with her fists, Elen-ai felt that the sparkling intelligence in her eyes would be just as deadly as any knife.

Kar-am had a habit of waving her hands around as she spoke, punctuating her comments with gestures from her curled fingers, as though she could almost push the point she was making into the mind of her audience.

"We will need to assemble a camp immediately," she said, her arm darting forward and a crooked finger extending in Silius' direction.

"Where?" Nikalus asked.

"In front of the city, of course. The Katan forces will come from either Harete or Bertak way. We have the opportunity to claim the favourable ground in front of the city. Gives our people some space to lose ground if they need to." Her arm waved back and forth, as though she were swatting away an insect flying around her head.

"Lose ground?" Kaine's expression was one of equal parts confusion and concern.

"Yes. Not all victories are earned on the front foot. We may not need the space, but I want to have it and not need it rather than not have it and need it." She did not spare the time to linger on further explanation, but moved on to the matter of the loyalist army's composition. She did not need to point out that the time until the Katan army arrived was short, and they would need all of it to give themselves the best chance to win. They all were far too keenly aware of that already.

The next day, Elen-ai accompanied the inspection of the Veertak forces as they were amalgamated into Herran's defenders, and a camp for the loyalist forces was properly established. For such a peace-loving family, the Veertaks had managed to muster a surprisingly large force. Under the guidance of

Kar-am, the two forces were maneuvered around the land so that the camp was more strategically positioned. Elen-ai had never seen so many people in an open space. It was almost overwhelming. For the most part, she stayed next to Varl and Valena, conversing quietly with them as the woman who had enjoyed their family's patronage now put a lifetime of study into effect. She directed where tents should go, how the various forces should be grouped, the exact placement of spear racks. At one point, she rushed forward and seized an enormous sword from a member of the Royal Guard – she had made members of the Royal Guard commanders due to their training – and began gesturing with it as she directed the arrangement of some fighters.

"She certainly seems to know what she's doing," Elen-ai said as the three of them watched Kar-am's exuberant gesturing.

"When she was a little more mobile, she used to be a truly phenomenal swordswoman," Varl said.

Elen-ai thought back to the duel that had been staged during the Council. The memory of Halen's sickly sweet breath and the menace he had exuded still evoked the profound sense of unease and discomfort she had felt at the time. She could have so easily ended his life in that moment. If she had acted then, would she still have been walking on what would soon be a battlefield now?

"Did she win any competitions?" she asked, realising that Varl and Valena were waiting for her to say something.

"Oh, several. She fought before Gidyon's grandmother," Valena said. The cold brushed pink along her cheekbones, emphasising the hauteur of her face. She would have been a truly striking woman in her youth. She was still a striking woman now.

"It makes sense that she would be interested in warfare," Elen-ai said.

"When she retired from competing, she became interested in the theory behind fighting on larger and larger scales," Varl said, his eyes on the people who were moving obediently at the instruction of the tiny old woman.

"She travelled into the Fourth Country by herself to conduct research," his wife added, respect for Kar-am's dedication to her field in her voice.

"Does she think that we will win?" Elen-ai readjusted her scarf against the wind that swept across the wide, open space. The fact that Valena and Varl seemed not particularly concerned by the icy wind left Elen-ai amazed.

Varl's loud exhale did not inspire confidence. "She does love a challenge," he said. "And she does seem positive. Although she has suggested that our chances might be improved with the addition of the Aadran and Tak forces."

It was obvious that he did not say she believed they would win.

Dinner that evening was sombre. There was still no word from Gidyon, and the concern elicited by this silence weighed on everybody. The worry made the food, despite it being as superb as ever, impossible to enjoy. The meal was finished quickly, and the little party moved into one of the sitting rooms to play a game of fa'thong. Up to eight competitors could play at a time, vying to remove each other's pieces from the board. The winner was the last person with any pieces remaining. It was a game of strategy, with the pieces restricted in how they could move across the squares, and it required consideration and the ability to correctly judge how opponents would behave. The more people who played, the more complex the elements to consider became. Some called fa'thong a game of war strategy. Elen-ai found it somewhere between appropriate and profane that it was the game that had been selected for that evening. It was, however, also one of the few games that was suitable for so many people.

Elen-ai had seen Gidyon play fa'thong at the Tak house in the previous spring. The game, against Arlena Aadran, and Karan and Serek Tak, had been outrageously intense. All were competitive people. Elen-ai had left the room to confront Zekken about her suspicions that he and Latana were lovers, but she had later found out from Gidyon that Arlena had won. He claimed his loss had been deliberate. To win would have been precocious he explained, but he had been certain that he could have.

This game was far less competitive – nobody really wanted to play, but they also wanted to fill the evening with something other than dwelling on the imminent arrival of the Katan forces. Elen-ai played a good game, but she was the second to be eliminated after Nikalus. Perhaps unsurprisingly, eventually Kar-am won, defeating Valena with a brilliant series of moves. It was a small comfort that the military strategian was victorious, but Elen-ai wondered if the woman's ability to win a game of logic and tactics meant she could successfully direct an army of people, rather than pieces that conformed to very specific rules in how they could move, and what they could do.

Silius half-heartedly suggested that one of the Palace minstrels play for them, but the Veertaks declined, citing lingering fatigue from the journey to Herran. The relief was palpable.

Nikalus offered to escort the Veertaks to their rooms – they were being housed in the Palace rather than their Herran residence. Silius regarded Elen-ai and Kaine across the table after Nikalus and the Veertaks had departed. The pompous figure Elen-ai had first met seemed to have vanished since her return from the Aadran estate without Gidyon. He looked old, and like he had not slept in several days. It seemed he was going to say something, but instead he simply gave a sigh and bade them both goodnight. He strode from the room with a purpose that Elen-ai suspected he did not feel.

Wordless accordance saw Elen-ai and Kaine walk back to his rooms in a companionable silence. The worries of the days and the coming battle hung over them both, but both were content to leave them unvoiced. There would be time enough for those fears to be said, to be lived.

Piles of books still littered Kaine's chambers, despite the fact that legal arguments against Halen were no longer any way to stop him. Elen-ai liked that his rooms were disordered. It felt like a home.

He drew her to him, and she let him hold her like they were sweethearts with no greater concern than the blossom of their love. She rested her head against the curve of his neck, enjoying the warmth of his skin. The pulse in his neck beat deafeningly against her temple. With each pulse, it reminded her how delicate people were, how easily they could be felled. It was both a comforting and unsettling thought.

At length, he drew away. "I understand if you still want to fight against Halen. I wish I could persuade you to stay back where it's safe, though."

She shrugged, not wanting to be drawn into conversations about war and death.

"I just want you to know that if I could, I would be beside you. But the only thing I'll do is get myself killed, or have you looking after me the whole time. If Halen wants to argue about the nuance of laws, I'll be the best person to—"

She interrupted him. She wanted to hang onto the moment in which they weren't inhabiting a world of worried anticipation just a little longer. "What was Gidyon like as a child?"

Memory clouded his golden eyes as he thought, acquiescing to the request which she had not put into words. "He was always more serious than other children. You know, we have some children here in the Palace – the servants who live here, some of them have children. Gidyon took his first lessons with them, even played with them, but he was always different from them, and not because he was a member of the Royal Family. He was so diligent with his lessons, so grave."

"It sounds as though he always knew he was going to rule," Elen-ai said.

Kaine bit his lip as he considered her observation. "He took the idea of being adviser to a sister who would be born after him very seriously. I suppose we always did tell him, from the moment he was born, that it would be his job to look after her."

Elen-ai felt a pang for a little boy with hair the colour of sunlight gravely nodding as someone told him that his whole life would be looking after someone who didn't even exist yet.

Kaine chuckled. "Once, Gid arranged the other children in a classroom and tried to teach them the principles of advanced mathematics. He couldn't have been more than eight or nine. None of them had any idea what he was saying – he'd surpassed the standard lessons by at least two years at that point. Those poor children, they were so polite. None of them said anything the whole time he was talking."

"He must have been so lonely," she murmured.

"He had us," Kaine protested. Faint hurt edged his words.

She had never been more grateful for the Brothers and Sisters beside whom she had grown up than she was in that moment.

"I know, we weren't enough." Kaine's voice was filled with regret. "I think that until he met you, he didn't really have a friend."

Elen-ai, daughter of the Family, was nearly brought to tears by the simple statement. "I can't..." She did not know how to put into words how inadequate she felt as Gidyon's friend. She could not imagine what it was like to be Gidyon, so solitary, and so strong. She had never admired anyone more.

"Do you think that we can win this?" Kaine's question came abruptly, concern giving him the illusion of looking much older than he was.

Elen-ai thought about Gidyon negotiating, wheedling, charming the Aadran and Tak families. She considered a little golden-haired boy with bright blue eyes trying to teach a room full of lowborn children about mathematics, and she found herself smiling, despite the fear and uncertainty that had descended over what seemed like the entire Second Country. "I have faith," she told Kaine.

SIXTEEN

Halen's army arrived three days after the Veertaks and their forces. Elen-ai stood alone on the walls of the Palace and watched the figures march onto the plain beyond the city. From such a distance, they looked more like smudges on the far-away field than people who could, and would, kill those who stood between them and the city. She shivered. The dark tide crept onward, seemingly without any end. Suddenly, the combined forces of Herran and the Veertaks encamped outside the city walls looked far less numerous. She wondered how they could possibly hold the city against the number of people that Halen had amassed. The ominous blue-black rainclouds overhead seemed a fitting backdrop as the Katan army set up camp.

She heard Silius approaching. She did not move, knowing he would use every moment of the journey to compose whatever thoughts were in his head. Eventually he came to stand beside her, his breath heavy from the walk, making tiny clouds in the cold air. Elen-ai did not think that he would appreciate the suggestion that he incorporate some light exercise into his daily routine.

"For a long time, I did not trust you," he said in the typically blunt manner to which she'd grown accustomed. She said nothing, letting him finish whatever he had come to say. She had learned to coexist with him well.

"You are a member of the Family. You are paid to kill. I thought my sister insane when she hired you to protect Gidyon. But you have ensured his safety. Kaine seems to trust you completely, although his judgment might be compromised given the nature of your relationship with him. Yet you have been a loyal subject to Gidyon, and a loyal friend to this family."

Elen-ai remained looking straight ahead, watching as Halen's army arrayed themselves opposite the loyalist forces. Somewhere among them was the man himself in all his vile glory. Her fingers curled into fists at the thought of him.

"We have received word from Gidyon," Silius said quietly.

Elen-ai's head snapped around to look at him. "And?" Desperate worry curled its way around the single word.

"He is returning to Herran as fast as possible. With Aadran and Tak forces."

Elen-ai's exhalation was a long plume of steam. The relief was almost overwhelming. She could see that relief reflected in Silius' face, too.

"Thank you for coming to tell me," she said.

"I wanted to thank you, also." He did not smile. His face remained as impassive as ever. "It is good that you have been with us."

At that moment, the rain promised by the clouds came down in a heavy sheet. Together, Elen-ai and Silius left the Palace wall and went back inside.

Kar-am had ensconced herself in Gidyon's favourite council chamber. The old scholar had liberally drawn over the maps pinned to the walls. The many coloured lines and squiggles made sense only to her, but she seemed content with her work, which Elen-ai supposed was the important thing.

"So, the other side has arrived," she said with what could only be described as restrained glee, the moment Elen-ai and Silius entered the room, shaking off the rain that had settled on them.

"Yes, and quite a lot of them, too," Silius said.

"So I saw. Our reports were reasonably accurate about their numbers." Kar-am sounded more impressed by the efforts of the scouts and informants than worried by the size of the Katan army. She turned to a map of Herran and its surrounds on a table and bent so far over it that her nose practically brushed the map's surface.

The rest of the room's inhabitants – Kaine, Nikalus, Varl and Valena, watched her with silent anticipation. Kar-am did not seem to be particularly aware of her audience. Her mouth moved silently as she thought, her fingers tapping some kind of rhythm on the map. Eventually she straightened.

"Nobody can fight while it's raining," she declared.

Her audience was a good one. No one said anything. Some consensus had led to the recognition that it was best for Kar-am simply to talk until she was finished.

"If they attack, we can stand firm and cut them down in the mud as they slip their way over to us. Same thing if we attack. Even after the rain, attacking on soaked ground creates the same problem, but with better visibility, so whoever's being attacked has time to prepare. We can't do anything. The good news, though, is that they can't either. Unless they're very stupid, in which case, that's good for us." She interlinked her hands and massaged her fingers, a slightly triumphant look on her face.

"So we need to wait until the rain stops and the ground dries?" Silius asked.

She nodded, the wispy white hair on her head flapping with the movement.

"Is there anything that we can or should be doing in the meantime?" Nikalus asked.

Kar-am tilted her head to one side, half closing her eyes as she thought. "Without knowing more about what sort of troops they have, not particularly. It looks as though they're building catapults."

"Catapults? But I thought they have only been used in the Fourth Country," Kaine said with alarm.

"That doesn't mean that Halen doesn't have them. I've instructed some of our people to try to build a few, but they're quite tricky to actually construct," Kar-am said. Her enthusiasm for the destructive devices was a little unsettling. No such things were necessary in the Second Country thanks to the peace maintained by the political structure. Knowledge of catapults came from reports and sketches brought to the ears of the powerful and the knowledge-hungry by people who had passed through the violent factional Fourth Country. There, the machines had been used in the power struggles between the various warmongers, destroying opponents' fortifications, or even simply destroying the towns that fell under opposing lands in order to force surrender. To think that they had come to the Second Country made the world feel as though it had tipped on its side.

"So what will give us an edge?" Nikalus asked.

Kar-am thought for a moment. "Knowing more about what he has. How many people are there, exactly? How many archers does he have? What sort of weapons are his hand-to-hand fighters using? Spears, swords? Do they have shields and, if so, what kind? If we know these things, we can adjust where and how we place our own people."

"How can we know any of this?" Silius asked.

The old woman shrugged, returning her attention to the map laid out in front of her. "We can't, unless someone is there in person. But that would be too dangerous."

"Unless you could get in unseen," Elen-ai said.

"Well, yes, then one could find out all of those things." Evidently assuming that getting into the enemy camp undetected was a hypothetical impossibility, Kar-am didn't even look up.

"I'll do it," Elen-ai said.

Kar-am lifted her head. She looked as though she was on the verge of objecting, but then she scrutinised Elen-ai properly. "I didn't see it at first," she muttered more to herself than anyone else. "Your people have a way of eluding notice."

For a moment, Elen-ai had overlooked that Kar-am didn't know she was a member of the Family. It seemed that her place within the Palace had become so familiar, so comfortable, that she had forgotten the need for secrecy about her identity – for a second, she had simply thought of herself as a part of the Palace apparatus. The moment of discomfort was alleviated by the fact that everybody else in the room was aware of who she was and did not seem to care that Kar-am now knew. Kar-am herself certainly seemed to have put no further thought into Elen-ai's identity as a member of the Family.

Elen-ai's eyes flicked to Kaine, wondering if he would object to her sneaking into the Katan fighters' camp, in the same way he had been against the idea of her fighting in any battle. But he simply looked preoccupied.

"I'll go there once it's dark," she said.

The rain stopped just as darkness fell. Elen-ai skipped over the peaks and troughs of slippery mud on the field of the would-be battleground, her steps so light that she barely collected any mud on her feet. Wearing dark clothes and with the shadows gathered around her, she was invisible to everyone.

The troops who Halen had convinced to join him, as well as though he had simply bought, were arrayed over a large space. Even from a distance, the sight of so many people amid the myriad of tents and campfires was incredible. Elen-ai's skin crawled at the prospect of that many bodies charging into battle. Until that moment, she had never truly appreciated how wonderful the absence of war within the Second Country had been.

Elen-ai circled around the unlucky souls squelching through the mud on patrol. Even had she not been wreathed in shadows, they were unable to see more than a little way in front of them. She was an invasion of one into the camp, and had she wished, she could have killed everybody in her path.

The sound of several thousand conversations was surprisingly soft as Elen-ai slipped into the camp and wove through the network of people, fires, and tents. Amid the songs, chuckles, and clatter of dice, gentle moans suggested some members of Halen's army were passing the time in a more private manner. Every noise that reached her ears was at once familiar yet strange. All of these activities were to be found in most establishments across the Second Country, yet it was as though she were hearing it all for the first time as they clashed together in the open air.

The people in the camp appeared so disconcertingly ordinary. Yet they were here because they were fighting for a man who was so despicable. It did not make sense, and left Elen-ai unsettled in a way she had not before felt.

Despite the fact that she had been trained in the use of every weapon imaginable, the composition of the army was a foreign music to Elen-ai. Yet she had undertaken to report on the army, so she persisted, trying to make sense of what she saw. Amid the hum of voices she could hear the elongated vowels of the Fourth Country's speech. The foreign fighters stayed together, declining to mingle with the inhabitants of the Second Country. Swords either strapped to their waists or placed within easy reached marked them as different to the Second Country fighters. Elen-ai's countrymen paid little heed to the spears neatly stacked far away from them, seeming more intent with the task of swapping stories. A disconcerting number of the campfires were surrounded by these foreign fighters. It took only a glance for her to know that all of them were hardened to fighting. These were the people who would carve through any battle, who would be the true threat. Near a particularly dense gathering of Fourth Country fighters she spied the huge shapes that could only be catapults. Counting four, she moved on.

She walked around a man relieving himself on the side of a tent – why he thought that was an appropriate place, she had no idea – and continued deeper into the camp. In the middle was Halen's tent, larger than any of the others and with the sun symbol of the Divine One stitched ostentatiously into the side . A minstrel played nearby, presumably for Halen's amusement. Elen-ai truly despised the Katan leader – who brought a minstrel to play for them on a campaign to usurp their rightful ruler?

Only one guard stood outside Halen's tent. It confirmed Elen-ai's suspicion the man was elsewhere. Lighter than breath, Elen-ai slipped past her. The opening flap to Halen's tent stirred as though by a passing breeze, but that was all that marked Elen-ai's entrance into the tent, and it certainly wasn't enough to arouse the suspicions of the guard. Elen-ai felt sorry for whoever had been tasked with erecting and dismantling the tent each day during the army's march toward Herran. It was enormous. She was certain she would find something more useful here than simply counting the soldiers in the camp. Kar-am had given her one other instruction: find out if there was a particular time when Halen was planning to send his people across the field to fight.

Despite the size of the tent, there was a surprising absence of any ornate furnishing. A small brazier smouldered near the entrance, offering the most meagre of light through a haze of smoke. It was more than enough illumination for Elen-ai. She crossed to a writing chest and rifled through its contents. This sort of reconnaissance she had done more times than she could remember. It was almost soothing to slip into that comfortable, known rhythm as she scanned each paper, trying to discern any information about what Halen was planning.

The Shadow God was evidently smiling upon her, for she found references to archer numbers, swords, and spears, amid the pages of correspondence and notes, all of which she memorised. Halen was obviously a man who organised himself with a painstaking attention to detail. That much was evident in the way he had gone about demanding the throne for his granddaughter. The timing, the execution, it all spoke of months, perhaps even years, of planning. There was no other way that he could have mustered this many people to fight for him so quickly. Perhaps he had anticipated Queen Latana's failure to produce a female heir years before anybody else, and recognised it as something of which he could take advantage.

There was, however, no information on when Halen was planning to send the people who he had managed to convince to risk their lives for him to try and take the capital. All she could find were messages about "being ready to muster when the word is given", or "ensuring weapons can be rapidly accessed". As she flicked through the communiqués, she breathed out a curse. A sense of desperation filled her. She wanted to find out everything she possibly could to help the people who were willing to die defending Herran and Gidyon's claim to the throne. She felt keenly the strain of knowing how many lives were going to be thrown so carelessly at one another. She spent another moment rereading every scrap of paper, but there was nothing that gave any indication of when exactly Halen was planning to attack. With nothing more she could glean, it was time to go. She replaced everything where she had found it with practised efficiency. But as she was about to close the final drawer, the tent flap was flung open and Halen strode in. Elen-ai silently cursed. She had been so absorbed in her task, shed missed the sound of his footsteps approaching the tent. She was caught. She prayed nobody in the Family would ever hear about this unforgivable lapse. She would almost certainly never be allowed to return to them if the fact she had allowed her emotion to blind her senses to her surroundings became known to them.

For a moment, Halen simply stared at the black-clothed figure on the other side of his tent. She bit down on her burning hatred and ensured her expression was settled into one of hard neutrality. Then she straightened, kicking the drawer closed with an effortless movement. Her eyes never left his, the hardness in her expression a thousandfold reflected in her eyes. The eyes of someone for whom taking life was a business. In the dim, hazy light given by the brazier, he would barely be able to make out her face, but her eyes would be shining like his, and she hoped he could discern her resolve in them.

Halen's mouth had opened in surprise, but he closed it, evidently deciding against calling for the guards who Elen-ai could sense – now that she was focusing – outside the tent.

"I assume that if I call for my people, I'll be dead before they can come in?" he asked. It would have been impossible for him not to know she was a member of the Family.

She lifted her shoulders in the most imperceptible shrug. It seemed he had not yet recognised her, but she was sure that he would quickly arrive at the correct conclusion. She could simply leave, but he would use the fact that a member of the Family had been in his tent to gather yet more support among the people of the Second Country. For all his faults, he was a clever man. She had little choice but to stay and try the best way out of this.

"I did not think that the Family interfered with matters related to the Royal Family," Halen said, slowly stepping farther into the tent. Elen-ai stayed where she was, waiting for him to identify her. She didn't know what he would do with the fact that one of Gidyon's advisers was a member of the Family, but she knew he would twist it to his advantage.

"If you're a member of the Family, why am I still alive?" Halen asked, taking another step toward her. While he could not see her face clearly, she could see his perfectly thanks to the skills of the Family. His forehead furrowed as he worked through the question. Then he arrived at the conclusion: "Lady Elen-ai."

She almost struck. It would have been so easy to close the distance between them. She could have done it in the space between heartbeats. But to leave Halen dead in the middle of his own camp would only point to some form of foul play. Questions would forever be asked about Gidyon as a ruler, and the Second Country had already been rended in two. The only way for something close to peace to return to the Second Country was if Halen was properly defeated. So the moment passed, and Halen's death at Elen-ai's hands slipped ignominiously away.

"So, the boy who would be king has a kept assassin. Or the Family has a kept king. I did wonder how he has remained so safe." A smirk worked its way across Halen's face. "It has been a question I could not answer: what compelled Gidyon to retain you, and why you seemed so loyal to him. Perhaps the rumours are true and you are his lover."

Elen-ai crossed the remaining distance between them in a move too quick for him to see. "Are you certain that you want to irritate me?"

Halen chuckled, apparently unfazed by the demonstration of her capabilities. He had been sucking on a candied lolly, and the sickly sweetness of his breath invaded her nose. Another flash of rage accompanied the realisation that he had been goading her.

"If I am found dead, then nobody in the Second Country will think that your king is legitimate in anything he does. I know you wouldn't harm a hair on my head." His confidence was foul.

Elen-ai seriously considered shearing off a lock of his hair to spitefully prove him wrong. "Don't worry, Halen, I won't hurt you. I'll leave that to

Gidyon, and the people who fight for him. Tell me, how many of the people here did you have to pay to get them to march on Herran?" She moved away from him, gliding to the only chair and seating herself.

His face tightened at her insubordination, but a pleasant lightness remained in his voice. "You would not be surprised to learn that there are a great many people who do not feel it is appropriate that a man should have the throne. Once they knew that my granddaughter had a claim ... well." He spread his hands in lieu of finishing the sentence.

"And of course you will have no hand whatsoever in her rule."

Halen laughed. They both knew that he would be king in all but name. Just like they both knew that he was practically drooling at the mere thought of such an eventuality. In her mind, Elen-ai flowed across the room and wrapped her hands around Halen's neck, and he died knowing that she had been the one to kill him.

"If so many people support your claim, why did you have to hire swords from the Fourth Country?" she asked instead of killing him in one the hundred ways she so desperately wanted to.

"There is no harm in being cautious, my lovely assassin," he said, not seeming to be even slightly embarrassed that she knew he had hired foreign mercenaries. "After all, once my beautiful granddaughter ascends to the throne, money will be the least of my concerns." The way he inclined his head meant that the meagre light from the brazier shone on his bald pate. It should have made him look ridiculous, but instead it gave his face an unexpectedly sinister cast.

"You do realise that you're insane?"

"If I were insane, would your pointing it out make me less so?"

The fact that Halen's logic had a point snapped the final slender thread of Elen-ai's self-control. If she couldn't kill him, she could at least scare him. Halen couldn't have seen Elen-ai draw or throw the knife, but he certainly felt its impact between his feet. He glanced down at it, surprise on his face. Before he could react, two more knives were on either side of his boots, so close that one had even nipped the leather.

"You'll be nothing more than a footnote in the pages of history," Elen-ai snarled. Despite the three knives at Halen's feet, it looked as though she hadn't moved in the chair at all.

He slowly lifted his gaze from the blades to her. "Even if that's true, at least I'll be remembered. Will the same be said of you?"

Elen-ai slithered across the room, collecting her knives with a movement that was too fast to be seen. Halen had to turn to find her at the entrance to his tent where she paused so that she could deliver one parting comment. "I don't need to be remembered. It's enough for me to know that I'm on the right side of history – the side against you."

Rendering herself invisible, she ran across the campsite so quickly that her feet barely touched the ground. No one noticed her passing. She was simply a part of the night breeze.

SEVENTEEN

Kar-am received Elen-ai's information on the Katan forces with much enthusiasm. The old scholar's eyes brightened, and she scribbled on a map, all the while muttering excitedly to herself. After several moments had passed, it appeared as though Kar-am had entirely forgotten that Elen-ai still stood there. Finally, it became apparent that Elen-ai would have to interrupt the woman's conversation with herself. "I can't be sure, but I think Halen will order his people to attack as soon as possible."

The prediction had caught Kar-am's attention. She looked up, hand poised above the page, her eyes refocusing on Elen-ai as though surprised to find her standing there. "Why do you say that?"

"He found me in his tent. He wouldn't know what I discovered, but I wouldn't be surprised if he attacks as soon as he can to forestall any advantage we might have. But," Elen-ai paused for a breath, trying to work out the best way to explain what she had seen in the man. "Even if he hadn't caught me, I think he would attack without caring about the lives he might lose. He already thinks that people are disposable. He won't care about how many lives are lost if mounting an attack sooner gives him some advantage – even just a small one. The fact that he's paying many of them to fight for him would only contribute to that decision." Elen-ai fought the urge to twist her hands together as she waited for Kar-am to consider the statement. She was certain of her conclusion, but that didn't mean others would readily accept her assessment. She had observed enough people from the shadows to know the kind of person Halen really was, though. And her encounter with Halen in his tent had merely confirmed what she had long thought of him.

After many moments of contemplation, the old woman nodded. "We'll muster an hour before dawn to be ready for such an attack from the Katan side. You should get some rest before then. I believe you will be fighting to-morrow, and you'll want to be alert."

Elen-ai went to Kaine's chamber, unsurprised to find him still awake and reading. This time, it was not some arcane legal text but a volume on warfare tactics.

"Not your normal bedtime reading," she said.

He jumped. She had entered his rooms and moved through them with her customary silence, not paying any thought to alerting him to her presence. But he did not seem upset by the surprise. She liked that. He placed the book aside and offered her a weary smile. "Kar-am was kind enough to lend it to me."

"Anything interesting?"

He shook his head. "I've no taste for in this sort of thing."

Elen-ai crossed the distance between them with deliberate steps, pulling him to her. "Kar-am believes that Halen will order his people to attack at the first chance that arises. I'll be on the field in a few hours with the rest of the soldiers."

She had kissed his mouth so many times that it was now wonderfully familiar against her own. His hands on her offered a certainty that she was still there, still alive, that things were still as they should be, for at least a little while longer.

That promise of normalcy had only been an illusion. While dawn was still some way from arriving, Elen-ai headed down to encampment of loyalist forces and took her place in the unit of sword fighters to which Kar-am had assigned her. Elen-ai had no idea what exactly a unit was supposed to be, but neither did any of the people around her. Kar-am's explanation had been simple enough, though. Move when the enemy moved, and try and stay close to one another in battle. The people around Elen-ai stamped their feet to keep warm, rubbing together hands that would soon clutch weapons. Kaine's chamber seemed a world away in the chill pre-dawn light. The cold seeped into Elen-ai. She stamped her feet to try and stay warm. The waiting made the anticipation and dread settle in her alongside the cold. She longed for a cloak, but when the fighting did commence, she could not afford to be en-cumbered by such a billowing garment. She had lost count of how many times she had checked to ensure all of her blades were in place, but she performed the action again, as much for her own comfort as the meagre warmth the movement offered.

The city had practically been stripped so that any cloth royal colours – purple and gold - could be given to the Herran fighters. They needed to be able to identify one another so that they did not mistakenly attack the wrong people. Kar-am had been most insistent about it. People wore purple or gold – yellow, really – cloth in a variety of manners. Some were fortunate enough to have shirts or jackets in the colours. Elen-ai herself wore a shirt of deep purple, pilfered from somewhere in the Palace. Most of the people around her simply had strips of yellow or purple securely tied around their arms or waists. Yet the colours gave the army a ragtag sort of unison.

Elen-ai glanced skyward. Clouds still covered the sky. Drizzle so fine that it could be mistaken for mist quickly set in. Elen-ai wondered if Halen would attack after all. If not, the entire loyalist army would have been waiting for the last half hour for nothing. Somewhere behind her, close to the safety of the city's walls and separate from any fighting, Kar-am and the rest of the Royal Family stood. They would be watching the progress of the battle, sending down orders to particular groups of fighters in response to whatever Halen's army was doing, but they were too far away to chart the progress of any individual fighter. The thought that Kaine would be looking at the fighting but unable to see her made Elen-ai double check that every blade, every buckle, every lace, was exactly where it should be. She wanted to see him again.

Finally, the sky began to lighten until it was possible to see further and further and some modicum of colour seeped into the landscape. The white-green of the frosted grass stood out starkly against the brown of the earth. Elen-ai's breath was a cloud in front of her.

She glanced up to the walls of the city – if you could call them that. The cities and towns of the Fourth Country were truly walled in preparation for an attack, but the peace that had gifted the Second Country for so long had made such protection unnecessary. The walls that denoted the beginning of Herran were more a collection of houses. Even the field in which they stood could have been called a part of Herran, filled as it was in summer with the makeshift camps of the poorest residents, those who came to scratch out a meagre living by performing the lowliest jobs that could be found, such as cleaning the refuse from the streets. In wintertime, those poor souls crammed into dwellings that should only have housed a third as many. Many a tragedy had gone unnoticed when such structures caught fire, and everybody inside perished. Some of those people stood beside Elen-ai now, their skeletal forms obvious even under the clothes that had been given to them by the Palace. The offer of food, clothing, and coin had brought a surprising number of people to fight for Gidyon. It was impossible to tell if their allegiance was to the king or the comforts they were offered. Elen-ai wondered uneasily if paying those desperate for sustenance to defend Herran was akin to Halen hiring mercenaries to fight for him. She wanted to say the actions were worlds apart, but she was no naïve child. The Palace's offer was using the lowborn of the Second Country just as Halen did. Such was the way of the world when the rich and powerful fought. At least these men and women beside her were fighting for their city.

Katan forces mounted their attack three long and tedious hours after dawn, once the drizzle had cleared. The unit leaders of Gidyon's army shouted for the defenders to hold their positions. Kar-am had ordered with a terrifying fierceness that no offensive action be taken. Where the ground wasn't frozen, it was wet and slippery. Any charge would result in people falling over, becoming stuck, losing their momentum. From there, it would be easy for the Katan fighters to cut them down as they struggled for purchase in the unforgiving earth. Halen must have felt he had fighters to waste on a charge across the treacherous ground.

The first wave of Katan fighters appeared as a dark line that became thicker as they approached. Horns blared as the Katan troops came closer and closer. Elen-ai hefted the sword she had been given, taking a small measure of comfort from its weight. The people around her – her unit – mirrored her action. Most of the other fighters in the loyalist army were equipped with spears, which were easier to use, especially with little training. Elen-ai did not allow herself to be distracted by worry about the under-trained army in which she stood. She pushed her mind instead to think of her own skill, to ready herself for the coming fight, for it would be the hardest fight of her life.

Alarmed shouts from the rear attracted Elen-ai's attention. One of the two catapults the Herran forces had managed to build had collapsed. Women and men scrambled around the debris. One or two unfortunates had been struck by beams or ropes. It was a gruesome sight. The other catapult appeared to still be intact, its cup filled with large rocks. Then its ropes snapped. The deadly projectiles flew across the battlefield and crashed into the line of Katan fighters, but because the ropes had snapped rather than been released, a few fell short, landing amid the Herran soldiers, too. Screams of pain and terror split the air. Fortunately, Elen-ai had not been in the path of the catapult, but she couldn't help but worry that this was some kind of sign as to how the battle would fall. The Katan catapults returned fire. They appeared to be slightly more successful. Deadly debris rained destruction onto the loyalist ranks. Some held shields, baskets, pieces of wood, anything they could find, above their heads in a desperate bid for some protection. But the Katans too were struggling with their own hastily erected catapults. Even as she watched, Elen-ai saw one of the shadowy mountains topple sideways. She glanced back one more time at the disasters that had been the loyalists' catapults. Such was the outcome when scholars tried to put into practice dangerous ideas without first testing them. Elen-ai wondered what else of Kar-am's theories would be proved wrong in practice before the day was out.

As the Katan forces drew closer, a wave of arrows from behind them came speeding from behind them. Once again, the loyalist forces held anything they could use to protect themselves above their heads. The thick thud of arrows raining down was almost deafening, but it was over quickly. The loyalist army held its position as its archers replied with their own volley of arrows onto the Katan forces which grew ever closer.

The archers of both sides sent over waves of arrows in a desperate bid to thin their enemies' ranks, and then the Katan army was too close, and the real battle began. The forces met in a cacophony of sound and blood and violence. Elen-ai threw herself into the battle with a vigour she had not realised she possessed. The sword was an extension of her arm, biting into flesh with hungry metal teeth. She gave herself to the blood song. This was everything that she had been made to do, fighting in the most pure of forms. She was not forged for the world of the court, or the subtleties of games played by those who did not truly have to bear their consequences. The only toys that she had ever been given were weapons, made to fit her tiny hands. She had been trained and broken, and trained again. She had been forged to be the victor in any fight. The months of constraint and intrigue in the court had almost made Elen-ai forget what and who she was, but that self came roaring out in the clash and crash of battle.

Elen-ai was vaguely aware that the light had become brighter as the morning wore on, and that people around her were falling with a distinct absence of any grace or poeticism. The Royal Guard, who only occasionally put their training into practice where they fended off robbers when escorting something for the Royal Family, were barely more efficient than the lowborn. If anything, many of the lowborn fought better thanks to the fact that in the less refined world of the Second Country, brawls were commonplace. As she hacked and slashed her way through any enemy who crossed her path, Elen-ai wondered if this battle bore any resemblance to the tomes and recollections that Kar-am had collected over her lifetime. Somehow, she doubted that this bloody, messy, disaster was the sort of thing documented in the records of tactics and battle outcomes. There was a difference between a tale recounted to an interested audience or words on a page, and the slick feel of blood, the ache of muscles, or the jagged cries of pain from those left wounded and dying on the ground.

A momentary lull hours later saw Elen-ai rouse herself from the bloodlust which had saturated her very being. The exertion of hours of fighting had covered her with a sheen of sweat. The chill of the morning had long since fled her. She looked at the battle surrounding her, and despair threatened to choke her when she saw how many Katan fighters still stood. They far outnumbered the people alongside whom Elen-ai fought. Despite the hope to which she had desperately clung, she could see no way that Halen would not win this battle. Indeed, it seemed a miracle that the loyalists had held out for so long. Once he had overpowered the defenders of Herran, Halen's troops would simply march through the city streets until he battered down the Palace doors and claimed the throne. Elen-ai forced down the sense of hopelessness and threw every last part of herself back into the fray. If Halen was victorious today, she would take down as many of his people as she possibly could. It was the only thought that gave her comfort and she drew on it to keep fighting with every last drop of her strength and speed.

The feel of wind whispering past her drew her out of her violent reverie. She knew what that sensation meant, even as she struggled to believe it could be true: members of the Family were amid the fighting. The grace with which they danced from person to person was quite beautiful. The bloody carnage they left behind was breathtakingly spectacular. The deadly skills of the Family were all too often used in secret. However, here on the battlefield, there was no need to hide themselves. They were fighting for their lives, for their city. The death they swiftly brought to any opponent they encountered made those loyalists around them fight even harder.

A tap on her shoulder had Elen-ai whipping around, blade in hand – she had lost the sword perhaps half an hour previously, leaving it in the belly of a man as she had swung to block a blow from a woman foolishly trying to surprise her. Instead of an attacker though, she came face to face with the grinning mountain that was one of her Brothers, Al-et.

"Are you really that surprised to see us, Sister?" he asked. A man charged at him before she could reply. He fended the attacker off with no obvious effort.

"I can't say I expected you," she gasped, her breath stolen by the surprise of her family's appearance rather than the exertion of the fighting.

"Why ever not?" He grinned. The gold tooth he had inserted after his fiftieth kill winked at her.

"I didn't think that the Family would fight." Elen-ai took a moment to parry a blow aimed at her head. The woman who held the offending blade was from the Fourth Country by the look of her. There was a silken manner to her movements that suggested she was very practised in the art of killing. It meant that Elen-ai had to concentrate a little and momentarily, her conversation with Al-et was ceased. She parried another blow, then whispered around the woman to stab her in the back of her neck.

Al-et shouted, "Good to see you haven't lost your touch."

She made an obscene gesture at him. "Why is the Family fighting for Gidyon?" she yelled back once he had finished dispatching two women. Unfortunately for them, they had decided that the fact he was conversing with Elen-ai would mean he would be an easy kill.

He twirled his axe. He was showing off, now. "You apparently made a good case to our Grandparents."

A smile broke Elen-ai's face in two. Despite the gore, the sweat, and the sweet ache that told her that her muscles were beginning to strain, she felt once more that victory might be possible. She threw herself back into the fight with renewed energy.

The members of the Family had woven themselves across the battle-field. They were phenomenal. Everyone they touched fell and stayed down. They were harmed by only the luckiest of blows. But even the influx of the Family and their deadly efficiency was not enough to truly turn the tide of battle. Members of the Family might have brought down anyone who came near them, but the battlefield was large, and the number of Katan fighters so very enormous.

"Keep them from entering the city." The cry boomed across the battle-field, taken up by those defending Herran from those seeking to take it for themselves. Soon it was a deafening roar, but the desperation within it could not be missed. There were too many Katan fighters for the defenders to keep at bay. Even the Family could only thin their numbers, perhaps provide a slight delay. But it would only be a matter of time until the attackers made their way into Herran.

Despair once again weighed down Elen-ai's heart. Despite all that she had done, despite the Family defying the impossible and coming to fight, it seemed that Herran would still be lost. A sob made its way up her throat as she slashed and danced. She could fight until there was nothing left of her but a blade and the will to hold it, but there was no way that it could be enough.

The sky seemed to mirror her anguish, having turned an ominous black. It was only the early afternoon, but darkness was seeping over the land. Rain, thunder and lightning looked as though they were ready to engulf the frenetic and bloody battlefield, throwing the entire scene into even further chaos.

And then the cries around her took on a different tenor. Wondering what Halen could possibly do now, what terrible and bloody force he could introduce to rip through the tired, bloodied defenders, and break into the streets of Herran where he would destroy anybody or anything that stood in the way between him and the Palace, Elen-ai hardly dared to raise her eyes beyond the immediate melee to see. There she saw the new fighters approaching the battlefield. Elen-ai's heart painfully tightened at the thought that Halen had somehow managed to hide a force of reserve fighters so that they could sweep in and destroy the tired and bloody loyalists who had been ensconced in battle all day. In that second, Halen seemed to her not a man, but a figure with godlike powers. She almost fell to her knees, giving up and letting the battle simple wash over her. But then she saw a flash of golden hair and her heart squeezed painfully with a wild joy she could barely contain as it pounded through her. Gidyon had finally arrived with fighters from the Tak and Aadran families.

EIGHTEEN

The arrival of the reinforcements was a magnificent sight. In the dark that had swept across the sky the land, Gidyon's hair glowed, drawing the eye to him amid the reinforcements. He rode his kittanae at a reckless pace, leading his forces.

The fighting stopped almost entirely as every single person in the fray turned to watch the King approach. The King of the Second Country was spectacular, almost like a vision. Even from far away, Elen-ai could see in the set of his face the determination that he would not lose this fight, that he would never see his throne lost. He was leading several mounted riders. Behind them was a mass of unmounted fighters. Gidyon drew his sword and held it aloft. On the graceful feline whose stride seemed more akin to flight, Gidyon looked like a figure straight out of legend.

The air was so still that from the other side of the battlefield, Halen's furious scream to his archers was clear. "What are you waiting for? Fire on him."

The cold of the day washed over Elen-ai for the first time since the fighting had begun. Gidyon wore leather armour, but his head was unprotected. If a lucky arrow struck him, then he would almost certainly die. She could only watch as the volley flew in an arc across the rapidly closing distance between Gidyon and the battlefield. The pale wood of the arrows stood out against the blue-blackness of the sky, almost beautiful in their flight. They hailed down around the King. A few struck people near him, but Gidyon was mercifully untouched.

The call to release came again, and another barrage of arrows arced across the air, seemingly suspended in flight. Once more, everybody – not just Elen-ai – appeared to hold their breath as they waited to see whether the battle would be ended by one lucky arrow. One arrow did find a mark of sorts, lodging in the neck of Gidyon's mount. The beautiful beast stumbled, then came crashing to the ground, the King falling with it. Elen-ai heard a strangled cry, then realised it was hers. A fall like that, especially with an animal as large as a kittanae, could be just as fatal as an arrow hitting home. Time seemed to stop as beast and boy tumbled. Elen-ai could hear her own heartbeat, thrumming through her body, feel the rasp of air against her throat.

Then Gidyon rolled clear of the falling animal and pushed himself to his feet. He barely seemed to worry about the other riders thundering past him who might trample him. Gidyon now stood alone, a solitary figure in the space between the two armies, the near-profane sight of the wounded kittanae beside him somehow serving to make him look even more startling. He had miraculously defied death three times in a row.

A cheer rose up from the loyalist fighters. Astonishment, pride, and relief made the women and men fighting in Gidyon's name scream in wordless rapture at what they had witnessed. The cry broke the spell of stillness that Gidyon's appearance had caused and the fighting resumed. Caught between three different assailants, Elen-ai was no longer able to watch Gidyon's progress. She was vaguely aware that another volley of arrows was released and sailed toward the King, but she could not look to make sure that he was not hit. She could only pray that he had once more managed to defy death.

The fighting took on a new intensity as the defenders found themselves reinvigorated by the sight of the reinforcements, their king, and his escape from harm. Elen-ai could feel the change across the battlefield as the line of mounted Tak and Aadran fighters swept through it. She too was caught up in that sensation; she didn't even realise that she was uttering a guttural cry until she felt the rawness of her throat when she paused to draw breath. She hacked, slashed, twisted, turned without thought. She didn't even notice whether she was running down men or women, all she could feel was the ache of her muscles and the resistance when blades met flesh. Elen-ai all but flew between her victims. Sometimes she would pause to properly engage an assailant who found themselves directly in her path, sometimes she would simply reach out an arm or leg, and whoever she had chosen as her unlucky target went down. Her legs covered in mud, her arms and face smeared with blood, she should have looked terrifying, and to anyone who she was about to strike, she did in fact look like a sending from their worst night terrors. People from both sides were falling, exhausted from the unrelenting hours of fighting. Some were even unharmed, simply lying in the mud, uncaring if death did in fact claim them, uncaring even if the end of the world came. But she still moved as though she could evade exhaustion itself, every turn, pivot, thrust, a graceful piece of poetry in action.

Elen-ai eventually came to the end of her dance and she paused to re-gather herself. She stood surrounded by people doing their utmost to remain alive, and in that moment of stillness, the reverie of bloodshed in which she had been caught up was broken. The salty smell of blood mingled with that of earth, opened bowel and bile. Even the four months she had spent working in a slaughterhouse at age nine, which she had thought had made her utterly indifferent to the unpleasant smell and sight of death, had failed to prepare her for this. The reek was overpowering. It seemed to rise from the earth and assail the senses with the same ferocity as any of the fighters on the field. It was almost overwhelming to see the number of fallen bodies that surround-ed her. So many forms covered the ground that it seemed impossible enough people were still able to continue fighting. Yet even as she stood, some opti-mistic fool rushed at her. She simply dropped low and pushed up with her blade, goring her enemy with a brutal efficiency. As she rose to stand fully upright once more, the sound of another feral battle cry reached her ears. The Tak and Aadran foot soldiers had finally reached the battle. The sound of weapons clashing mixed with cries of pain, deafeningly loud as both loyalists and usurpers were invigorated by the arrival of these new fighters.

Nearby, a wounded Herran fighter dragged herself through the muck of battle towards the tents where the wounded were being treated. Something about the woman's desperate determination to try to save herself pulled Elen-ai away from the call of fighting. In swift strides, Elen-ai went to the woman's side, pulled her up, and slung one arm around her shoulder.

"Can you walk?" Elen-ai asked.

The woman gave a feeble nod.

"Come on."

They half-crawled, half-ran back toward Herran, weaving through what had once been ranks of men and women and was now simply chaos.

The woman collapsed completely as they neared the edge of the battle-ground, and Elen-ai carried her the rest of the way. She laid the woman down among the unending lines of bodies inside the first tent she reached. As soon as the woman was out of her arms, Elen-ai would have struggled to find her amid the pain, mud, and blood that left everybody in the tent looking exactly like one another.

She took the moment to stretch and ease the ache that had taken root deep within her muscles. The sound of battle was muffled by the walls of the sheets of canvas slung over an array of poles to keep the bloodied wounded under cover that a generous soul might call a tent. Somewhere further along, there were actual tents, but as the battle had continued and more people had dragged themselves away to seek help, the structures that had been erected to offer them even the most meagre of shelter had become increasingly crude.

Elen-ai called for help and one of the few attendants yelled at her to wait. There were all too few people in the tent with the training to help those who needed it. Many of the wounded would die as relatively minor wounds went untended and became fatal. The smell of the injured was almost worse than it had been on the battlefield. It was a certainty that, on the other side of the battlefield, there were Katan fighters arrayed in an almost identical way. Elen-ai was struck by the pointlessness of the battle that raged on even as she stood surrounded by the wounded and dying. The thought brought to life the anger at Halen that Elen-ai nursed within her. Here was a man willing to knowingly end so many lives simply for the sake of his own greed, his own ego. In that moment, she vowed to the Shadow God that even if he won this battle, even if he claimed the throne for his inept granddaughter, she would still bring death to Halen Katan. If it came to Halen residing in the Palace, all but sitting on the throne himself, it would almost certainly mean that Gidyon and his uncles were dead, that the country she knew and loved was irrevocably changed. If that eventuated, the only thing that Elen-ai could do would be to end the miserable life of Halen Katan, no matter if it meant that she would be never allowed back to the Family, even it meant her own death. As she stood in the tent, surrounded by the stench of blood and gore, she prayed to the Shadow God and promised that if the worst came to pass, she would take Halen's life with her own hands.

Elen-ai left the area devoted to the wounded. The tents had been placed on a rise so that if rain did come, the casualties wouldn't be lying in pools of water. Of course, the ground was already cold and damp from the preceding days of rain, and lines of bodies almost completely filled the tent. If the battle continued for much longer, there was no more room even for makeshift tents on the slight hill; the wounded would be forced to lie outside.

Elen-ai turned to the battle raging below, the crash of weapons and the guttural cries of pain and rage filled the air. Gidyon was somewhere in the melee, but amid the sea of people, it was impossible to pick him out. The terrible thought occurred to Elen-ai that he might be wounded or dead, rendered anonymous by mud and blood. If that were the case, then this terrible fight was continuing for no reason. The prospect that Gidyon might be dead filled Elen-ai with dread that left a sour taste in her mouth. That taste became more bitter as she looked out across the battlefield and realised that despite the reinforcements from Tak and Aadran, the Katan fighters still had superior numbers. Moreover, after battling rain and mud during their march across the Second Country to arrive at Herran in time, the Tak and Aadran fighters were tired. Elen-ai could see it in the sluggishness of their movements. They were being slaughtered.

The vantage point laid the battle out before her like a map. The members of the Family were not visible, but where they went could not be missed for the trails of dead they left in their wakes. The hired fighters from the Fourth Country were brutal, giving no ground. Their movements were efficient, practised. They were unshaken by the chaos of the battleground or the extent of the carnage through which they waded. And then there was everybody else, the citizens of the Second Country who had been conscripted through the promise of a meal, money, or some ideology. Some had broken and were fleeing toward Herran, or the dubious safety of the plains. A surprising number held their ground, though fatigue shone through their sluggish movements. It was safe to assume that all were desperately praying that their waking nightmare would soon be over.

The light was bleeding quickly from the land as Elen-ai made her way toward the fray. With the clouds pregnant with rain, it would soon be too dark to tell friend from foe. Elen-ai grabbed a sword from a fallen body and cut her way through the crush of exhausted bodies to the heart of the battle. Three times, she came across her Brothers and Sisters, and she exchanged a tired, knowing nod with them. She wondered how many of them would fall before the battle was over. Their deaths would be on her conscience. Fighting anybody who was stupid enough to engage her, she searched in the fading light for Gidyon. Finally, she saw a flash of gold. Of course, he was in the thick of battle, despite the danger. It was just one more reason she would follow him to the ends of the earth if he asked. Or even if he didn't.

She hacked her way through to Gidyon's side. Six soldiers fought alongside him: two members of the Royal Guard and two each from the household guards of Tak and Aadran, ensuring his sides and rear were protected. A fighter from the Fourth Country towered in front of Gidyon. Elen-ai didn't hesitate. She ran the woman through, pushing her body aside as it fell. The corpse fell to the earth with a thud, leaving Elen-ai and Gidyon staring at one another across it.

"Your Highness." Elen-ai looked Gidyon over to ensure he was uninjured. Other than a thorough coating of mud, he seemed miraculously unharmed.

"It's good to see you." Gidyon gave her a smile that managed to reach his eyes. "Your lessons have been very helpful today." His words ignited comfort in her at knowing that even though she hadn't been by his side, she had still been able to protect him.

Before Elen-ai had the opportunity to reply, she was forced to parry a swing from an attacker who had managed to sneak between two members of Gidyon's guard. While their blades were locked, Elen-ai stomped on his foot, then stabbed him in the eye with one of her blades.

Once, Gidyon would have been horrified by the demonstration of her brutal skills, but all he said was "Thank you," once it was clear that the man was not going to get up again.

"We won't be able to keep this up." Elen-ai had to shout across the roar of battle which had suddenly crescendoed around them.

The expression on his face told her that he had already arrived at that conclusion. Any reply was curtailed as a group of Katan fighters charged them, intent on ending the battle by killing the king. Precious light fled even further as for several moments, Elen-ai and Gidyon became preoccupied with dispatching their attackers. Two of Gidyon's guards fell and Elen-ai was forced to fight three people at once before loyalists came to their aid and they were momentarily clear of enemies.

A flash of lightning from the harbour side of Herran was proceeded by a growl of thunder that temporarily drowned out the cacophony of battle.

"Gid, if it starts to rain, we'll be in trouble. Most people will barely be able to see if it gets dark. With the rain, they won't know who they're fighting," Elen-ai yelled.

Gidyon didn't respond; his blade remained at a 'guard' position, but his thoughts were clearly not on defending himself.

"Gidyon," Elen-ai yelled. "I don't know how we're supposed to win this." At last she voiced what she had tried so hard to not admit. No matter how she considered it, the battle did not seem as though it could be won. Elen-ai had not realised until that moment how much she had hoped that Gidyon had some brilliant plan to defy the odds. She had not realised the extent of her faith in Gidyon until she felt that faith beginning to be shaken.

Gidyon closed his eyes. It seemed a foolish thing to do in the middle of a battle. His lips moved, but she could not hear what he said. She moved close to him, looking around for potential attackers.

"What?" She placed her ear so close to his lips that she could feel the warmth of his breath against her face. It was a poor position for her to be in if they were attacked.

"Don't you believe in me, Elen-ai?" She could hear a sad smile in his voice. "Step back."

She didn't hesitate, didn't question; she simply obeyed the order of her king.

Gidyon let his sword fall to the ground and raised his hands high above his head. Elen-ai wondered what he was doing, but she did not interrupt him. Her task now was to ensure he was undisturbed. She raised her blade, watching with keen eyes for anyone who might come toward her king. The land was almost completely dark now, that blackness only punctuated only by distant lightning strikes. It was possible that the storm would pass them by, but Elen-ai had her doubts. She parried one attacker, lost a blade as she threw it into the eye of a second would-be assailant, then thrust her sword into the face of her first attacker.

The man fell. His blood seemed impossibly red in the dark, even with her Family-gifted sight. Then Elen-ai realised she wasn't seeing with the skills of the Family. Gidyon's hands were glowing, possible to almost be mistaken for a ray of light which had managed to break through the thick, dark clouds. , the light unwavering like a sunbeam breaking through cloud. Then it became stronger. Then it was so bright that Elen-ai's eyes watered. The fighting around them had stopped as people looked for the source of this sudden light.

The light became so bright that Elen-ai couldn't look directly at it. Instead, she dropped her gaze to Gidyon's face. His eyes were closed, the expression on his face was serene. The glow grew even brighter, piercing the darkness of the battleground to touch everybody, and Elen-ai could not even look at Gidyon's face any longer. Now no one fought. Silence reigned. Everybody was looking to Gidyon – the king who was summoning the sun amid the darkness.

It was impossible to know who knelt first, but from wherever it started, the action spread like a ripple until every person on the battlefield, including Elen-ai, was kneeling in the mud and blood, beside the bodies of those who had fallen, beside the person who until a moment ago they had been fighting alongside or against, bowing their heads in reverence to the king – their king, who held the sun in his hands.

NINETEEN

Three days after the battle for Herran and still Elen-ai's muscles ached from the hours of fighting. She spared a thought for the others who had not been trained from birth by the Family. They must be in agony.

The bustle of the Palace reached her ears as she lay on the bed in her rooms. The sounds were familiar to her by now; servants moving discreetly through the building, the Royal Guard performing a drill – they must have been in immense discomfort returning to such work so soon – the snip of shears as the gardens were tended. It was different to the near meditative quiet of the Family's house, interspersed with the occasional hum of conversation, the thuds and whisper-soft grunts of training. Even the creak of the old house moving in the weather was a far more unobtrusive noise than the sounds of the Palace. Yet the everyday noises of the Palace had resolved themselves into a familiar tune that no longer struck her anew each time she heard it.

At some point during the fighting, she had sustained a shallow but long slash across her shoulder blades. Only once it had been pointed out to her amid the disarray of the battlefield's dismantling had it begun hurting. Since then it had stung with an intrusive constancy. Never more had Elen-ai wished for Freya's presence and her healing skills.

The knock on the door which rang through her chambers was followed immediately by Gidyon. Since the battle she had spent very little time by his side. So many things had demanded his attention that it had been impossible for Elen-ai to keep up with what he was doing. Or at least, that was what she had told herself.

He closed the door behind him. "Am I interrupting?"

"No." Elen-ai sat up. She winced as the movement pulled scabs across her shoulders.

The King approached her, his uncertainty obvious in the sound of his steps as he crossed the small sitting room to enter her bedchamber. Rather than come and sit beside her, he remained standing in the doorway. After a hesitant moment, Elen-ai patted the space next to her on the bed. He sat.

"Everything all right?" she asked.

He gave a little shrug, looking down at the embroidery on the bed's coverlet rather than at her. "I suppose. Judging and sentencing people is not exactly my favourite thing to do."

"I'm sorry I haven't been—" she began, but he cut her off with a wave of his hand.

"You have done more than enough. You deserve a rest."

"And you? You came all the way across the country, threw yourself into the fighting, and now you're still going."

"A ruler does not live for themselves but in service to their people." Gidyon was obviously reciting something he had been told often, yet that made it no less moving to be reminded of how seriously Gidyon took his duty.

"Halen never would have understood that," Elen-ai said with quiet firmness.

Gidyon gave another little shrug. "I do not know. He might have. Sometimes I think that deep underneath it all, he honestly did believe he was doing the right thing. But then he became so caught up with his ego and greed that it was impossible to separate the two."

"He never wanted to do right by the people of the Second Country. Not in the way that you do." The fierceness in Elen-ai's tone caught her by surprise. Gidyon was long past needing protection or reassurance. He had proved that time and time again.

"Do you know what they are calling me?" He didn't look at her, instead gazing at the painting of Herran's harbour on the wall.

Elen-ai had, but she chose to let him tell her.

"The Sun King."

"Better than the Pretender King or Boy-King," she said.

"They think that my reign is blessed by the Divine One. That I am some form of Divine incarnation."

"Don't you believe that?"

Gidyon was silent, giving due consideration to the question. "I do not know what I believe."

"Well, with the support that you have, you could do anything you like," she pointed out.

"That scares me, though," he said. "I do not want to be able to do anything. The reason we have justices, the reason we have the power of the Seven Families, is so that whoever sits on the throne cannot simply do what they want."

Elen-ai slung an arm across the King's shoulders, giving him a quick hug. "If you want, I can always tell you when you're being stupid."

A smile tugged at his lips. "Ah yes. 'I am terribly sorry, but my friend thinks I am being stupid, so I will not be proceeding with this particular idea, after all'. I am sure that will be well received."

She laughed, resting her head against his shoulder. In reply, he tilted his head to gently brush against hers. For a moment, she forgot what had transpired on the battlefield. Rather than being the Sun King who had brought two armies to their knees, he was once more simply her friend.

"Have you spoken with Kaine?" Gidyon asked.

"A little."

Gidyon opened his mouth to say something further, then hesitated. She knew why. Like her, like everyone, Gidyon's uncles had been unsure how they should approach their nephew. Unlike Elen-ai, though, whose struggle lay in the uncertainty of how to treat as a friend someone who had inspired awe across an entire country, and as a result, someone whose every command would be obeyed without any question, Gidyon's uncles were still struggling to understand what magic Gidyon had within him that allowed him to summon light. For them, Gidyon had gone from being their king to being a figure who walked hand-in-hand with their god. It was one of the other reasons that Elen-ai had secluded herself over the past three days. She did not want to have any discussion of Gidyon's acts with Kaine. She did not want to have those sorts of discussions with anyone.

"I feel very alone," Gidyon said, so softly that it was almost as though had hadn't even meant to actually voice the feeling aloud.

Elen-ai pulled her friend more closely to her. "Don't say that."

He shook his head ever so slightly. The catch in his breath spoke of a battle to contain tears.

"You're never alone," she promised him. "You'll always have me."

They left her rooms and walked together through the Palace corridors. Almost certainly Gidyon had somewhere to be, but there was no sense of urgency in his demeanour. Elen-ai looked at the walls as they passed. It was as though she was seeing them again for the first time. The careful arrangement of the coloured tiles formed beautiful patterns that gave the corridor a sense of light and beauty. Elen-ai couldn't begin to imagine how painstaking it must have been to envisage such a design, let alone place the tiles so that every small square fit together as part of a larger whole.

"It's a shame that the tiles will be destroyed if you knock down this wing," she commented.

Gidyon looked at her in confusion before casting a glance at the walls. "They are terribly outdated."

"But they're so beautiful."

"Elen-ai, nobody tiles their walls anymore. It has not been done for at least thirty years." Gidyon sounded amused.

"So? Don't you think this is beautiful?" Elen-ai stopped in front of a section that had been tiled only in blue and white. The blue tiles were arranged in a growing spiral radiating out from a small centre. Against the starkness of the white, it was quite arresting. The windowsills of that section had been painted alternately white and blue, too.

"It is very visually impressive," Gidyon admitted.

"So you're the Sun King. If you like it, just have them put in tiles. Who's going to dare to say you have old-fashioned taste?"

It was good to hear him laugh.

They continued on to the council chamber. The maps had been removed from the walls and the stacks of papers and books that had transformed the space into a veritable maze had been returned to their appropriate places. Elen-ai thought she should cease to call it the war room in her mind. Yet she could not think of it as anything else. Gidyon's uncles were waiting for him. Elen-ai's eyes met Kaine's. He looked as though he had a world of questions to ask her, but she immediately dropped her gaze.

"We have a problem," Silius said the moment the door closed behind them.

"Another attempt to take my throne?" The wry amusement in Gidyon's tone suggested he did not think that was very likely.

"No. But we need to decide what we are to do with Halen and the rest of the Katan family."

"Execution is a possibility," Nikalus suggested.

Gidyon shook his head. "If he had won, he would have executed all of us. I do not want to be like him in any way."

"Well, he can't remain in the Second Country. Even if he's imprisoned, he may still have enough influence and intelligence to cause trouble," Silius said.

Gidyon turned to Kaine. "What legal options do we have?"

Gidyon's uncles were all noticeably wary of him. They hesitated before speaking, and didn't allow their gaze to meet the King's for an overly long time. Elen-ai could see the faintest edge of hurt in Gidyon's eyes at the treatment he was receiving. In summoning light, he had elevated himself to something that separated him from others beyond the mere fact that he was their King.

Kaine looked at the wall in an almost convincing pretence of consideration. "We could definitely throw them all in the jail."

"Remember, we have to deal with the Rasatan and Bertak families as well."

Nikaus' reminder was either directed at his nephew or his brother. It meant that he conveniently did not need to look at Gidyon as he spoke but could instead turn to Kaine.

"They placed their support behind Halen and the Katan claim. And, of course, the Bertak family has been breaching the law with the illegal workers." When the Royal Guard had arrived at the Bertak estate to place the family under house arrest until Gidyon decided what to do with them, they had discovered that supporting the Katan army was not the only morally questionable thing the Bertaks had been doing. Citizens from the Fourth Country who had fled the violence there were working in the Bertak mines. Not only was such a proliferation of undocumented workers illegal, but after a brief preliminary investigation, it had been determined that the Bertaks were woefully underpaying the refugees – another crime within the Second Country.

"I think we imprison the heads of the Bertak and Rasatan families," Gidyon said. "And impose several sanctions and taxes onto those who adopt the leadership."

Kaine nodded. "That would all fall within some form of law or legal precedent."

"But the Katan family?" Silius prompted. "I do think we should consider execution, like Nik said."

"I will not kill them. Not even Halen. Serenah is my cousin and your niece. And Serenah's mother is your sister. I do not understand how you can suggest this." The sharpness to Gidyon's voice when addressing his uncles was not new. What Elen-ai had never seen, though, was his uncles practically cower in reply to his firmness.

"My apologies." Silius looked somewhere over Gidyon's shoulder rather than meeting the King's eyes. Nikalus immediately dropped his gaze to his feet like a chastened child, and Kaine remained staring at the wall in a magnificent pretence of contemplation.

A hand squeezed Elen-ai's heart when she thought of Gidyon's earlier quiet confession, that he felt isolated from everyone around him. His uncles' responses to him would do nothing other than reinforce this. With time, hopefully, they would drop this posturing and return to the relationship they once had with their nephew.

"What about exile?" Kaine suggested.

Gidyon nodded thoughtfully. "If we do this, do I have the right to take their land from them?"

His question earned him a surprised look from even Elen-ai.

"There is no law permitting it," Kaine said. "But then again, there is no law to prevent it."

"All right then. That is what I want to do. Strip them of their land and wealth, leaving them enough coin to survive, and exile them until Serenah dies."

There was a certain brutality to the decision that Elen-ai quite liked.

"What if they try to garner support while in exile?" Nikalus asked.

"What, try to overthrow the Sun King?" Silius smirked.

Elen-ai felt Gidyon tense. It was one thing for him to refer to himself as the Sun King, or for her to do it in jest. It was another thing entirely to hear his own family use this title.

"I will not let Halen make me into his executioner. Jail is too good for him. Let him live with his shame," Gidyon said finally, carefully emphasising each word so that there could be no mistaking his intent.

"I'm sure I could draft a list of laws that set out your right to take their land," Kaine offered awkwardly.

"I would like to have the warrants and precedents ready within the next two days," Gidyon said. "I want them locked up or about to leave by the time we hold some kind of memorial for the fallen. Now, if you will excuse me, I believe there is a builder waiting to discuss the new wing. I have told him that I particularly like the curly bits in his design." Gidyon caught Elen-ai's eye. The tension with which he had addressed his uncles had vanished, replaced by a mischievous smile playing about the corners of his mouth. She bit her lip to keep from laughing. The shift from severe king to playful friend was disconcerting, but she was reassured to see that the Gidyon with whom she could share a joke, or playfully deride, was not overshadowed by the Sun King.

"It's a good idea to make an alteration to the Palace, especially after this victory," Silius said, approval on his face even though he still did not quite meet his nephew's eyes.

"I was thinking that we would put a room in there called the assassin's room," Gidyon said, still looking at Elen-ai. The cautious smile that he offered her warmed her heart. Even though he might now be known as the Sun King, a figure more steeped in legend and reverence than truth, he was still her friend and always would be.

"We can discuss where exactly we can send our friends from the Katan family later. I would assume the Fourth Country would be a fitting place for him, though, given his obvious affinity with their hired fighters. Elen-ai, did you want to come along to the meeting?"

Elen-ai responded with an expression that perfectly conveyed what she thought about the prospect of discussing building styles and techniques at length.

Gidyon laughed. "All right then. I will find you later," he said, and with that promise, he left.

Elen-ai made to leave once Gidyon had departed, but was arrested by Silius clearing his throat in a manner that left no doubt he wished to say something to her. "Do you have a moment?"

The way he spoke made it clear that he wasn't asking her at all.

Elen-ai obliged by staying where she was, even though being given a command rankled somewhat. By some unspoken accord, the three brothers stepped closer to her. She chose to wait until one of them spoke. She had a growing sense that she was not going to like what followed.

Silius spoke with his characteristic bluntness. "You have to choose. Stay here, or go back to the Family."

"I'm a daughter of the Family. I can't just leave them. And I can't leave Gidyon, either." She recalled her promise to Gidyon only an hour or so earlier, and the way his three uncles had been so distant from him, so wary of him. Perhaps she was the only person who was not waylaid by such sentiments and could treat him normally. She simply could not leave him alone.

"Think about it, Elen-ai," Kaine urged her, his golden eyes earnest. "He will have to marry soon. You won't be able to just stroll in and out of his rooms then. How will that seem to his wife? What about his children? How will your inconsistent presence be explained to them, a lowborn aunt who happens to kill people for a living? And what if his friendship with you – who you truly are – is discovered? People may now think that ... whatever power he may possess has been bestowed upon him from the Divine One, but if there is enough substance to the rumour that he consorts with assassins, how long until people begin to whisper that he has made some pact with a malevolent demon, courtesy of the Family?"

Elen-ai began to disagree, but he cut her off.

"I know that the Family does not harness the power of demons. But consider it from the perspective of the other lowborn, of the other inhabitants of the Second Country." His golden eyes implored her to understand the logic behind his words.

"I—" Elen-ai felt as though he had just pushed a knife between her ribs. The knife sat there, making each breath a sharp jab in her side.

"Don't mistake what we are saying," Nikalus said. "What you have done for Gidyon and the Second Country can never be overstated. But you cannot endanger everything that you have helped build."

Elen-ai curled her hands into fists. "So I'm a liability to Gidyon, now."

"You always were." For someone normally so brusque, when he spoke, Silius' voice was surprisingly gentle. "But there were larger risks to his position than you."

"So if I choose to stay here, what would you do with me?" She scanned the three faces before her. The earnest expressions they all wore made it so much worse. They, like her, were only looking to protect their king's best interests.

"You would officially take on the mantle of King's adviser, like us," Kaine said.

"The Veertak would confer upon you some form of qualification that would make such a title legitimate," Nikalus added.

"Adviser?" Elen-ai crossed her arms. She hoped they would not see that her hands were trembling. "And you would give me duties to perform under this title?" She restrained herself from adding 'like a trained animal'.

Silius nodded. "You would be ideal for travelling, as well. Your unique set of skills means that you would be safe, and able to spot what others might not. You could ensure that the Seven," he caught himself, "Six families are all behaving, not seeking to undermine Gidyon in any way."

Tears of anger now threatened to force their way into her eyes, but Elen-ai blinked slowly, refusing to let them be seen. "You want me to spy for you. So I'd barely be here, and I'd be spying for you."

"If that's how things work. But you wouldn't be spying for us. You'd be doing it for Gidyon," Silius said.

Elen-ai stared straight ahead. She dared not look at Kaine. She didn't know what she would see in his face, and she was afraid of what she may see there if she did turn her eyes to him.

She fought past the desire to scream, run, fight. She truly had been in the Court for too long. Instead of doing what came naturally to her, she raised her chin, allowing her arms to fall down to her sides, her hands open. "I will consider your proposal," she said, her voice even. It was the kind of response that would have made Gidyon proud.

With that, she left the room, her back as perfectly straight as ever. The air in the corridor was particularly chilling after the stuffiness of the war room. She told herself that it was the shock of the cold that was making her eyes water. She almost believed it.

She did not turn at the sound of running footsteps. She didn't need to. She knew the sound of Kaine's footfalls. She sped up but he drew level with her nevertheless. She did not look back.

"Elen-ai, please wait." Kaine gasped for breath, pausing for a moment, then jogging to catch up with her again. "Could you please stop for a moment?"

When she did not acknowledge his request, he grabbed her hand.

Faster than thought, Elen-ai put him on the ground, one of her blades drawn and a whisper away from his eye.

To his credit, Kaine kept his nerve, staying perfectly still on the cold floor. "I know this is a difficult thing to ask of you."

Elen-ai straightened up in a movement too fast to see. "Get away from me," she snarled.

Kaine clambered awkwardly back to his feet. "Please."

She remained completely inert while he laboured to stand. She stared at him, her face a mask.

"Please," he repeated. "You know we're correct."

She took a step toward him. He looked very much as though he wanted to take a step back, but restrained himself.

"How would you feel if I asked you to choose between your family and someone you loved?" Despite her desire to shout, she asked the question in a voice that was so soft that the anger and anguish behind it could almost be missed. Almost.

"I know. I know it's not fair. I'm sorry." His handsome features were distorted with emotion, and she saw how hard it was for him to ask this of her.

It was the apology that broke her. Anger, violence, even betrayal, she could deal with and still come through. But that heartfelt apology twisted the knife that he had lodged in her, and she felt the tears slide down her cheeks.

He pulled her to him and she had nothing left in her to resist any longer. She cried softly into his shoulder, letting him put his arm around her and whisper "I'm sorry" into her ear over and over.

TWENTY

After the chill of the outside air, the warmth in the Family's home was almost overwhelming. The tip of Elen-ai's numbed nose bloomed into sensation. She had never been able to tell what discrete scents comprised the smell of the Family's home. All she had ever known for certain was that it was the comforting smell of home.

The sound of muted activity within the depth of the house made its way to Elen-ai's ears. The efficient clang of cooking noises and light-hearted chatter came from the kitchen where lunch was being prepared. The home felt alive, exactly as Elen-ai had known it for her entire life. Unlike her most recent visits, there was nobody to greet her. Something about it made her feel less like a visitor and more like she was merely stepping back home after a day on the streets.

Elen-ai followed her nose to the kitchen, craving the camaraderie of her family. Her stomach gave an angry growl at the familiar scent of a family recipe, learned by observation and refined by years of practice.

A brief silence descended when Elen-ai entered the kitchen. She stared back at the four Family members who seemed shocked to see her. Their expressions made her pause, uncertain of what to do or say. Two of her Brothers and one of her Sisters were holding knives. It occurred to Elen-ai that those kitchen knives were lethal enough on their own, let alone in the hands of those trained to use anything and everything as a weapon. Once, she wouldn't have given that truth a second thought.

"Good. We could use the help," the Father who was standing near a bubbling pot said. With his comment, activity resumed as though it had never stopped.

Elen-ai took a proffered knife and began to slice vegetables. The dish they were cooking was one she knew well, a vegetable-based stew that nourished the soul. Unlike at the Palace, meat was a rarity that the Family consumed only once or twice a week. It was so with most of the Second Country's lowborn.

It had been so long since she had done this sort of work that it felt almost like a dream to be once more in the kitchen surrounded by her family, performing a task as menial as chopping vegetables for lunch. Undertaking the chore offered Elen-ai a certain sense of comfort that she had never felt living in the Palace. Easy, casual chatter surrounded her. It was hard to reconcile the mundane harmony of the scene with the fact that all four members of the Family who worked in the kitchen had fought in the battle for Herran.

"Have you heard that cloth from the Fourth Country has doubled in price?" Elen-ai's Brother El-en said as he peeled a long mallenroot with deft movements.

"Mm. There's fighting there between six houses now. It'll be a wonder if we can get anything from the Fourth Country before long," their Father replied from his position at the stove. The finely diced moash frying there was the culprit of the smell that had sent Elen-ai's stomach into a flutter.

Her Sister, Tan-ai, heaved a lump of dough onto a countertop and began kneading it with rhythmic thuds. "There'll always be something coming in from the Fourth Country. It'll just be so expensive you'll have to sell yourself to buy it."

"Better ready yourself now, El-en. I know how much you love the candied nuts from the Fourth Country," their Father said.

"Who'd want to buy El-en?" asked Tan-ai, evoking a chuckle from everyone in the room.

Elen-ai chuckled along with them. It was good to be among the intimate banter, free from the rigid social mores of the Court. It was what she had known her whole life.

"What about my fruit seller? He seems to like me just fine." El-en put a hand to his chest in feigned hurt.

"Yes El-en, that's because he's blind," their Father said with exaggerated patience, eliciting yet more chuckles.

Once the meal was prepared, Elen-ai took a bowl of the stew and climbed up to the roof, easily balancing the bowl as she negotiated the climb. The weak sunlight offered a pathetic warmth that could not dispel the shock of the rooftop's cold. Despite the chill seeping into her backside, Elen-ai sat happily, enjoying looking at the sea of haphazard rooftops cobbled together in an unintentionally graceful array. It was a sight she had known and loved her whole life.

Mari-am's appearance by her side was announced by only the slightest whisper.

"Is it a nicer view from the Palace?"

"Nothing's nicer than this view." Elen-ai's answer came immediately.

"You don't have to lie."

"I'm not. No view of the city will ever be as nice as this one."

For many minutes after that, they sat in silence and ate, as they had done from the first time they both were able to climb to the rooftop. This was their spot, and everybody in the Family knew better than to try to claim it for themselves.

Finally, Elen-ai could restrain her curiosity no longer. "Why were you fighting for Gidyon?" She had glimpsed her Sister on the battlefield, handling herself with deadly grace. In the days since the battle, she had pondered Mari-am's motives many times.

She tore her eyes away from the view and looked at Mari-am. Her Sister's brown eyes were, as always, sharp with intelligence and consideration. "Gidyon was the better choice. A Katan on the throne would have been unacceptable."

"You still don't support Gidyon, then?"

"No man should ever sit on the throne." Mari-am's voice indicated this was not a belief she was willing to debate.

"I'm sorry that I hurt you," Elen-ai said after the silence between them had stretched for too long.

Mari-am dispensed with the spoon that she was using and slurped up the remainder of her lunch straight from the bowl. Elen-ai suppressed a laugh, imagining the expressions of horror the inhabitants of the Palace would wear if someone were to do that in front of them.

"Are you coming home?" Mari-am asked, ignoring Elen-ai's apology.

Elen-ai looked out over the city. This was the sight that she had known her whole life. Sitting on the rooftop next to her Sister was where she felt the most comfortable. More than anything, she wanted to hold onto the moment, preserving it in time so that she never had to move into a future full of un-knowns.

"No."

Mari-am exhaled slowly. "I guess life in the Palace really is that good."

"I made a promise." Elen-ai forced herself to look at Mari-am, to etch into her memory the slope of her nose, the blush that spread across Mari-am's cheek in reply to the cold air, the way the strands of hair played across her eyes. If it was the last time she was going to be with her Sister, she wanted to remember everything.

"What will happen to your skills? Who can you train against that will actually push you? Who can ensure that you are the finest weapon that you can possibly be?" Mari-am paused for a moment, looking out over the city with a slight squint. "I was on that battlefield. I saw you. You were magnificent. Nobody who approached you was your equal. Do you really believe that if you leave, you'll be able to maintain that skill?"

Elen-ai said nothing. Mari-am was correct. The truth was uncomfortable to hear. "I suppose if I stay by his side, I can't be an assassin any longer. So perhaps it's right that I'm not..." She couldn't finish the sentence. Her throat constricted at the prospect of losing the edge that her whole life had been spent honing. It was almost as awful as the prospect of never seeing any of her family again.

"Do you really love him that much?" Mari-am asked. "I can't imagine loving anyone so much that I'd give away being a member of the Family." The obstinate certainty in her Sister's tone was so characteristic of Mari-am that the familiarity was like an iron band around Elen-ai's heart.

Elen-ai shook her head, buying herself some time to work past the tightness in her throat. "I don't love him in the way you think I do."

Laughter arose from the street below, incongruous with the moment between the sisters. It seemed they were at a total impasse.

"I'll miss you." Elen-ai offered that truth in place of all the other things that she wanted to say.

"I'll miss you, too." Mari-am's dark eyes were unreadable. "Here, give me your bowl. I'll take it down to the kitchen." She held out her hand.

Within the offer was the painfully clear message that there was no need for Elen-ai to re-enter the Family's home. Mari-am's rebuff made her chest ache. She wanted so badly to take it all back, to say instead that she was coming home. She did not know what she would be if she wasn't a member of the Family, if her skills became dulled. She desperately wished that she could simply come home. But she had promised Gidyon that she would not leave him.

She turned her gaze back to the rooftops. It really was a beautiful view. She took a deep breath. The cold air burned her nose and throat. When she turned her head back to where Mari-am had been sitting, her Sister was gone.

She couldn't remember the walk up to the Palace. Her grief and shock at the enormity of what she had done had numbed her far more effectively than the frozen air. Walking back through the Palace gates had felt surreal. No matter how long she lived in the Palace, she would never fail to find it unusual that the Guards recognised her, stood aside for her, greeted her with obvious respect. She had been trained to live in the shadows, to slip unnoticed from place to place. Such conspicuousness felt so wrong.

In the Palace's driveway, she stood for several minutes, not even really noticing the cold. Her first thought was to find Gidyon, but she was not ready to explain to him what she had just done. Then, she thought about going to her rooms. But that prospect was too much a reminder of the home she had just lost. So her feet took her to the stables and the comforting presence of the kittanae.

The stables were warm, and Elen-ai slipped into the pen where she was met with a slow blink from one of the animals. They numbered only four now. Gidyon's mount had died on the battlefield. There was something forlorn about the remaining animals. They curled even more tightly together now. Being close to them and their grief made Elen-ai feel less alone.

She didn't know how long she had been there before Gidyon found her. She was sitting against the wooden wall of the pen, the massive paw of one kittanae thrown across her lap when she recognised his footfalls. His face appeared over the wall. "I thought I'd find you here," he said.

"How did you know?"

"I know you," he said. He vaulted over the wall – less nimbly than she had. All four of the kittanae raised their heads at his entrance. Gidyon walked to the nearest kittanae, a beast with rich brown fur, and held out a hand for it to smell. Once it had satisfied itself that Gidyon was not a threat, the king idly scratched under its chin, eliciting a purr of contentment.

"Are you going to go back to the Family?" he asked in a voice smaller than she thought possible.

She didn't reply. To that, she had no answer. With Gidyon's appearance, Elen-ai's grief had condensed and lodged itself in her chest. The realisation that she had would never again see her family was a weight that pressed down upon her. If she allowed herself to contemplate the enormous finality of her decision – of never going back to the home, of never laughing with her Brothers and Sisters, of never belonging so completely – breathing became difficult. She hadn't truly considered what it meant to never go back. Now, all she could think of were the things she would never get to do. Suddenly the rest of her life, devoid of any link to who she was, seemed terribly long.

The King left the side of the kittanae and came to sit next to her. The straw sighed as he sat on it. The solidity of Gidyon's presence next to her roused her enough to answer him.

"I'm not going back."

"Ever?"

She shook her head, too exhausted by her grief to do anything else.

"Why?" Even though she wasn't looking at him, she could feel the intensity of his gaze. It gave her the resolve to be able to speak in a full sentence.

"I belong here, by your side."

Gidyon did not try to comfort her with the lie that she was able to visit. She appreciated that. "But you're miserable. I don't want you to be sad."

She took his hand. "I told you I'd never leave you, Gid."

Instead of replying, he squeezed her hand. His eyes were bright with tears. "You would do that for me?"

"I would do anything for you, Gidyon," Elen-ai told him. And with that, somehow, the grief that had placed itself on her chest with what seemed like an immutable weight, shifted slightly, and she found that she could breathe a little easier.

The initial shock and grief evoked by the enormity of her decision gradually abated. There was an almost unsettling normalcy to life in the Palace that removed the edge from her despondency. Preparations began for the construction of the new wing, and Elen-ai was forced to vacate her old rooms. She could not help but notice that her new rooms were in the wing where Kaine's were, and she knew Gidyon was behind this. She and Kaine did not exchange more than a few words whenever they saw one another, which happened infrequently. Elen-ai worked hard to ensure she spent as little time near him as possible. She did not yet know what she wanted to say to him.

She shadowed Gidyon wherever he went, taking comfort from the presence of her friend. As Elen-ai had predicted, the legend that surrounded Gidyon as the Sun King meant that no objection was raised to his decision to claim the Katan holdings as sovereign land. When he privately suggested in jest that he offer the lands to the Family, Elen-ai had given him a stare that would have withered most people.

"You're the Sun King. The sun doesn't shine from your backside," she told him.

He threw back his head and laughed.

She liked that she could make him laugh. It was good to see the King smile. Among the shining gold of his hair, she sometimes thought that she could see threads of silver. He wasn't even eighteen years old.

A month passed. Elen-ai still ached for home but she no longer wore the sadness like a shroud. A great celebration was planned to commemorate the victory against the Katan insurgency. Gidyon invited the new heads of the Bertak and Rasatan families. It was a clear message that he considered the treasonous behaviour of their families to be decisions made solely by their elders, regardless of what the truth may have been. Nikalus and Kaine vigorously opposed their inclusion, arguing that Gidyon had imprisoned their family members and imposed harsh taxes against them, and so there was no way that they would be loyal to Gidyon. Silius and Gidyon countered that while that much was obvious, it was better to show that the crown was willing to pretend otherwise and offer them the opportunity to redeem themselves. Elen-ai agreed with Kaine and Nikalus. She had, however, thought that bringing them to Court meant that they could be observed, which might be useful. But she didn't say anything, seeking to draw as little attention to herself from Gidyon's uncles as possible. They all might have Gidyon's best interests at heart, but she still could not help but feel betrayed by the three men.

She was praying in her rooms before the grand party when a rap at the door roused her. She was glad for the interruption. There was no way that she could not pray to the Shadow God, but every time she did, it brought forth a sharp bloom of sorrow at the life she no longer had. She opened the door to find Gidyon flanked by a small army of people.

"Do you need something?" she asked.

His face was totally serious. "I have a debt to collect."

"A debt?" She made no effort to hide her bewilderment.

"If I recall correctly, I won a bet. Silius danced at midwinter. I have yet to collect my winnings." Gidyon linked his arms behind his back.

"Are you serious?" Elen-ai took a panicked step back.

"Deadly." Gidyon advanced on her. The people he had brought with him remained at the threshold. Uncertainty clouded their faces as they peered at her. While the truth behind her origins was unknown, rumours about Elen-ai, especially after her performance on the battlefield, were certainly rife. Fortunately, they were all too enamoured with the fact that they worked for the Sun King to be overly bothered.

"I fought on a battlefield for you," Elen-ai said with a fierceness that she did not feel. The prospect of him putting her in skirts was terrifying.

"You swore on your honour that you would wear skirts if I could get Silius to dance. You were so certain that he would not." Gidyon smirked, enjoying her discomfort.

"Please, Gidyon. Anything but this." Elen-ai was not one for begging, but here she threw away her dignity in a desperate attempt to avoid this impending torture.

"Do you really expect me to show you any mercy?" Gidyon grinned wickedly, indicating to the people he had brought with him that they should enter her room. They did so, with obvious trepidation.

"I hate you," Elen-ai told him.

His smile simply broadened. Gidyon slipped his hands into his pockets and tilted his head to one side as he examined her. It was a predatory sort of examination. "Hmm. What about a nice flared skirt? In a delightful shade of sky-blue?"

"I beg that you do not," Elen-ai said.

Gidyon laughed at the panic on her face. "Don't worry. I'll make sure it's tasteful," he said. Somehow, the promise did not reassure her.

It took three hours to prepare Elen-ai for the evening's festivities. Her hair was brushed with the finest comb she had ever seen. Any snarl or kink in the short strands was removed by the careful hands of the man who seemed blissfully unconcerned that Elen-ai was capable of snapping his neck with very little effort. In fact, there were several points throughout the entire process when she considered exacting a bloody vengeance upon the people who pampered, plucked, brushed, and combed every part of her. All through it, Gidyon watched her, amusement making his blue eyes even more vibrant than normal. This time, however, she was not glad that she was making him amused. Elaborate silver cords were threaded through her short hair, her face was painted with a slender brush, and finally she was squashed into a dress of blood red. The colour, she could only assume, was Gidyon's idea of a private joke.

Finally, she was ready. A mirror was held in front of her and the elegant woman who stared back at her with enormous dark eyes seemed a complete stranger.

"What have you done to me?" She demanded, standing with no small amount of difficulty.

"I think I've managed to actually transform you," Gidyon said, resplendent in his own dress clothes. Unlike her, he looked totally comfortable in his garb.

"Shall we?" He offered her his arm.

Grudgingly, she took it and they left her room together. Her torture was complete when they came across Gidyon's three uncles, obviously waiting for the King before they entered the grand hall in which all of the Palace's guests were gathered.

Kaine glanced at her, looked away, then did a double take. Elen-ai felt profoundly uncomfortable in the tight-fitting bodice and flared skirts that Gidyon had chosen for her. She wished that more paint had been put on her face so that she was totally unrecognisable. But unfortunately for her, Gidyon had sat opposite while his own face was made up, directing the lines and colours that should be drawn onto her features, emphasising rather than hiding them. How he had picked up this interest in dress and fashion, she had no idea.

"You look—" Kaine's lips parted slightly as his eyes once more traversed her length, from the dainty shoes on her feet, to the way the low cut of the bodice emphasised the curve of her breasts, to the blood red that stained her lips.

"Yes?" Elen-ai put her hands on her hips and arched an eyebrow that, to her chagrin, had been painted so as to 'accentuate' her eyes. She had no idea what that meant, exactly, but the man who had done it had been very excited about it.

Kaine shook his head slightly as though to clear it. "You look ridiculous," he said finally.

"The Shadow's blessings be upon you. Can you tell that to your nephew!" she exclaimed.

"Oh, I'm sure that was exactly what he was trying to achieve," Kaine told her.

"The thanks I get. I fight in his Shadow-cursed army, I protect his secrets, and this is what he does to me? I could ruin him, you know." Elen-ai crossed her arms, awkwardly realising that that action pushed her breasts higher. She dropped her arms so that they swung by her side.

She realised that Gidyon, Nikalus and Silius were watching the exchange between her and Kaine with mixtures of undisguised amusement and curiosity. This was the longest exchange between them since the day the brothers had told Elen-ai she had to choose between the Family and Gidyon, and it was obvious that they all knew that. Elen-ai pressed her lips together in mortification at the spectacle that was being made of her.

"Shall we go in?" Gidyon asked once the silence had stretched longer than necessary. A slight smirk crossed his face as Elen-ai and he locked eyes.

"I'm going to get back at you for this," Elen-ai promised him.

His smile broadened into an outright grin, and he proffered his arm once again. She made a rude gesture at him that caused Silius' eyes to widen with shock and Gidyon to throw back his head in laughter.

"I'm intrigued to see what you will do to me," he told her before the doors opened to admit them. Together, they stepped into the room.

THE LOVERS

Anticipation set her skin aflame. She paced the chamber impatiently, taking no note of the luxury which surrounded her. Her thoughts were consumed by him and the promise of his nearness. It had been months since they'd last met. While her days had been occupied with duty, her nights had been filled with longing.

She glanced at the door. Worry gripped her with insidious hands. Had he been delayed or caught? What explanation could he offer if he were found sneaking to her room? The danger of their illicit romance had made his allure all the more powerful when this started, but she'd come to realise just how much she risked by continuing their relationship. Often, she tried to end it, to remove him and the threat he represented. But while in almost every other aspect of her life, she was able to exert a powerful self-control, she found herself unable to countenance the prospect of a life devoid of him, even if all they could have was this secret, half-grasped existence. She thought the years might have dulled her ardour, but they'd only deepened it into love. He saw her as she was – not as a symbol, or leader, or woman of power, but as a person whose fears and imperfections sometimes weighed down heavily enough to make her worry that she may not be enough. Thus, what had at first started as an act almost of rebellion, had become something that sustained her in ways so profound and powerful that it made her afraid as much as it exhilarated her.

She glanced at the timepiece, her fear building. Their years of furtive meetings had not been without close calls. Once, he'd had to hide for a whole day behind a set of curtains – without a stitch of clothing. The incident seemed funny in hindsight, although his absence now made the humour seem pale, a foolish response to what should have been a call to sensibly end things.

These thoughts always traversed her mind when he was late. Yet that did not stop her fear from being as real as ever. Perhaps finally, their time had run out. Her mind began to whirl with the steps that would need to be taken if he'd been discovered. There was a certain comfort in falling back to the methods of intrigue and machination that had been taught to her from the time she was young. It distracted her from terror and sadness strong enough to sweep her away.

Then the door opened, and relief flooded through her at the sight of him.

"My love." His voice soothed the raging storm within her. "I'm so sorry – I had to wait for some servants to pass."

The last vestiges of queenly composure melted away. "I began to worry."

"I know." He opened his arms and she flew across the room to land in his embrace.

"I missed you," she whispered, heady with that indefinable combination of scents that she could associate only with him. Here, with him, was the only time she ever uttered such phrases, ever felt as though underneath the title, the grooming and the weight of her responsibilities was a person who as ordinary as anyone else. It was both a dangerous thing to realise and something which made her stronger – better at the task she had been born to do.

"And I you. But I'm here now." He placed a finger under her chin and tilted her face up so he could draw his down to meet her.

His lips met hers and it felt there was no way that what lay between them could be wrong, or could lead to any harm.

ACKNOWLEDGEMENTS

Wow. I can't believe I'm *relaunching* Queendom and King. I'm so proud of this little duology, and am so immeasurably grateful to it for all the wonderful people I have met along the journey of its publication.

As I have said many, many times before, I must always thank my family first. My parents, my sister, my grandparents, and my friends, your collective support and enthusm (and patience), have meant the world. Papa, I miss you so much, but every story you ever told me has wound its way around my heart and is such a strong part of the storyteller I am today.

To my technical team – Jason who takes my words and makes them better, Marcus and Nicole who take my ideas and give them beautiful covers, and Kim, who takes my vague 'market strategy' and makes it into an actual plan; you guys are all so talented. Thank you.

To my LoveOzYA and OzAuthorsOnline fam, working with you is amazing, and putting something wonderful out into the world is so special, especially when done alongside incredible, passionate, talented people.

Biggest thanks – especially for this one – go to my bookstagrammers. I've listed you before, and will do it again. Alphabetically: Abi, Blue, Jayse, Jem, Jess, Jess, Julie Kat, Laura, Laura, Madi, Mel, Nat, Roz, Sam, Tay, Teagan, and those I *know*, I've missed (forgive me, please!!). You've been with me from the beginning. In particular, Kat – hours of conversation, advice, and support have made everything better. Debut Books will flourish because you are behind it.

Of course, all my love to Mitch for never waivering in your belief in me. You're better than Gid (almost).

ABOUT THE AUTHOR

Alice Jane Boer-Endacott is a born and bred Melbournian. That means she's very particular about her coffee, complaining about the cold (or the heat), and loves a good brunch.

Queendom of the Seven Lakes was written when she was 22 and finishing her Masters degree in Executive Management. She is not pursuing a career in Executive Management.

She is currently the Secretary for LoveOzYA, as well as on the organizing team for OzAuthors Online.

You can check out more of her work at her website, **www.abendacott.com** or follow her on twitter (@ajendacott) or on Instagram (@alicejaneboere).

If you enjoyed this book, she would love you forever if you left a review saying as much on Goodreads!

IF YOU ENJOYED THE QUEENDOM DULOGY, MAKE SURE YOU CHECK OUT THE OTHER LEGENDS OF THE GODSKISSED CONTINENT

Get ready to enter the final country in the Godskissed Continent, The First Country, coming in the second half of 2020.

Like all Blessed in the First Country, Kaylene is kept behind the stone walls of the Sanctuary to ensure the protection of others. Life has not been unbearable, though. She has found friends – and in Luka, even love. Then Luka dies in a terrible accident and Kaylene's entire world falls apart.

Life itself seems devoid of any hope until a chance encounter with a stranger gives Kaylene a purpose that sets her on a path that challenges everything she's ever believed: To reach beyond death itself and bring him back.

Follow Lexa's journey in the standalone story set in the Fourth Country...

THE RUTHLESS LAND

"Lying is not simply about telling a plausible story, it's about being able to tell what someone will want to believe"

To outsiders, the Fourth Country is an unforgiving place. Under the leadership of ruthless women, powerful families regularly wage brutal campaigns against one another to increase their land and wealth, and men live in a state of complete subjugation.

Lexana, heiress to the Farwan family, is sent to the Academy, an elite institution where the daughters of powerful families learn and refine techniques to maintain and gain power. There, she finds herself attracted to Jaxen, one of the teachers who defies convention and often goes about unveiled. His apparent disregard for what is expected of him leaves her both uneasy and fascinated.

Then the impossible comes to pass and disaster befalls the Farwan family. Lexa must leave the Academy to find her mother and help restore her family to power. Jaxen insists upon accompanying her, arguing that she cannot survive without his help. Lexa can't be certain that she can trust Jaxen, but she needs his help if she is to succeed.

Or follow Freya's story in the Dark Trilogy, beginning with...

DARK INTENT

"You can either live in the world that surrounds you, or you can fight for the world you want."

Many years after the brutal Kade takeover of the Third Country, Freya Kuch, a healer, has succeeded when many Pious have failed: she is a perfect Kade citizen. However, this life of willing subjugation is torn apart when she is caught in an attack perpetrated by the anarchic followers of the Dark Gods and is assigned to care for Zarech, their captured leader. Contrary to her expectations, he is not a raving madman but charismatic and quite rational.

Over the long months of his treatment she unwillingly becomes close to Zarech and she begins to reconsider everything, especially as he reveals the supernatural abilities bestowed upon those with true piety.

Her obedience to the strict Kade regime is further complicated by her attraction to Ashtyn, a member of the Pious Resistance movement. She tries to ignore her feelings knowing full well the brutal punishments for adultery and dissidence. But soon, she is forced to decide: will she maintain her life of careful safety, or give in to her heart's dark desires and join the fight against the Kade's regime?